A Day Of Fate

By

Edward Payson Roe

Double9
BOOKS

A Day Of Fate
by Edward Payson Roe

Copyright © 2023

All Rights reserved.

ISBN: 978-93-61154-69-0
Published by

DOUBLE 9 BOOKS

2/13-B, Ansari Road
Daryaganj, New Delhi – 110002
info@double9books.com
www.double9books.com
Tel. 011-40042856

ABOUT THE AUTHOR

Edward Payson Roe was an American novelist, Presbyterian clergyman, gardener, and historian. Edward Payson Roe was born in the settlement of Moodna, which is now part of New Windsor, New York. He attended Williams College and the Auburn Theological Seminary. In 1862, he was appointed chaplain of the Second New York Cavalry, United States Volunteers, and in 1864, chaplain of Hampton Hospital in Virginia. From 1866 to 1874, he was pastor of the First Presbyterian Church in Highland Falls, New York. In 1874, he moved to Cornwall-On-Hudson, where he focused on fiction writing and horticulture. During the American Civil War, he published weekly letters to the New York Evangelist and later lectured on the conflict and wrote for publications. He married Anna Paulina Sands in 1863 and had a number of children. Sarah married Olympic fencer Charles T. Tatham, while Pauline married landscape painter Henry Charles Lee. His writings were well-received in their day, particularly among middle-class readers in England and America, and were translated into other European languages. Their strong moral and theological aim helped to overcome America's Puritan prejudice toward works of fiction. One of his most common criticisms was that his writing resembled sermons.

CONTENTS

PREFACE

"Some shallow story of deep love."

—Shakespeare

BOOK FIRST

CHAPTER I
AIMLESS STEPS

"Another month's work will knock Morton into 'pi,'" was a remark that caught my ear as I fumed from the composing-room back to my private office. I had just irately blamed a printer for a blunder of my own, and the words I overheard reminded me of the unpleasant truth that I had recently made a great many senseless blunders, over which I chafed in merciless self-condemnation. For weeks and months my mind had been tense under the strain of increasing work and responsibility. It was my nature to become absorbed in my tasks, and, as night editor of a prominent city journal, I found a limitless field for labor. It was true I could have jogged along under the heavy burden with comparatively little wear and loss, but, impelled by both temperament and ambition, I was trying to maintain a racer's speed. From casual employment as a reporter I had worked my way up to my present position, and the tireless activity and alertness required to win and hold such a place was seemingly degenerating into a nervous restlessness which permitted no repose of mind or rest of body. I worked when other men slept, but, instead of availing myself of the right to sleep when the world was awake, I yielded to an increasing tendency to wakefulness, and read that I might be informed on the endless variety of subjects occupying public attention. The globe was becoming a vast hunting-ground, around which my thoughts ranged almost unceasingly that I might capture something new, striking, or original for the benefit of our paper. Each day the quest had grown more eager, and as the hour for going to press approached I would even become feverish in my intense desire to send the paper out with a breezy, newsy aspect, and would be elated if, at the last moment, material was flashed in that would warrant startling head-lines, and correspondingly depressed if the weary old world had a few hours of quiet and peace. To make the paper "go," every faculty I possessed was in the harness.

The aside I had just overheard suggested, at least, one very probable result. In printer's jargon, I would soon be in "pi."

The remark, combined with my stupid blunder, for which I had blamed an innocent man, caused me to pull up and ask myself whither I was hurrying so breathlessly. Saying to my assistant that I did not wish to be disturbed for a half hour, unless it was essential, I went to my little inner room. I wished to take a mental inventory of myself, and see how much was left. Hitherto I had been on the keen run—a condition not favorable to introspection.

Neither my temperament nor the school in which I had been trained inclined me to slow, deliberate processes of reasoning. I looked my own case over as I might that of some brother-editors whose journals were draining them of life, and whose obituaries I shall probably write if I survive them. Reason and Conscience, now that I gave them a chance, began to take me to task severely.

"You are a blundering fool," said Reason, "and the man in the composing-room is right. You are chafing over petty blunders while ignoring the fact that your whole present life is a blunder, and the adequate reason why your faculties are becoming untrustworthy. Each day you grow more nervously anxious to have everything correct, giving your mind to endless details, and your powers are beginning to snap like the overstrained strings of a violin. At this rate you will soon spend yourself and all there is of you."

Then Conscience, like an irate judge on the bench, arraigned me. "You are a heathen, and your paper is your car of Juggernaut. You are ceasing to be a man and becoming merely an editor—no, not even an editor—a newsmonger, one of the world's gossips. You are an Athenian only as you wish to hear and tell some new thing. Long ears are becoming the appropriate symbols of your being. You are too hurried, too eager for temporary success, too taken up with details, to form calm, philosophical opinions of the great events of your time, and thus be able to shape men's opinions. You commenced as a reporter, and are a reporter still. You pride yourself that you are not narrow, unconscious of the truth that you are spreading yourself thinly over the mere surface of affairs. You have little comprehension of the deeper forces and motives of humanity."

It is true that I might have pleaded in extenuation of these rather severe judgments that I was somewhat alone in the world, living in bachelor apartments, without the redeeming influences of home and family life. There were none whose love gave them the right or the motive to lay a restraining hand upon me, and my associates in labor were more inclined to applaud my zeal than to curb it. Thus it had been left to the casual remark of a nameless printer and an instance of my own failing powers to break the spell that ambition and habit were weaving.

Before the half hour elapsed I felt weak and ill. The moment I relaxed the tension and will-power which I had maintained so long, strong reaction set in. Apparently I had about reached the limits of endurance. I felt as if I were growing old and feeble by minutes as one might by years. Taking my hat and coat I passed out, remarking to my assistant that he must do the best he could—that I was ill and would not return. If the Journal had never appeared again I could not then have written a line to save it, or read another proof.

Saturday morning found me feverish, unrefreshed, and more painfully conscious than ever that I was becoming little better than the presses on which the paper was printed. Depression inevitably follows weariness and exhaustion, and one could scarcely take a more gloomy view of himself than I did.

"I will escape from this city as if it were Sodom," I muttered, "and a June day in the country will reveal whether I have a soul for anything beyond the wrangle of politics and the world's gossip."

In my despondency I was inclined to be reckless, and after merely writing a brief note to my editorial chief, saying that I had broken down and was going to the country, I started almost at random. After a few hours' riding I wearied of the cars, and left them at a small village whose name I did not care to inquire. The mountains and scenery pleased me, although the day was overcast like my mind and fortunes. Having found a quiet inn and gone through the form of a dinner, I sat down on the porch in dreary apathy.

The afternoon aspect of the village street seemed as dull and devoid of interest as my own life at that hour, and in fancy I saw myself, a broken-down man, lounging away days that would be like eternities, going through my little round like a bit of driftwood, slowly circling in an eddy of the world's great current. With lack-lustre eyes I "looked up to the hills," but no "help" came from them. The air was close, the sky leaden; even the birds would not sing. Why had I come to the country? It had no voices for me, and I resolved to return to the city. But while I waited my eyes grew heavy with the blessed power to sleep—a boon, for which I then felt that I would travel to the Ultima Thule. Leaving orders that I should not be disturbed, I went to my room, and Nature took the tired man, as if he were a weary child, into her arms.

At last I imagined that I was at the Academy of Music, and that the orchestra were tuning their instruments for the overture. A louder strain than usual caused me to start up, and I saw through the open window a robin on a maple bough, with its tuneful throat swelled to the utmost. This was the leader of my orchestra, and the whole country was alive with musicians, each one giving out his own notes without any regard for the others, but apparently the score had been written for them all, since the innumerable strains made one divine harmony. From the full-orbed song from the maple by my window, down to the faintest chirp and twitter, there was no discord; while from the fields beyond the village the whistle of the meadow-larks was so mellowed and softened by distance as to incline one to wonder whether their notes were real or mere ideals of sound.

For a long time I was serenely content to listen to the myriad-voiced chords without thinking of the past or future. At last I found myself idly querying whether Nature did not so blend all out-of-door sounds as to make them agreeable, when suddenly a catbird broke the spell of harmony by its flat, discordant note. Instead of my wonted irritation at anything that jarred upon my nerves, I laughed as I sprang up, saying,

"That cry reminds me that I am in the body and in the same old world. That bird is near akin to the croaking printer."

But my cynicism was now more assumed than real, and I began to wonder at myself. The change of air and scene had seemingly broken a malign influence, and sleep—that for weeks had almost forsaken me—had yielded its deep refreshment for fifteen hours. Besides, I had not sinned against my life so many years as to have destroyed the elasticity of early manhood. When I had lain down to rest I had felt myself to be a weary, broken, aged man. Had I, in my dreams, discovered the Fountain of Youth, and unconsciously bathed in it? In my rebound toward health of mind and body I seemed to have realized what the old Spaniard vainly hoped for.

I dressed in haste, eager to be out in the early June sunshine. There had been a shower in the night, and the air had a fine exhilarating quality, in contrast with the close sultriness of the previous afternoon.

Instead of nibbling at breakfast while I devoured the morning dailies, I ate a substantial meal, and only thought of papers to bless their absence, and then walked down the village street with the quick glad tread of one whose hope and zest in life have been renewed. Fragrant June roses were opening on every side, and it appeared to me that all the sin of man could not make the world offensive to heaven that morning.

I wished that some of the villagers whom I met were more in accord with Nature's mood; but in view of my own shortcomings, and still more because of my fine physical condition, I was disposed toward a large charity. And yet I could not help wondering how some that I saw could walk among their roses and still look so glum and matter-of-fact. I felt as if I could kiss every velvet petal.

"You were unjust," I charged back on Conscience; "this morning proves that I am not an ingrained newsmonger. There is still man enough left within me to revive at Nature's touch;" and I exultantly quickened my steps, until I had left the village miles away.

Before the morning was half gone I learned how much of my old vigor had ebbed, for I was growing weary early in the day. Therefore I paused before a small gray building, old and weather-stained, that seemed neither a barn, nor a dwelling, nor a school-house. A man was in the act of unlocking the door, and his garb suggested that it might be a Friends' meeting-house. Yielding to an idle curiosity I mounted a stone wall at a point where I was shaded and partially screened by a tree, and watched and waited, beguiling the time with a branch of sweetbriar that hung over my resting-place.

Soon strong open wagons and rockaways began to appear drawn by sleek, plump horses that often, seemingly, were gayer than their drivers. Still there was nothing sour in the aspect or austere in the garb of the people. Their quiet appearance took my fancy amazingly, and the peach-like bloom on the cheeks of even well-advanced matrons suggested a serene and quiet life.

"These are the people of all others with whom I would like to worship to-day," I thought; "and I hope that that rotund old lady, whose face beams under the shadow of her deep bonnet like a harvest moon through a fleecy cloud, will feel moved to speak." I plucked a few buds from the sweet-briar bush, fastened them in my button-hole, and promptly followed the old lady into the meeting-house. Having found a vacant pew I sat down, and looked around with serene content. But I soon observed that something was amiss, for the men folk looked at each other and then at me. At last an elderly and substantial Friend, with a face so flushed and round as to suggest a Baldwin apple, arose and creaked with painful distinctness to where I was innocently infringing on one of their customs.

"If thee will follow me, friend," he said, "I'll give thee a seat with the men folks. Thee's welcome, and thee'll feel more at home to follow our ways."

His cordial grasp of my hand would have disarmed suspicion itself, and I followed him meekly. In my embarrassment and desire to show that I had no wish to appear forward, I persisted in taking a side seat next to the wall, and quite near the door; for my guide, in order to show his goodwill and to atone for what might seem rudeness, was bent on marshalling me almost up to the high seats that faced the congregation, where sat my rubicund old Friend lady, whose aspect betokened that she had just the Gospel message I needed.

I at once noted that these staid and decorous people looked straight before them in an attitude of quiet expectancy. A few little children turned on me their round, curious eyes, but no one else stared at the blundering stranger, whose modish coat, with a sprig of wild roses in its buttonhole, made him rather a conspicuous contrast to the other men folk, and I thought—

"Here certainly is an example of good-breeding which could scarcely be found among other Christians. If one of these Friends should appear in the most fashionable church on the Avenue, he would be well stared at, but here even the children are receiving admonitory nudges not to look at me."

I soon felt that it was not the thing to be the only one who was irreverently looking around, and my good-fortune soon supplied ample motive for looking steadily in one direction. The reader may justly think that I should have composed my mind to meditation on my many sins, but I might as well have tried to gather in my hands the reins of all the wild horses of Arabia as to curb and manage my errant thoughts. My only chance was for some one or something to catch and hold them for me. If that old Friend lady would preach I was sure she would do me good. As it was, her face was an antidote to the influences of the world in which I dwelt, but I soon began to dream that I had found a still better remedy, for, at a fortunate angle from my position, there sat a young Quakeress whose side face arrested my attention and held it. By leaning a little against the wall as well as the back of my bench, I also, well content, could look straight before me like the others.

The fair profile was but slightly hidden by a hat that had a perceptible leaning toward the world in its character, but the brow was only made to seem a little lower, and her eyes deepened in their blue by its shadow. My sweet-briar blossoms were not more delicate in their pink shadings than was the bloom on her rounded cheek, and the white, firm chin denoted an absence of weakness and frivolity. The upper lip, from where I sat, seemed one half of Cupid's bow. I could but barely catch a glimpse of a ripple of hair that, perhaps, had not been smoothed with sufficient pains, and thus seemed in league with the slightly worldly bonnet. In brief, to my kindled fancy, her youth and loveliness appeared the exquisite human embodiment of the June morning, with its alternations of sunshine and shadow, its roses and their fragrance, of its abounding yet untarnished and beautiful life.

No one in the meeting seemed moved save myself, but I felt as if I could become a poet, a painter, and even a lover, under the inspiration of that perfect profile.

CHAPTER II
A JUNE DAY-DREAM

Moment after moment passed, but we all sat silent and motionless. Through the open windows came a low, sweet monotone of the wind from the shadowing maples, sometimes swelling into a great depth of sound, and again dying to a whisper, and the effect seemed finer than that of the most skilfully touched organ. Occasionally an irascible humble-bee would dart in, and, after a moment of motionless poise, would dart out again, as if in angry disdain of the quiet people. In its irate hum and sudden dartings I saw my own irritable fuming and nervous activity, and I blessed the Friends and their silent meeting. I blessed the fair June face, that was as far removed from the seething turmoil of my world as the rosebuds under her home-windows.

Surely I had drifted out of the storm into the very haven of rest and peace, and yet one might justly dread lest the beauty which bound my eyes every moment in a stronger fascination should evoke an unrest from which there might be no haven. Young men, however, rarely shrink from such perils, and I was no more prudent than my fellows. Indeed, I was inclining toward the fancy that this June day was the day of destiny with me; and if such a creature were the remedy for my misshapen life it would be bliss to take it.

In our sweet silence, broken only by the voice of the wind, the twitter of birds beguiling perhaps with pretty nonsense the hours that would otherwise seem long to their brooding mates on the nests, and the hum of insects, my fancy began to create a future for the fair stranger—a future, rest assured, that did not leave the dreamer a calm and disinterested observer.

"This day," I said mentally, "proves that there is a kindly and superintending Providence, and men are often led, like children in the dark, to just the thing they want. The wisdom of Solomon could not have led me to a place more suited to my taste and need than have my blind, aimless steps; and before me are possibilities which suggest the vista through which Eve was led to Adam."

My constant contact with men who were keen, self-seeking, and often unscrupulous, inclined me toward cynicism and suspicion. My editorial life made me an Arab in a sense, for if there were occasion, my hand might be against any man, if not every man. I certainly received many merciless blows, and I was learning to return them with increasing zest. My column in the paper was often a tilting-ground, and whether or no I inflicted wounds that amounted to much, I received some that long rankled. A home such as yonder woman might make would be a better solace than newspaper files. Such lips as these might easily draw the poison from any wound the world could make. Wintry firelight would be more genial than even June sunlight, if her eyes would reflect in into mine. With such companionship, all the Gradgrinds in existence would prose in vain; life would never lose its ideality, nor the world become a mere combination of things. Her woman's fancy would embroider my man's reason and make it beautiful, while not taking from its strength. Idiot that I was, in imagining that I alone could achieve success! Inevitably I could make but a half success, since the finer feminine element would be wanting. Do I wish men only to read our paper? Am I a Turk, holding the doctrine that women have no souls, no minds? The shade of my mother forbid! Then how was I, a man, to interpret the world to women? Truly, I had been an owl of the night, and blind to the honest light of truth when I yielded to the counsel of ambition, that I had no time for courtship and marriage. In my stupid haste I would try to grope my way through subjects beyond a man's ken, rather than seek some such guide as yonder maiden, whose intuitions would be unerring when the light of reason failed. In theory, I held the doctrine that there was sex in mind as truly as in the material form. Now I was inclined to act as if my doctrine were true, and to seek to double my power by winning the supplemental strength and grace of a woman's soul.

Indeed, my day-dream was becoming exceedingly thrifty in its character, and I assured ambition that the companionship of such a woman as yonder maiden must be might become the very corner-stone of success.

Time passed, and still no one was "moved." Was my presence the cause of the spiritual paralysis? I think not, for I was becoming conscious of reverent feeling and deeper motives. If the fair face was my Gospel message, it was already leading me beyond the thoughts of success and ambition, of mental power and artistic grace. Her womanly beauty began to awaken my moral nature, and her pure face, that looked as free from guile as any daisy with its eye turned to the sun, led me to ask, "What right have you to approach such a creature? Think of her needs, of her being first, and not your own. Would you drag her into the turmoil of your world because she would be a solace? Would you disturb the maidenly serenity of that brow with knowledge of evil and misery, the nightly record of which you have collated so long that you are callous? You, whose business it is to look behind the scenes of life, will you disenchant her also? It is your duty to unmask hypocrisy, and to drag hidden evil to light, but will you teach her to suspect and distrust? Should you not yourself become a better, truer, purer man before you look into the clear depths of her blue eyes? Beware, lest thoughtlessly or selfishly you sully their limpid truth."

"If she could be God's evangel to me, I might indeed be a better man," I murmured.

"That is ever the way," suggested Conscience; "there is always an 'if' in the path of duty; and you make your change for the better depend on the remote possibility that yonder maiden will ever look on you as other than a casual stranger that caused a slight disturbance in the wonted placidity of their meeting hour."

"Hush," I answered Conscience, imperiously; "since the old Friend lady will not preach, I shall endure none of your homilies. I yield myself to the influences of this day, and during this hour no curb shall be put on fancy. In my soul I know that I would be a better man if she is what she seems, and could be to me all that I have dreamed; and were I tenfold worse than I am, she would be the better for making me better. Did not Divine purity come the closest to sinful humanity? I shall approach this maiden in fancy, and may seek her in reality, but it shall be with a respect so sincere and an homage so true as to rob my thoughts and quest of bold irreverence or of mere selfishness. Suppose I am seeking my own good, my own salvation it may be, I am not seeking to wrong her. Are not heaven's best gifts best won by giving all for them? I would lay my manhood at her feet. I do not expect to earn her or buy her, giving a quid pro quo. A woman's love is like the grace of heaven—a royal gift; and the spirit of the suitor is more regarded than his desert. Moreover, I do not propose to soil her life with the evil world that I must daily brush against, but through her influence to do a little toward purifying that world. Since this is but a dream, I shall dream it out to suit me.

"That stalwart and elderly Friend who led me to this choice point of observation is her father. The plump and motherly matron on the high seat, whose face alone is a remedy for care and worry, is her mother. They will invite me home with them when meeting is over. Already I see the tree-embowered farmhouse, with its low, wide veranda, and old-fashioned roses climbing the lattice-work. In such a fragrant nook, or perhaps in the orchard back of the house, I shall explore the wonderland of this maiden's mind and heart. Beyond the innate reserve of an unsophisticated womanly nature there will be little reticence, and her thoughts will flow with the clearness and unpremeditation of the brook that I crossed on my way here.

What a change they will be from the world's blotted page that I have read too exclusively of late!

"Perhaps it will appear to her that I have become smirched by these pages, and that my character has the aspect of a printer at the close of his day's tasks.

"This source of fear, however, is also a source of hope. If she has the quickness of intuition to discover that I know the world too well, she will also discern the truth that I would gladly escape from that which might eventually destroy my better nature, and that hers could be the hand which might rescue my manhood. To the degree that she is a genuine woman there will be fascination in the power of making a man more manly and worthy of respect. Especially will this be true if I have the supreme good-fortune not to offend her woman's fancy, and to excite her sympathy; without awakening contempt.

"But I imagine I am giving her credit for more maturity of thought and discernment than her years permit. She must be young, and her experiences would give her no means of understanding my life. She will look at me with the frank, unsuspecting gaze of a child. She will exercise toward me that blessed phase of charity which thinketh no evil because ignorant of evil.

"Moreover, while I am familiar with the sin of the world, and have contributed my share toward it, I am not in love with it; and I can well believe that such a love as she might inspire would cause me to detest it. If for her sake and other good motives, I should resolutely and voluntarily; turn my back on evil, would I not have the right to walk at the side of one who, by the goodhap of her life, knows no evil? At any rate, I am not sufficiently magnanimous to forego the opportunity should it occur. Therefore, among the lengthening shadows of this June day I shall woo with my utmost skill one who may be able to banish the deeper shadows that are gathering around my life; and if I fail I shall carry the truth of her spring-time beauty and girlish innocence back to the city, and their memory will daily warn me to beware lest I lose the power to love and appreciate that which is her pre-eminent charm.

"But enough of that phase of the question. There need be no failure in my dream, however probable failure may be in reality. Let me imagine that in her lovely face I may detect the slight curiosity inspired by a stranger passing into interest. She will be shy and reserved at first; but as the delicious sense of being understood and admired gains mastery, her thoughts will gradually reveal her heart like the opening petals of a rose, and I can reverently gaze upon the rich treasures of which she is the unconscious possessor, and which I may win without impoverishing her.

"Her ready laugh, clear and mellow as the robin's song that woke me this morning, will be the index of an unfailing spring of mirthfulness—of that breezy, piquant, laughing philosophy which gives to some women an indescribable charm, enabling them to render gloom and despondency rare inmates of the home over which they preside. When I recall what dark depths of perplexity and trouble my mother often hid with her light laugh, I remember that I have never yet had a chance even to approach her in heroism. In my dream, at least, I can give to my wife my mother's laugh and courage; and surely Nature, who has endowed yonder maiden with so much beauty, has also bestowed every suitable accompaniment. Wherefore I shall discover in her eyes treasures of sunshine that shall light my home on stormy days and winter nights.

"As I vary our theme of talk from bright to sad experiences, I shall catch a glimpse of that without which the world would become a desert—woman's sympathy. Possibly I may venture to suggest my own need, and emphasize it by a reference to Holy Writ. That would be appropriate in a Sunday wooing. Surely she would admit that if Adam could not endure being alone in Eden, a like fate would be far more deserving of pity in such a wilderness as New York.

"Then, as a sequel to her sympathy, I may witness the awakening of that noble characteristic of woman—self-sacrifice—the generous impulse to give happiness, even though at cost to self.

"As the winged hours pass, and our glances, our words, our intuitions, and the subtle laws of magnetism that are so powerful, and yet so utterly beyond the ken of reason, reveal us to each other, I detect in the depths of her blue eyes a light which vanishes when I seek it, but returns again—a principle which she does not even recognize, much less understand, and yet which she already unconsciously obeys. Her looks are less frank and open, her manner grows deliciously shy, she hesitates and chooses her words, but is not so happy in their choice as when she spoke without premeditation. Instead of the wonted bloom on her cheek her color comes and goes. Oh, most exquisite phase of human power! I control the fountain of her life; and by an act, a word, a glance even, can cause the crimson tide to rise even to her brow, and then to ebb, leaving her sad and pale. Joy! joy! I have won that out of which can be created the best thing of earth, and the type of heaven—a home!"

At this supreme moment in my day-dream, an elderly Friend on the high seat gave his hand to another white-haired man who had, for the last hour, leaned his chin on his stout cane, and meditated under the shadow of his broad-brimmed hat, and our silent meeting was over. The possessor of the exquisite profile who had led me through a flight of romance such as I had never known before, turned and looked directly at me.

The breaking of my dream had been too sudden, and I had been caught too high up to alight again on the solid ground of reality with ease and grace. The night-editor blushed like a school-girl under her glance, at which she seemed naturally surprised. She, of course, could imagine no reason why her brief look of curiosity should cause me confusion and bring a guilty crimson to my face. I took it as a good omen, however, and said mentally, as I passed out with the others,

"My thoughts have already established a subtle influence over her, drawing her eyes and the first delicate tendril of interest toward one to whom she may cling for life."

CHAPTER III
THE SHINING TIDE

As I was strenuously seeking to gain possession of my wits, so that I could avail myself of any opportunity that offered, or could be made by adroit, prompt action, the stalwart and elderly Friend, who had seemed thus far one of the ministers of my impending fate, again took my hand and said:

"I hope thee'll forgive me for asking thee to conform to our ways, and not think any rudeness was meant."

"The grasp of your hand at once taught me that you were friendly as well as a Friend," I replied.

"We should not belie our name, truly. I fear thee did not enjoy our silent meeting?"

"You are mistaken, sir. It was just the meeting which, as a weary man, I needed."

"I hope thee wasn't asleep?" he said, with a humorous twinkle in his honest blue eyes.

"You are quite mistaken again," I answered, smiling; but I should have been in a dilemma had he asked me if I had been dreaming.

"Thee's a stranger in these parts," he continued, in a manner that suggested kindness rather than curiosity.

"Possibly this is the day of my fate," I thought, "and this man the father of my ideal woman." And I decided to angle with my utmost skill for an invitation.

"You are correct," I replied, "and I much regret that I have wandered so far from my hotel, for I am not strong."

"Well, thee may have good cause to be sorry, though we do our best; but if thee's willing to put up with homely fare and homely people, thee's welcome to come home with us."

Seeing eager acquiescence in my face, he continued, without giving me time to reply, "Here, mother, thee always provides enough for one more. We'll have a stranger within our gates to-day, perhaps."

To my joy the Friend lady, with a face like a benediction, turned at his words. At the same moment a large, three-seated rockaway, with a ruddy boy as driver, drew up against the adjacent horse-block, while the fair unknown, who had stood among a bevy of young Quakeresses like a tall lily among lesser flowers, came toward us holding a little girl by the hand. The family group was drawing together according to my prophetic fancy, and my heart beat thick and fast. Truly this was the day of fate!

"Homely people" indeed! and what cared I for "fare" in the very hour of destiny!

"Mother," he said, with his humorous twinkle, "I'm bent on making amends to this stranger who seemed to have a drawing toward thy side of the house. Thee didn't give him any spiritual fare in the meeting-house, but I think thee'll do better by him at the farmhouse. When I tell thee that he is not well and a long way from home, thee'll give him a welcome."

"Indeed," said the old lady, taking my hand in her soft, plump palm, while her face fairly beamed with kindness; "it would be poor faith that did not teach us our duty toward the stranger; and, if I mistake not, thee'll change our duty into a pleasure."

"Do not hope to entertain an angel," I said.

"That's well," the old gentleman put in; "our dinner will be rather too plain and substantial for angels' fare. I think thee'll be the better for it though."

"I am the better already for your most unexpected kindness, which I now gratefully accept as a stranger. I hope, however, that I may be able to win a more definite and personal regard;" and I handed the old gentleman my card.

"Richard Morton is thy name, then. I'll place thee beside Ruth Yocomb, my wife. Come, mother, we're keeping Friend Jones's team from the block. My name is Thomas Yocomb. No, no, take the back seat by my wife. She may preach to thee a little going home. Drive on, Reuben," he added, as he and his two daughters stepped quickly in, "and give Friend Jones a chance. This is Adah Yocomb, my daughter, and this is little Zillah. Mother thought that since the two names went together in Scripture they ought to go together out of it, and I am the last man in the world to go against the Scripture. That's Reuben Yocomb driving. Now thee knows all the family, and I hope thee don't feel as much of a stranger as thee did;" and the hearty old man turned and beamed on me with a goodwill that I felt to be as warm and genuine as the June sunshine.

"To be frank," I exclaimed, "I am at a loss to understand your kindness. In the city we are suspicious of strangers and stand aloof from them; but you treat me as if I had brought a cordial letter of introduction from one you esteemed highly."

"So thee has, so thee has; only the letter came before thee did. 'Be not forgetful to entertain strangers'—that's the way it reads, doesn't it, mother?"

"Moreover, Richard Morton," his wife added, "thee has voluntarily come among us, and sat down with us for a quiet hour. Little claim to the faith of Abraham could we have should we let thee wander off to get thy dinner with the birds in the woods, for the village is miles away."

"Mother'll make amends to thee for the silent meeting," said Mr. Yocomb, looking around with an impressive nod.

"I trust she will," I replied. "I wanted to hear her preach. It was her kindly face that led to my blunder, for it so attracted me from my perch of observation on the wall that I acted on my impulse and followed her into the meeting-house, feeling in advance that I had found a friend."

"Well, I guess thee has, one of the old school," laughed her husband.

The daughter, Adah, turned and looked at me, while she smiled approvingly. Oh, blessed day of destiny! When did dream and reality so keep pace before? Was I not dreaming still, and imagining everything to suit my own fancy? When would the perverse world begin to assert itself?

Sitting just before me, on the next seat, so that I could often see the same perfect profile, was the maiden that I had already wooed and won in fancy. Though she was so near and in the full sunlight, I could detect no cloudiness in her exquisite complexion, nor discover a fault in her rounded form. The slope of her shoulders was grace itself. She did not lean back weakly or languidly, but sat erect, with a quiet, easy poise of vigor and health. Her smile was frank and friendly, and yet not as enchanting as I expected. It was an affair of facial muscles rather than the lighting up of the entire visage. Nor did her full face—now that my confusion had passed away and I was capable of close observation—give the same vivid impression of beauty made by her profile. It was pretty, very pretty, but for some reasons disappointing. Then I smiled at my half-conscious criticism, and thought, "You have imagined a creature of unearthly perfection, and expect your impossible ideal to be realized. Were she all that you have dreamed, she would be much too fine for an ordinary mortal like yourself. In her rich, unperverted womanly nature you will find the beauty that will outlast that of form and feature."

"I fear thee found our silent meeting long and tedious," said Mrs. Yocomb, deprecatingly.

"I assure you I did not," I replied, "though I hoped you would have a message for us."

"It was not given to me," she said meekly. Then she added, "Those not used to our ways are troubled, perhaps, with wandering thoughts during these silent hours."

"I was not to-day," I replied with bowed head; "I found a subject that held mine."

"I'm glad," she said, her face kindling with pleasure. "May I ask the nature of the truth that held thy meditations?"

"Perhaps I will tell you some time," I answered hesitatingly; then added reverently, "It was of a very sacred nature."

"Thee's right," she said, gravely. "Far be it from me to wish to look curiously upon thy soul's communion."

For a moment I felt guilty that I should have so misled her, but reassured myself with the thought, "That which I dwelt upon was as sacred to me as my mother's memory."

I changed the subject, and sought by every means in my power to lead her to talk, for thus, I thought, I shall learn the full source of womanly life from which the peerless daughter has drawn her nature.

The kind old lady needed but little incentive. Her thoughts flowed freely in a quaint, sweet vernacular that savored of the meeting-house. I was both interested and charmed, and as we rode at a quiet jog through the June sunlight felt that I was in the hands of a kindly fate that, in accordance with the old fairy tales, was bent on giving one poor mortal all he desired.

At last, on a hillside sloping to the south, I saw the farmhouse of my dream. Two tall honey locusts stood like faithful guardians on each side of the porch. An elm drooped over the farther end of the piazza. In the dooryard the foliage of two great silver poplar or aspen trees fluttered perpetually with its light sheen. A maple towered high behind the house, and a brook that ran not far away was shadowed by a weeping willow. Other trees were grouped here and there as if Nature had planted them, and up one a wild grape-vine clambered, its unobtrusive blossoms filling the air with a fragrance more delicious even than that of the old-fashioned roses which abounded everywhere.

"Was there ever a sweeter nook?" I thought as I stepped out on the wide horse-block and gave my hand to one who seemed the beautiful culmination of the scene.

Miss Adah needed but little assistance to alight, but she took my hand in hers, which she had ungloved as she approached her home. It was her mother's soft, plump hand, but unmarked, as yet, by years of toil. I forgot we were such entire strangers, and under the impulse of my fancy clasped it a trifle warmly, at which she gave me a look of slight surprise, thus suggesting that there was no occasion for the act.

"You are mistaken," I mentally responded; "there is more occasion than you imagine; more than I may dare to tell you for a long time to come."

A lady who had been sitting on the piazza disappeared within the house, and Adah followed her.

"Now, mother," said Mr. Yocomb, "since thee did so little for friend Morton's spiritual man, see what thee can do for the temporal. I'll take the high seat this time, and can tell thee beforehand that there'll be no silent meeting."

"Father may seem to thee a little irreverent, but he doesn't mean to be. It's his way," said his wife, with a smile. "If thee'll come with me I'll show thee to a room where thee can rest and prepare for dinner."

I followed her through a wide hall to a stairway that changed its mind when half-way up and turned in an opposite direction. "It suggests the freedom and unconventionality of this home," I thought, yielding to my mood to idealize everything.

"This is thy room so long as thee'll be pleased to stay with us," she said, with a genial smile, and her ample form vanished from the doorway.

I was glad to be alone. The shining tide of events was bearing me almost too swiftly. "Can this be even the beginning of true love, since it runs so smoothly?" I queried. And yet it had all come about so simply and naturally, and for everything there was such adequate cause and rational explanation, that I assured myself that I had reason for self-congratulation rather than wonder.

Having seen such a maiden, it would be strange indeed if I had not been struck by her beauty. With an hour on my hands, and thoughts that called no one master, it would have been stranger still if I had not been beguiled into a dream which, in my need, promised so much that I was now bent on its fulfilment. Kind Mr. and Mrs. Yocomb had but carried out the teachings of their faith, and thus I was within the home of one who, developing under the influences of such a mother and such surroundings, would have the power beyond most other women of creating another home. I naturally thought that here, in this lovely and sheltered spot, and under just the conditions that existed, might be perfected the simple, natural flower of womanhood that the necessities of my life and character required.

I was too eager to prove my theories, and too strongly under the presentiment that my hour of destiny had come, to rest, and so gladly welcomed the tinkle of the dinner-bell.

The apparent mistress of my fate had not diminished her unconscious power by exchanging her Sunday-morning costume for a light muslin, that revealed more of her white throat than the strict canons of her sect would warrant perhaps, but none too much for maidenly modesty and artistic effect. Indeed, the gown harmonized with her somewhat worldly hat. I regarded these tendencies as good omens, however, felicitating myself with the thought that while her Quaker antecedents would always give to her manner and garb a beautiful simplicity, they would not trammel her taste with arbitrary custom. Though now more clearly satisfied that the beauty of her full face by no means equalled that of her profile, I was still far more than content with a perfection of features that sustained a rigorous scrutiny.

"Richard Morton," said Mrs. Yocomb, "let me make thee acquainted with Emily Warren."

I turned and bowed to a young woman, who seemed very colorless and unattractive to my brief glance, compared with the radiant creature opposite me. It would appear that I made no very marked impression on her either, for she chatted with little Zillah, who sat beyond her, and with Reuben across the table, making no effort to secure my attention.

If Mrs. Yocomb's powers as a spiritual provider were indicated by the table she had spread for us, the old meetinghouse should be crowded every Sunday, on the bare possibility that she might speak. From the huge plate of roast-beef before her husband to the dainty dish of wild strawberries on the sideboard, all was appetizing, and although it was the day of my destiny, I found myself making a hearty meal. My beautiful vis-a-vis evidently had no thoughts of destiny, and proved that the rich blood which mantled her cheeks had an abundant and healthful source. I liked that too. "There is no sentimental nonsense about her," I thought, "and her views of life will never be dyspeptic."

I longed to hear her talk, and yet was pleased that she was not garrulous. Her father evidently thought that this was his hour and opportunity, and he seasoned the ample repast with not a little homely wit and humor, in which his wife would sometimes join, and again curb and deprecate.

I began to grow disappointed that the daughter did not manifest some of her mother's quaint and genial good sense, or some sparkle and piquancy that would correspond to her father's humor: but the few remarks she made had reference chiefly to the people at the meeting, and verged toward small gossip.

I broached several subjects which I thought might interest her, but could obtain little other response than "Yes," with a faint rising inflection. After one of these unsuccessful attempts I detected a slight, peculiar smile on Miss Warren's face. It was a mischievous light in her dark eyes more than anything else. As she met my puzzled look it vanished instantly, and she turned away. Everything in my training and calling stimulated alertness, and I knew that smile was at my expense. Why was she laughing at me? Had she, by an intuition, divined my attitude of mind? A plague on woman's intuitions! What man is safe a moment?

But this could scarcely be, for the one toward whom my thoughts had flown for the last three hours, and on whom I had bent glances that did her royal homage, was serenely unconscious of my interest, or else supremely indifferent to it. She did not seem unfriendly, and I imagined that she harbored some curiosity in regard to me. My dress, manner, and some slight personal allusions secured far more attention than any abstract topic I could introduce. Her lips, however, were so exquisitely chiselled that they made, for the time, any utterance agreeable, and suggested that only tasteful thoughts and words could come from them.

"Now, mother," said Mr. Yocomb, leaning back in his chair after finishing a generous cup of coffee, "I feel inclined to be a good Christian man. I have a broad charity for about every one except editors and politicians. I am a man of peace, and there can be no peace while these disturbers of the body politic thrive by setting people by the ears. I don't disparage the fare, mother, that thee gives us at the meetinghouse, that is, when thee does give us any, but I do take my affirmation that thee has prepared a gospel feast for us since we came home that has refreshed my inner man. As long as I am in the body, roast-beef and like creature comforts are a means of grace to me. I am now in a contented frame of mind, and am quite disposed to be amiable. Emily Warren, I can even tolerate thy music—nay, let me speak the truth, I'd much like to hear some after my nap. Thee needn't shake thy head at me, mother, I've caught thee listening, and if thee brings me up before the meeting, I'll tell on thee. Does thee realize, Emily Warren, that thee is leading us out of the straight and narrow way?"

"I would be glad to lead you out of a narrow way," she replied, in a tone so quiet and yet so rich that I was inclined to believe I had not yet seen Miss

Warren. Perhaps she saw that I was becoming conscious of her existence, for I again detected the old mirthful light in her eyes. Was I or Mr. Yocomb's remark the cause?

Who was Emily Warren anyway, and why must she be at the farmhouse at a time when I so earnestly wished "the coast clear?" The perverse world at last was asserting its true self, and there was promise of a disturbance in my shining tide. Moreover, I was provoked that the one remark of this Emily Warren had point to it, while my perfect flower of womanhood had revealed nothing definitely save a good appetite, and that she had no premonitions that this was the day of her destiny.

CHAPTER IV
REALITY

"Father," said my fair ideal abruptly, as if a bright idea had just struck her, "did thee notice that Friend Jones's rockaway had been painted and all fixed up? I guess he rather liked our keeping him there before all the meeting."

"Mother, I hope thee'll be moved to preach about the charity that thinketh no evil," said her father gravely.

The young girl tossed her head slightly as she asserted, "Araminta Jones liked it anyway. Any one could see that."

"And any one need not have seen it also," her mother said, with a pained look. Then she added, in a low aside, as we rose from the table, "Thee certainly need not have spoken about thy friend's folly."

The daughter apparently gave little heed to her mother's rebuke, and a trivial remark a moment later proved that she was thinking of something else.

"Adah, thee can entertain Richard Morton for a time, while mother attends to the things," said her father.

The alacrity with which she complied was flattering at least, and she led me out on the piazza, that corresponded with my day-dream.

"Zillah," called Mrs. Tocomb to her little girl, "do not bother Emily Warren. She may wish to be alone. Stay with Adah till I am through."

"Oh, mother, please, let me go with Emily Warren. I never have a good time with Adah."

"There, mother, let her have her own way," said Adah, pettishly. "Emily Warren, thee shouldn't pet her so if thee doesn't want to be bothered by her."

"She does not bother me at all," said Miss Warren quietly. "I like her."

The little girl that had been ready to cry turned to her friend a radiant face that was eloquent with the undisguised affection of childhood.

"Zillah evidently likes you, Miss Warren," I said, "and you have given the reason. You like her."

"Not always a sufficient reason for liking another," she answered.

"But a very good one," I urged.

"There are many better ones."

"What has reason to do with liking, anyway?" I asked.

The mirthfulness I had noted before glimmered in her eyes for a moment, but she answered demurely, "I have seen instances that gave much point to your question, but I cannot answer it," and with a slight bow and smile she took her hat from Zillah and went down the path with an easy, natural carriage, that nevertheless suggested the city and its pavements rather than the country.

"What were you two talking about?" asked Adah, with a trace of vexed perplexity on her brow, for I imagined that my glance followed Miss Warren with some admiration and interest.

"You must have heard all we said."

"Where was the point of it?"

"What I said hadn't any point, so do not blame yourself for not seeing it. Don't you like little Zillah? She seems a nice, quiet child."

"Certainly I like her—she's my sister; but I detest children."

"I can't think that you were detested when you were a child."

"I don't remember: I might have been," she replied, with a slight shrug.

"Do you think that, as a child, you would enjoy being detested?"

"Mother says it often isn't good for us to have what we enjoy."

"Undoubtedly your mother is right."

"Well, I don't see things in that way. If I like a thing I want it, and if I don't like it I don't want it, and won't have it if I can help myself."

"Your views are not unusual," I replied, turning away to hide my contracting brow. "I know of others who cherish like sentiments."

"Well, I'm glad to meet with one who thinks as I do," she said complacently, and plucking a half-blown rose that hung near her, she turned its petals sharply down as if they were plaits of a hem that she was about to stitch.

"Here is the first harmonic chord in the sweet congeniality of which I dreamed," I inwardly groaned; but I continued, "How is it that you like Zillah as your sister, and not as a little girl?"

"Oh, everybody likes their brothers and sisters after a fashion, but one doesn't care to be bothered with them when they are little. Besides, children rumple and spoil my dress," and she looked down at herself approvingly.

"Now, there's Emily Warren," continued my "embodiment of June." "Mother is beginning to hold her up to me as an example. Emily Warren is half the time doing things that she doesn't like, and I think she's very foolish. She is telling Zillah a story over there under that tree. I don't think one feels like telling stories right after dinner."

"Yes, but see how much Zillah enjoys the story."

"Oh, of course she enjoys it. Why shouldn't she, if it's a good one?"

"Is it not possible that Miss Warren finds a pleasure in giving pleasure?"

"Well, if she does, that is her way of having a good time."

"Don't you think it's a sweet, womanly way?"

"Ha, ha, ha! Are you already smitten with Emily Warren's sweet, womanly ways?"

I confess that I both blushed and frowned with annoyance and disappointment, but I answered lightly, "If I were, would I be one among many victims?"

"I'm sure I don't know," she replied, with her slight characteristic shrug, which also intimated that she didn't care.

"Miss Warren, I suppose, is a relative who is visiting you?"

"Oh, no, she is only a music teacher who is boarding with us. Mother usually takes two or three boarders through the summer months, that is if they are willing to put up with our ways."

"I suppose it's correct to quote Scripture on Sunday afternoon. I'm sure your mother's ways are those of pleasantness and peace. Do you think she would take me as a boarder?"

"I fear she'll think you would want too much city style."

"That is just what I wish to escape from."

"I think city style is splendid."

"Why?"

"Oh, the city is gay and full of life and people. I once took walks down Fifth Avenue when making a visit in town, and I would be perfectly happy if I could do so every day."

"Perfectly happy? I wish I knew of something that would make me perfectly happy. Pardon me, I am only a business man, and can't be expected to understand young ladies very well. I don't understand why walking down Fifth Avenue daily would make you happy."

"Of course not. A man can't understand a girl's feelings in such matters."

"There is nothing in New York so beautiful as this June day in the country."

"Yes, it's a nice day: but father says we need more rain dreadfully."

"You have spoiled your rose."

"There are plenty more."

"Don't you like roses?"

"Certainly. Who does not like roses?"

"Let me give you another. See, here is one that has the hue of your cheeks."

"I suppose a city pallor like Emily Warren's is more to your taste."

"I am wholly out of humor with the city, and I do not like that which is colorless and insipid. I think the rose I have just given you very beautiful."

"Thanks for your roundabout compliment," and she looked pleased.

"I suppose your quiet life gives you much time for reading?"

"I can't say that I enjoy father and mother's books."

"I doubt whether I would myself, but you have your own choice?"

"I read a story now and then; but time slips away; and I don't do much reading. We country girls make our own clothes, and you have no idea how much time it takes."

"Will you forgive me if I say that I think you make yours very prettily?"

Again she looked decidedly pleased; and, as if to reward me, she fastened the rose on her bosom. "If she would only keep still," I thought, "and I could simply look at her as at a draped statue, I could endure another half-hour; but every word she speaks is like the note of that catbird which broke the spell of harmony this morning. I have not yet seen a trace of ideality in her mind. Not a lovable trait have I discovered beyond her remarkable beauty, which mocks one with its broken promise. What is the controlling yet perverse principle of her life which makes her seem an alien in her own home? I am glad she does not use the plain language to me, since by nature she is not a Friend."

Miss Yocomb interrupted my thoughts by saying:

"I thought my dress would be much too simple and country-like for your taste. I can see myself that Emily Warren's dress has more style."

Resolving to explore a little, I said:

"I know a great many men in town."

"Indeed!" she queried, with kindling interest.

"Yes, and some of them are fine artists; and the majority have cultivated their tastes in various ways, both at home and abroad: but I do not think many of them have any respect for what you mean by 'style.' Shop-boys, clerks, and Fifth Avenue exquisites give their minds to the arbitrary mode of the hour; but the men in the city who amount to anything rarely know whether a lady's gown is of the latest cut. They do know, however, whether it is becoming and lady-like. The solid men of the city have a keen eye for beauty, and spend hundreds of thousands of dollars to enjoy its various phases. But half of the time they are anathematizing mere style. I have seen fashion transform a pretty girl into as near an approach to a kangaroo as nature permitted. Now, I shall be so bold as to say that I think your costume this afternoon has far better qualities than mere style. It is becoming, and in keeping with the day and season, and I don't care a fig whether it is the style or not."

My "perfect flower of womanhood" grew radiant, and her lips parted in a smile of ineffable content. In bitter disappointment I saw that my artifice had succeeded, and that I had touched the key-note of her being. To my horror, she reminded me of a pleased, purring kitten that had been stroked in the right direction.

"Your judgment is hasty and harsh," I charged myself, in half-angry accusation, loth to believe the truth. "You do not know yet that a compliment to her dress is the most acceptable one that she can receive. She probably takes it as a tribute to her good taste, which is one of woman's chief prerogatives."

I resolved to explore farther, and continued:

"A lady's dress is like the binding of a book—it ought to be suggestive of her character. Indeed, she can make it a tasteful expression of herself. Our eye is often attracted or repelled by a book's binding. When it has been made with a fine taste, so that it harmonizes with the subject under consideration, we are justly pleased; but neither you nor I believe in the people who value books for the sake of their covers only. Beauty and richness of thought, treasures of varied truth, sparkling wit, droll humor, or downright earnestness are the qualities in books that hold our esteem.

A book must have a soul and life of its own as truly as you or I; and the costliest materials, the wealth of a kingdom, cannot make a true book any more than a perfect costume and the most exquisite combination of flesh and blood can make a true woman." (I wondered if she were listening to me; for her face was taking on an absent look. Conscious that my homily was growing rather long, I concluded.) "The book that reveals something new, or puts old truths in new and interesting lights—the book that makes us wiser, that cheers, encourages, comforts, amuses, and makes a man forget his stupid, miserable self, is the book we tie to. And so a man might well wish himself knotted to a woman who could do as much for him, and he would naturally be pleased to have her outward garb correspond with her spiritual beauty and worth."

My fair ideal had also reached a momentous conclusion, for she said, with the emphasis of a final decision:

"I won't cut that dress after Emily Warren's pattern. I'll cut it to suit myself."

I had been falling from a seventh heaven of hope for some time, but at this moment I struck reality with a thump that almost made me sick and giddy. The expression of my face reminded her of the irrelevancy of her remark, and she blushed slightly, but laughed it off, saying:

"Pardon me, that I followed my own thoughts for a moment rather than yours. These matters, no doubt, seem mere trifles to you gentlemen, but they are weighty questions to us girls who have to make a little go a great way. Won't you, please, repeat what you said about that lady who wrote a book for the sake of its binding? I think it's a pretty idea."

I was so incensed that I answered as I should not have done. "She was remarkably successful. Every one looked at the binding, but were soon satisfied to look no farther."

I was both glad and vexed that she did not catch my meaning, for she said, with a smile:

"It would make a pretty ornament."

"It would not be to my taste," I replied briefly. "The beautiful binding would hold out the promise of a good book, which, not being fulfilled, would be tantalizing."

"Do you know the lady well?"

"Yes, I fear I do."

"How strangely you look at me!"

"Excuse me," I said, starting. "I fear I followed your example and was thinking of something else."

But I let what I was thinking about slip out.

"It was indeed a revelation. My thoughts will not interest you, I fear. The experience of a man who saw a mirage in the desert came into my mind."

"I don't see what put that into your head."

"Nor do I, now. The world appears to me entirely matter-of-fact."

"I'm glad to hear you say that. Mother is always talking to me about spiritual meanings and all that. Now I agree with you. Things are just what they are. Some we like, and some we don't like. What more is there to say about them? I think people are very foolish if they bother themselves over things or people they don't like. I hope mother will take you to board, for I would like to have some one in the house who looks at things as I do."

"Thanks. Woman's intuition is indeed unerring."

"I declare, there comes Silas Jones with his new top-buggy. You won't mind his making one of our party, will you?"

"I think I will go to my room and rest awhile, and thus I shall not be that chief of this world's evils—the odious third party." And I rose decisively.

"I'd rather you wouldn't go," she said. "I don't care specially for him, and he does not talk half so nicely as you do. You needn't go on his account. Indeed, I like to have half a dozen gentlemen around me."

"You are delightfully frank."

"Yes, I usually say what I think."

"And do as you please," I added.

"Certainly. Why shouldn't I when I can? Don't you?"

"But I came from the wicked city." "So does Emily Warren."

"Is she wicked?"

"I don't know; she keeps it to herself if she is; and, by the way, she is very quiet, I can never get her to talk much about herself. She appears so good that mother is beginning to quote her as an example, and that, you know, always makes one detest a person. I think there is some mystery about her. I'm sorry you will go, for I've lots of questions I'd like to ask you now we are acquainted."

"Pardon me; I'm not strong, and must have a rest. Silas Jones will answer just as well."

"Not quite," she said softly, with a smile designed to be bewitching.

As I passed up the hall I heard her say, "Silas Jones, I'm pleased to see thee."

I threw myself on the lounge in my room in angry disgust.

"O Nature!" I exclaimed, "what excuse have you for such perverseness? By every law of probability—by the ordinary sequence of cause and effect—this girl should have been what I fancied her to be. This, then, forsooth, is the day of my fate! It would be the day of doom did some malicious power chain me to this brainless, soulless, heartless creature. What possessed Nature to make such a blunder, to begin so fairly and yet reach such a lame and impotent conclusion? To the eye the girl is the fair and proper outcome of this home and beautiful country life. In reality she is a flat contradiction to it all, reversing in her own character the native traits and acquired graces of her father and mother.

"As if controlled and carried forward by a hidden and malign power, she goes steadily against her surrounding influences that, like the winds of heaven, might have wafted her toward all that is good and true. Is not sweet, quaint Mrs. Yocomb her mother? Is not the genial, hearty old gentleman her father? Has she not developed among scenes that should ennoble her nature, and enrich her mind with ideality? There is Oriental simplicity and largeness in her parents' faith. Abraham sitting at the door of his tent, could scarcely have done better. Hers is the simplicity of silliness, which reveals what a woman of sense, though no better than herself, would not speak of. It is exasperating to think that her eyes and fingers are endowed with a sense of harmony and beauty, so that she can cut a gown and adorn her lovely person to perfection, and yet be so idiotic as to make a spectacle of herself in her real womanhood. As far as I can make out, Nature is more to blame than the girl. There is not a bat blinking in the sunlight more blind than she to every natural beauty of this June day; and yet her eyes are microscopic, and she sees a host of little things not worth seeing. A true womanly moral nature seems never to have been infused into her being. She detests children, her little sister shrinks from her; she speaks and surmises evil of the absent; to strut down Fifth Avenue in finery, to which she has given her whole soul, is her ideal of happiness—there, stop! She is the daughter of my kind host and hostess. The mystery of this world's evil is sadly exemplified in her defective character, from which sweet, true womanliness was left out. I should pity her, and treat her as if she were deformed. Poor Mrs. Yocomb! Even mother-love cannot blind her to the truth that her fair daughter is a misshapen creature." After a little, I added wearily, "I wish I had never seen her; I am the worse for this day's mirage," and I closed my eyes in dull apathy.

CHAPTER V
MUTUAL DISCOVERIES

I must have slept for an hour or more, for when I awoke I saw through the window-lattice that the sun was declining in the west. Sleep had again proved better than all philosophy or medicine, for it had refreshed me and given something of the morning's elasticity.

I naturally indulged in a brief retrospect, conscious that while nothing had happened, since the croaking printer's remark, that I would care to print in the paper, experiences had occurred that touched me closer than would the news that all the Malays of Asia were running amuck. I felt as if thrown back on to my old life and work in precisely their old form. My expedition into the country and romance had been disappointing. It is true I had found rest and sleep, and for these I was grateful, and with these stanch allies I can go on with my work, which I now believe is the best thing the world has for me. I shall go back to it to-morrow, well content, after this day's experience, to make it my mistress. The bare possibility of being yoked to such a woman as in fancy I have wooed and won to-day makes me shiver with inexpressible dread. Her obtuseness, combined with her microscopic surveillance, would drive me to the nearest madhouse I could find. The whole business of love-making and marriage involves too much risk to a man who, like myself, must use his wits as a sword to carve his fortunes. I've fought my way up alone so far, and may as well remain a free lance. The wealthy, and those who are content to plod, can go through life with a woman hanging on their arm. Rich I shall never be, and I'll die before I'll plod. My place is in the midst of the world's arena, where the forces that shall make the future are contending, and I propose to be an appreciable part of those forces. I shall go back the wiser and stronger for this day's folly, and infinitely better for its rest, and I marched down the moody stairway, feeling that I was not yet a crushed and broken man, and cherishing also a secret complacency that I had at last outgrown my leanings toward sentimentality.

As I approached the door of the wide, low-browed parlor, I saw Miss Warren reading a paper; a second later and my heart gave a bound: it was the journal of which I was the night editor, and I greeted its familiar aspect as the face of an old friend in a foreign land. It was undoubtedly the number that had gone to press the night I had broken down, and I almost hoped to see some marks of the catastrophe in its columns. How could I beguile the coveted sheet from Miss Warren's hands and steal away to a half-hour's seclusion?

"What! Miss Warren," I exclaimed, "reading a newspaper on Sunday?"

She looked at me a moment before replying, and then asked:

"Do you believe in a Providence?"

Thrown off my guard by the unexpected question, I answered:

"Assuredly; I am not quite ready to admit that I am a fool, even after all that has happened."

There was laughter in her eyes at once, but she asked innocently:

"What has happened?"

I suppose my color rose a little, but I replied carelessly, "I have made some heavy blunders of late. You are adroit in stealing away from a weak position under a fire of questions, but your stratagem shall not succeed," I continued severely. "How can you explain the fact, too patent to be concealed, that here in good Mrs. Yocomb's house, and on a Sunday afternoon, you are reading a secular newspaper?"

"You have explained my conduct yourself," she said, assuming a fine surprise.

"I?"

"You, and most satisfactorily. You said you believed in a Providence. I have merely been reading what he has done, or what he has permitted, within the last twenty-four hours."

I looked around for a chair, and sat down "struck all of a heap," as the rural vernacular has it.

"Is that your definition of news?" I ventured at last.

"I'm not a dictionary. That's the definition of what I've been reading this afternoon."

"Miss Warren, you may score one against me."

The mischievous light was in her eyes, but she said suavely:

"Oh, no, you shall have another chance. I shall begin by showing mercy, for I may need it, and I see that you can be severe."

"Well, please, let me take breath and rally my shattered wits before I make another advance. I understand you, then, that you regard newspapers as good Sunday reading?"

"You prove your ability, Mr. Morton, by drawing a vast conclusion from a small and ill-defined premise. I don't recall making any such statement."

"Pardon me, you are at disadvantage now. I ask for no better premise than your own action; for you are one, I think, who would do only what you thought right."

"A palpable hit. I'm glad I showed you mercy. Still it does not follow that because I read a newspaper, all newspapers are good Sunday reading. Indeed, there is much in this paper that is not good reading for Monday or any other day."

"Ah!" I exclaimed, looking grave, "then why do you read it?"

"I have not. A newspaper is like the world of which it is a brief record—full of good and evil. In either case, if one does not like the evil, it can be left alone."

"Which do you think predominates in that paper?"

"Oh, the good, in the main. There is an abundance of evil, too, but it is rather in the frank and undisguised record of the evil in the world. It does not seem to have got into the paper's blood and poisoned its whole life. It is easily skipped if one is so inclined. There are some journals in which the evil cannot be skipped. From the leading editorial to the obscurest advertisement, one stumbles on it everywhere. They are like certain regions in the South, in which there is no escape from the snakes and malaria. Now there are low places in this paper, but there is high ground also, where the air is good and wholesome, and where the outlook on the world is wide. That is the reason I take it."

"I was not aware that many young ladies looked, in journals of this character, beyond the record of deaths and marriages."

"We studied ancient history. Is it odd that we should have a faint desire to know what Americans are doing, as well as what the Babylonians did?"

"Oh, I do not decry your course as irrational. It seems rather—rather—"

"Rather too rational for a young lady."

"I did not say that; but here is my excuse," and I took from a table near a periodical entitled "The Young Lady's Own Weekly," addressed to Miss Adah Yocomb.

"Have not young men their own weeklies also—which of the two classes is the more weakly?"

"Ahem! I decline to pursue this phase of the subject any further. To return to our premise, this journal," and I laid my hand on the old paper caressingly. "It so happens that I read it also, and thus learn that we have had many thoughts in common; though, no doubt, we would differ on some of the questions discussed in it. What do you think of its politics?"

"I think they are often very bad."

"That's delightfully frank," I said, sitting back in my chair a little stiffly. "I think they are very good—at any rate they are mine."

"Perhaps that is the reason they are so good?"

"Now, pardon me if I, too, am a trifle plain. Do you consider yourself as competent to form an opinion concerning politics as gray-headed students of affairs?"

"Oh, certainly not; but do I understand that you accept, unquestioningly, the politics of the paper you read?"

"Far from it: rather that the politics of this paper commend themselves to my judgment."

"And you think 'judgment' an article not among a young woman's possessions?"

"Miss Warren, you may think what you please of the politics of this paper. But how comes it that you think about them at all? I'm sure that they interest but comparatively few young ladies."

Her face suddenly became very grave and sad, and a moment later she turned away her eyes that were full of tears. "I wish you hadn't asked that question; but I will explain my seeming weakness," she said, in a low, faltering voice. "I lost my only brother in the war—I was scarcely more than a child; but I can see him now—my very ideal of brave, loyal manhood. Should I not love the country for which he died?"

Politics! a word that men so often utter with contempt, has been hallowed to me since that moment.

She looked away for a moment, swiftly pressed her handkerchief to her eyes, then turning toward me said, with a smile, and in her former tones:

"Forgive me! I've been a bit lonely and blue this afternoon, for the day has reminded me of the past. I won't be weak and womanish any more. I think some political questions interest a great many women deeply. It must be so. We don't dote on scrambling politicians; but a man as a true statesman makes a grand figure."

I was not thinking of statecraft or the craftsmen.

"By Jove!" I exclaimed mentally, "this girl is more beautiful than my 'perfect flower of womanhood.' Night-owl that I am, I am just gaining the power to see her clearly as the sun declines."

I know my face was full of honest sympathy as I said, gently and reverently:

"Tell me more of your brother. The thoughts of such men make me better."

She shot a quick, grateful glance, looked down, trembled, shook her head as she faltered:

"I cannot—please don't; speak of something far removed."

The feeling was so deep, and yet so strongly curbed, that its repression affected me more deeply than could its manifestation. Her sorrow became a veiled and sacred mystery of which I could never be wholly unconscious again; and I felt that however strong and brilliant she might prove in our subsequent talk, I should ever see, back of all, the tender-hearted, sensitive woman.

"Please forgive me. I was cruelly thoughtless," I said, in a voice that trembled slightly. Then, catching up the paper, I continued, with attempted lightness, "We have found this journal, that we mutually read, a fruitful theme. What do you think of its literary reviews?"

Mirth and tears struggled for the mastery in her eyes; but she answered, with a voice that had regained its clear, bell-like tone:

"In some I have seen indisputable proof of impartiality and freedom from prejudice."

"In what did that proof consist?"

"In the evident fact that the reviewer had not read the book."

"You are severe," I said, coloring slightly.

She looked at me with a little surprise, but continued:

"That does not happen very often. It is clear that there are several contributors to this department, and I have come to look for the opinions of one of them with much interest. I am sure of a careful and appreciative estimate of a book from his point of view. His one fault appears to be that he sees everything from one perspective, and does not realize that the same thing may strike other intelligent people very differently. But he's a fixed and certain quantity, and a good point to measure from. I like him because he is so sincere. He sits down to a book as a true scientist does to a phase of nature, to really learn what there is in it, and not merely to display a little learning, sarcasm, or smartness. I always feel sure that I know something about a book after reading one of his reviews, and also whether I could afford to spend a part of my limited time in reading it."

"I have singled out the same reviewer, and think your estimate correct. On another occasion, when we have more time, I am going to ask how you like the musical critic's opinions; for on that subject you would be at home."

"What makes you think so?"

"Miss Yocomb told me that you taught music in the city, and music is about the only form of recreation for which I have taken time in my busy life. There are many things concerning the musical tendencies of the day that I would like to ask you about. But I hear the clatter of the supper dishes. What do you think of the editorial page, and its moral tendencies? That is a good Sunday theme."

"There is evidence of much ability, but there is a lack of earnestness and definite purpose. The paper is newsy and bright, and, in the main, wholesome. It reflects public opinion fairly and honestly, but does little to shape it. It is often spicily controversial, sometimes tiresomely so. I do a good deal of skipping in that line. I wish its quarrels resulted more from efforts to right some wrong; and there is so much evil in our city, both in high and low places, that ought to be fought to the death. The editor has exceptional opportunities, and might be the knight-errant of our age. If in earnest, and on the right side, he can forge a weapon out of public opinion that few evils could resist. And he is in just the position to discover these dragons and drive them from their hiding-places. If, for instance, the clever paragraphist in this column, whose province, it seems, is to comment at the last moment on the events of the day, were as desirous of saying true, strong, earnest words, as bright and prophetic ones, in which the news of the morrow is also outlined-why, Mr. Morton, what is the matter?"

"Are you a witch?"

She looked at me a moment, blushed deeply, and asked hesitatingly:

"Are-are you the paragraphist?"

"Yes," I said, with a burst of laughter, "as truly as yours is the only witchcraft in which I believe-that of brains." Then putting my finger on my lips, I added, *sotto voce*: "Don't betray me. Mr. Yocomb would set all his dogs on me if he knew I were an editor, and I don't wish to go yet."

"What have I been saying!" she exclaimed, with an appalled look.

"Lots of clever things. I never got so many good hints in the same time before."

"It wasn't fair in you, to lead me on in the dark."

"Oh, there wasn't any 'dark,' I assure you. Your words were coruscations. Never was the old journal so lighted up before."

There were both perplexity and annoyance in her face as she looked dubiously at me. Instantly becoming grave, I stepped to her side and took her hand, as I said, with the strongest emphasis:

"Miss Warren, I thank you. I have caught a glimpse of my work and calling through the eyes of a true, refined, and, permit me to add, a gifted woman. I think I shall be the better for it, but will make no professions. If I'm capable of improvement this column will show it."

Her hand trembled in mine as she looked away and said:

"You are capable of sympathy."

Then she went hastily to the piano.

Before she could play beyond a bar or two, little Zillah bounded in, exclaiming:

"Emily Warren, mother asks if thee and Richard Morton will come out to tea?"

"I may be in error, but is not a piano one of the worldly vanities?" I asked, as she turned to comply. "I did not expect to see one here."

"Mrs. Yocomb kindly took this in with me. I could scarcely live without one, so you see I carry the shop with me everywhere, and am so linked to my business that I can never be above it."

"I hope not, but you carry the business up with you. The shop may be, and ought to be, thoroughly respectable. It is the narrow, mercenary spirit of the shop that is detestable. If you had that, you would leave your piano in New York, since here it would have no money value."

"You take a nice view of it."

"Is it not the true view?"

In mock surprise she answered:

"Mr. Morton, I'm from New York. Did you ever meet a lady from that city who was not all that the poets claimed for womanhood?"

CHAPTER VI
A QUAKER TEA

"Richard Morton," said Mrs. Yocomb genially, "thee seems listening very intently to something Emily Warren is saying, so thee may take that seat beside her."

"Richard Morton," said Mr. Yocomb from the head of the table, "has thee made the acquaintance of Emily Warren?"

"No, sir, but I am making it."

"So am I, and she has been here a week."

"I should esteem that one of the highest of compliments," I said; then turning to her, I added, in an aside, "You found me out in half an hour."

"Am I such a sphinx?" she asked Mr. Yocomb with a smile; while to me she said, in a low tone: "You are mistaken. You have had something to say to me almost daily for a year or more."

"I am not acquainted with the article, and so can't give an opinion," Mr. Yocomb replied, with a humorous twinkle in his eye. "If the resemblance is close, so much the better for the sphinxes."

"Now, father, thee isn't a young man that thee should be complimenting the girls," his wife remarked.

"I've persuaded Silas Jones to stay," said Adah, entering.

"Silas Jones, I hope thee and thy parents are well," Mrs. Yocomb answered, with a courtesy somewhat constrained. "Will thee take that seat by Adah? Let me make thee acquainted with Richard Morton and Emily Warren."

We bowed, but I turned instantly to Miss Warren and said.

"Do you note how delightfully Mrs. Yocomb unites our names? I take it as an omen that we may become friends in spite of my shortcomings. You should have been named first in the order of merit."

"Mrs. Yocomb rarely makes mistakes," she replied.

"That confirms my omen."

"Omens are often ominous."

"I'm prepared for the best."

"Hush!" and she bowed her head in the grace customary before meals in this house.

I had noted that Mr. Yocomb's bow to Mr. Jones was slightly formal also. Remembering the hospitable traits of my host and hostess, I concluded that the young man was not exactly to their taste. Indeed, a certain jauntiness in dress that verged toward flashiness would not naturally predispose them in his favor. But Adah, although disclaiming any special interest in him, seemed pleased with his attentions. She was not so absorbed, however, but that she had an eye for me, and expected my homage also. She apparently felt that she had made a very favorable impression on me, and that we were congenial spirits. During the half hour that followed I felt rather than saw that this fact amused Miss Warren exceedingly.

For a few moments we sat in silence, but I fear my grace was as graceless as my morning worship had been. Miss Warren's manner was reverent. Were her thoughts also wandering? and whither? She certainly held mine, and by a constraint that was not unwelcome.

When she lifted her expressive eyes I concluded that she had done better than merely comply with a religious custom.

"The spirit of this home has infected you," I said.

"It might be well for you also to catch the infection."

"I know it would be well for me, and wish to expose myself to it to the utmost. You are the only obstacle I fear."

"I?"

"Yes. I will explain after supper."

"To explain that you have good cause to ask for time,"

"Richard Morton, does thee like much sugar in thy tea?" Mrs. Yocomb asked.

"No-yes, none at all, if you please."

My hostess looked at me a little blankly, and Adah and Silas Jones giggled.

"A glass of milk will help us both out of our dilemma," I said, with a laugh.

"An editor should be able to think of two things at once," Miss Warren remarked, in a low aside.

"That depends on the subject of his thoughts. But don't breathe that word here, or I'm undone."

"Richard Morton," said Mr. Yocomb, "I hope thee feels the better for mother's ministrations since we came home. Will thee pass thy plate for some more of the same kind?"

"Mrs. Yocomb has done me good ever since I followed her into the meeting-house," I replied. "I am indeed the better for her dinner, and I ought to be. I feared you would all be aghast at the havoc I made. But it is your kindness and hospitality that have done me the most good, I would not have believed yesterday afternoon that my fortunes could have taken so favorable a turn."

"Why, what was the matter with you then?" asked Adah, with wide-eyed curiosity; and little Zillah looked at me with a pitying and puzzled glance.

"A common complaint in the city. I was committing suicide, and yesterday became conscious of the fact."

"Mr. Morton must have hit on an agreeable method of suicide, since he could commit it unconsciously," Miss Warren remarked mischievously. "I read in Emily Warren's newspaper this afternoon," said Silas Jones, with awkward malice, "of a young fellow who got a girl to marry him by pretending to commit suicide. He didn't hurt himself much though."

The incident amused Adah exceedingly, and I saw that Miss Warren's eyes were full of laughter. Assuming a shocked expression, I said:

"I am surprised that Miss Warren takes a paper so full of insidious evil." Then, with the deepest gravity, I remarked to Silas Jones, "I have recently been informed, sir, on good authority, that each one instinctively finds and reads in a newspaper that which he likes or needs. I sincerely hope, my dear sir, that the example you have quoted will not lead you to adopt a like method."

Adah laughed openly to her suitor's confusion, and the mouths of the others were twitching. With the complexion of the rose at his button-hole Mr. Jones said, a trifle vindictively:

"I thought the paragraph might refer to you, sir, you seem so slightly hurt."

"I don't like to contradict you, but I cannot be this ingenious youth whose matrimonial enterprise so deeply interests you, since I am not married, and I was hurt severely."

"Thee had been overworking," said Mrs. Yocomb kindly.

"Working foolishly rather. I thought I had broken down, but sleep and your kindness have so revived me that I scarcely know myself. Are you accustomed to take in tramps from New York?"

"That depends somewhat upon the tramps. I think the right leadings are given us."

"If good leadings constitute a Friend, I am one to-day, for I have been led to your home." "Now I'm moved to preach a little," said Mr. Yocomb. "Richard Morton, does thee realize the sin and folly of overwork? If thee works for thyself it is folly. If thee toils for the good of the world, and art able to do the world any good, it is sin; if there are loved ones dependent on thee, thee may do them a wrong for which there is no remedy. Thee looks to me like a man who has been over-doing."

"Unfortunately there is no one dependent on me, and I fear I have not had the world's welfare very greatly at heart. I have learned that I was becoming my own worst enemy, and so must plead guilty of folly."

"Well, thee doesn't look as if thee had sinned away thy day of grace yet. If thee'll take roast-beef and common-sense as thy medicine, thee'll see my years and vigor."

"Richard Morton," said his wife, with a gentle gravity, "never let any one make thee believe that thee has sinned away thy day of grace."

"Mother, thee's very weak on the 'terrors of the law.' Thee's always for coaxing the transgressors out of the broad road. Thee's latitudinarian; now!"

"And thee's a little queer, father."

"Emily Warren, am I queer?"

"You are very sound and sensible in your advice to Mr. Morton," she replied. "One may very easily sin against life and health beyond the point of remedy. I should judge from Mr. Morton's words that he is in danger."

"Now, mother, thee sees that Emily Warren believes in the terrors of the law."

"Thee wouldn't be a very good one at enforcing them, Emily," said Mrs. Yocomb, nodding her head smilingly toward her favorite.

"The trouble is," said Miss Warren a little sadly, "that some laws enforce themselves. I know of so many worn-out people in New York, both men and women, that I wish that Mr. Yocomb's words were printed at the head of ail our leading newspapers."

"Yes," said Mr. Yocomb, "if editors and newspaper writers were only as eager to quiet the people as they are to keep up the hubbub of the world, they might make their calling a useful one. It almost takes away my breath to read some of our great journals."

"Do you not think laziness the one pre-eminent vice of the world?" tasked.

"Not of native-born Americans. I think restlessness, nervous activity, is the vice of our age. I am out of the whirl, and can see it all the more clearly. Thee admits that thy city life was killing thee—I know it would kill me in a month."

"I would like to have a chance to be killed by it," said Adah, with a sigh.

"Thy absence would be fatal to some in the country," I heard Silas Jones remark, and with a look designed to be very reproachful.

"Don't tell me that. Melissa Bunting would soon console thee."

"Thee stands city life quite well, Emily," said Mrs. Yocomb.

"Yes, better than I once did. I am learning how to live there and still enjoy a little of your quiet; but were it not for my long summers in the country I fear it would go hard with me also."

"You have suggested my remedy," I said. "My business does not permit much chance for rest, unless it is taken resolutely; and, like many other sinners, I have great reforms in contemplation."

"It must be a dreadful business that came so near killing you," Adah remarked, looking at me curiously. "What can it be?"

Mrs. Yocomb glanced at her daughter reprovingly, but Miss Warren's eyes were dancing, and I saw she was enjoying my rather blank look immensely.

T decided, however, that honesty and audacity would be my best allies, and at the same time I hoped to punish Adah a little through her curiosity.

"I must admit that it is a dreadful business. Deeds of darkness occupy much of my time; and when good, honest men, like your father, are asleep, my brain, and hand are busiest. Now you see what a suspicious character your father and mother have harbored in their unquestioning hospitality."

The young lady looked at me with a thoroughly perplexed and half alarmed expression.

"My gracious!" she exclaimed. "What do you do?"

"You do not look as if 'inclined to mercy,'" I replied. "Mr. Yocomb and Miss Warren believe in the terrors of the law, so I have decided to make a full confession to Mrs. Yocomb after supper. I think that I am one of the 'transgressors' that she could 'coax.'"

After a momentary and puzzled glance at my laughing critic, Mrs. Yocomb said:

"Emily Warren knows thy secret."

"So you have told Emily Warren, but will not tell us," Adah complained, in a piqued tone and manner.

"Indeed, you are mistaken. Miss Warren found me out by intuition. I am learning that there is no occasion to tell her things: she sees them."

Mr. Yocomb's face wore a decidedly puzzled look, and contained also the suggestion of an apt guess.

"Well," he said, "thee has shown the shrewdness of an editor, and a Yankee one at that."

Miss Warren now laughed outright.

"Thee thinks," he continued, "that if thee gets mother on thy side thee's safe. I guess I'll adopt a common editorial policy, and sit safely on the fence till I hear what mother says to thy confession."

"Are you laughing at me?" I asked Miss Warren, with an injured air.

"To think that one of your calling should have got into such a dilemma!" she said, in a low tone. "It's delicious!"

"My cheeks may become bronzed, but never brazen, Miss Warren. My guilelessness should touch your sympathies."

"Well," said Adah, with rather a spiteful look at Miss Warren, "I'm glad I've not got a prying disposition. I talked with you half the afternoon and did not find you out."

Even Mrs. Yocomb laughed at this.

"Now, Miss Warren," I said, turning to her with a triumphant look, "I hope you feel properly quenched."

"Is there any record of your crime, or misfortune, or whatever it may be, in Miss Warren's newspaper?" asked Silas Jones, with a slight sneer.

"Yes, sir, of both, if the truth must be told," I replied. "That is the way she found me out."

This unexpected admission increased the perplexity all around, and also added to Miss Warren's merriment.

"Where is the paper?" said Adah, quickly.

At this peculiar proof of his daughter's indifference Mr. Yocomb fairly exploded with laughter. He seemingly shared his wife's confidence in Miss Warren to that degree that the young lady's knowledge of my business, combined with her manner, was a guarantee against anything seriously wrong. Moreover, the young girl's laugh was singularly contagious. Its spontaneity and heartiness were irresistible, and I feared that her singing would not be half so musical.

"Richard Morton," said Mrs. Yocomb, rising, "if thee wishes to free thy mind, or conscience, or heart, I will now give thee an opportunity."

"My fate is in your hands. If you send me back to my old life and work I will go at once."

"Ah!" exclaimed Miss Warren, in mock gravity, "now there is a touch of tragedy in your words. Must we all hold our breaths till you return, absolved or condemned?"

"And were I condemned would you breathe freely?"

"Yes, indeed I would, if Mrs. Yocomb condemned you. But after my sense of justice was satisfied I might be moved to pity."

"And you think I may become a pitiable object?"

"You would be, indeed, if Mrs. Yocomb condemned you."

"Lead on," I exclaimed, with a gesture of mock tragedy; "this is the hour of destiny."

CHAPTER VII
A FRIEND

"Richard Morton," said Mrs. Yocomb, as she sat down encouragingly near me in the low-studded parlor, "thee does not look into my eyes as if thee had a great burden on thy conscience."

"I have a great fear in my heart," I said.

"The two should go together," she remarked a little gravely; "and strength will be given thee to cast away both."

The spirit of jesting left me at once, and I know that I looked into her kind motherly face very wistfully and appealingly. After a moment I asked:

"Mrs. Yocomb, did you ever treat an utter stranger so kindly before?"

"I think so," she said, with a smile. "Emily Warren came to us an entire stranger and we already love her very much."

"I can understand that. Miss Warren is a genuine woman—one after your own heart. I was not long in finding that out. But I am a man of the world, and you must have noted the fact from the first."

"Richard Morton, supposing thee is a sinner above all others in Galilee, where do I find a warrant for the 'I am better than thou' spirit?"

She said these words so gently and sincerely that they touched my very soul, and I exclaimed:

"If evil had been my choice a thousand years, you might me from it."

She shook her head gravely as she said:

"Thee doesn't understand. Weak is the arm of flesh."

"But kindness and charity are omnipotent."

"Yes, if thee turns to Omnipotence for them. But far be it from me to judge thee, Richard Morton. Because thee does not walk just where I am walking is no proof that thou art not a pilgrim."

"I must tell you in all sincerity that I am not. My brain, heart, and soul have been absorbed by the world, and not by its best things either. Fifteen years ago, when scarcely more than a child, I was left alone in it. I have feared it inexpressibly, and with good reason. I have fought it, and have often been worsted. At times I have hated it; but as I began to succeed I learned to love it, and to serve it with an ambition that gave me so little respite that yesterday I thought that I was a broken and worn-out man. If ever the world had a slave, I am one; but there have been times during this June day when I earnestly wished that I might break my chains; and your serene, kindly face, that is in such blessed contrast to its shrewd, exacting, and merciless spirit, gave hope from the first."

"So thee has been alone in the world since thee was a little boy," she said, in a tone that seemed the echo of my dead mother's voice.

"Since I was twelve years of age," I replied, after a moment, and looking away. I could not meet her kind eyes as I added: "My mother's memory has been the one good, sacred influence of my life; but I have not been so true to it as I ought to have been—nothing like so true."

"Has thee no near friends or relatives?"

"I have acquaintances by the hundred, but there is no one to whom I could speak as I have to you, whom I have known but a few hours. A man has intuitions sometimes as well as a woman."

"How strange it all is!" said Mrs. Yocomb, with a sigh, and looking absently out of the window to where the sun glowed not far above the horizon. Its level rays lighted up her face, making it so beautiful and noble that I felt assured that I had come to the right one for light and guidance. "Every heart seems to have its burden when the whole truth is known," she added, meditatively. "I wonder if any are exempt. Thee seemed indeed a man of the world when jesting at the table, but now I see thy true self Thee is right, Richard Morton; thee can speak to me as to thy friend."

"I fear your surmise is true, Mrs. Yocomb; for in two instances to-day have I caught glimpses of burdens heavier than mine." She looked at me hastily, and her face grew pale. I relieved her by quietly continuing:

"Whether you have a burden on your heart or not, one thing I know to be true—the burdened in heart or conscience would instinctively turn to you. I am conscious that it is this vital difference between your spirit and that of the world which leads me to speak as I do. Except as we master and hold our own in the world, it informs us that we are of little account—one of millions; and our burdens and sorrows are treated as sickly sentimentalities. There is no isolation more perfect than that of a man of the world among people of his own kind, with whom manifestations of feeling are weaknesses, securing prompt ridicule. Reticence, a shrewd alertness to the main chance of the hour, and the spirit of the entire proverb, 'Every man for himself,' become such fixed characteristics that I suppose there is danger that the deepest springs in one's nature may dry up, and no Artesian shaft of mercy or truth be able to find anything in a man's soul save arid selfishness. In spite of all that conscience can say against me—and it can say very much—I feel sure that I have not yet reached that hopeless condition."

"No, Richard Morton, thee has not."

"I honestly hope I never may, and yet I fear it. Perhaps the turning-point has come when I must resolutely look my old life and its tendencies in the face and as resolutely work out such changes as true manhood requires. If you will permit a metaphor, I feel like a shipmaster whom a long-continued and relentless gale has driven into an unexpected and quiet harbor. Before I put to sea again I would like to rest, make repairs, and get my true bearings, otherwise I may make shipwreck altogether. And so, impelled by my stress and need, I venture to ask if you will permit me to become an inmate of your home for a time on terms similar to those that you have made with Miss Warren. That you may very naturally decline is the ground of the fear to which I referred."

"Richard Morton," said the old lady heartily, "thee's welcome to stay with us as long as thee pleases, and to come whenever thee can. The leadings in this case are plain, and I shall pray the kind Heavenly Father that all thy hopes may be realized."

"One has been realized truly. You cannot know how grateful I am."

"Thee's welcome, surely, and father will tell thee so, too. Come," and she led me out to the further end of the veranda, where Mr. Yocomb sat with Miss Warren, his daughters, and Silas Jones grouped near him.

"Well," exclaimed Adah eagerly, "what is Mr. Morton's calling? It must, indeed, be a dreadful business, since you have had such a long and serious time."

Mrs. Yocomb looked at me a little blankly.

"I declare," I exclaimed, laughing, "I forgot to tell you."

"Forgot to tell!" cried Adah. "Why, what on earth did you tell? There is nothing about you in this paper that I can find."

Mr. Yocomb looked perplexed, and I saw Miss Warren's quick glance at Mrs. Yocomb, who smiled back reassuringly.

"Father," she said, "Richard Morton wishes to stay with us for a time, I have told him that he was welcome, and that thee would tell him so, too. I think thee will. Thee may ask him any questions thee pleases. I am satisfied."

"Thee is mistress of thy home, mother, and if thee's satisfied I am. Richard Morton, thee's welcome. Thee was wise to get mother on thy side."

"So I instinctively felt ever since I saw her at the meeting-house door."

"Perhaps mother gave thee a bit of a sermon?"

"She has given me two things that a man can't be a man without—hope and courage."

"Well, thee does kind of look as if thee had plucked up heart."

"You, too, are catching the infection of this home," Miss Warren said, in a low voice, as she stood near me.

"So soon? I feel that I shall need an exposure of several weeks. There is now but one obstacle in the way."

"Ah, yes! I remember what you said. It's time you explained."

"Not yet." And I turned and answered Adah's perplexed and frowning brow.

"You will find me in that paper, Miss Adah, as one of its chief faults. I am one of its editors, and this fact will reveal to you the calling from which I and many others, no doubt, have suffered. Thus you see that, after all, I have revealed my secret to you only. To your mother I revealed myself. I hope, sir, you will not reverse your decision?" I said to Mr. Yocomb.

The old gentleman laughed heartily as he answered, "I have had my say about editors in general. Mother and—I may add—something in thy own manner, has inclined me to except present company. But I'll read thy paper since Emily Warren takes it, so thee'd better beware."

I saw that Adah was regarding me with complacency, and seemed meditating many other questions. I had fully decided, however, that while I should aim to keep her goodwill I would not permit her to make life a burden by her inane chatter, or by any sense of proprietorship in me. She must learn, as speedily as possible, that I was not one of her "half-dozen young men."

"Richard Morton, thee can keep thy room, and I hope thee will not find our quiet, homely ways irksome, since we cannot greatly change them," said my hostess.

"I have a request to make, Mrs. Yocomb," I replied earnestly; "and I shall derive no pleasure or benefit from my sojourn with you unless you grant it. It is, that your family life may go on just the same as if I were not here. As surely as I see that I am a source of restraint or extra care and trouble, you will drive me out into the wilderness again. You know why I wish to stay with you," I added meaningly.

"We shall take thee at thy word," said Mrs. Yocomb, with a smile on her lips but a very wistful, kindly light in her eyes.

"Reuben, tell Richard Morton the truth," said his father. "Would it give thee a great deal of trouble or much pleasure to take Dapple and drive to the village for friend Morton's valise?"

The youth, who was a good-natured and manly boy, to whom Sundays passed a trifle slowly, sprang up with such alacrity that I laughed as I said, "No need of words, Reuben, but I owe you a good turn all the same." Then turning to Miss Warren, I continued:

"You have been here a week. Will your conscience permit you to teach me a little topography? It would be no worse than reading that newspaper."

"Indeed, I think it might be better. It will be a useful task, at least; for, left to yourself, you might get lost, and make Mr. Yocomb no end of trouble. Did you not tell me, sir (to our host), that on one occasion you had to hunt some one up with fish-horns, lanterns, etc.?"

"Yes, and he was from New York, too," said Mr. Yocomb.

"If I get lost, leave me to my fate. There will be one editor the less."

"Very true; but I'd rather have thee on thy paper than on my conscience. So Emily Warren, thee look after him, and show him the right and proper ways, for I am now too old to enjoy a night hunt, even with the music of fish-horns to cheer us on. I ask thee, Emily, for some of thine instead when thee comes back."

CHAPTER VIII
THE MYSTERY OF MYSTERIES

"Is it a task, then, to show me the right paths and proper ways?" I asked, as we strolled away, leaving Adah looking as if—in her curiosity to know more of the new species, a night editor—she wished Silas Jones in the depths of the Dead Sea.

"That may depend on how apt and interesting a scholar you prove. I'm a teacher, you know, and teaching some of my scholars is drudgery, and others a pleasure."

"So I'm put on my good behavior at once."

"You ought to be on your good behavior anyway—this is Sunday."

"Yes, and June. If a man is not good now he'll never be. And yet such people as Mrs. Yocomb—nor will I except present company—make me aware that I am not good—far from it."

"I am glad Mrs. Yocomb made just that impression on you."

"Why?"

"Because it proves you a better man than your words suggest, and, what is of more consequence, a receptive man. I should have little hope for any one who came from a quiet talk with Mrs. Yocomb in a complacent mood or merely disposed to indulge in a few platitudes on the sweetness and quaintness of her character, and some sentimentalities in regard to Friends. If the depths of one's nature were not stirred, then I would believe that there were no depths. She is doing me much good, and giving me just the help I needed."

"I can honestly say that she uttered one sentence that did find soundings in such shallow depths as exist in my nature, and I ought to be a better man for it hereafter."

"She may have found you dreadfully bad, Mr. Morton: but I saw from her face that she did not find you shallow. If she had, you would not have touched her so deeply."

"I touched her?"

"Yes. Women understand each other. Something you said—but do not think I'm seeking to learn what it was—moved her sympathies."

"Oh, she's kind and sympathetic toward every poor mortal."

"Very true; but she's intensely womanly; and a woman is incapable of a benevolence and sympathy that are measured out by the yard—so much to each one, according to the dictates of judgment. You were so fortunate as to move Mrs. Yocomb somewhat as she touched your feelings; and you have cause to be glad; for she can be a friend that will make life richer."

"I think I can now recall what excited her sympathies, and may tell you some time, that is, if you do not send me away."

"I send you away?"

"Yes, I told you that you were the one obstacle to my remaining."

She looked at me as if perplexed and a little hurt. I did not reply at once, for her countenance was so mobile, so obedient to her thought and feeling, that I watched its varied expressions with an interest that constantly deepened. In contrast to Adah Yocomb's her face was usually pale; and yet it had not the sickly pallor of ill-health, but the clear, transparent complexion that is between the brunette and the blonde. Her eyes were full, and the impression of largeness, when she looked directly at you, was increased by a peculiar outward curve of their long lashes.

Whether her eyes could be called blue I could not yet decide, and they seemed to darken and grow a little cold as she now looked at me; but she merely said, quietly:

"I do not understand you."

"This was your chosen resting-place for the summer, was it not, Miss Warren?"

"Yes."

"Well, then, what right have I, an entire stranger, to come blundering along like a June beetle and disturb your rest? You did not look forward to associations with night editors and like disreputable people when you chose this sheltered nook of the world, and nestled under Mrs. Yocomb's wing. You have the prior right here."

As I spoke, her face so changed that it reminded me of the morning of this eventful day when I first looked out upon its brightness, and as I ceased her laugh rang out heartily.

"So after all your fate is in my hands."

"It is. You have pre-empted this claim."

"Suppose I am a little non-committal, and should say, You may spend the evening, you may stay till to-morrow; would you be content?"

"No, indeed, but I would have to submit."

"Well, this is rich. Who ever heard of an editor—and the shrewd, alert, night editor at that—in such a dilemma! Do you realize what an unwise step you have taken? Mr. Yocomb justly complimented your shrewdness in getting Mrs. Yocomb on your side, and having won her over you were safe, and might have remained in this Eden as long as you chose. Now you place it within the power—the caprice even—of an utter stranger to send you out into the wilderness again."

I said, with a smile, "I am satisfied that you differ from your mother Eve in one respect."

"Ah! in what respect?"

"You are not the kind of woman that causes banishment from Eden."

"You know very little about me, Mr. Morton."

"I know that."

She smiled and looked pleased in spite of herself.

"I think I'll let you stay till—till to-morrow," she said, with an arch side glance; then added, with a laugh, "What nonsense we are talking! As if you had not as good a right to be here as I have."

"I beg your pardon. I spoke in downright sincerity. You found this quiet place first. In a large hotel, all kinds of people can meet almost as they do on Broadway; but here we must dwell together as one family, and I feel that I have no right to force on you any association without your leave, especially as you are here alone. In a certain sense I introduce myself, and compel you to meet me socially without your permission. You may have formed a very different plan for your summer's rest."

"It is rather rare for a music-teacher to receive so much consideration. It bewilders me a little."

"Pardon me. I soon discovered that you possessed woman's highest rank."

"Indeed! Am I a princess in disguise?"

"You are more than many princesses have been—a lady. And, as I said before, you are here alone."

She turned and looked at me intently, and I felt that if I had not been sincere she would have known it. It was a peculiar and, I eventually learned, a characteristic act. I am now inclined to think that she saw the precise attitude of my mind and feeling toward her; but my awakening interest was as far removed from curiosity as is our natural desire to have a melody completed, the opening strains of which are captivating.

Her face quickly lost its aspect of grave scrutiny, and she looked away, with a slight accession of color.

"Do you want to stay very much?" she asked.

"Miss Warren," I exclaimed, and my expression must have been eager and glad, "you looked at me then as you would at a doubtful stranger, and your glance was searching. You looked as only a woman can—as one who would see her way rather than reason it out. Now tell me in sincerity what you saw."

"You know from my manner what I saw," she said, smiling and blushing slightly.

"No, I only hoped; I have not a woman's eyesight."

She bit her lip, contracted her wide, low brow for a moment, then turned and said frankly:

"I did not mean to be rude in my rather direct glance. Even though a music-teacher, I have had compliments before, and I have usually found them as empty and insincere as the people who employed them. I am somewhat alone in the world, Mr. Morton, and I belong to that class of timid and rather helpless creatures whose safety lies in their readiness to run to cover. I have found truth the best cover for me, situated as I am. I aim to be just what I seem—neither more nor less; and I am very much afraid of people who do not speak the truth, especially when they are disposed to say nice things."

"And you saw?"

"I saw that bad as you are, I could trust you," she said, laughing; "a fact that I was glad to learn since you are so bent on forcing your society upon us all for a time."

"Thank Heaven!" I exclaimed, "I thought yesterday that I was a bankrupt, but I must have a little of the man left in me to have passed this ordeal. Had I seen distrust in your eyes and consequent reserve in your manner, I should have been sorely wounded."

"No," she replied, shaking her head, "when a man's character is such as to excite distrust, he could not be so sorely wounded as you suggest."

"I'm not sure of that," I said. "I think a man may know himself to be weak and wicked, and yet suffer greatly from such consciousness."

"Why should he weakly suffer? Why not simply do right? I can endure a certain amount of honest wickedness, but there is a phase of moral weakness that I detest," and for a moment her face wore an aspect that would have made any one wronging her tremble, for it was pure, strong, and almost severe.

"I do believe," I said, "that men are more merciful to the foibles of humanity than women." "You are more tolerant, perhaps. Ah! there's Dapple," and she ran to meet the spirited horse that was coming from the farmyard. Reuben, driving, sat confidently in his light open wagon, and his face indicated that he and the beautiful animal he could scarcely restrain shared equally in their enjoyment of young, healthful life. I was alarmed to see Miss Warren run forward, since at the moment Dapple was pawing the air. A second later she was patting his arched neck and rubbing her cheek against his nose. He looked as if he liked it. Well he might.

"Oh, Reuben," she cried, "I envy you. I haven't seen a horse in town that could compare with Dapple."

The young fellow was fairly radiant as he drove away.

She looked after him wistfully, and drew a long sigh.

"Ah!" she said, "they do me good after my city life. There's life for you, Mr. Morton—full, overflowing, innocent life—in the boy and in the horse. Existence, motion, is to them happiness. It seems a pity that both must grow old and weary! My hand fairly tingles yet from my touch of Dapple's neck, he was so alive with spirit. What is it that animates that great mass of flesh and blood, bone and sinew, making him so strong, yet so gentle. At a blow he would have dashed everything to pieces, but he is as sensitive to kindness as I am. I sometimes half think that Dapple has as good a right to a soul as I have. Perhaps you are inclined toward Turkish philosophy, and think so too."

"I should be well content to go to the same heaven that receives you and Dapple. You are very fearless, Miss Warren, thus to approach a rearing horse."

Her answer was a slight scream, and she caught my arm as if for protection. At the moment I spoke a sudden turning in the lane brought us face to face with a large matronly cow that was quietly ruminating and switching away the flies. She turned upon us her large, mild, "Juno-like" eyes, in which one might imagine a faint expression of surprise, but nothing more.

My companion was trembling, and she said hurriedly:

"Please let us turn back, or go some other way."

"Why, Miss Warren," I exclaimed, "what is the matter?"

"That dreadful cow! Cows are my terror."

I laughed outright as I said, "Now is the time for me to display courage, and prove than an editor can be the knight-errant of the age. Upon my soul, Miss Warren, I shall protect you whatever horn of this dilemma I may be impaled upon." Then advancing resolutely toward the cow, I added, "Madam, by your leave, we must pass this way."

At my approach the "dreadful cow" turned and ran down the lane to the pasture field, in a gait peculiarly feminine.

"Now you know what it is to have a protector," I said, returning.

"I'm glad you're not afraid of cows," she replied complacently. "I shall never get over it. They are my terror."

"There is one other beast," I said, "that I am sure would inspire you with equal dread."

"I know you are going to say a mouse. Well, it may seem very silly to you, but I can't help it. I'm glad I wasn't afraid of Dapple, for you now can think me a coward only in streaks."

"It does appear to me irresistibly funny that you, who, alone and single-handed, have mastered this great world so that it is under your foot, should have quailed before that inoffensive cow, which is harmless as the milk she gives."

"A woman, Mr. Morton, is the mystery of mysteries—the one problem of the world that will never be solved. We even do not understand ourselves."

"For which truth I am devoutly thankful. I imagine that instead of a week, as Mr. Yocomb said, it would require a lifetime to get acquainted with some women. I wish my mother had lived. I'm sure that she would have been a continuous revelation to me. I know that she had a great deal of sorrow, and yet my most distinct recollection of her is her laugh. No earthly sound ever had for me so much meaning as her laugh. I think she laughed when other people would have cried. There's a tone in your laugh that has recalled to me my mother again and again this afternoon."

"I hope it is not a source of pain," she said gently.

"Far from it," I replied. "Memories of my mother give me pleasure, but I rarely meet with one to whom I would even think of mentioning her name."

"I do not remember my mother," she said sadly.

"Come," I resumed hastily, "you admit that you have been dull and lonely to-day. Look at that magnificent glow in the west. So assuredly ended in brightness the lives of those we loved, however clouded their day may have been at times. This June evening, so full of glad sounds, is not the time for sad thoughts. Listen to the robins, to that saucy oriole yonder on the swaying elm-branch. Beyond all, hear that thrush. Can you imagine a more delicious refinement of sound? Let us give way to sadness when we must, and escape from it when we can. I would prefer to continue up this shady lane, but it may prove too shadowy, and so color our thoughts. Suppose we return to the farmyard, where Mr. Yocomb is feeding the chickens, and then look through the old garden together. You are a country woman, for you have been here a week; and so I shall expect you to name and explain everything. At any rate you shall not be blue any more to-day if I can prevent it. You see I am trying to reward your self-sacrifice in letting me stay till to-morrow."

"You are so considerate that I may let you remain a little longer."

"What is that fable about the camel? If he once gets his head in—"

"He next puts his foot in it, is the sequel, perhaps," she replied, with the laugh that was becoming to me like a refrain of music that I could not hear too often.

CHAPTER IX
"OLD PLOD"

"Emily Warren, why does thee bring Richard Morton back so soon?" asked Mr. Yocomb, suspending for a moment the sweep of his hand that was scattering grain.

"You are mistaken, sir," I said; "I brought Miss Warren back. I thought she would enjoy seeing you feed the poultry, the horses, and especially the cows."

"Thee's more self-denying than I'd a been," he resumed, With his humorous twinkle. "Don't tell mother, but I wouldn't mind taking a walk with Emily Warren myself on a June evening like this."

"I will take a walk with you whenever you wish," laughed Miss Warren; "but I'll surely tell Mrs. Yocomb."

"Oh! I know I'd get found out," said the old man, shaking his head ruefully; "I always do."

"I'm sure you would if Miss Warren were here," I added. "I'm at a loss to know how early in the day she found me out."

"Well, I guess thee's a pretty square sort of a man. If thee'd been stealing sheep Emily Warren wouldn't laugh at thee so approvingly. I'm finding out that she rather likes the people she laughs at. At least, I take that view, for she laughs at me a great deal. I knew from Emily Warren's laugh that thee hadn't anything very bad to tell mother."

"I admit that, at the time, I enjoyed being laughed at—a rather rare experience."

"You needn't, either of you, plume yourselves that you are irresistibly funny. I laugh easily. Mr. Yocomb, why do you feed the chickens so slowly? I have noticed it before. Now Reuben and Hiram, the man, throw the corn all down at once."

"They are in more of a hurry than I am. I don't like to do anything in a hurry, least of all to eat my dinner. Now, why should these chickens, turkeys and ducks gobble everything right down? The corn seems to taste good to them; so, after a handful, I wait till they have had a chance to think how good the last kernel was before they get another. You see I greatly prolong their pleasure."

"And in these intervals you meditate on Thanksgiving Day, I suppose," she said.

"Emily Warren, thee's a good Yankee. I admit that that young gobbler there did suggest a day on which I'm always very thankful, and with good reason. I had about concluded before thee came that, if we were both spared—i.e., that gobbler and I—till next November, I would probably survive him."

"How can you have the heart to plan against that poor creature's life so coolly? See how he turns his round, innocent eyes toward you, as if in gratitude. If he could know that the hand that feeds him would chop off his head, what a moral shock he would sustain! That upturned beak should be to you like a reproachful face."

"Emily Warren, we expect thee to eat thy Thanksgiving dinner with us; and that young gobbler will probably be on the table. Now what part of him will thee take on that occasion?"

"A piece of the breast, if you please."

"Richard Morton, is not Emily Warren as false and cruel as I am?"

"Just about."

"Is thee not afraid of her?"

"I would be if she were unfriendly."

"Oh, thee thinks everybody in this house is friendly. Emily Warren, thee must keep up our good name," he added, with a mischievous nod toward her.

"Mr. Yocomb, you are forgetting the chickens altogether. There are some staid and elderly hens that are going to bed in disgust, you have kept them waiting so long."

"See how quick they'll change their minds," he said, as he threw down a handful of corn. "Now isn't that just like a hen?" he added, as they hastened back.

"And just like a woman also, I'm sure you want to suggest," said Miss Warren.

"I suppose thee never changes thy mind."

"I'm going to change the subject. Poultry with their feathers on don't interest me very much. The male birds remind me of a detestable class of conceited men, that one must see daily in the city, whose gallantry is all affectation, and who never for a moment lose sight of themselves or their own importance. That strutting gobbler there, Mr. Morton, reminds me of certain eminent statesmen whom your paper delights to honor, and I imagine that that ridiculous creature embodies their idea of the American eagle. Then the hens have such a simple, unthinking aspect. They act as if they expected to be crowed over as a matter of course; and thus typify the followers of these statesmen, who are so pre-eminent in their own estimation. Their exalted perches seem to be awarded unquestioningly."

"So you think, Miss Warren, that I have the simple, unthinking aspect typified by the physiognomy of these hens?"

"Mr. Morton, I was generalizing. We always except present company. Remember, I disagree with your paper, not you; but why you look up to these human species of the gobbler is something I can't understand, and being only a *woman*, that need not seem strange to you."

"Since I must tell you the truth on all occasions, *nolens volens*, you have hit on a subject wherein I differ from my paper. Human phases of the gobbler are not pleasant."

"But the turkey phase *is, very*," said Mr. Yocomb, throwing a handful of corn down before his favorite, which, like certain eminent statesmen, immediately looked after his own interests.

"Mr. Yocomb, please, let me help you feed the horses," said Miss Warren, leading the way into the barn, where on one side were mows for hay and grain, and, on the other, stalls for several horses. The sleek and comfortable animals seemed to know the young girl, for they thrust out their black and brown noses toward her and projected their ears instead of laying them back viciously, as when I approached; and one old plow-horse that had been much neglected, until Miss Warren began to pet him, gave a loud ecstatic whinny.

"Oh, you big, honest old fellows!" she exclaimed, caressing one and another, "I'd rather teach you than half my pupils."

"In which half do you place me?" I asked.

"You? oh, I forgot; I was to teach you topography. I will assign you by and by, after you have had a few lessons."

"A man ought to do as well as a horse, so I hope to win your favor."

"I wish all men did as well as Mr. Yocomb's horses. They evidently feel they have the family name and respectability to keep up. Mr. Yocomb, what is it that smells so sweetly?"

"That is the red-top clover we cut last week."

"Oh, isn't it good? I wouldn't mind having some myself," and she snatched down a fragrant handful from the mow. "Here, Old Plod," she said, turning to the plow-horse, "the world has rather snubbed you, as it has honest worth before. Mr. Yocomb, you and Reuben are much too fond of gay horses."

"Shall I tell Reuben that thee'd rather ride after Old Plod, as thee calls him?"

"No, I thank you; I'll go on as I've begun. I'm not changeable."

"Now, Friend Morton, is not Emily Warren as bad as I am about gay horses?"

"I'm inclined to think she is about as bad as you are in all respects."

"Emily Warren, thee needn't put on any more airs. Richard Morton thinks thee isn't any better than I am, and there's nothing under the sun an editor doesn't know."

"I wish he were right this time," she said, with a laugh and sigh curiously blended. "It seems to me, Mr. Yocomb, that you have grown here in the country like your clover-hay, and are as good and wholesome. In New York it is so different, especially if one has no home life; you breathe a different atmosphere from us in more respects than one. This fragrant old barn appears to me more of a sanctuary than some churches in which I have tried to worship, and its dim evening light more religious." "According to your faith," I said, "no shrine has ever contained so precious a gift as a manger."

"According to *our* faith, if you please, Mr. Morton."

By an instinct that ignored a custom of the Friends, but exemplified their spirit, the old man took off his hat as he said, "Yes, friend Morton, according to *our* faith. The child that was cradled in a manger tends to make the world innocent."

"The old barn has indeed become a sanctuary," I thought, in the brief silence that followed. Miss Warren stepped to the door, and I saw a quick gesture of her hands to her eyes. Then she turned and said, in her piquant way:

"Mr. Yocomb, our talk reminds me of the long grace in Latin which the priests said before meals, and which the hungry people couldn't understand. The horses are hinting broadly that oats would be more edifying. If it were Monday, I'd wager you a plum that they would all leave your oats to eat clover-hay out of my hand."

"We'll arrange about the bet to-morrow, and now try the experiment," said Mr. Yocomb, relapsing into his genial humor at once.

I was learning, however, that a deep, earnest nature was hidden by this outward sheen and sparkle. Filling his four-quart measure from the cobwebbed bin, he soon gave each horse his allowance.

"Now, Richard Morton, thee watch her, and see that she doesn't coax too much, or come it over them with any unlawful witchery. Take the hay thyself, Emily, and we'll stand back."

I went to the further end of the barn, near Old Plod, and stood where I could see the maiden's profile against the light that streamed through the open door. Never shall I forget the picture I then saw. The tall, ample figure of the old Quaker stood in the background, and his smile was broad and genial enough to have lighted up a dungeon. Above him rose the odorous clover, a handful of which Miss Warren held out to the horse in the first stall. Her lips were parted, her eyes shining, and her face had the intent, eager interest of a child, while her attitudes and motions were full of unstudied and unconscious grace.

The first horse munched stolidly away at his oats. She put the tempting wisp against his nose, at which he laid back his ears and looked vicious. She turned to Mr. Yocomb, and the old barn echoed to a laugh that was music itself as she said:

"You have won your plum, if it is Sunday. I shall try all the other horses, however, and thus learn to value correctly the expressions of affection I have received from these long-nosed gentlemen."

One after another they munched on, regardless of the clover. Step by step she came nearer to me, smiling and frowning at her want of success. My heart thrilled at a beauty that was so unconventional and so utterly self-forgetful. The blooming clover, before it fell at a sweep of the scythe, was the fit emblem of her then, she looked so young, so fair, and sweet.

"They are as bad as men," she exclaimed, "who will forgive any wrong rather than an interruption at dinner."

She now stood at my side before Old Plod, that thus far, in his single-minded attention to his oats, had seemingly forgotten her presence; but, as he lifted his head from the manger and saw her, he took a step forward, and reached his great brown nose toward her, rather than for the clover. In brief, he said, in his poor dumb way:

"I like you better than hay or oats."

The horse's simple, undisguised affection, for some reason, touched the girl deeply; for she dropped the hay and threw her arm around the horse's head, leaning her face against his. I saw a tear in her eye as she murmured:

"You have more heart than all the rest put together. I don't believe any one was ever kind to you before, and you've been a bit lonely, like myself." Then she led the way hastily out of the barn, saying, "Old Plod and I are sworn friends from this time forth; and I shall take your advice, Old Plod."

I was soon at her side, and asked:

"What advice did Old Plod give you?"

For some inexplicable reason she colored deeply, then laughed as she said:

"It's rarely wise to think aloud; but impulsive people will do it sometimes. I suppose we all occasionally have questions to decide that to us are perplexing and important, though of little consequence to the world. Come; if we are to see the old garden, we must make the most of the fading light. After my interview with Old Plod, I can't descend to cows and pigs; so good-by, Mr. Yocomb."

CHAPTER X
A BIT OF EDEN

"This is my first entrance into Eden," I said, as we passed through the rustic gate made of cedar branches and between posts green with American ivy.

"Like another man, you won't stay here long."

"Like Adam, I shall certainly go out when you do."

"That will be before very long, since I have promised Mr. Yocomb some music."

"Even though a Bohemian editor, as you may think, I am conscious of a profound gratitude to some beneficent power, for I never could have chosen so wisely myself. I might have been in Sodom and Gomorrah—for New York in contrast seems a union of both—receiving reports of the crimes and casualties of the day, but I am here with this garden in the foreground and music in the background."

"You don't know anything about the music, and you may yet wish it so far in the background as to be inaudible."

"I admit that I will be in a dilemma when we reach the music, for no matter how much I protest, you will know just what I think."

"Yes, you had better be honest."

"Come, open for me the treasures of your ripe experience. You have been a week in the country. I know you will give me a rosebud—a rare old-fashioned one, if you please, with a quaint, sweet meaning, for I see that such abound in this garden, and I am wholly out of humor with the latest mode in everything. Recalling your taste for homely, honest worth, as shown by your passion for Old Plod, I shall seek a blossom among the vegetables for you. Ah, here is one that is sweet, white, and pretty," and I plucked a cluster of flowers from a potato-hill. "By the way, what flower is this?" I asked demurely.

She looked at it blankly for a moment, then remarked, with a smile, "You have said that it was sweet, white, and pretty. Why inquire further?"

"Miss Warren, you have been a week in the country and don't know a potato-blossom."

"Our relations may be changed," she said, "and you become the teacher."

"Oh, here comes Zillah. We will settle the question according to Scripture. Does it not say, 'A little child shall lead them'? Who are you so glad to see, little one, Miss Warren or me?"

"I don't know thee very well yet," she said shyly.

"Do you know Miss Warren very well?"

"Oh, yes, indeed."

"How soon did you come to know her well?"

"The first day when she kissed me."

"I think that's a very nice way of getting acquainted. Won't you let me kiss you good-night when you get sleepy."

She looked at me with a doubtful smile, and said, "I'm afraid thy mustache will tickle me."

The birds were singing in the orchard near, but there was not a note that to my ear was more musical than Miss Warren's laugh. I stooped down before the little girl as I said:

"Suppose we see if a kiss tickles you now, and if it don't now, you won't mind it then, you know." She came hesitatingly to me, and gave the coveted salute with a delicious mingling of maidenly shyness and childish innocence and frankness.

"Ah!" I exclaimed, "Eden itself contained nothing better than that. To think that I should have been so honored—I who have written the records of enough crimes to sink a world!"

"Perhaps if you had committed some of them she wouldn't have kissed you."

"If I had to live in a ninety-nine story tenement-house, as so many do, I think I would have committed them all. Well, I may come to it. Life is a risky battle to such as I, but I'm in heaven now."

"You do seem very happy," she said, looking at me wistfully.

"I am very happy. I have given myself up wholly to the influences of this day, letting them sway me, lead me whithersoever they will. If this is a day of destiny, no stupid mulishness of mine shall thwart the happy combination of the stars. That the Fates are propitious I have singular reason to hope. Yesterday I was a broken and dispirited man. This evening I feel the influence of all this glad June life. Good Mrs. Yocomb has taken me in hand. I'm to study topography with a teacher who has several other bumps besides that of locality, and Zillah is going to show us the garden of Eden."

"Is this like the garden of Eden?" the little girl asked, looking up at me in surprise.

"Well, I'm not sure that it's just like it, but I'm more than content with this garden. In one respect I think it's better—there are no snakes here. Now, Zillah, lead where you please, I'm in the following mood. Do you know where any of these birds live? Do you think any of them are at home on their nests? If so, we'll call and pay our respects. When I was a horrid boy I robbed a bird's nest, and I often have a twinge of remorse for it." "Do you want to see a robin's nest?" asked Zillah excitedly.

"Yes, indeed."

"Then come and walk softly when I do. There's one in that lilac-bush there. If we don't make a noise, perhaps we can see mother robin on the nest. Sh—, sh—, very softly; now lift me up as father did—there, don't you see her?"

I did for a moment, and then the bird flew away on a swift, silent wing, but from a neighboring tree the paternal robin clamored loudly against our intrusion. Nevertheless, Zillah and I peeped in.

"Oh, the queer little things!" she said, "they seem all mouth and swallow."

"Mrs. Robin undoubtedly thinks them lovely. Miss Warren, you are not quite tall enough, and since I can't hold you up like Zillah, I'll get a box from the tool-house. Isn't this the jolliest housekeeping you ever saw? A father, mother, and six children, with a house six inches across and open to the sky. Compare that with a Fifth Avenue mansion!"

"I think it compares very favorably with many mansions on the Avenue," she said, after I returned with a box and she had peered for a moment into the roofless home.

"I thought you always spoke the truth," I remarked, assuming a look of blank amazement.

"Well, prove that I don't."

"Do you mean to say that you think that a simple house, of which this nest is the type, compares favorably with a Fifth Avenue mansion?"

"I do."

"What do you know about such mansions?"

"I have pupils in some of the best of them."

"I hear the voices of many birds, but you are the *rara avis* of them all," I said, looking very incredulous.

"Not at all; I am simply matter-of-fact. Which is worth the more, a furnished house or the growing children in it?"

"The children ought to be."

"Well, many a woman has so much house and furniture to look after that she has no time for her children. The little brown mother we have frightened away can give nearly all her time to her children; and, by the way, they may take cold unless we depart and let her shelter them again with her warm feathers. Besides, the protesting paterfamilias on the pear-tree there is not aware of our good-will toward him and his, and is naturally very anxious as to what we human monsters intend. The mother bird keeps quiet, but she is watching us from some leafy cover with tenfold his anxiety."

"You will admit, however, that the man bird is doing the best he can."

"Oh, yes, I have a broad charity for all of his kind."

"Well, I am one of his kind, and so shall take heart and bask in your general good-will. Stop your noise, old fellow, and go and tell your wife that she may come home to the children. I differ from you, Miss Warren, as I foresee I often shall. You are not matter-of-fact at all. You are unconventional, unique—" "Why not say queer, and give your meaning in good plain English?"

"Because that is not my meaning. I fear you are worse—that you are romantic. Moreover, I am told that girls who dote on love in a cottage all marry rich men if the chance comes." She bit her lip, colored, and seemed annoyed, but said, after a moment's hesitation, "Well, why shouldn't they, if the rich men are the right men?"

"Oh, I think such a course eminently proper and thrifty. I'm not finding fault with it in the least. They who do this are a little inconsistent, however, in shunning so carefully that ideal cottage, over which, as young ladies, they had mild and poetic raptures. Now, I can't associate this kind of thing with you. If you had 'drawings or leadings,' as Mrs. Yocomb would say, toward a Fifth Avenue mansion, you would say so in effect. I fear you are romantic, and are under the delusion that love in a cottage means happiness. You have a very honest face, and you looked into that nest as if you liked it."

"Mr. Morton," she said, frowning and laughing at the same time, "I'm not going to be argued out of self-consciousness. If we don't know what we know, we don't know anything. I insist upon it that I am utterly matter-of-fact in my opinions on this question. State the subject briefly in prose. Does a family exist for the sake of a home, or a home for the sake of a family? I know of many instances in which the former of these suppositions is true. The father toils and wears himself out, often gambles—speculating, some call it—and not unfrequently cheats and steals outright in order to keep up his establishment. The mother works and worries, smooths her wrinkled brow to curious visitors, burdens her soul with innumerable deceits, and enslaves herself that her house and its belongings may be as good or a little better than her neighbor's. The children soon catch the same spirit, and their souls become absorbed in wearing apparel. They are complacently ignorant concerning topics of general interest and essential culture, but would be mortified to death if suspected of being a little off on 'good form' and society's latest whims in mode. It is a dreary thraldom to mere things in which the soul becomes as material, narrow, and hard as the objects which absorb it. There is no time for that which gives ideality and breadth."

"Do you realize that your philosophy would stop half the industries of the world? Do you not believe in large and sumptuously furnished houses?"

"Yes, for those who have large incomes. One may live in a palace, and yet not be a slave to the palace. Our home should be as beautiful as our taste and means can make it; but, like the nest yonder, it should simply serve its purpose, leaving us the time and means to get all the good out of the world at large that we can."

A sudden cloud of sadness overcast her face as she continued, after a moment, half in soliloquy:

"The robins will soon take wing and leave the nest; so must we. How many have gone already!"

"But the robins follow the sun in their flight," I said gently, "and thus they find skies more genial than those they left."

She gave me a quick, appreciative smile as she said:

"That's a pleasant thought."

"Your home must be an ideal one," I remarked unthinkingly.

She colored slightly, and laughed as she answered:

"I'm something like a snail; I carry my home, if not my house, around with me. A music-teacher can afford neither a palace nor a cottage."

I looked at her with eager eyes as I said, "Pardon me if I am unduly frank; but on this day I'm inclined to follow every impulse, and say just what I think, regardless of the consequences. You make upon me a decided impression of what we men call comradeship. I feel as if I had known you weeks and months instead of hours. Could we not have been robins ourselves in some previous state of existence, and have flown on a journey together?"

"Mrs. Yocomb had better take you in hand, and teach you sobriety."

"Yes, this June air, laden with the odors of these sweet old-style roses and grape-blossoms, intoxicates me. These mountains lift me up. These birds set my nerves tingling like one of Beethoven's symphonies, played by Thomas's orchestra. In neither case do I know what the music means, but I recognize a divine harmony. Never before have I been conscious of such a rare and fine exhilaration. My mood is the product of an exceptional combination of causes, and they have culminated in this old garden. You know, too, that I am a creature of the night, and my faculties are always at their best as darkness comes on. I may seem to you obtuseness itself, but I feel as if I had been endowed with a spiritual and almost unerring discernment. In my sensitive and highly wrought condition, I know that the least incongruity or discord in sight or sound would jar painfully. Yes, laugh at me if you will, but nevertheless I'm going to speak my thoughts with no more restraint than these birds are under. I'm going back for a moment to the primitive condition of society, when there were no disguises. You are the mystery of this garden—you who come from New York, where you seem to have lived without the shelter of home life, to have obtained your livelihood among conventional and artificial people, and to whom the false, complicated world must be well known, and yet you make no more discord in this garden than the first woman would have made. You are in harmony with every leaf, with every flower, and every sound; with that child playing here and there; with the daisies in the orchard; with the little brown mother, whose children you feared might take cold. Hush!" I said, with a deprecatory gesture, "I will speak my mind. Never before in my life have I enjoyed the utter absence of concealment. In the city one must use words to hide thoughts more often than to express them, but here, in this old garden, I intend to reproduce for a brief moment one of the conditions of Eden, and to speak as frankly as the first man could have spoken. I am not jesting either, nor am I irreverent. I say, in all sincerity, you are the mystery of this garden—you who come from New York, and from a life in which your own true womanhood has been your protection; and yet if, as of old, God should walk in this garden in the cool of the day, it seems to me you would not be afraid. Such is the impression—given without reserve—that you make on me—you whom I have just seen, as it were!"

As she realized my sincerity she looked at me with an expression of strong perplexity and surprise.

"Truly, Mr. Morton," she said slowly, "you are in a strange, unnatural mood this evening."

"I seem so," I replied, "because absolutely true to nature. See how far astray from Eden we all are! I have merely for a moment spoken my thoughts without disguise, and you look as if you doubted my sanity."

"I must doubt your judgment," she said, turning away.

"Then why should such a clearly defined impression be made on me? For every effect there must be a cause."

She turned upon me suddenly, and her look was eager, searching, and almost imperious in its demand to know the truth.

"Are you as sincere as you are unconventional?" she asked.

I took off my hat, as I replied, with a smile, "A garden, Miss Warren, was the first sacred place of the world, and never were sincerer words spoken in that primal garden."

She looked at me a moment wistfully, and even tearfully. "I wish you were right," she said, slowly shaking her head; "your strange mood has infected me, I think; and I will admit that to be true is the struggle of my life, but the effort to be true is often hard, bitterly hard, in New York. I admit that for years truthfulness has been the goal of my ambition. Most young girls have a father and mother and brothers to protect them: I have had only the truth, and I cling to it with the instinct of self-preservation."

"You cling to it because you love it. Pardon me, you do not cling to it at all. Truth has become the warp and woof of your nature. Ah! here is your emblem, not growing in the garden, but leaning over the fence as if it would like to come in, and yet, among all the roses here, where is there one that excels this flower?" And I gathered for her two or three sprays of sweetbrier.

"I won't mar your bit of Eden by a trace of affectation," she said, looking directly into my eyes in a frank and friendly manner; "I'd rather be thought true than thought a genius, and I will make allowance for your extravagant language and estimate on the ground of your intoxication. You surely see double, and yet I am pleased that in your transcendental mood I do not seem to make discord in this old garden. This will seem to you a silly admission after you leave this place and recover your everyday senses. I'm sorry already I made it—but it was such an odd conceit of yours!" and her heightened color and glowing face proved how she relished it.

It was an exquisite moment to me. The woman showed her pleasure as frankly as a happy child. I had touched the keynote of her character as I had that of Adah Yocomb's a few hours before, and in her supreme individuality Emily Warren stood revealed before me in the garden.

She probably saw more admiration in my face than she liked, for her manner changed suddenly.

"Being honest doesn't mean being made of glass," she said brusquely; "you don't know anything about me, Mr. Morton. You have simply discovered that I have not a leaning toward prevarication. That's all your fine words amount to. Since I must keep up a reputation for telling the truth, I'm obliged to say that you don't remind me of Adam very much."

"No, I probably remind you of a night editor, ambitious to be smart in print."

She bit her lip, colored a little. "I wasn't thinking of you in that light just then," she said. "And—and Adam is not my ideal man."

"In what light did you see me?"

"It is growing dusky, and I won't be able to see you at all soon."

"That's evasion."

"Come, Mr. Morton, I hope you do not propose to keep up Eden customs indefinitely. It's time we returned to the world to which we belong."

"Zillah!" called Mrs. Yocomb, and we saw her coming down the garden walk.

"Bless me! where is the child!" I exclaimed.

"When you began to soar into the realms of melodrama and forget the garden you had asked her to show you, she sensibly tried to amuse herself. She is in the strawberry-bed, Mrs. Yocomb."

"Yes," I said, "I admit that I forgot the garden; I had good reason to do so."

"I think it is time we left the garden. You must remember that Mrs. Yocomb and I are not night editors, and cannot see in the dark."

"Mother," cried Zillah, coming forward, "see what I have found;" and her little hands were full of ripe strawberries. "If it wasn't getting so dark I could have found more, I'm sure," she added,

"What, giving them all to me?" Miss Warren exclaimed, as Zillah held out her hands to her favorite. "Wouldn't it be nicer if we all had some?"

"Who held you up to look into the robin's nest?" I asked reproachfully.

"Thee may give Richard Morton my share," said the little girl, trying to make amends.

I held out my hand, and Miss Warren gave me half of them.

"Now these are mine?" I said to Zillah. "Yes!"

"Then I'll do what I please with them."

I picked out the largest, and stooping down beside her, continued: "You must eat these or I won't eat any."

"Thee's very like Emily Warren," the little girl laughed; "thee gets around me before I know it."

"I'll give you all the strawberries for that compliment."

"No, thee must take half."

"Mrs. Yocomb, you and I will divide, too. Could there possibly be a more delicious combination!" and Miss Warren smacked her lips appreciatively.

"The strawberry was evolved by a chance combination of forces," I remarked.

"Undoubtedly," added Miss Warren, "so was my Geneva watch."

"I like to think of the strawberry in this way," said Mrs. Yocomb. "There are many things in the Scriptures hard to understand; so there are in Nature. But we all love the short text: 'God is love.' The strawberry is that text repeated in Nature."

"Mrs. Yocomb, you could convert infidels and pagans with a gospel of strawberries," I cried.

"There are many Christians who prefer tobacco," said Mrs. Yocomb, laughing.

"That reminds me," I exclaimed, "that I have not smoked to-day. I fear I shall fall from grace to-morrow, however."

"Yes, I imagine you will drop from the clouds by tomorrow," Miss Warren remarked.

"By the way, what a magnificent cloud that is rising above the horizon in the southwest. It appears like a solitary headland in an azure sea."

"Ah—h!" she said, in satirical accent.

"Mrs. Yocomb, Miss Warren has been laughing at me ever since I came. I may have to claim your protection."

"No! thee and father are big enough to take care of yourselves."

"Emily Warren, is thee and Richard Morton both lost?" called Mr. Yocomb from the piazza. "I can't find mother either. If somebody don't come soon I'll blow the fish-horn."

"We're all coming," answered Mrs. Yocomb, and she led the way toward the house.

"You have not given me a rose yet," I said to Miss Warren.

"Must you have one?"

"A man never uses the word 'must' in seeking favors from a lady."

"Adroit policy! Well, what kind of a one do you want?"

"I told you long ago."

"Oh, I remember. An old-fashioned one, with a pronounced meaning. Here is a York and Lancaster bud. That has a decided old-style meaning."

"It means war, does it not?"

"Yes."

"I won't take it. Yes I will, too," I said, a second later, and I took the bud from her hand. "You know the law of war," I added: "To the victor belong the spoils."

She gave me a quick glance, and after a moment said, a trifle coldly,

"That remark seems bright, but it does not mean anything."

"It often means a great deal. There, I'm out of the garden and in the ordinary world again. I wonder if I shall ever have another bit of Eden in my life."

"Oh, indeed you shall. I will ask Mr. Yocomb to give you a day's weeding and hoeing there."

"What will you do in the meantime?"

"Sit under the arbor and laugh at you."

"Agreed. But suppose it was hot and I grew very tired, what would you do?"

"I fear I would have to invite you under the arbor."

"You fear?"

"Well, I would invite you if you had been of real service in the garden."

"That would be Eden unalloyed."

"Since I am not intoxicated, I cannot agree with you."

CHAPTER XI
"MOVED"

"Mr. Yocomb," I said, as we mounted the piazza, "what is the cause of the smoke rising above yonder mountain to the east of us? I have noticed it several times this afternoon, and it seems increasing."

"That mountain was on fire on Saturday. I hoped the rain of last night would put it out, but it was a light shower, and the fire is under headway again. It now seems creeping up near the top of the mountain, for I think I see a faint light."

"I do distinctly; the mountain begins to remind me of a volcano."

"The moon will rise before very long, and you may be treated to a grand sight if the fire burns, as I fear it will."

"This is a day of fate," I said, laughing, "and almost any event that could possibly happen would not surprise me."

"It has seemed a very quiet day to me," said the old gentleman. "Neither mother nor any one on the high seat had a message for us this morning, and this afternoon I took a very long nap. If thee had not come and stirred us up a little, and Emily Warren had not laughed at us both, I would call it almost a dull day, as far as any peaceful day can be dull. Such days, however, are quite to my mind, and thee'll like 'em better when thee sees my age."

"I'm inclined to think," I replied, "that the great events of life would rarely make even an item in a newspaper."

Mrs. Yocomb looked as if she understood me, but Miss Warren remarked, with a mischievous glance:

"Personals are generally read."

"Editors gossip about others, not themselves."

"You admit they gossip."

"That one did little else seems your impression."

"News and gossip are different things; but I'm glad your conscience so troubles you that you exaggerate my words."

"Emily Warren, thee can squabble with Richard Morton all day to-morrow after thy amiable fashion, but I'm hankering after some of thy music."

"I will keep you waiting no longer, sir, and would have come before, but I did not wish you to see Mr. Morton while he was in a very lamentable condition."

"Why, what was the matter with him?" asked Adah, who had just joined us in the lighted hall; "he seems to have very queer complaints."

"He admits that he was intoxicated, and he certainly talked very strangely."

"Miss Adah, did I talk strangely or wildly this afternoon?"

"No, indeed, I think you talked very nicely; and I told Silas Jones that I never met a gentleman before who looked at things so exactly as I did."

This was dreadful. I saw that Miss Warren was full of suppressed merriment, and was glad that Mrs. Yocomb was in the parlor lighting the lamps.

"I suppose Mr. Jones was glad to hear what you said," I remarked, feeling that I must say something.

"He may have been, but he did not look so."

"Mr. Yocomb, you have your daughter's testimony that I was sober this afternoon, and since that time I have enjoyed nothing stronger than milk and the odor of your old-fashioned roses. If I was in a lamentable condition in the garden, Miss Warren was the cause, and so is wholly to blame."

"Emily Warren, does thee know that thy mother Eve made trouble in a garden?"

"I've not the least intention of taking Mr. Morton out of the garden. He may go back at once, and I have already suggested that you would give him plenty of hoeing and weeding there."

"I'm not so sure about that; I fear he'd make the same havoc in my garden that I'd make in his newspaper."

"Then you think an editor has no chance for Eden?"

"Thee had better talk to mother about that. If there's any chance for thee at all she'll give thee hope. Now, Emily Warren, we are all ready. Sing some hymns that will give us all hope—no, sing hymns of faith."

Adah took a seat on the sofa, and glanced encouragingly at me, but I found a solitary chair by an open window, where I could look out across the valley to the burning mountain, and watch the stars come out in the darkening sky. Within I faced Miss Warren's profile and the family group.

I had not exaggerated when I told Miss Warren that I was conscious of a fine exhilaration. Sleep and rest had banished all dragged and jaded feelings. For hours my mind had been free from a sense of hurry and responsibility, which made it little better than a driving machine. In the mental leisure and quiet which I now enjoyed I had grown receptive—highly sensitive indeed—to the culminating scenes of this memorable day. Even little things and common words had a significance that I would not have noted ordinarily, and the group before me was not ordinary. Each character took form with an individuality as sharply defined as their figures in the somewhat dimly lighted room, and when I looked without into the deepening June night it seemed an obscure and noble background, making the human life within more real and attractive.

Miss Warren sat before her piano quietly for a moment, and her face grew thoughtful and earnest. It was evident that she was not about to perform some music, but that she would unite with her sincere and simple friends, Mr. and Mrs. Yocomb, in giving expression to feelings and truths that were as real to her as to them.

"How perfectly true she is!" I thought, as I noted the sweet, childlike gravity of her face. Then, in a voice that proved to be a sympathetic, pure soprano, well trained, but not at all great, she sang:

"My faith looks up to Thee."

Their faith seemed very real and definite, and I could not help feeling that it would be a cruel and terrible thing if that pronoun "Thee" embodied no living and loving personality. The light in their faces, like that of a planet beaming on me through the open window, appeared but the inevitable reflection of a fuller, richer spiritual light that now shone full upon them.

One hymn followed another, and Reuben, who soon came in, seemed to have several favorites. Little Zillah had early asked for those she liked best, and then her head had dropped down into her mother's lap, and Miss Warren's sweet tones became her lullaby, her innocent, sleeping face making another element in a picture that was outlining itself deeply in my memory.

Adah, having found that she could not secure my attention, had fallen into something like a revery. Very possibly she was planning out the dress that she meant to "cut to suit herself," but in their repose her features became very beautiful again.

Her face to me, however, was now no more than a picture on the wall; but the face of the childlike woman that was so wise and gifted, and yet so simple and true, had for me a fascination that excited my wonder. I had seen scores of beautiful women—I lived in a city where they abounded—but I had never seen this type of face before. The truth that I had not was so vivid that it led to the thought that, like the first man, I had seen in the garden the one woman of the world, the mistress of my fate. A second later I was conscious of a sickening fear. To love such a woman, and yet not be able to win her—how could one thereafter go on with life! Beware, Richard Morton! On this quiet June evening, in this home of peace and the peaceful, and with hymns of love and faith breathed sweetly into your ears, you may be in the direst peril of your life. From this quiet hour may come the unrest of a lifetime. Then Hope whispered of better things. I said to myself, "I did not come to this place. I wandered hither, or was led hither; and to every influence of this day I shall yield myself. If some kindly Power has led me to this woman of crystal truth, I shall be the most egregious fool in the universe if I do not watch and wait for further possibilities of good."

How sweet and luminous her face seemed in contrast with the vague darkness without! More sweet and luminous would her faith be in the midst of the contradictions, obscurities, and evils of the world. The home that enshrined such a woman would be a refuge for a man's tempted soul, as well as a resting-place for his tired body.

"Sing 'Tell me the Old, Old Story,'" said Mr. Yocomb, in his warm, hearty way. Was I a profane wretch because the thought would come that if I could draw, in shy, hesitating admission, another story as old as the world it would be heavenly music?

Could it have been that it was my intent gaze and concentrated thought that made her turn suddenly to me after complying with Mr. Yocomb's request? She colored slightly as she met my eyes, but said quietly, "Mr. Morton, you have expressed no preference yet."

"I have enjoyed everything you have sung," I replied, and I quietly sustained her momentary and direct gaze.

She seemed satisfied, and smiled as she said, "Thank you, but you shall have your preference also."

"Miss Warren, you have sung some little time, and perhaps your voice is tired. Do you play Chopin's Twelfth Nocturne? That seems to me like a prayer."

"I'm glad you like that," she said, with a pleased, quick glance. "I play it every Sunday night when I am alone."

A few moments later and we were all under the spell of that exquisite melody which can fitly give expression to the deepest and tenderest feelings and most sacred aspirations of the heart.

Did I say all? I was mistaken. Adah's long lashes were drooping, her face was heavy with sleep, and it suggested flesh and blood, and flesh and blood only.

Miss Warren's eyes, in contrast, were moist, her mouth tremulous with feeling, and her face was a beautiful transparency, through which shone those traits which already made her, to me, pre-eminent among women.

I saw Mrs. Yocomb glance from one girl to the other, then close her eyes, while a strong expression of pain passed over her face. Her lips moved, and she undoubtedly was speaking to One near to her, though so far, seemingly, from most of us.

A little later there occurred one or two exquisite movements in the prayer harmony, and I turned to note their effect on Mrs. Yocomb, and was greatly struck by her appearance. She was looking fixedly into space, and her face had assumed a rapt, earnest, seeking aspect, as if she were trying to see something half hidden in the far distance. With a few rich chords the melody ceased. Mr. Yocomb glanced at his wife, then instantly folded his hands and assumed an attitude of reverent expectancy. Reuben did likewise. At the cessation of the music Adah opened her eyes, and by an instinct or habit seemed to know what to expect, for her face regained the quiet repose it had worn at the meeting-house in the morning.

Miss Warren turned toward Mrs. Yocomb, and sat with bowed head. For a few moments we remained in perfect silence. There was a faint flash of light, followed after an interval by a low, deep reverberation. The voices in nature seemed heavy and threatening. The sweet, gentle monotone of the woman's voice, as she began to speak, was divine in contrast. Slowly she enunciated the sentences:

"What I do, thou knowest not now: but thou shalt know hereafter."

After a pause she continued: "As the dear young friend was playing, these words were borne in upon my mind. They teach the necessity of faith. Thanks be to the God of heaven and earth, that He who spake these words is so worthy of the faith He requires! The disciple of old could not always understand his Lord; no more can we. We often shrink from that which is given in love, and grasp at that which would destroy. Though but little, weak, erring children, we would impose on the all-wise God our way, instead of meekly accepting His way. Surely, the One who speaks has a right to do what pleases His divine will. He is the sovereign One, the Lord of lords; and though He slay me, yet will I trust in Him.

"But though it is a King that speaks, He does not speak as a king. He is talking to His friends; He is serving them with a humility and meekness that no sinful mortal has surpassed. He is proving, by the plain, simple teaching of actions, that we are not merely His subjects, but His brethren, His sisters; and that with Him we shall form one household of faith, one family in God. He is teaching the sin of arrogance and the folly of pride. He is proving, for all time, that serving—not being served—is God's patent of nobility. We should not despise the lowliest, for none can stoop so far as He stooped."

Every few moments her low, sweet voice had, as an accompaniment, distant peals of thunder, that after every interval rolled nearer and jarred heavier among the mountains. More than once I saw Miss Warren start nervously, and glance apprehensively at the open window where I sat, and through which the lightning gleamed with increasing vividness. Adah maintained the same utterly quiet, impassive face, and it seemed to me that she heard nothing and thought of nothing. Her eyes were open; her mind was asleep. She appeared an exquisite breathing combination of flesh and blood, and nothing more. Reuben looked at his mother with an expression of simple affection; but one felt that he did not realize very deeply what she was saying; but Mr. Yocomb's face glowed with an honest faith and strong approval.

"The Master said," continued Mrs. Yocomb, after one of the little pauses that intervened between her trains of thought, "'What I do, thou knowest not now.' There He might have stopped. Presuming is the subject that asks his king for the why and wherefore of all that he does. The king is the highest of all; and if he be a king in truth, he sees the furthest of all. It is folly for those beneath the throne to expect to see so far, or to understand why the king, in his far-reaching providence, acts in a way mysterious to them. Our King is kingly, and He sees the end from the beginning. His plans reach through eternities. Why should He ever be asked to explain to such as we? Nevertheless, to the fishermen of Galilee, and to us, He does say, 'Thou shalt know hereafter.'

"The world is full of evil. We meet its sad mysteries on every side, in every form. It often touches us very closely—" For a moment some deep emotion choked her utterance. Involuntarily, I glanced at Adah. Her eyes were drooping a little heavily again, and her bosom rose and fell in the long, quiet breath of complete repose. Miss Warren was regarding the suffering mother with the face of a pitying angel.

"And its evils *are* evil," resumed the sad-hearted woman, in a tone that was full of suppressed anguish; "at least, they seem so, and I don't understand them—I can't understand them, nor why they are permitted; but He has promised that good shall come out of the evil, and has said, 'Thou shalt know hereafter.' Oh, blessed hereafter! when all clouds shall have rolled away, and in the brightness of my Lord's presence every mystery that now troubles me shall be made clear. Dear Lord, I await Thine own time. Do what seemeth good in Thine own eyes;" and she meekly folded her hands and bowed her head. For a moment or two there was the same impressive silence that fell upon us before she spoke. Then a louder and nearer peal of thunder awakened Zillah, who raised her head from her mother's lap and looked wonderingly around, as if some one had called her.

Never had I witnessed such a scene before, and I turned toward the darkness that I might hide the evidence of feelings that I could not control.

A second later I sprang to my feet, exclaiming, "Wonderful!"

Miss Warren came toward me with apprehension in her face, but I saw that she noted my moist eyes.

I hastened from the room, saying, "Come out on the lawn, all of you, for we may now witness a scene that is grand indeed."

CHAPTER XII
ONE OF NATURE'S TRAGEDIES

I had been so interested in Mrs. Yocomb's words, their effect on the little group around her, and the whole sacred mystery of the scene, that I had ceased to watch the smoking mountain, with its increasingly lurid apex. In the meantime the fire had fully reached the summit, on which stood a large dry tree, and it had become a skeleton of flame. Through this lurid fire and smoke the full moon was rising, its silver disk discolored and partially obscured.

This scene alone, as we gathered on the piazza and lawn below it, might well have filled us with awe and wonder; but a more impressive combination was forming. Advancing from the southwest, up the star-lit sky, which the moon was brightening momentarily, was a cloud whose blackness and heaviness the vivid lightning made only the more apparent.

"I am an old man," said Mr. Yocomb, "but I never saw anything so grand as this before."

"Mother, mother," said little Zillah, "I'm afraid. Please take me upstairs and put me to bed." And the mother, to whom the scene in the heavens was a glorious manifestation of the God she loved rather than feared, denied herself of what was almost like a vision, for the sake of the child.

"It's awful," said Adah; "I won't look at it any longer. I don't see why we can't have nice quiet showers that one can go to sleep in;" and she disappeared within the house. Reuben sat down on the piazza, in his quiet, undemonstrative way. Miss Warren came down and stood close to Mr. Yocomb's side, as if she half unconsciously sought the good man's protection.

Incessant lightnings played from some portion of the cloud, zigzagging in fiery links and forkings, while, at brief intervals, there would be an exceptionally vivid flash, followed more and more closely by heavier and still heavier explosions. But not a leaf stirred around us: the chirp of a cricket was sharply distinct in the stillness. The stars shone serenely over our heads, and the moon, rising to the left out of the line of the smoke and fire, was assuming her silvery brightness, and at the same time rendering the burning mountain more lurid from contrast.

"Herbert, Herbert, now I know how brave you were," I heard Miss Warren exclaim, in a low, awed tone.

I saw by the frequent flashes that she was very pale, and that she was trembling.

"You mean your brother," I said gently.

With her eyes fixed on the threatening and advancing cloud as if fascinated by it, she continued in the same tone, that was full of indescribable dread: "Yes, yes, I never realized it so fully before, and yet I have lain awake whole nights, going, by an awful necessity, over every scene of that terrible day. He stood in his place in the line of battle on an open plain, and he watched battery after battery come down from the heights above and open fire. He stood there till he was slain, looking steadily at death. This cloud that is coming makes me understand the more awful storm of war that he faced. Oh, I wish this hadn't happened," and there was almost agony in her tone. "I'm not brave as he was, and every nearer peal of thunder shakes my very soul."

Mr. Yocomb put his hand tenderly on her shoulder as he said:

"My dear, foolish little child—as if thy Father in heaven would hurt thee!"

"Miss Warren," I said earnestly, "I have too little of Mr. and Mrs. Yocomb's faith; but it seems impossible that anything coming from heaven could harm you."

She drew closer to Mr. Yocomb's side, but still looked at the cloud with the same wide-eyed dread, as if spellbound by it.

"To me," she resumed in her former tone, that only became more hurried and full of fear as the tempest approached, "these awful storms are no part of heaven. They are wholly of earth, and seem the counterparts of those wild outbreaks of human passion from which I and so many poor women in the past have suffered;" and a low sob shook her frame. "I wish I had more of good Mr. Yocomb's spirit; for this appalling cloud seems to me the very incarnation of evil. Why *does* God permit such things?"

With a front as calm and serene as that of any ancient prophet could have been, Mr. Yocomb began repeating the sublime words, "The voice of Thy thunder was in the heavens; the lightnings lightened the world."

"Oh, no, no!" cried the trembling girl, "the God I worship is not in the storm nor in the fire, but in the still small voice of love. You may think me very weak to be so moved, but truly I cannot help it. My whole nature shrinks from this." I took her hand as I said warmly, "I do understand you, Miss Warren. Unconsciously you have fully explained your mood and feeling. It's in truth your nature, your sensitive, delicate organism, that shrinks from this wild tumult that is coming. In the higher moral tests of courage, when the strongest man might falter and fail, you would be quietly steadfast."

She gave my hand a quick, strong pressure, and then withdrew it as she said, "I hope you are right; you interpret me so generously that I hope I may some day prove you right."

"I need no proof. I saw your very self in the garden."

"How strange—how strange it all is!" she resumed, with a manner that betokened a strong nervous excitability. "Can this be the same world—these the same scenes that were so full of peace and beauty an hour ago? How tremendous is the contrast between the serene, lovely June day and evening just passed and this coming tempest, whose sullen roar I already hear with increasing dread! Mr. Morton, you said in jest that this was a day of fate. Why did you use the expression? It haunts me, oppresses me. Possibly it is. I rarely give way to presentiments, but I dread the coming of this storm inexpressibly. Oh!" and she trembled violently as a heavier peal than we had yet heard filled the wide valley with awful echoes.

"Not even a sparrow shall fall to the ground without your Father. We are safe, my child. God will shield thee more lovingly than I;" and he drew her closer to him.

"I know what you say is true, and yet I cannot control this mortal fear and weakness."

"No, Miss Warren, you cannot," I said; "therefore do not blame yourself. You tremble as these trees and shrubs will be agitated in a few moments, because you cannot help it."

"You are not so moved."

"No, nor will that post be moved," I replied, with a reckless laugh. "I must admit that I am very much excited, however, for the air is full of electricity. I can't help thinking of the little robins in a home open to the sky."

Her only answer was a low sob, but not for a moment did she take her wide, terror-stricken gaze from the cloud whose slow, deliberate advance was more terrible than gusty violence would have been.

The phenomena had now become so awful that we did not speak again for some moments. The great inky mass was extending toward the eastward, and approaching the fire burning on the mountain-top, and the moon rising above and to the left of it; and from beneath its black shadow came a heavy, muffled sound that every moment deepened and intensified.

Suddenly, as if shaken by a giant's hands, the tree-tops above us swayed to and fro; then the shrubbery along the paths seemed full of wild terror and writhed in every direction.

Hitherto the moon had shone on the cloud with as serene a face as that with which Mr. Yocomb had watched its approach, but now a scud of vapor swept like a sudden pallor across her disk, giving one the odd impression that she had just realized her peril, and then an abyss of darkness swallowed her up. For a few moments longer the fire burned on, and then the cloud with its torrents settled down upon it, and the luridly luminous point became opaque.

The night now alternated between utter darkness and a glare in which every leaf and even the color of the tossing roses were distinct.

After the first swirl of wind passed, there fell upon nature round us a silence that was like breathless expectation, or the cowering from a blow that cannot be averted, and through the stillness the sound of the advancing tempest came with awful distinctness, while far back among the mountains the deep reverberations scarcely ceased a moment.

Broken masses of vapor, the wild skirmish line of the storm, passed over our heads, blotting out the stars. The trees and shrubbery were bending helplessly to the gust, and Miss Warren could scarcely stand before its violence. The great elm swayed its drooping branches over the house as if to protect it. The war and whirl of the tempest was all about us, the coming rain reminded one of the resounding footsteps of an innumerable host, and great drops fell here and there like scattering shots.

"Come in, my child," said Mr. Yocomb; "the storm will soon be passed, and thee and the robins shall yet have quiet sleep to-night. I've seen many such wild times among the mountains, and nothing worse than clearer skies and better grain followed. You will hear the robins singing—"

A blinding flash of lightning, followed by such a crash as I hope I may never hear again, prevented further reassuring words, and he had to half support her into the house.

I had never been in a battle, but I know that the excitement which mastered me must have been akin to the grand exaltation of conflict, wherein a man thinks and acts by moments as if they were hours and years. Well he may, when any moment, may end his life. But the thought of death scarcely entered my mind. I had no presentiment of harm to myself, but feared that the dwelling or outbuildings might be struck.

Almost with the swiftness of lightning came the calculation:

"Estimating distance and time, the next discharge of electricity will be directly over the house. If there's cause, which God forbid, may I have the nerve and power to serve those who have been so kind!"

As I thought, I ran to an open space which commanded a view of the farmhouse. Scarcely had I reached it before my eyes were blinded for a second by what seemed a ball of intense burning light shot vertically into the devoted home.

"O God!" I gasped, "it is the day of fate." For a moment I seemed paralyzed, but the igniting roof beside the chimney roused me at once.

"Reuben!" I shouted.

A flash of lightning revealed him still seated quietly on the piazza, as if he had heard nothing. I rushed forward, and shook him by the shoulder.

"Come, be a man; help me. Quick!" and I half dragged him to a neighboring cherry-tree, against which I had noticed that a ladder rested.

By this time he seemed to recover his senses, and in less than a moment we had the ladder against the house. Within another moment he had brought me a pail of water from the kitchen.

"Have two more pails ready," I cried, mounting the low, sloping roof.

The water I carried, and rain, which now began to fall in torrents, extinguished the external fire, but I justly feared that the woodwork had been ignited within. Hastening back at perilous speed, I said to Reuben, who stood ready: "Take one of the pails and lead the way to the attic and the rooms upstairs."

The house was strangely and awfully quiet as we rushed in.

I paused a second at the parlor door. Miss Warren lay motionless upon the floor, and Mr. Yocomb sat quietly in his great armchair.

A sickening fear almost overwhelmed me, but I exclaimed loudly, "Mr. Yocomb, rouse yourself; I smell fire; the house is burning!"

He did not move nor answer, and I followed Reuben, who was half-way up the stairs. It took but a few seconds to reach the large, old-fashioned garret, which already was filling with smoke.

"Lead the way to the chimney," I shouted to Reuben in my terrible excitement. "Do not waste a drop of water. Let me put it on when I find just where the fire is."

Through the smoke I now saw a lurid point. A stride brought me thither, and I threw part of the water in my pail up against it. The hissing and sputtering proved that we had hit on the right spot, while the torrents falling on the roof so dampened the shingles that further ignition from without was impossible.

"We must go down a moment to breathe," I gasped, for the smoke was choking us.

As we reached the story in which were the sleeping apartments, I cried:

"Great God! Why don't some of the family move or speak?"

Hitherto Reuben had realized only the peril of his home; but now he rushed into his mother's room, calling her in a tone that I shall never forget.

A second later he uttered my name in a strange, awed tone, and I entered hesitatingly. Little Zillah apparently lay sleeping in her crib, and Mrs. Yocomb was kneeling by her bedside.

"Mother!" said Reuben, in a loud whisper.

She did not answer.

He knelt beside her, put his arm around her, and said, close to her ear, "Mother! why don't you speak to me?" She made no response, and I saw that she leaned so heavily forward on the bed as to indicate utter unconsciousness.

The boy sprang up, and gazed at me with wild questioning in his eyes.

"Reuben!" I said quickly, "she's only stunned by the lightning. Will you prove yourself a man, and help me in what must be done? Life may depend upon it."

"Yes," eagerly.

"Then help me lift your mother on the bed; strong and gentle, now — that's it."

I put my hand over her heart.

"She is not dead," I exclaimed joyously; "only stunned. Let us go to the attic again, for we must keep shelter this wild night."

We found that the smoke had perceptibly lessened; I dashed the other pail of water on the spot that had been burning, then found that I could place my hand on it. We had been just in time, for there was light woodwork near that communicated with the floor, and the attic was full of dry lumber, and herbs hanging here and there, that would have burned like tinder. Had these been burning we could not have entered the garret, and as it was we breathed with great difficulty. The roof still resounded to the fall of such torrents that I felt that the dwelling was safe, unless it had become ignited in the lower stories, and it was obviously our next duty to see whether this was the case.

"Reuben," I said, "fill the pails once more, while I look through the house and see if there's fire anywhere else. It's clear that all who were in the house were stunned—even you were, slightly, on the piazza—so don't give way to fright on their account. If you do as I bid, you may do much to save their lives; but we must first make sure the house is safe. If it isn't, we must carry them all out at once."

He comprehended me, and went for the water instantly.

I again looked into Mrs. Yocomb's room. It was impregnated with a strong sulphurous odor, and I now saw that there was a discolored line down the wall adjoining the chimney, and that little Zillah's crib stood nearer the scorching line of fire than Mrs. Yocomb had been. But the child looked quiet and peaceful, and I hastened away.

My own room was dark and safe. I opened the door of Miss Warren's room, and a flash of lightning, followed by complete darkness, showed that nothing was amiss.

I then opened another door, and first thought the apartment on fire, it was so bright; but instantly saw that two lamps were burning, and that Adah lay dressed upon the bed, with her face turned toward them. By this common device she had sought to deaden the vivid lightning. Her face was white as the pillow on which it rested; her eyes were closed, and from her appearance she might have been sleeping or dead. Even though almost overwhelmed with dread, I could not help noting her wonderful beauty. In my abnormal and excited condition of mind, however, it seemed a natural and essential part of the strange, unexpected experiences of the day.

I was now convinced that there was no fire in the second story, and the thought of Miss Warren drew me instantly away. I already had a strange sense of self-reproach that I had not gone to her at once, feeling as if I had discarded the first and most sacred claim. I met Reuben on the stairway, and told him that the second story was safe, and asked him to look through the first story and cellar, and then to go for a physician as fast as the fleetest horse could carry him.

CHAPTER XIII
THE LIGHTNING AND A SUBTLER FLAME

On entering the parlor, I found Mr. Yocomb standing up and looking around in a dazed manner. He did not seem to know me, and in my deep anxiety I did not heed him. Kneeling beside Miss Warren, I found that her pulse was very feeble. I lifted her gently upon the sofa, and threw open a window, so that the damp, gusty wind, full of spray from the rain, might blow in upon her.

Mr. Yocomb laid his hand heavily on my shoulder, and asked, in a thick voice, "What does it all mean?"

I saw that he was deathly pale, and that he tottered. Taking his arm, I supported him to a lounge in the hall, and said, "Mr. Yocomb, you were taken ill. You must lie down quietly till the physician comes."

He seemed so confused and unable to think that he accepted my explanation. Indeed, he soon became so ill from the effects of the shock that he could not rise.

Again I knelt at Miss Warren's side, and began chafing her hands; but the cool wind and spray did the most to revive her. She opened her eyes, looked at me fixedly a few moments, and then tried to rise.

"Please keep quiet," I said, "till I bring you some brandy;" and I hastened to my room, tore open my valise, and was soon moistening her lips from a small flask. After swallowing a little she regained self-possession rapidly.

"What happened?" she asked.

"I fear you swooned."

She passed her hand over her brow, and looked around as if in search, of some one, then said, "Where is Mrs. Yocomb?"

"She is in her room with Zillah."

"Please let me go to her;" and she again essayed to rise.

"Miss Warren," I said gently, "I have no right to ask a favor of you, but I will thank you very much if you will just remain quietly on this sofa till you are better. You remember we had a frightful storm. I never knew such heavy thunder."

"Ah! there it is again," she said, shuddering, as a heavy peal rolled away to the north.

"Miss Warren, you said once to-day that you could trust me. You can. I assure you the storm is past; there is no more danger from it, but there is danger unless you do as I bid you. Remain quietly here till you have recovered from—from your nervous prostration. I happen to have some knowledge in a case of this kind, and I know that much depends on your being quiet for an hour or more. You need not be alarmed if you do as I bid you. I will see to it that some one is within call all the time;" and I tried to speak cheerfully and decisively.

She smiled as she said, "Since you have assumed the role of doctor, I'll obey, for I know how arbitrary the profession is."

Then she again reclined wearily on the sofa, and I went out, closing the door.

I found Reuben beside his father, who certainly needed care, for the terrible nausea which attends recovery from a severe shock from electricity had set in.

"Reuben," I urged, "*do* go for the doctor; I'll do everything for your father that I can, but we must have a good physician at once. Go in your buggy as fast as you can drive in the dark—can't you take a lantern?—and bring the doctor with you. First tell him what has happened, so that he can bring the proper remedies. Be a man, Reuben; much depends on you to-night."

Within five minutes I heard the swift feet of Dapple splash out upon the road. The night was growing still and close, and the gusts occurred at longer intervals. The murky cloud had covered the sky, utterly obscuring the moonlight, and there was a steady and heavy fall of rain.

After Reuben had gone, a terrible sense of isolation and helplessness oppressed me. I remembered strange tales of lightning and its effects that I had heard. Would the mother and her two daughters survive? Was Mr. Yocomb seriously ill? But I found that the anxiety which tortured me most was in behalf of the one who gave the best promise of speedy recovery; and it was my chief hope that she would remain quietly where I had left her till the physician arrived. I had pretended to a far greater knowledge than I possessed, since in truth I had had very little experience in illness. If Miss

Warren should leave the parlor, and thus learn that the farmhouse might become the scene of an awful tragedy, the effect upon her would probably be disastrous in the extreme.

These and like thoughts were coursing swiftly through my mind as I waited upon Mr. Yocomb, and sought to give him relief.

"Ice!" he gasped; "it's in cellar."

I snatched up the candle that Reuben had left burning on the hall-table, and went for it. The place was strange, and I was not as quick and deft as many others would have been, and so was absent some moments.

Great was my surprise and consternation when I returned, for Miss Warren stood beside Mr. Yocomb, holding his head.

"Why are you here?" I asked, and my tone and manner betokened deep trouble.

"I'm better," she said, quietly and firmly.

"Miss Warren," I remonstrated, "I won't answer for the consequences if you don't go back to the parlor and remain there till the doctor comes. I know what I'm about."

"You don't look as if master of the situation. You are haggard—you seem half desperate—"

"I'm anxious about you, and if—"

"Mr. Morton, you are far more anxious about others. I've had time to think. A swoon is not such a desperate affair. You guessed rightly—a thunderstorm prostrates me, but as it passes I am myself again."

After aiding Mr. Yocomb to recline feebly on the lounge, she came to the table where I was breaking the ice, and said, in a low tone:

"Something very serious has happened."

I could not look at her. I dared not to speak even, for I was oppressed with the dread of a worse tragedy. With her morbid fear of lightning she might almost lose her reason if now, in her weak, unnerved condition, she saw its effect on Mrs. Yocomb and Adah.

"Mother," moaned Mr. Yocomb; "why don't mother come?"

"She's with Zillah upstairs," I faltered. "Zillah's ill!"

"Then why does not Adah come to her father?" Miss Warren questioned, looking at me keenly.

I felt that disguise was useless.

"Mr. Morton, your hand so trembles that you can scarcely break the ice. Something dreadful has happened—there's the smell of smoke and fire in the house. Tell me, tell me!" and she laid her hand appealingly on my arm.

"Oh, Miss Warren," I groaned, "let me shield you. If further harm should come to you to-night—"

"Further harm will come unless you treat me as a woman, not as a child," she said firmly. "I know you mean it kindly, and no doubt I have seemed weak enough to warrant any amount of shielding."

At this moment there came a peal of thunder from the passing storm, and she sank shudderingly into a chair. As it passed she sprang up and said:

"I can't help that, but I can and will help you. I understand it all. The house has been struck, and Zillah, Adah, and Mr. Yocomb have been hurt. Let me feed Mr. Yocomb with the ice. Are you sure he should have ice? I would give him brandy first if I had my way, but you said you knew—"

"Miss Warren, I don't know—I'm in mortal terror in behalf of the family; but my chief dread has been that you would come to know the truth, and now I can't keep it from you. If you can be brave and strong enough to help me in this emergency, I will honor you and thank you every day of my life."

"Mother! mother! why doesn't mother come?" Mr. Yocomb called.

Miss Warren gave me a swift glance that was as reassuring as sunlight, and then went quietly into the parlor. A moment later she was giving Mr. Yocomb brandy and water, and quieting him with low, gentle words.

"You remember, Mr. Yocomb," she said, "that Zillah was greatly frightened by the storm. You would not have the mother leave the child just yet. Mr. Morton, will you go upstairs and see if I can be of any assistance? I will join you there as soon as I have made Mr. Yocomb a little more comfortable," and she went to the parlor and brought out another pillow, and then threw open the hall-door in order that her patient might have more air, for he respired slowly and laboriously. Her words seemed to quiet him, and he gave himself into her hands. I looked at her wonderingly for a moment, then said, in a low tone:

"You are indeed a woman and a brave one. I recognize my superior officer, and resign command at once."

She shook her head as she gave me a glimmer of a smile, but urged, in a whisper, "Hasten, we must not lose a moment."

I swiftly mounted the stairs, relieved of my chief anxiety.

Through the open door I saw Adah's fair white face. She had not stirred. I now ventured in and spoke to her, but she was utterly unconscious. Taking her hand I was overjoyed to find a feeble pulse.

"It may all yet be well. God grant it," I muttered.

"He will," said Miss Warren, who had joined me almost immediately; "this is not a day of fate, I trust;" and she began moistening Adah's lips with brandy, and trying to cause her to swallow a little, while I chafed her pretty hands and rubbed brandy on her wrists.

"It seems to me as if an age, crowded with events, had elapsed since I started on my aimless walk this morning," I said, half in soliloquy.

"That you were directed hither will be cause for lasting gratitude. Was not the house on fire?"

"Yes, but Reuben was invaluable. He was out on the piazza, and so was not hurt."

"Was Mrs. Yocomb hurt?" she asked, looking at me in wild alarm.

"Please do not fail me," I entreated; "you have been so brave thus far. Mrs. Yocomb will soon revive, I think. You were unconscious at first."

She now realized the truth that Mrs. Yocomb was not caring for Zillah, and hastened to their room, impelled by an overmastering affection for the woman who had treated her with motherly kindness.

I followed her, and assured her that her friend was living. It needed but a moment to see that this was true, but little Zillah scarcely gave any sign of life. Both were unconscious.

The young girl now looked at me as if almost overwhelmed, and said, in a low shuddering tone, "This is awful—far worse than I feared; I do wish the doctor was here."

"He must be here soon. I know you won't give way. In great emergencies a true woman is great. You may save—"

A thunder-peal from the retreating storm drowned my words. She grew white, and would have fallen had I not caught her and supported her to a chair.

"Give me—a few moments," she gasped, "and I'll be—myself again. This shock is awful. Why, we would all have burned up—had you not put the fire out," and her eyes dilated with horror.

"We have no time for words," I said, brusquely. "Here, take this brandy, and then let us do everything in our power to save life. I scarcely know what to do, but something must be done. If we can only do the right thing, all may yet be well."

In a moment the weakness passed, and she was her brave, quiet self once more.

"I won't fail you again," she said resolutely, as she tried to force a little brandy between Mrs. Yocomb's pallid lips.

"You are a genuine woman," I replied heartily, as I chafed Mrs. Yocomb's wrists with the spirits; "I know how terrible the ordeal has been for you, and most young ladies would have contributed to the occasion nothing but hysterics."

"And you feared I would."

"I feared worse. You are morbidly timid in a thunder-storm, and I dreaded your learning what you now know beyond measure."

"You were indeed burdened," she said, looking at me with strong sympathy.

"No matter. If you can keep up and suffer no ill consequences from this affair, I believe that the rest will come through all right. After all, they are affected only physically, but you—"

"I have been a little weak-minded. I know it. But if it doesn't thunder any more I'll keep up. Ever since I was a child the sound of thunder paralyzed me. Thank God, Mrs. Yocomb is beginning to revive."

"I will leave her in your care, and see if I can do anything for Mr. Yocomb. I thus show that I trust you fully."

As I passed out I heard a faint voice call, "Mother!"

Going to the door of Adah's room I saw that she was conscious, and feebly trying to rise. As I entered she looked at me in utter bewilderment, then shrank with instinctive fear from the presence of a seeming intruder. I saw the impulse of her half-conscious mind, and called Miss Warren, who came at once, and her presence seemed reassuring.

"What's the matter?" she asked, with the same thick utterance that I had noted in Mr. Yocomb's voice. It seemed as if the organs of speech were partially paralyzed.

"You have been ill, my dear, but now you are much better. The doctor will be here soon," Miss Warren said soothingly.

She seemed to comprehend the words imperfectly, and turned her wondering eyes toward me.

"Oh, that the doctor would come!" I groaned. "Here you have two on your hands, and Mr. Yocomb is calling."

"Who's that?" asked Adah, feebly pointing to me.

"You remember Mr. Morton," Miss Warren said quietly, bathing the girl's face with cologne. "You brought him home from meeting this morning."

The girl's gaze was so fixed and peculiar that it held me a moment, and gave the odd impression of the strong curiosity of one waking up in a new world. Suddenly she closed her eyes and fell back faint and sick. At that moment, above the sound of the rain, I heard the quick splash of a horse's feet, and hastened down to greet the doctor.

In a few hasty words I added such explanation of the catastrophe as Reuben's partial account rendered necessary, and by the time I had finished we were at Mrs. Yocomb's door. Mr. Yocomb seemed sufficiently at rest to be left for a while.

"This is Miss Warren," I said. "She will be your invaluable assistant, but you must be careful of her, since she, too, has suffered very severely, and, I fear, is keeping up on the strength of her brave will, mainly."

The physician, fortunately, was a good one, and his manner gave us confidence from the start.

"I think I understand the affair sufficiently," he said; "and the best thing you can do for my patients, and for Miss Warren also, Mr. Morton, is to have some strong black coffee made as soon as possible. That will now prove an invaluable remedy, I think."

"I'll show you where the coffee is," Miss Warren added promptly. "Unfortunately—perhaps fortunately—Mrs. Yocomb let the woman who assisted her go away for the night. Had she been here she might have been another burden."

Even though I had but a moment or two in the room, I saw that the doctor was anxious about little Zillah.

As Miss Warren waited on me I said earnestly, "What a godsend you are!"

"No," she replied with a tone and glance that, to me, were sweeter and more welcome than all the June sunshine of that day. "I was here, and you were sent." Then her eyes grew full of dread, reminding me of the gaze she had bent on the storm before which she had cowered. "The house was on fire," she said; "we were all helpless—unconscious. You saved us. I begin to realize it all."

"Come, Miss Warren, you now are 'seeing double.' Here, Reuben," I said to the young fellow, who came dripping in from the barn. "I want to introduce you in a new light. Miss Warren doesn't half know you yet, and I wish her to realize that you are no longer a boy, but a brave, level-headed man, that even when stunned by lightning could do as much as I did."

"Now, Richard Morton, I didn't do half as much as thee did. How's mother?" and he spoke with a boy's ingenuousness.

"Doing well under the care of the doctor you brought," I said; "and if you will now help me make this dying fire burn up quickly, she will have you to thank more than any one else when well again."

"I'm going to thank you now," Miss Warren exclaimed, seizing both of his hands. "God bless you, Reuben! You don't realize what you have done for us all."

The young fellow looked surprised. "I only did what Richard Morton told me," he protested, "and that wasn't much."

"Well, there's a pair of you," she laughed. "The fire put itself out, and Dapple went after the doctor." Then, as if overwhelmed with gratitude, she clasped her hands and looked upward, as she said, in low, thrilling tones: "Thank God, oh thank God! what a tragedy we have escaped!"

"Yes," I said, "it might have been a day of fate indeed. Life would have been an unendurable burden if what you feared had happened. What's more, I would have lost my faith in God had such a home and its inmates been destroyed. The thought of it makes me sick," and I sank into a chair.

"We must not think of it," she cried earnestly, "for there's much to be done still. There, I've helped you all I can here. When the coffee's ready, call me, and I'll come for it. Get on dry clothes as soon as you can, Reuben, for you can be of great service to us upstairs. I'm astonished at you, Mr. Morton, you haven't any nerve at all—you who have dealt in conflagrations, murders, wars, pestilences, earthquakes, writing them up in the most harrowing, blood-curdling style; you have absolutely turned white and faint because the inmates of a farmhouse were shocked. I won't believe you are an editor at all unless you call me within five minutes."

Whether because her piquant words formed just the spur I needed, or because she had a mysterious power over me which made her will mine, I threw off the depression into which I had reacted from my overwhelming excitement and anxiety, and soon had my slowly kindling fire burning furiously, dimly conscious in the meantime that deep in my heart another and subtler flame was kindling also.

CHAPTER XIV
KINDLING A SPARK OF LIFE

I soon had coffee made that was as black as the night without. Instead of calling Miss Warren, I took a tray from the dining-room, and carried it with several cups upstairs.

"Bring it here!" called the doctor.

I entered Mrs. Yocomb's room, and found that she had quite fully revived, and that Reuben had supported his father thither also. He reclined on the lounge, and his usually ruddy face was very pale. Both he and his wife appeared almost helpless; but the doctor had succeeded in arresting, by the use of ice, the distressing nausea that had followed consciousness. They looked at me in a bewildered manner as I entered, and could not seem to account for my presence at once. Nor did they, apparently, try to do so long, for their eyes turned toward little Zillah with a deeply troubled and perplexed expression, as if they were beginning to realize that the child was very ill, and that events of an extraordinary character had happened.

"Let me taste the coffee," said the doctor. "Ah! that's the kind—black and strong. See how it will bring them around," and he made Mr. and Mrs. Yocomb each swallow a cup of it.

"Miss Warren," he called, "give some of this to Miss Adah, if she is quiet enough to take it. I cannot leave the child."

Miss Warren came at once. Her face was clouded and anxious, and she looked with eager solicitude toward the still unconscious Zillah, whose hands Reuben was chafing.

"I think Miss Adah will soon be better," she replied to the doctor's inquiring glance, and she went back to her charge.

"Take some yourself," said the physician to me, in a low tone. "I fear we are going to have a serious time with the little girl."

"You do not realize," I urged, "that Miss Warren needs keeping up almost as truly as any of them."

"You'll have to take care of her then," said the doctor hastily; "she seems to be doing well herself, and doing well for others. Take her some coffee, and say that I said she must drink it."

I knocked at Adah's door and called, "Miss Warren, the doctor says you must drink this coffee."

"In a few moments," she answered, and after a little time she came out.

"Where's your cup?" she asked. "Have you taken any?"

"Not yet, of course."

"Why of course? If you want me to drink this you must get some at once."

"There may not be enough. I don't know how much the doctor may need."

"Then get a cup, and I'll give you half of this."

"Never," I answered promptly. "Do as the doctor bade you."

She went swiftly to Mrs. Yocomb's room and filled another cup.

"I pledge you my word I won't touch a drop till you have taken this. You don't realize what you have been through, Mr. Morton. Your hand so trembled that you could scarcely carry the cup; you are all unnerved. Come," she added gravely, "you must be in a condition to help, for I fear Zillah is in a critical condition."

"I'm not going to break down," I said resolutely. "Give it to Reuben. Poor fellow, he was very wet."

She looked at my clothes, and then exclaimed:

"Why, Mr. Morton, don't you know you are wet through and through?"

"Am I?" and I looked down at my soaked garments.

"I don't believe you have a dry thread on you."

"I've been too excited to think of it. Of course, I got wet on the roof; but what's a summer shower! Your coffee's getting cold."

"So is yours."

"You have the doctor's orders."

"I would be glad if my wishes weighed a little with you," she said, appealingly.

"There, Miss Warren, if you put it that way I'd drink gall and vinegar," and I gulped down the coffee.

She vanished into Adah's room, saying, "You must take my word for it that I drink mine. I shall sip it while waiting on my patient."

Having insisted on Reuben's taking some also, I returned to the kitchen and made a new supply. Mr. and Mrs. Yocomb's extreme prostration, both mental and physical, perplexed me. Their idolized child was still unconscious, and yet they could only look on in wondering and perplexed anxiety. I afterward learned that a partial paralysis of every faculty, especially of memory, was a common effect of a severe shock of electricity. It was now evident that Miss Warren, from some obscure cause, escaped harm from lightning. The words I had employed to reassure her turned out to be true—she had merely swooned—and thus, on recovery, had full possession of all her faculties.

"I would be glad if my wishes weighed a little with you," she had said. In wonder at myself, I asked, "What weighs more with me? By what right is this maiden, whom I have met but to-day, taking such absolute control of my being? Am I overwrought, morbid, fanciful, deluded by an excited imagination into beliefs and moods that will vanish in the clear sunlight and clearer light of reason? or has the vivid lightning revealed with absolute distinctness the woman on whom I can lean in perfect trust, and yet must often sustain in her pathetic weakness? The world would say we are strangers; but my heart and soul and every fibre of my being appear to recognize a kinship so close that I feel we never can be strangers again. It is true the lightning fuses the hardest substances, making them one; however, I am beginning to think that my hitherto callous nature has been smitten by a diviner fire. If so, Heaven grant that I'm not the only one struck.

"Well, it's a queer world. When I broke down, last Friday night, and sat cowering before the future in my editorial sanctum, I little dreamed that on Sunday night I should be making coffee in a good old Quaker's kitchen, and, what is still more strange, making a divinity out of a New York music-teacher!"

A moment later I added, "That's a stupid way of putting it. I'm not making a divinity out of her at all. She is one, and I've had the wit to recognize the truth. Are her gentlemen friends all idiots that they have not—"

"What! talking to yourself, Mr. Morton? I fear the events of this day are turning your head." And Miss Warren entered.

"Speak of an angel—you know the saying." "Indeed! The only word I heard as I entered was 'idiot.'"

"Pardon me, you overheard the word 'idiots,' so can gather nothing from that."

"No, your mutterings are dark indeed. I see no light or sense in them; but the doctor came to Adah's door and asked me for more coffee."

"How is Miss Adah?"

"Doing nicely. She'll sleep soon, I think."

"I do hope little Zillah is recovering."

"Yes, Reuben put a radiant face within the door, a few minutes since, and said Zillah was 'coming to,' as he expressed it. Adah is doing so well that I feel assured about the others. Now that she is becoming quiet, I think I can leave her and help with Zillah."

"And you're not exhausting yourself?"

"I've not yet reached the stage of muttering delirium. Mr. Morton, will you permit me to suggest that you go to your room and put on dry clothes. You are not fit to be seen. Moreover, there is a mark athwart your nose that gives to your face a sinister aspect, not becoming in one whose deeds of darkness this night will bear the light of all coming time. It might be appropriate in a printing-office; but I don't intend to have little Zillah frightened. Oh, I'm so glad and grateful that we have all escaped! There, that will do; give me the tray."

"Beg your pardon: I shall carry it up myself. What on earth would I have done without you in this emergency?"

"Come, Mr. Morton, I'm not used to being disobeyed. Yes, you did look as helpless as only a man can look when there's illness; and there's no telling what awful remedies you might have administered before the doctor came. I think I shall take the credit of saving all our lives, since you and Reuben won't."

She pushed open the door of Mrs. Yocomb's room, and her face changed instantly.

Little Zillah lay on the bed and was still unconscious. Mrs. Yocomb had been moved into an armchair, and every moment comprehension of the truth grew clearer, and her motherly solicitude was intensified.

Reuben evidently was frightened, and the doctor's brow was knitted into a frown of perplexity.

"We thought she was coming to," said Reuben to Miss Warren, "but she's gone back worse than ever."

"Mr. Morton, I wish you to give to all a cup of that coffee and take some yourself," said the physician, in a quiet but authoritative voice. "Mr. Yocomb, you must not rise; you will be ill again, and I now need all the help I can get with this child. We must try artificial respiration, spraying the chest with cold water, and every possible means."

"Would to God that I could help thee!" cried Mrs. Yocomb.

"You can help by keeping absolutely quiet. Mr. Morton, in this emergency you must become as a brother or one of the family."

"I am one with them to-night," I said earnestly; "let me help you in any way."

"You three must rub her with flannel and spirits, while I lift her arms slowly up and down to try to induce respiration."

The poor limp little body—how sacred it seemed to me!

We worked and worked till the perspiration poured from our faces. Every expedient was tried, until the physician at last desisted and stood back for a moment in anxious thought.

Then, in a tone broken with anguish, Mr. Yocomb exclaimed:

"Would to God the bolt had fallen on my head, and not on this dear little lamb."

In bitter protest against it all I cried, "The bolt has fallen on your heart, Mr. Yocomb. How is it that God has thunderbolts for lambs?"

"Richard Morton, thee's unjust," began Mrs. Yocomb, in a voice that she tried to render quiet and resigned. "Who art thou to judge God? 'What I do thou knowest not now, but thou shalt know—' Oh, my child, my child!" broke out her wailing cry, and motherhood triumphed.

Reuben was sobbing over his sister with all the abandon of boyish grief, but Miss Warren stood before the little form, apparently lifeless, with clasped hands and dilated eyes.

"I can't—I won't give her up," she exclaimed passionately, and darted from the room.

I followed wonderingly. She was already in the kitchen, and had found a large tub.

"Fill this with hot water," she said to me. "No! let me do it; I'll trust no one. Yes, you may carry it up, but please be careful. I'll bring some cold water to temper it. Doctor," she exclaimed, re-entering the room, "we must work till we know there is no chance. Yes, and after we know it. Is not hot water good?"

"Anything is good that will restore suspended circulation," he replied; "we'll try it. But wait a moment. I've employed a nice test, and if there's life I think this little expedient will reveal it." He held the child's hand, and I noted that a string had been tied around one of the small white fingers, and that he intently watched the part of the finger beyond the string. I comprehended the act at once, and recognized the truth that there would be little hope of life if this test failed. If there was any circulation at all the string would not prevent the blood flowing out through the artery, but it would prevent its return, and, therefore, if there was life a faint color would manifest itself in the finger. I bent over and held my breath in my eager scrutiny.

"The child's alive!" I exclaimed.

By a quick, impressive gesture the physician checked my manifestation of feeling and excitement as he said:

"Yes, she's alive, and that's about all. We'll try a plunge in the hot bath, and then friction and artificial respiration again."

We set to work once more with double zeal under the inspiration of Miss Warren's words and manner, but especially because assured that life still lingered. In less than a quarter of an hour there was a perceptible pulse. At last she was able to swallow a little stimulant, and the faint spark of life, of which we scarcely dared to speak lest our breath might extinguish it, began to kindle slowly. When at last she opened her eyes, Miss Warren turned hers heavenward with a fulness of gratitude that must have been sweet to the fatherly heart of God if the words be true, "Like as a father pitieth his children."

Mrs. Yocomb threw herself on her knees by the bedside, sobbing, "Thank God! thank God!"

Reuben was growing wild with joy, and the father, overwhelmed with emotion, was struggling to rise, when the doctor said, in low, decided tones:

"Hush! Nothing must be said or done to excite or surprise her. Mr. and Mrs. Yocomb, as you love your child, control yourselves. You, Mr. Morton, would seem strange to her, and, with Reuben, had better leave us now. Miss Warren will help me, and I think all will be well."

"Don't overtax Miss Warren," I urged, lingering anxiously at the door a moment.

She gave me a smiling, reassuring nod, as much as to say that she would take care of herself.

"God bless her!" I murmured, as I sought my room. "I believe she has saved the child."

CHAPTER XV
MY FATE

Having lighted the lamp in my room, I looked around it with a delicious sense of proprietorship. Its quaint, homely comfort was just to my taste, and now appeared doubly attractive. Chief of all, it was a portion of the home I had had some part in saving, and we instinctively love that which ministers to our self-complacency. An old house seems to gain a life and being of its own, and I almost imagined it conscious of gratitude that its existence had not been blotted out. Mrs. Yocomb's cordial invitation to come and stay when I could gave me at the time a glad sense that I had found a country refuge to which I could occasionally escape when in need of rest. I felt now, however, as if the old walls themselves would welcome me. As to the inmates of the home, I feared that their grateful sense of the services I was so fortunate as to render might make their boundless sense of obligation embarrassing to me. It would be their disposition to repay an ordinary favor tenfold, and they would always believe that Reuben and I had saved their lives, and the old home which no doubt had long been in their family.

"Well, I'll never complain of fortune again," I thought, "since I've been permitted to do for these people what I have;" and I threw myself down on the lounge, conscious of the warm, comfortable glow imparted by dry clothes and the strong coffee, still more conscious of an inner satisfaction that the threatening events of the night had ended just as I could have wished.

"Since it was to be, thank God I was here and was able to act for the best," I murmured. "The June sunshine and the lightning have thrown considerable light on my future. I said to Emily Warren, 'What could I have done without you in this emergency?' With still greater emphasis I feel like asking, What would life be without you? It seems absurd that one person should become essential to the life of another in a few brief hours. And yet, why absurd? Is it not rather in accord with the deepest and truest philosophy of life? Is the indissoluble union of two lives to result from long and careful calculations of the pros and cons? In true marriage it seems to me the soul should recognize its mate when meeting it."

It thus may be seen that I was no exception to that large class who accept or create a philosophy pleasing to it, and there is usually enough truth in any system to prevent its being wholly unreasonable.

I heard a step in the hall, and as I had left my door open so that at any sound I could spring up, I was so fortunate as to intercept the object of my thoughts. Her face was full of deep content, but very pale. To the eager questioning of my manner, she replied:

"The doctor says Zillah is doing as well as we could expect. Oh, I'm so glad!" "Miss Warren, you don't know how pale you are. When are *you* going to rest? I've been lying down, and my conscience troubled me as I thought of you still working."

"I never imagined that editors had such tender consciences," she said, with a low laugh, and she vanished into Adah's room.

I knew she wouldn't stay long, and remained at the end of the hall, looking out of the window. The lightning flashes had grown faint and distant, but they were almost incessant, and they revealed that the clouds were growing thin toward the west, while near the horizon a star glimmered distinctly.

"Miss Warren," I called, as she came out of Adah's room, "I've a good omen to show you. Do you see that star in the west? I think the morning will be cloudless?"

"But those flashes prove that the storm is causing fear and loss to other and distant homes."

"Not at all. It is, no doubt, causing 'better grain and clearer skies,' as Mr. Yocomb said. Such an experience as we have had to-night, while having its counterparts not infrequently, take the world over, is by no means common."

"Oh, I hope we may have no more heavy thunderstorms this summer. They are about the only drawback to this lovely season."

"You are perfectly safe so long as you remain here," I laughed; "you know the lightning never strikes twice in the same place."

"I hope to stay here, but for better reasons than that."

"So do I."

"I should think you would. You, certainly, are no longer homeless. Mr. and Mrs. Yocomb will adopt you in spite of yourself as soon as they realize it all. The string of the latch will always hang outside of the door for you, I can tell you; and a nice place it will be for a city man to come."

"And for a city woman, too. Mrs. Yocomb had adopted you before all this happened, and I don't believe she'll forget that you really saved little Zillah's life."

"The dear little thing!" she exclaimed, tears starting to her eyes. "How pathetic her little unconscious form was!"

"To me," I replied earnestly, "it was the most exquisite and sacred thing I ever saw. I don't wonder you felt as you did when you said, 'I can't—I won't give her up,' for it seemed at the moment almost as if my life depended on her life, so powerful was her hold on my sympathy. The doctor spoke truer than he thought, for it seems as if the lightning had fused me into this family, and my grief would have been almost as great as Reuben's had little Zillah not revived."

"I feel as if it would have broken my heart," and her tears fell fast. Dashing them away she said, "I cry as well as laugh too easily, and I'm often so provoked that I could shake myself. I must say that I think we're all becoming well acquainted for people who have met so recently."

"Oh, as for you," I replied, "I knew you well in some previous state of existence, and have just met you again."

"Mr. Morton," she said, turning on me brusquely, "I shall not be quite sure as to your entire sanity till you have had a long sleep. You have seemed a little out of your head on some points ever since our extended acquaintance began. You have appeared impressed or oppressed with the hallucination that this day—is it to-day or to-morrow?"

"It's to-day for a little while longer," I replied, looking at my watch.

"Well, then, that to-day was 'a day of fate,' and you made me nervous on the subject—"

"Then I'm as sane as you are."

"No, I hadn't any such nonsense in my mind till you suggested it, but having once entertained the idea it haunted me."

"Yes, and it haunts you still," I said, eagerly.

"What time is it, Mr. Morton?"

"It lacks but a few moments of midnight."

"No," she said, laughingly, "I don't believe anything more will happen to-day, and as soon as the old clock downstairs strikes twelve I think the light of reason will burn again in your disordered mind. Good-night."

Instead of going, however, she hesitated, looked at me earnestly a moment, then asked:

"You said you found me unconscious?"

"Yes."

"How did you revive me?"

"I carried you to the sofa under the window, which I opened. I then chafed your hands, but I think the wind and spray restored you."

"I don't remember fainting before; and—oh, well, this whole experience has been so strange that I can't realize it."

"Don't try to. If I'm a little out of my head, your soul will be out of your body if you don't take better care of yourself. You might as well be killed by lightning as over-fatigue. That doctor seems to think you are made of india-rubber."

"I've laughed to myself more than once at your injunctions to the doctor since Zillah revived. We've had such a narrow escape that I feel as if I ought not to laugh again for a year, but I can't help it. I won't thank you as I meant to—it might make you vain. Good-night," and she gave my hand a quick, strong pressure, and went swiftly back to Mrs. Yocomb's room.

Had my hand clasped only flesh and blood, bone and sinew? No, indeed. I felt that I had had within my grasp a gratitude and friendly regard that was so full and real that the warm-hearted, impulsive girl would not trust herself to express it in words. Her manner, however, was so frank and unconstrained that I knew her feelings to be only those of gratitude and friendly regard, seeing clearly that she entertained no such thoughts as had come unbidden to me.

In spite of my fatigue, the habit of my life and the strong coffee would have banished all thought of sleep for hours to come, if there had been no other cause, but the touch of a little hand had put more glad awakening life within me than all the stimulants of the world.

I went downstairs and looked through the old house to see that all was right, with as much solicitude as if it were indeed my own home. Excepting the disorder I had caused in the kitchen and hall, it had the midnight aspect of quiet and order that might have existed for a century.

"I would not be afraid of the ghosts that came back to this home," I muttered. "Indeed, I would like to see Mr. and Mrs. Yocomb's ancestors; and, now I think of it, some one of them should wear a jaunty, worldly hat to account for Adah. By Jove! but she was beautiful as she lay there, with her perfect physical life suspended instantaneously. If the lightning would only create a woman within the exquisite casket, the result would well repay what we have passed through. Her mother would say, as I suppose, that another and subtler fire from heaven were needed for such a task."

As I came out into the hall the great clock began to strike, in the slow, dignified manner befitting its age—

"One, two, three—twelve."

The day of fate had passed. I knew Emily Warren was laughing at me softly to herself as she and the physician watched with the patients in Mrs. Yocomb's room.

I was in no mood to laugh, for every moment the truth was growing clearer that I had met my fate.

I looked into the parlor, in which a lamp was burning, and conjured up the scene I had witnessed there. I saw a fair young face, with eyes turned heavenward, and heard again the words, "My faith looks up to Thee."

Their faith had been sorely tried. The burning bolt from heaven seemed a strange response to that faith; the crashing thunder a wild, harsh echo to the girl's sweet, reverent tones.

"Is it all chance?" I queried, "or all inexorable law? Who or what is the author of the events of this night?" As if in answer, Mrs. Yocomb's text came into my mind: "What I do thou knowest not now, but thou shalt know hereafter."

"Well," I muttered, "perhaps there is as much reason in their philosophy as in any other. Somebody ought to be in charge of all this complex life and being."

I went out on the piazza. The rain was still falling, but softly and lightly. A freshening breeze was driving the thin, lingering clouds before it, and star after star looked out, as if lights were being kindled in the western sky. The moon was still hidden, but the vapor was not dense enough to greatly obscure her rays. In the partial light the valley seemed wider, the mountains higher, and everything more beautiful, in contrast with the black tempest that had so recently filled the scene.

I sat down on the piazza to watch with those who were watching with the child. I made up my mind that I certainly should not retire until the physician departed; and in my present mood I felt that my midsummer night's dream would be to me more interesting than that of Will Shakespeare. Hour after hour passed almost unnoted. The night became serene and beautiful. The moon, like a confident beauty, at last threw aside her veil of clouds, and smiled as if assured of welcome. Raindrops gemmed every leaf; and when the breeze increased, myriads of them sparkled momentarily through the silver light. As morning approached the air grew so sweet that I recognized the truth that the new flowers of a new day were opening, and that I was inhaling their virgin perfume.

I rose and went softly to the ivy-covered gateway of the old garden, and the place seemed transfigured in the white moonlight. Even the kitchen vegetables lost their homely, prosaic aspect. I stole to the lilac-bush, and peered at the home that had been roofless through all the wild storm. My approach had been so quiet that the little brown mother sat undisturbed, with her head under her wing; but the paternal robin, from an adjacent spray, regarded me with unfeigned surprise and alarm. He uttered a note of protest, and the mother-bird instantly raised her head and fixed on me her round, startled eyes. I stole away hastily, smiling to myself as I said:

"Both families will survive unharmed, and both nests are safe."

I went to the spot where I had stood with Emily Warren at the time I had half-jestingly, half-earnestly indulged my fancy to reproduce a bit of Eden-like frankness. Under the influence of the hour and my mood I was able to conjure up the maiden's form almost as if she were a real presence. I knew her far better now. With her I had passed through an ordeal that would test severely the best and strongest. She had been singularly strong and very weak; but the weakness had left no stain on her crystal truth, and her strength had been of the best and most womanly kind. As in the twilight, so in the white moonlight, she again made perfect harmony in the transfigured garden.

"There is but one woman in the world for me," I murmured, "as truly as there was only one for the first lonely man. I know not how it is with her, but I hope—oh, what would life now be to me without this hope!—that she cannot have inspired this absolute conviction that she is essential to my being without some answering sympathy in her own woman's heart. But whether this is true or not, or whether it ever can be true, *I have met my fate.*"

As I returned from the garden I saw that the dawn was coming, and I sat down and watched it brighten with the feeling that a new and happy life was also coming.

BOOK SECOND

CHAPTER I
THE DAY AFTER

The epochs of one's life are not divided according to the calendar, nor are they measured by the lapse of time. Within a few brief hours I had reached a conclusion that left no shadow of doubt on my mind. As I sat there in the beautiful June dawn I turned a page in my history. The record of future joys and ills would have to be kept in double entry, for I felt with absolute conviction that I could entertain no project and decide no question without instinctively and naturally consulting the maiden who had quietly and as if by divine right obtained the mastery of my soul. But a day since I would have said that my present attitude was impossible, but now it seemed both right and inevitable. The doubt, the sense of strangeness and remoteness that we justly associate with a comparative stranger, had utterly passed away, and in their place was a feeling of absolute trust and rest. I could place in her hands the best treasures of my life, without a shadow of hesitancy, so strongly had I been impressed with her truth.

And yet it all was a beautiful mystery, over which I could have dreamed for hours.

–I had not shunned society in the past, and had greatly admired other ladies. Their voices had been sweet and low, as a woman's tones should be, and their glances gentle and kind, but not one of them had possessed the power to quicken my pulse or to disturb the quiet slumber of my heart; but this woman spoke to me as with authority from heaven. "My whole being," I murmured, "bows down to her by a constraint that I could scarcely resist, and no queen in the despotic past ever had a more loyal subject than I have become. To serve her, even to suffer for her and to stand between her and all evils the world could inflict, are privileges that I covet supremely. My regard is not a sudden passion, for passion is selfish and inconsiderate. My love is already united with honor and reverence, and my strongest impulse is to promote her happiness before my own. The thought of her is an inspiration toward a purer, better manhood than I have yet known. Her truth and innate nobility produce an intense desire to become like her, so that she may look into my eyes and trust also."

I scarcely know how long my bright-hued dream would have lasted, but at length the door of Mrs. Yocomb's room opened, and steps were on the stairs. A moment later the physician came out, and Miss Warren stood in the doorway.

"They are all sleeping quietly," he said, in answer to my inquiry. "Yes; all danger in Zillah's case is now passed, I think; but she's had a serious time of it, poor little thing!"

"There's no need of your walking home to-night," protested Miss Warren. "We can make you comfortable here, and Reuben will gladly drive you over in the morning."

"It's morning now," he said, smiling, "and I'll enjoy the walk in the fresh air. I'll call again before very long. Good-day!" and he walked lightly down the path, as if all were very satisfactory to him.

"What are you doing here, Mr. Morton?" Miss Warren asked, assuming an expression of strong surprise.

"Helping to watch."

"What a waste! You haven't done Zillah a bit of good."

"Didn't you know I was here?"

"Yes; but I hope you don't think that I need watching?"

"I was within call." "So you would have been if sleeping. I could have blown the great tin horn if it had been necessary to waken you, and you had remained undisturbed by other means."

"Oh, well, then, if it made no difference to you, I'll merely say I'm a night editor, and kept awake from habit."

"I didn't say it made no difference to me," she answered. "You ought to have known better than to have made that speech."

"Miss Warren," I urged anxiously, "you look white as a ghost in this mingling of moonlight and morning. When *will* you rest?"

"When the mind and heart are at rest a tired body counts for little. So you're not afraid of ghosts?"

I looked at her intently as I replied: "No, I would like to be haunted all my life."

It was not wholly the reflection of the dawn that tinged the pallor of her face as I spoke these words.

After a moment's hesitation she apparently dismissed a thought, and maintained her old frank manner.

"Oh, how beautiful, how welcome the morning is!" she exclaimed, coming out on the piazza. "To think that this is the same world that we saw last night—it's almost impossible."

"Mr. Yocomb's words will yet prove true," I said, "and clearer skies and better grain will be the result of the storm."

"Oh, I'm so glad, I'm so very glad," she murmured. "This morning is like a benediction;" and its brightness and beauty glowed in her face.

"I can tell you something that will please you greatly," I continued. "I have visited the little home in the garden that was open to last night's sky. The father and mother robins are well, and I'm sure all the little ones are too, for the mother robin had her head under her wing—a thing impossible, I suppose, if anything was amiss with the children."

"Oh, I'm so glad!" she again repeated, and there was a joyous, exquisite thrill in her tones.

At that moment there came a burst of song from the top of the pear-tree in the garden, and we saw the head of the little household greeting the day.

Almost as sweetly and musically my companion's laugh trilled out:

"So it wasn't the day of fate after all."

Impelled by an impulse that for the moment seemed irresistible, I took her hand as I said earnestly:

"Yes, Miss Warren, for me it was, whether for a lifetime of happiness or of disappointment."

At first she appeared startled, and gave me a swift, searching glance; then a strong expression of pain passed over her face. She understood me well, for my look and manner would have been unmistakable to any woman.

She withdrew her hand as she said gently:

"You are overwrought from watching—from all that's happened; let us both forget that such rash words were spoken."

"Do not think it," I replied, slowly and deliberately. "I have learned to know you better since we have met than I could in months or years amid the conventionalities of society. In you I recognize my fate as vividly and distinctly as I saw you in the lightning's gleam last night. Please hear and understand me," I urged, as she tried to check my words by a strong gesture of dissent. "If you had parents or guardians, I would ask them for the privilege of seeking your hand. Since you have not, I ask you. At least, give me a chance. I can never prove worthy of you, but by years of devotion I can prove that I appreciate you."

"Oh, I'm so sorry, so very sorry you feel so," she said, and there was deep distress in her tones; "I was in hopes we should be life-long friends."

"We shall be," I replied quietly. She looked at me hesitatingly a moment, then said impulsively:

"Mr. Morton, you are too honorable a man to seek that which belongs to another. There," she added, flushing deeply, "I've told you what I've acknowledged to no one—scarcely to myself."

I know that the light of hope faded out of my face utterly, for I felt ill and faint. If in truth she belonged to another, her absolute truth would make her so loyal to him that further hope would be not only vain but an insult, which she would be the first to resent.

"I understand you too well," I began despondently, "to say another word. Miss Warren. I—I wish—it seems rather odd I should have felt so toward you when it was no use. It was as inevitable as our meeting. The world and all that's in it is an awful muddle to me. But God bless you, and if there's any good God, you will be blessed." I shivered as I spoke, and was about to leave the piazza hastily, when her eager and entreating tones detained me.

"Mr. Morton, you said that in spite of all we should be friends; let me claim my privilege at once. I'm sure I'm right in believing that you're overwrought and morbid, from the strange experiences you have just passed through. Do not add to your exhaustion by starting off on another aimless walk to-day; though you may think it might lead you to a better fate, it cannot bring you to those who care so deeply for you. We'll be merry, true-hearted friends after we've had time to rest and think it all over."

"True-hearted, anyway," I said emphatically. "What's more, I'll be sane when we meet again—entirely matter-of-fact, indeed, since I already foresee that I shall be troubled by no more days of fate. Good-by now; go and sleep the sleep of the just; I'll rest quietly here;" and I held out my hand.

She took it in both of hers, and said gently: "Mr. Morton, I believe you saved my—our lives last night."

"I had some hand in it—yes, that should be happiness enough. I'll make it answer; but never speak of it again."

"When I cease to think of it I shall cease to think at all," she said, in strong emphasis; and with a lingering wistful glance she passed slowly in and up the winding stairway.

I watched her as I would a ship that had left me on a desolate rock.

"She is one that could not change if she would," I thought. "It's all over. No matter; possibly I saved her life."

I sat down again in a rustic chair on the piazza, too miserable and disheartened to do more than endure the pain of my disappointment. Indeed there was nothing else to do, for seemingly I had set my heart on the impossible. Her words and manner had made but one impression—that she had given her love and faith to an earlier and more fortunate suitor.

"It would be strange if it were otherwise," I muttered. "I was the 'idiot,' in thinking that her gentlemen friends were blind; but I protest against a world in which men are left to blunder so fatally. The other day I felt broken down physically; I now know that I'm broken and disabled in all respects. The zest and color have wholly gone out of life. If I ever go back to my work I shall find my counterpart in the most jaded and dispirited stage-horse in the city. Miss Warren will have no more occasion to criticise light, smart paragraphs. Indeed, I imagine that I shall soon be restricted to the obituary notices, and I now feel like writing my own. Confound these birds! What makes them sing so? Nature's a heartless jade anyway. Last night she would have burned us up with lightning, and this morning there would have been not a whit less of song and sunshine. Oh, well, it's far better that my hopes are in ashes than that this house should be. I, and all there is of me, is a small price to pay for this home and its inmates; and if I saved her little finger from being scorched, I should be well content. But why the devil did I feel so toward her when it was of no use! That fact irritates me. Is my whole nature a lie, and are its deepest intuitions and most sacred impulses false guides that lead one out into the desert to perish? In the crisis of my life, when I had been made to see that past tendencies were wrong, and I was ready for any change for the better, my random, aimless steps led to this woman, and, as I said to her, the result was inevitable. All nature seemed in league to give emphasis to the verdict of my own heart, but the moment I reached the conviction that she was created for me and I for her, I am informed that she was created for another. I must therefore be one of the odd ones, for whom there is no mate. Curse it all! I rather feel as if another man were going to marry my wife, and I must admit that I have a consuming curiosity to see him.

"But this can't be. Her heart must have recognized the true kinship in this other man—blast him! no, bless him, if she marries him—for she's the last one in the world to enter into merely legal relations, unsanctioned by the best and purest instincts of her womanly nature.

"It's all the devil's own muddle."

And no better conclusion did I reach that dismal morning—the most dismal I can remember, although the hour abounded in beauty and the glad, exuberant life that follows a summer rain. I once heard a preacher say that hell could be in heaven and heaven in hell. I thought him a trifle irreverent at the time, but now half believed him right.

My waking train of thought ended in a stupor in which I do not think I lost for a moment the dull consciousness of pain. I was aroused by a step upon the gravel-path, and, starting up, saw the woman who served Mrs. Yocomb in the domestic labors of the farmhouse. She stopped and stared at me a moment, and then was about to continue around the house to the kitchen entrance.

"Wait a moment, my good woman," I said; "and you'll now have a chance to prove yourself a good woman, and a very helpful and considerate one, too. The house was struck by lightning last night."

"Lord a massy!" she ejaculated, and she struck an attitude with her hands on her hips, and stared at me again, with her small eyes and capacious mouth opened to their utmost extent.

"Yes," I continued, "and all were hurt except Reuben. The doctor has been here, and all are now better and sleeping, so please keep the house quiet, and let us sleep till the doctor comes again. Then have a good fire, so that you can get ready at once whatever he orders for the patients."

"Lord a massy!" she again remarked very emphatically, and scuttled off to her kitchen domains in great excitement.

I now felt that my watch had ended, and that I could give the old farmhouse into the hands of one accustomed to its care. Therefore I wearily climbed the stairs to my room, and threw myself, dressed, on the lounge.

After a moment or two Miss Warren's door opened, and her light step passed down to the kitchen. She, too, had been on the watch for the coming of the domestic, and, if aware that I had seen the woman, did not regard me as competent to enlighten her as to her duties for the day. The kitchen divinity began at once:

"Lord a massy, Miss Em'ly, what a time yer's all had! The strange man told me. There hain't no danger now, is there?"

In response to some remark from Miss Warren she continued, in shrill volubility:

"Yes, he told me yer's all struck but Reub'n. I found him a-sittin' on the stoop, and a-lookin' all struck of a heap himself. Is that the way lightning 'fects folks? He looked white as a ghost, and as if he didn't keer ef he was one afore night. 'Twas amazin' —" and here Miss Warren evidently silenced her.

I heard the murmur of her voice as she gave a few brief directions, and then her steps returned swiftly to her room.

"She can be depended upon," I sighed, "to do all she thinks right. She must have been wearied beyond mortal endurance, and worried by my rash and unlooked-for words, and yet she keeps up till all need is past. Every little act shows that I might as well try to win an angel of heaven as sue against her conscience, she is so absolutely true. You're right, old woman; I *was* 'struck,' and I wish it had been by lightning only."

Just when I exchanged waking thoughts for hateful dreams I do not remember. At last I started to my feet, exclaiming:

"It's all wrong; he shall not marry my wife!" and then I sat down on the lounge and tried to extricate myself from the shadows of sleep, and thus become able to recognize the facts of the real world that I must now face. Slowly the events of the previous day and night came back, and with them a sense of immeasurable loss. The sun was low in the west, thus proving that my unrefreshing stupor had lasted many hours. The clatter of knives, and forks indicated preparations for supper in the dining-room below. I dreaded meeting the family and all words of thanks, as one would the touching of a diseased nerve. More than all, I dreaded meeting Miss Warren again, feeling that we both would be under a wretched constraint. My evil mood undoubtedly had physical causes, for my mouth was parched, my head throbbed and ached, and I felt so ill in body and mind, so morbid and depressed, that I was ready to escape to New York without seeing a soul, were the thing possible.

The door opened softly, and I saw Reuben's ruddy, happy face.

"Oh, I'm so glad thee's awake," he said. "They're all doing well. Adah's got well so fast that she actually looks better than Emily Warren. Even Zillah's quite bright this evening, only she's so weak she can't sit up much, but the doctor says it'll wear away. Thee doesn't look very extra, and no wonder, thee did so much. Father, mother, and Emily Warren have been talking about thee for the last two hours, and Adah can't ask questions enough about thee, and how thee found her. She says the last thing she saw was thee on the lawn, and thee was the first thing she saw when she came to, and now she says she can't help seeing thee all the time. Emily Warren said we must let thee sleep as long as thee would, for that, she said, was what thee needed most of all."

"She's mistaken," I muttered, starting up. "Reuben," I continued aloud, "you're a good, brave fellow. I'll come down to supper as soon, as I can fairly wake up. I feel as stupid as an owl at midday, but I'm exceedingly glad that all are doing well."

When he left me I thought, "Well, I will keep up for two or three hours, and then can excuse myself. To-morrow I can return to New York, since clearly this will be no place for me. Miss Warren thinks that a little sleep will cure me, and that I will be sane and sensible now that I am awake. She will find me matter-of-fact indeed, for I feel like a bottle of champagne that has stood uncorked for a month; but may the devil fly away with me if I play the forlorn, lackadaisical lover, and show my wounds."

I bathed my face again and again, and made as careful a toilet as circumstances permitted.

In their kind-hearted simplicity they had evidently planned a sort of family ovation, for as I came out on the piazza, they were all there except Miss Warren, who sat at her piano playing softly; but as Mr. Yocomb rose to greet me she turned toward us, and through the open window could see us and hear all that passed. The old gentleman still bore marks of his shock and the illness that followed, but there was nothing weak or limp in his manner as he grasped my hand and began warmly:

"Richard Morton, last night I said thee was welcome; I now say this home is as truly thine as mine. Thee saved mother and the children from—" and here his voice was choked by emotion.

Mrs. Yocomb seized my other hand, and I saw that she was "moved" now if ever, for her face was eloquent with kindly, grateful feeling.

"Please don't," I said, so sharply as to indicate irritation, for I felt that I could not endure another syllable. Then, slapping Reuben brusquely on the shoulder, I added, "Reuben was quite as helpful as I: thank him. Any tramp from New York would try to do as much as I did, and might have done better. Ah, here is Zillah!" And I saw that the little girl was propped up on pillows just within the parlor window, where she could enjoy the cool evening air without too great exposure. "If she'll give me another kiss we'll call it all square and say no more about it," and I leaned over the window-sill.

The child put her arms around my neck and clung to me for a moment. There could have been no better antidote for my mood of irritable protest against my fate than the child's warm and innocent embrace, and for a moment it was balm indeed.

"There," I cried, kissing her twice, "now I'm overpaid." Raising my eyes, I met those of Miss Warren as she sat by her piano.

"Yes," she said, with a smile, "after that I should think you would be more than content."

"I certainly ought to be," I replied, looking at her steadily.

"Zillah's very grateful," Miss Warren continued. "She knows that you watched with her till morning."

"So did other night-owls, Zillah, and they were quite as useful as I was."

She reached up her hand and pulled me down. "Mother said," she began.

"You needn't tell a stranger what mother said," and I put my finger on her lips.

"Thee's no more of a stranger than Emily Warren," said the little girl reproachfully. "I can't think of thee without thinking of her."

I raised my eyes in a quick flash toward the young lady, but she had turned to the piano, and her right hand was evoking a few low chords.

"Miss Warren can tell you," I said, laughing, "that when people have been struck by lightning they often don't think straight for a long time to come."

"Crooked thinking sometimes happens without so vivid a cause," Miss Warren responded, without looking around

"Zillah's right in thinking that thee can never be a stranger in this home," said Mrs. Yocomb warmly.

"Mrs. Yocomb, please don't think me insensible to the feelings which are so apparent. Should I live centuries, the belief that I had served you and yours after your kindness would still be my pleasantest thought. But you overrate what I have done: it was such obvious duty that any one would have done the same, or else his ears should have been cropped. It gives me a miserably mean feeling to have you thank me so for it. Please don't any more."

"We forget," said Miss Warren, advancing to the window, "that Mr. Morton is versed in tragedies, and has daily published more dreadful affairs."

"Yes, and has written 'paragraphs' about them that no doubt seemed quite as lurid as the events themselves, suggesting that I gloated over disasters as so much material."

"Mr. Morton, isn't it nearly as bad to tell fibs about one's self as about other people?"

"My depravity will be a continuous revelation to you, Miss Warren," I replied.

With a low laugh she answered, "I see you make no secret of it," and she went back to her piano.

I had bowed cordially to Adah as I joined the family group, and had been conscious all the time of her rather peculiar and fixed scrutiny, which I imagined suggested a strong curiosity more than anything else.

"Well, Richard Morton," said Mr. Yocomb, as if the words were irrepressible, "thee knows a little of how we feel toward thee, if thee won't let us say as much as we would like. I love this old home in which I was born and have lived until this day. I could never build another home like it if every leaf on the farm were a bank-note. But I love the people who live here far more. Richard Morton, I know how it would all have ended, and thee knows. The house was on fire, and all within it were helpless and unconscious. I've seen it all to-day, and Reuben has told us. May the Lord bless thee for what them hast done for me and mine! I'm not going to burden thee with our gratitude, but truth is truth, and we must speak out once for all, to be satisfied. Thee knows, too, that when a Friend has anything on his mind it's got to come; hasn't it, mother? Richard Morton, thee has saved us all from a horrible death."

"Yes, Mr. Morton," said Miss Warren, coming again to the window and laughing at my crimson face and embarrassment, "you *must* face that truth—there's no escaping it. Forgive me, Mr. Yocomb, for laughing over so serious a subject, but Reuben and Mr. Morton amuse me greatly. Mr. Morton already says that any tramp from New York would have done the same. By easy transition he will soon begin to insist that it was some other tramp. I now understand evolution."

"Emily Warren, thee needn't laugh at Richard Morton," said Reuben a little indignantly; "thee owes more to him than to any other man living."

She did not turn to the piano so quickly now but that I saw her face flush at the unlooked-for speech.

"That you are mistaken, Reuben, no one knows better than Miss Warren herself," I replied irritably.

She turned quickly and said, in a low tone, "You are right, Mr. Morton. Friends do not keep a debit and credit account with each other. I shall not forget, however, that Reuben is right also, even though I may seem to sometimes," and she left the room.

I was by the open window, and I do not think any one heard her words except Zillah, and she did not understand them.

I stood looking after her, forgetful of all else, when a hand laid upon my arm caused me to look around, and I met Adah's gaze, and it was as fixed and intent as that of a child.

"She doesn't owe thee any more than I do," she said gravely. "I wish I could do something for thee."

"Why do you say 'thee' to me now?—you always said 'you' before," I asked.

"I don't know. It seems as if I couldn't say 'you' to thee any more," and a delicate color stole into her face.

"We all feel as if thee were one of us now," explained Mrs. Yocomb gently, "and I trust that life will henceforth seem to Adah a more sacred thing, and worthy of more sacred uses." And she passed into the house to prepare for supper.

Mr. Yocomb followed her, and Reuben went down to the barn.

"If you live to grow like your mother, Miss Adah, you will be the most beautiful woman in the world," I said frankly, for I felt as if I could speak to her almost as I would to Zillah.

Her eyes drooped and her color deepened as she shook her head and murmured:

"I'd rather be Emily Warren than any other woman in the world."

Her words and manner so puzzled me that I thought she had not fully recovered from the effects of the shock, and I replied, in an off-hand way:

"After a few weeks of teaching stupid children to turn noise into music you would gladly be yourself again."

She paid no heed to this remark, but, with the same intent, exploring look, asked:

"Thee was the first one I saw when I came to last night?"

"Yes, and you were much afraid of me."

"I was foolish—I fear mother's right, and I've always been foolish."

"Your manner last night was most natural. I was a stranger, and a hard-looking customer, too, when I entered your room."

"I hope I didn't look very—very bad."

"You looked so like a beautiful piece of marble that I feared you were dead."

"Thee wouldn't have cared much."

"Indeed I would. If you knew how anxious I was about Zillah—"

"Ugh!" she interrupted, with an expression of strong disgust, "I might have been a horrid, blackened thing if it hadn't been for thee."

"Oh, hush!" I cried; "I merely threw a couple of pails of water on the roof. Please say no more about it."

She passed her hand over her brow, and said hesitatingly:

"I'm so puzzled—I feel so strangely. It seems an age since yesterday."

"You've had a very severe shock, Miss Adah."

"Yes, that may be it; but it's so strange that I was afraid of thee."

"Why, Miss Adah, I was wet as a drowned rat, and had a black mark across my nose. I would have made an ideal burglar."

"That oughtn't to have made any difference; thee was trying to save my life."

"But you didn't know it."

"I don't believe I know anything rightly. I—I feel so strange—just as if I had waked up and hadn't got anything clear. But I know this much, in spite of what Reuben said," she added impulsively; "Emily Warren doesn't owe thee any more than I do." And she turned like a flash and was gone.

"Poor child," I muttered, "she hasn't recovered so fully as the others."

I had been holding one of Zillah's hands during the interview, and she now pulled me down and whispered:

"What's the matter with thee, Richard Morton?"

"Heaven grant you may never know, little one. Good-by." I had scarcely left the piazza, however, before Mrs. Yocomb called:

"Richard Morton, thee must be famished. Come to supper."

CHAPTER II
"IT WAS INEVITABLE"

I ought to have had a ravenous appetite but I had none at all. I ought to have been glad and thankful from the depths of my heart, but I was so depressed that everything I said was forced and unnatural. My head felt as if it were bursting, and I was enraged with myself and the wretched result of my bright dream. Indeed I found myself inclined to a spirit of recklessness and irritation that was wellnigh irresistible.

Miss Warren seemed as wholly free from any morbid, unnatural tendencies as Mr. Yocomb himself, and she did her utmost to make the hour as genial as it should have been. At first I imagined that she was trying to satisfy herself that I had recovered my senses, and that my unexpected words, spoken in the morning, were the result of a mood that was as transient as it was abnormal. I think I puzzled her; I certainly did not understand myself any better than did poor Adah, whose mind appeared to be in solution from the effects of the lightning, and I felt that I must be appearing worse than idiotic.

Miss Warren, resolutely bent on banishing every unnatural constraint, asked Mr. Yocomb:

"How is my genuine friend, Old Plod? Did the lightning wake him up?"

"No, he plods as heavily as ever this morning. Thee only can wake him up."

"You've no idea what a compliment that is," she said, with a low laugh. "Old Plod inspires me with a sense of confidence and stability that is very reassuring in a world full of lightning flashes."

"Yes," I said, "he is safe as a horse-block, and quite as exhilarating. Give me Dapple."

She looked at me quickly and keenly, and colored slightly. She evidently had some association in her mind with the old plow-horse that I did not understand.

"Exhilaration scarcely answers as a steady diet, Mr. Morton."

"Little chance of its lasting long," I replied, "even in a world overcharged with electricity."

"I prefer calm, steady sunshine to these wild alternations."

"I doubt it; 'calm, steady sunshine' would make the world as dry and monotonous as a desert."

"That's true, Richard Morton," said Mr. Yocomb. "I like peace and quiet more than most men, but even if we had all burned up last night, this part of the world would have been wonderfully the better for the storm. I reckon it was worth a million or more dollars to the county."

"That's the right way to look at it, Mr. Yocomb," I said carelessly. "The greatest good to the greatest number. Individuals are of no account."

"Your philosophy may be true, but I don't like it," Miss Warren protested. "A woman doesn't generalize."

"Thy philosophy is only half true, Richard Morton. God cares for each one of His children, and every one in my house counts for much to me."

"There's no getting ahead of thee, mother. If we want to talk heresy, Richard Morton, we must go off by ourselves."

"I think God showed His love for us in a queer way last night," said Adah, abruptly.

Both her father and mother looked pained at this speech, and Mrs. Yocomb said gravely:

"Thee'll see things in the true light some day, I hope. The lightning bolt may have been a message from Heaven to thee."

"It seems to me that Zillah got more of the message than I did, and she didn't need any," said the matter-of-fact Adah, "At any rate I hope Richard Morton may be here if I ever get another message."

"I shall surely be struck next time," I laughed, a trifle bitterly; "for according to Mrs. Yocomb's view I need a message more than any of you."

It was evident that neither Adah nor I was in a frame of mind that Mrs. Yocomb could commend.

"As you suggested, Mr. Morton, if some other tramp from New York had been present, what a thrilling narrative you could write for your paper," Miss Warren began. Seemingly she had had enough of clouds the previous evening, and was bent on clear skies to-night.

She found me incorrigible, however, for I said briefly:

"Oh, no, it would only make an item among the crimes and casualties."

Undaunted, she replied: "And such might have been its appropriate place had not the doctor arrived so promptly. The casualty had already occurred, and I'm quite sure you would have finished us all with original remedies if left to yourself."

"I agree with you, Miss Warren; blunders are worse than crimes, and I've a genius for them."

"Well, I'm not a genius in any sense of the word. Miss Adah and I look at things as they are. One would think, Mr. Morton, accepting your view of yourself, that you could supply your paper with all the crimes and casualties required, as the result of the genius you claim."

"Stupid blunders would make stupid reading."

"Oh, that column in your paper is very interesting, then?"

"Why shouldn't it be? I've never had the bad taste to publish in it anything about myself."

"I fail to find any logic in that remark. Have you a conscience, Mr. Morton?"

"The idea of an editor having a conscience! I doubt whether you have ever seen New York, Miss Warren, you are so unsophisticated."

"Emily, thee shouldn't be afraid of lightning when thee and Richard Morton are so ready to flash back and forth at one another."

"My words are only heat lightning, very harmless, and Mr. Morton's partake of the aurora in character—they are cool and distant."

"I hope they are not so mysterious," I replied.

"Their cause is, quite."

"I think I understand the cause," said Mrs. Yocomb as we rose from the table; and she came and took my hand. "Richard Morton, thee has fever; thy hands are hot and thy temples are throbbing."

I saw that Miss Warren was looking at me with an expression that was full of kind, regretful interest; but with the perversity of a child that should have been shaken, I replied, recklessly:

"I've taken cold, I fear. I sat on the piazza like an owl last night, and I learned that an owl would have been equally useful there. I fear I'm going to be ill, Mrs. Yocomb, and I think I had better make a precipitate retreat to my den in New York."

"Who'll take care of thee in thy den?" she asked, with a smile that would have disarmed cynicism itself.

"Oh, they can spare a devil from the office occasionally," I said carelessly; but I felt that my remark was brutal. In answer to her look of pained surprise I added, "Pardon me that I used the vile slang of the shop; I meant one of the boys employed in the printing-rooms. Mrs. Yocomb, I have now satisfied you that I'm too much of a bear to deserve any gentler nurse. I truly think I had better return to town at once. I've never been very ill, and have no idea how to behave. It's already clear that I wouldn't prove a meek and interesting patient, and I don't want to lose your good opinion."

"Richard Morton, if thee should leave us now I should feel hurt beyond measure. Thee's not thyself or thee wouldn't think of it."

"Richard Morton, thee cannot go," said Mr. Yocomb in his hearty way. "If thee knew mother as I do, thee'd give right in. I don't often put my foot down, but when I do, it's like old South Mountain there. Ah, here comes the doctor. Doctor Bates, if thee doesn't prescribe several weeks of quiet life in this old farmhouse for Friend Morton, I'll start right off to find a doctor who will."

"Please stay, and I'll gather wild strawberries for thee," said Adah, in a low tone. She had stolen close to my side, and still had the wistful, intent look of a child.

"You might do worse," Doctor Bates remarked.

"You'll never make him believe that," laughed Miss Warren, who evidently believed in tonic treatment and counter-irritants. "He would much prefer sultry New York and an imp from the printing-rooms."

"Thee may drive Dapple all thee wishes if thee'll only stay," said Reuben, his round, boyish face shadowed with unwonted anxiety.

We were standing in the hallway, and Zillah heard our talk, for her little figure came tottering out of the parlor in her trailing wrapper, and her eyes were full of tears.

"Richard Morton, if thee doesn't stay I'll cry myself sick."

I caught her up in my arms and carried her back to the sofa, and I whispered in her ear:

"I'll stay, Zillah; I'll do anything for you."

The child clapped her hands gleefully as she exclaimed:

"Now I've got thee. He's promised me to stay, mother."

"Yes," said the physician, after feeling my pulse, "you certainly must, and you ought to be in bed this moment. Your pulse indicates a very high fever. What's more, you seem badly run down. I shall put you under active treatment at once; that is, if you'll trust me."

"Go ahead, doctor," I said, "and get me through one way or the other before very long. Because these friends are so good and kind is no reason why I should become a burden to them," and I sank down on the sofa in the hall.

"Thee'll do us a great wrong if thee ever thinks that, Richard Morton," said Mrs. Yocomb earnestly. "Adah, thee see that his room is ready. I'm going to take thee in hand myself;" and she bustled off to the kitchen.

"You couldn't be in better hands, Mr. Morton," said the physician; "and Mrs. Yocomb can do more for you than I can. I'll try and help a little, however, and will prescribe for you after I've seen Zillah;" and he and Mr. Yocomb went into the parlor, while Reuben, with a triumphant chuckle, started for the barn.

Now that I was alone for a moment, Miss Warren, who had been standing in the doorway, and a little aloof, came to me, and her face was full of trouble as she said hurriedly, in a low tone:

"I fear I'm to blame for this. You'll never know how sorry I am. I *do* owe you so much! Please get well quickly or I'll—" and she hesitated.

"You are the only one who did not ask me to stay," I said reproachfully.

"I know it; I know, too, that I'd be ill in your place if I could."

"How could I help loving you!" I said impetuously. "There, forgive me," I added hastily as I saw her look of pain and almost fright. "Remember I'm ill, delirious it may be; but whatever happens, also remember that I said I wouldn't change anything. Were it all to do over again I'd do the same It was inevitable: I'm sane enough to know that. You are not in the least to blame."

She hung on my last words as if I were giving her absolution from a mortal sin.

"It's all a mistake. Oh, if you but knew how I regret—"

Steps were approaching. I shook my head, with a dreary glimmer of a smile.

"Good-by," I said in a whisper, and wearily closed my eyes.

Everything soon became very confused. I remembered Mr. Yocomb's helping me to my room. I saw Adah's intent, wistful look as I tried to thank her. Mrs. Yocomb's kind, motherly face changed into the features of my own mother, and then came a long blank.

CHAPTER III
RETURNING CONSCIOUSNESS

I seemed to waken as if from a long, troubled sleep. At first I was merely conscious that I was awake, and I wondered how long I had slept. Then I was glad I was awake, and that my confused and hateful dreams, of which no distinct memory remained, had vanished. The only thing I could recall concerning them was an indefinite and oppressive sense of loss of some kind, at which I had vaguely and impotently protested.

I knew I was awake, and yet I felt too languid to open my eyes. I was little more than barely conscious of existence, and I rather enjoyed this negative condition of complete inertia. The thought floated through my mind that I was like a new-born child, that knows nothing, fears nothing, thinks nothing, but simply breathes, and I felt so tired and "gone" that I coveted an age of mere respiration.

But thought slowly kindled in a weak, fitful fashion. I first became slightly curious about myself. Why had I slept so profoundly? Why was I so nerveless and stupid after such a sleep?

Instead of answering these questions, I weakly wandered off into another train of thought. "My mind seems a perfect blank," I said to myself. "I don't remember anything; I don't know where I am, and don't much care; nor do I know what my experience will be when I fully rouse myself. This is like beginning a new existence. What shall be the first entry on the blank page of my wakening mind? Perhaps I had better rouse up and see whether I am truly alive."

And yet I did not rise, but just lay still, heavy with a strange, painless inertia, over which I puzzled in a vague, weak way.

At last I was sure I heard a child crying. Then there was a voice, that I thought I had heard before, trying to hush and reassure the child, and I began to think who they were, and yet I did not seem to care enough to open my eyes to see.

I next heard something like a low sob near me, and it caused a faint thrill among my sluggish nerves. Surely I had heard that sound before, and curiosity so far asserted itself that I opened my eyes and looked wonderingly around.

The room was unfamiliar, and yet I was certain I had seen it on some previous occasion. Seated at a window, however, was a lady who soon absorbed my whole weak and wavering attention. My first thought was: "How very pretty she is!" Then, "What is she looking at so steadfastly from the window?" After a moment I mentally laughed at my stupidity. "She's looking at the sunset. What else should she be looking at? Can I have slept all day?"

I saw her bosom heave with another convulsive sob, and that tears fast followed each other down her cheeks. I seemed to have the power of noting everything distinctly, but I couldn't understand or account for what I saw. Who was that sweet-faced girl? Beyond a doubt I had seen her before, but where? Why was she crying? Why was she in my room?

Then I thought, "It must be all imaginary; I doubt whether I am awake yet. If she were only smiling instead of crying, I would like to dream on forever. How strangely familiar her face is! I must have seen it daily for years, and yet I can't recognize it."

The loud whinny of a horse seemed to give my paralyzed memory an impetus and suggestion, by means of which I began to reconstruct the past.

"That's Old Plod!" I exclaimed mentally. "And—and—why, that's Miss Warren sitting by the window. I remember now. We were in the barn together, and I was jealous of the old horse how absurd! Then we were in the garden, and she was laughing at me. How like a dream it all is! It seemed as if she were always laughing, and that the birds might well stop singing to listen. Now she is crying here in my room. I half believe it's an apparition, and that if I speak it will vanish. Perhaps it is a warning that she's in trouble somewhere, and that I ought to go to her help. How lovely she looks, with her hands lying in her lap, forgetful of the work they hold, and her tearful eyes fixed on the glowing west! Her face is very pale in contrast. Surely she's only a shadow, and the real maiden is in need of my aid;" and I made an effort to rise.

It seemed exceedingly strange that I could scarcely lift my hand; but my slight movement caused her to look around, and in answer to my gaze of eager inquiry she came softly and hesitatingly toward me.

"Miss Warren," I said, "can it be you in very truth?"

"Yes," she replied, with a sudden and glad lighting up of her face, "but please don't talk."

"How you relieve me," I tried to say joyfully, but I found I could only whisper. "What the mischief—makes my voice—so weak? Do you know—that I had the odd—impression—that you were an apparition—and had come to me—as a token—that—you were in trouble—and I tried to rise—to go to your aid—then it seemed yourself—that looked around. But you *are* in trouble—why can't I get up and help you?"

She trembled, and by her gesture tried to stop my words.

"Will you do what I ask?" she said, in a low, eager tone.

I smiled as I replied, "Little need of your asking that question."

"Then please try to get well speedily; don't talk, but just keep every little grain of strength. Oh, I'm so glad you are in your right mind. You have been very ill, but will soon get well now if only careful. I'll call Mrs. Yocomb."

"Please don't go," I whispered. "Now that I know you—it seems so natural—that you should be here. So I've been ill—and you have taken care of me;" and I gave a deep sigh of satisfaction. "I did not know you at first—idiot!—but Old Plod whinnied—and then it all began to come back."

At the word "Old Plod" she turned hastily toward the door. Then, as if mastered by an impulse, she returned, and said, in a tone that thrilled even my feeble pulse:

"Oh, live! in mercy live, or else I can never forgive myself."

"I'll live—never fear," I replied, with a low laugh. "I'm not such a fool as to leave a world containing you."

A rich glow overspread her face, she smiled, then suddenly her face became very pale, and she even seemed frightened as she hastily left the room.

A moment later Mrs. Yocomb came in, full of motherly solicitude.

"Kind Mrs. Yocomb," I murmured, "I am glad I'm in such good hands."

"Thank God, Richard Morton," she said, in low, fervent tones, "thee's going to get well. But don't speak a word."

"Wasn't that Zillah crying?"

"Yes, she was heart-broken about thee being so sick, but she'll laugh now when I tell her thee's better. Take this, and sleep again."

"Bless her kind heart!" I said.

Mrs. Yocomb laid her finger on my lips. I saw her pour out something, which I swallowed unquestioningly, and after a moment sank into a quiet sleep.

CHAPTER IV
IN THE DARK

"Yes, Mrs. Yocomb, good nursing and nourishment are all that he now requires," were the reassuring words that greeted my waking later in the evening. I opened my eyes, and found that a physician was feeling my pulse.

I turned feebly toward my kind hostess, and smilingly whispered:

"There's no fear of my wanting these where you are, Mrs. Yocomb; but don't let me make trouble. I fear I've made too much already."

"The only way thee can make trouble, Richard, is to worry about making trouble. The more we can do for thee the better we shall be pleased. All thee's got to do is to get well and take thy time about it."

"That's just like you. How long have I been ill?"

"That's none of thy business at present. One thing at a time. The doctor has put thee in my hands, and I'm going to make thee mind."

"I've heard that men were perfect bears when getting well," I said.

"Thee can be a bear if thee feels like it, but not another word to-night—not another syllable; am I not right, doctor?"

"Yes, I prescribe absolute quiet of mind and body; that and good living will bring you around in time. You've had a narrow graze of it, but if you will mind Mrs. Yocomb you will yet die of old age. Good-night."

My nurse gave me what she thought I needed, and darkened the room. But it was not so dark but that I saw a beautiful face in the doorway.

"Miss Warren," I exclaimed.

"It was Adah," said Mrs. Yocomb quietly; "she's been very anxious about thee."

"You are all so kind. Please thank her for me," I replied eagerly. "Mother, may I speak to Richard Morton?" asked a timid voice from the obscurity of the hallway.

"Not to-night, Adah—to-morrow." "Forgive me if I disobey you this once," I interrupted hastily. "Yes, Miss Adah, I want to thank you."

She came instantly to my side, and I held out my hand to her. I wondered why hers throbbed and trembled so strangely.

"It's I who should thank thee: I can never thank thee enough. Oh, I feared I might—I might never have a chance."

"There, Adah, thee mustn't say another word; Richard's too weak yet."

Her hand closed tightly over mine. "Good-by," she breathed softly, and vanished.

Mrs. Yocomb sat down with her knitting by a distant and shaded lamp.

Too weak to think, or to realize aught except that I was surrounded by an atmosphere of kindness and sympathy, I was well content to lie still and watch, through the open window, the dark foliage wave to and fro, and the leaves grow distinct in the light of the rising moon, which, though hidden, I knew must be above the eastern mountains. I had the vague impression that very much had happened, but I would not think; not for the world would I break the spell of deep quietude that enthralled every sense of my body and every faculty of my mind.

"Mrs. Yocomb," I said at last, "it must be you who creates this atmosphere of perfect peace and restfulness. The past is forgotten, the future a blank, and I see only your serene face. A subdued light seems to come from it, as from the shaded lamp."

"Thee is weak and fanciful, Richard. The doctor said thee must be quiet."

"I wish it were possible to obey the doctor forever, and that this exquisite rest and oblivion could last, I am like a ship becalmed on a summer sea in a summer night. Mind and body are both motionless."

"Sleep, Richard Morton, and when rested and well, may gales from heaven spring up and carry thee homeward. Fear not even rough winds, if they bear thee toward the only true home. Now thy only duty is to rest."

"You are not going to sit up to-night, Mrs. Yocomb."

She put her finger on her lips.

"Hush!" she said.

"Oh, delicious tyranny!" I murmured. "The ideal government is that of an absolute and friendly power."

I had a vague consciousness of being wakened from time to time, and of taking something from Mrs. Yocomb's hand, and then sinking back into an enthrallment of blessed and refreshing slumber. With every respiration life and health flowed back.

At last, as after my first long sleep in the country, I seemed to hear exquisite strains of music that swelled into richer harmony until what seemed a burst of song awoke me. Opening my eyes, I looked intently through the open, window and gladly welcomed the early day. The air was fresh, and I felt its exhilarating quality. The drooping branches of the elm swayed to and fro, and the mountains beyond were bathed in light. I speedily realized that it was the song of innumerable birds that had supplied the music of my waking dream.

For a few moments I gazed through the window, with the same perfect content with which I had watched the foliage grow distinct in the moonlight the previous evening, and then I looked around the room.

I started slightly as I encountered the deep blue eyes of Adah Yocomb fixed on me with an intent, eager wistfulness. "Can I do anything for thee, Richard Morton?" she asked, rising from her chair near the door. "Mother asked me to stay with thee awhile, and to let her know if thee woke and wanted anything."

"With you here this bright morning, how could I want anything more?" I asked, with a smile, for her young, beautiful face comported so well with the early morning of the summer day as to greatly please both my eye and fancy. The color of the early morning grew richer in her face as she replied:

"I'm glad thee doesn't want me to go away, but I must go and have thy breakfast brought up."

"No, stay; tell me all that's happened. I seem to have forgotten everything so strangely! I feel as if I had known you all a long time, and yet that can't be, for only the other day I was at my office in New York."

"Mother says thee's too weak to talk yet, and that I must not answer questions. She says thee knows thee's-been sick and thee knows thee's getting well, and that must do till thee's much stronger."

"Oh, I feel ever so much stronger. Sleep and the good things your mother has given me have made a new man of me."

"Mother says thee has never been sick, and that thee doesn't know how to take care of thyself, and that thee'll use thy strength right up if we don't take good care of thee."

"And are you going to take care of me?"

"Yes, if thee pleases. I'll help mother."

"I should be hard to please were I not glad. I shall have so nice a time getting well that I shall be tempted to play sick."

"I'll—I'll wait on thee as long as thee'll let me, for no one owes thee more than I do."

"What in the world do you owe me?" I asked, much perplexed. "If you are going to help me to get well, and will come to my room daily with a face like this summer morning, I shall owe you more than I can ever repay."

"My face would have been black enough but for thee; but I'm glad thee thinks I look well. They are all saying I look pale and am growing thin, but if thee doesn't think so I don't care," and she seemed aglow with pleasure.

"It would make a sick man well to look at you," I said, smiling. "Please come and sit by me and help me to get my confused brain straight once more. I have the strangest sense of not knowing what I ought to know well. You and your kind father and mother brought me home from meeting. Your mother said I might stay here and rest. Miss Warren was here—she was singing in the parlor. Where is Miss Warren?"

"She has gone out for a walk," said the girl a little coldly.

Her manner perplexed me, and, together with my thought of Miss Warren, there came a vague sense of trouble—of something wrong. I tried to raise my hand to my brow, as if to clear away the mist that obscured my mind, and my hand was like lead, it was so heavy.

"A plague on my memory!" I exclaimed. "We were in the parlor, and Miss Warren was singing. Your mother spoke—would that I might hear her again!—it's all tolerably clear up to that time, and then everything is confused."

"Adah, how's this?" said Mrs. Yocomb reproachfully. "Thee was not to let Richard Morton talk."

"I only am to blame, Mrs. Yocomb: I would talk. I'm trying to get the past straightened out; I know that something happened the other evening when you spoke so beautifully to us, but my memory comes up to that point as to an abyss, and I can't bridge it over."

"Richard Morton, doesn't thee believe that I'm thy friend?"

"My mind would indeed be a total blank if I doubted that."

"Well, then, do what I ask thee: don't question, don't think. Isn't it sufficient to know that thee has been ill, and that thy life depends on quiet? Thee can scarcely lift thy hand to thy head; thy words are slow and feeble. Can't thee realize that it is thy sacred duty to rest and grow strong before taking up the cares and burdens that life brings to us all? Thee looks weak and exhausted."

"I am indeed weak enough, but I felt almost well when I awoke."

"Adah, I fear I can't trust thee as a nurse," her mother began gravely.

"Please don't blame her; it was wholly my fault," I whispered. "I'll be very good now, and do just what you bid me."

"Well, then, thee must take what I have prepared, and thy medicine, and sleep again."

"Good-by, Adah," I said, smiling. "Don't look so concerned; you haven't done me a bit of harm. Your face was as bright and welcome as the sunshine."

"If it hadn't been for thee—" she began.

Mrs. Yocomb raised a warning finger, and the girl stole away.

"Can—can I not see Miss Warren this morning?" I asked hesitatingly.

"Thee must sleep first."

The medicine she gave evidently contained a sedative, or else sleep was the remedy that Nature instinctively grasped, for it gave back part of the strength that I had lost.

When I awoke again I felt wonderfully the better for a long rest that had not been broken, but made more beneficial from the fact that I was slightly roused from time to time to take stimulants and nourishment. The heat and glare of the summer day had passed. This I could perceive even through the half-closed window-blinds. At first I thought myself alone, but soon saw that Reuben was seated in the furthest corner, quietly carving on some woodwork that interested his boyish fancy. His round, fresh face was like a tonic.

"Well, old fellow," I laughed, "so you are playing nurse?"

"Is thee awake for good, Richard Morton?" he asked, springing up.

"I hope so."

"'Cause mother said that as soon as thee really waked up I must call her."

"Oh, wait a moment, and tell me all the news."

"Mother said I mustn't tell thee anything but to get well."

"I'm never going to get well."

"What!" exclaimed the boy, in consternation.

"Your mother and Miss Adah take such good care of me that I am going to play sick the rest of my life," I explained, laughing. "How is Dapple?"

"Oh, thee's only joking, then. Well, all I ask of thee is to get well just enough to drive Dapple around with me. He'll put life into thee—never fear. When I get hold of the reins he fairly makes my hands tingle. But there, mother said I shouldn't let thee talk, but tell her right away," and he started for the door.

"How is Miss Warren? Is she never coming to see me?"

"Emily Warren's been dreadfully anxious about thee. I never saw any one change so. But to-day she has been like a lark. She went with me to the village this morning, and she had almost as much spirit and life as Dapple. She's a jolly good girl. I like her. We're all so glad thee's getting well we don't know what to do. Father said he felt like jumping over a five-bar fence. Only Adah acts kind of queer and glum."

"I think I hear talking," said Mrs. Yocomb, entering.

"Dear Mrs. Yocomb," I laughed, "you are the most amiable and beneficent dragon that ever watched over a captive."

"Thee wants watching. The moment my back's turned thee's into mischief, and the young people are just as bad. Reuben, I might better have left Zillah here."

"Do let her come," I exclaimed; "she'll do more good than medicine."

"Well, she shall bring thee up thy chicken broth; that will please her wonderfully. Go away, Reuben, and tell Zillah to bring the broth—not another word. Does thee feel better, Richard?"

"Oh, I am almost well. I'm ashamed to own how hungry I am."

"That's a good sign—a very good sign."

"Mrs. Yocomb, how did I become so ill? I'm haunted by the oddest sense of not remembering something that happened after you spoke to us the other evening."

"There's nothing strange in people's being sick—thee knows that. Then thee had been overworking so long that thee had to pay the penalty."

"Yes, I remember that. Thank Heaven I drifted into this quiet harbor before the storm came. I should have died in New York."

"Well, thee knows where to come now when thee's going to have another bad turn. I hope, however, that thee'll be too good a man to overwork so again. Now thee's talked enough."

"Can I not see Mr. Yocomb, and—and—Miss Warren this evening?"

"No, not till to-morrow. Father's been waiting till I said he could come; but he's so hearty-like that I won't trust him till thee's stronger."

"Is—is Miss Warren so hearty-like also? It seems to me her laugh would put life into a mummy."

"Well, thee isn't a mummy, so she can't come till to-morrow."

She had been smoothing my pillow and bathing my face with cologne, thus creating a general sense of comfort and refreshment. Now she lifted my head on her strong, plump arm, and brushed my hair. Tears came into my eyes as I said brokenly:

"I can remember my mother doing this for me when I was ill once and a little fellow. I've taken care of myself ever since. You can have no idea how grateful your manner is to one who has no one to care for him specially."

"Thee'll always have some one to care for thee now; but thee mustn't say anything more;" and I saw strong sympathy in her moist eyes.

"Yes," I breathed softly, "I should have died in New York."

"And thee said an imp from the printing-house could take care of thee," she replied, with a low laugh.

"Did I say that? I must have been out of my head."

"Thee'll see that all was ordered for the best, and be content when thee gets strong. People are often better every way after a good fit of sickness. I believe the Good Physician will give His healing touch to thy soul as well as thy body. Ah, here is Zillah. Come in, little girl. Richard wishes to see thee."

Bearing a bowl in both hands, she entered hesitatingly.

"Why, Zillah, you waiting on me, too! It's all like a fairy tale, and I'm transformed into a great prince, and am waited on right royally. I'm going to drink that broth to your health, as if you were a great lady. It will do me more good than all the drugs of all the doctors, just because you are such a good little fairy, and have bewitched it."

The child dimpled all over with pleasure as she came and stood by my side.

"Oh, I'm so glad thee's getting well!" she cried. "Thee talks queer, but not so queer as thee did before. Thee—"

A warning gesture from her mother checked her, and she looked a little frightened.

"That will do, Zillah. After Richard has taken this I'm not going to let him talk for a long time."

"Do you want to make me all well, Zillah?" I asked, smiling into her troubled and sympathetic face.

She nodded eagerly and most emphatically.

"Then climb on a chair and give me a kiss."

After a quick, questioning look at her mother, she complied, laughing.

"Ah, that puts life into me," I said. "You can tell them all that you did me more good than the doctor. I'll go with you to see the robins soon."

"I've got something else for thee downstairs," she whispered, "something that Emily Warren gathered for thee," and she was gone in a flash.

A moment later she stood in the doorway, announced in advance by the perfume of an exquisite cluster of rosebuds arranged in a dainty vase entwined and half hidden with myrtle.

"Put the vase on the table by Richard, and then thee mustn't come any more."

"Thee surely are from the Garden of Eden," I exclaimed. "These and your kiss, Zillah, will make me well. Tell Miss Warren that I am going to thank her myself. Good-by now," and she flitted out of the room, bright with the unalloyed happiness of a child.

"Dear me," said Mrs. Yocomb, "thee must indeed get strong fast, for I do have such a time keeping the young people out of thy room. Reuben asks a dozen times a day if he can see thee, and father's nearly as bad. No more shall see thee to-day, I promise thee. Now thee must rest till to-morrow."

I was well content, for the roses brought a presence very near. In their fragrance, their beauty, their dewy freshness, their superiority to other flowers, they seemed the emblem of the maiden who had made harmony in the garden when Nature was at her best. The scene, as we had stood there together, grew so vivid that I saw her again almost in reality, her face glowing with the undisguised, irrepressible pleasure that had been caused by my unexpected tribute to the absolute truthfulness of her character. Again I heard her piquant laugh; then her sweet, vibratory voice as she sang hymns that awakened other than religious emotions, I fear. By an odd freak of fancy the flowers seemed an embodied strain from Chopin's nocturne that she had played, and the different shades of color the rising and falling of the melody.

"What do they mean?" I murmured to myself. "At any rate I see no York and Lancaster buds among them."

"Is thee so very fond of roses that thee gazes so long and intently at them?" Mrs. Yocomb quietly asked.

I started, and I had still sufficient blood to crimson my pallid face.

Turning away I said, "They recalled a scene in the garden where they grew. It seemed to me that Miss Warren had grown there too, she was so like them; and that this impression should have been made by a girl bred in the city struck me as rather strange."

"Thy impression was correct—she's genuine," Mrs. Yocomb replied gravely, and her eyes rested on me in a questioning and sympathetic way that I understood better as I thought it over afterward.

"Yes," I said, "she made just that impression on me from the first. We met as strangers, and in a few hours, without the slightest effort on her part, she won my absolute trust. This at first greatly surprised me, for I regret to say that my calling has made me distrustful. I soon learned, however, that this was just the impression that she should make on any one capable of understanding her."

A deep sigh was my companion's only answer.

"Mrs. Yocomb," I continued, earnestly, "was I taken ill while you were speaking? I have a vague, tormenting impression that something occurred which I cannot recall. The last that I can remember was your speaking to us; and then—and then—wasn't there a storm?"

"There may have been. We've had several showers of late. Thee had been overdoing, Richard, and thee felt the effects of the fever in thy system before thee or any of us knew what was the matter. Thy mind soon wandered; but thee was never violent; thee made us no trouble—only our anxiety. Now I hope I've satisfied thee."

"How wondrously kind you've all been to such a stranger! But Miss Adah made reference to something that I can't understand."

Mrs. Yocomb looked perplexed and annoyed. "I'll ask Adah," she said, gravely. "It's time thee took this medicine and slept."

The draught she gave me was more quieting than her words had been, for I remembered nothing more distinctly until I awoke in the brightness of another day.

CHAPTER V
A FLASH OF MEMORY

I found my spirits attuned to the clear sunshine of the new day, and congratulated myself that convalescence promised to be so speedy. Again I had the sense that it was my body only that was weak and exhausted by disease, for my mind seemed singularly elastic, and I felt as if the weight of years and toil had dropped away, and I was entering on a new and higher plane of existence. An unwonted hopefulness, too, gave buoyancy to my waking thoughts.

My first conscious act was to look for my flowers. They had been removed to a distant table, and in their place was a larger bouquet, that, for some reason, suggested Adah. "It's very pretty," I thought, "but it lacks the dainty, refined quality of the other. There's too much of it. One is a bouquet; the other suggests the bushes on which the buds grew, and their garden home."

From the sounds I heard, I knew the family was at breakfast, and before very long a musical laugh that thrilled every nerve with delight rang up the stairway, and I laughed in sympathy without knowing why.

"Happy will the home be in which that laugh makes music," I murmured. "Heaven grant it may be mine. Can it be presumption to hope this, when she showed so much solicitude at my illness? She was crying when my recovery was doubtful, and she entreated me to live. Reuben's words suggested that she was depressed while I was in danger, and buoyant after the crisis had passed. That she feels as I do I cannot yet hope. But what the mischief do she and Adah mean by saying that they owe me so much? It's I who owe them everything for their care during my illness. How long *have* I been ill? There seems to be something that I can't recall; and now I think of it, Mrs. Yocomb's account last night was very indefinite."

My further musings were interrupted by the entrance of Mrs. Yocomb with a steaming bowl that smelt very savory.

"Mrs. Yocomb," I cried, "you're always welcome; and that bowl is, too, for I'm hungry as a cub."

"Glad to hear it," said Mr. Yocomb's hearty voice from the doorway. "I'll kill for you a young gobbler that Emily Warren thinks is like the apple of my eye, if you will promise to eat him."

"No, indeed," I answered, reaching out my hand. "He is already devoted to Miss Warren's Thanksgiving dinner. May he continue to gobble until that auspicious day."

"What! do you remember that?" and Mr. Yocomb cast a quick look of surprise at his wife.

"Yes, I remember everything up to a certain point, and then all comes to a full stop. I wish you would bridge over the gap for me."

"Richard," interposed Mrs. Yocomb, quickly, "it wouldn't do thee any good to have father tell thee what thee said when out of thy mind from fever. I can tell thee, however, that thee said nothing of which thee need be ashamed."

"Well, I can't account for it. I must have been taken very suddenly. One thing is clear: you are the kindest people I ever heard of. You ought to be put in a museum."

"Why, Friend Morton, is it queer that we didn't turn thee out of doors or give thee in charge of the poormaster?"

"I certainly am the most fortunate man in the world," I said, laughing. "I had broken myself down and was about to become very ill, and I started off in the dark and never stopped till I reached the shelter of Mrs. Yocomb's wing. If I should tell my experience in New York there'd be an exodus to the country among newspaper men."

"Thee mustn't do it," protested Mr. Yocomb, assuming a look of dismay. "Thee knows I'm down on editors: I make thee an exception."

"I should think you had; but they would not expect to be treated one hundredth part so well as you have treated me."

"Well, bring thy friends, editors or otherwise. Thy friends will be welcome."

"I fear I'll be selfish; I feel as if I had made too rich a discovery to show it to others."

"Now, father, thee's had thy turn, and must go right out and let Richard take his breakfast and his medicine. I'm bent on making Dr. Bates say I'm the best nurse in town, and between such a lively patient and such a lively family I have a hard time of it."

"Well, thee knows I always mind, mother," said the old gentleman, putting on a rueful look. "I do it, thee knows, to set the children an example. Good-by now; mother will make thee as hearty as I am if thee'll mind her."

"Oh, I'm well enough to see *everybody* to-day," I said with emphasis, and I imagine that Mrs. Yocomb gave as definite a meaning to my indefinite term as I did.

"No one can stay long yet, but if thee continues to improve so nicely, we can move thee downstairs part of the day before very long."

"At that prospect I'll mind as well as Mr. Yocomb himself," I cried gladly. "Mr. Yocomb, they are spoiling me. I feel like a great petted boy, and behave like one, I fear; but having never been ill, I don't know how to behave."

"Thee's doing very well for a beginner. Keep on—keep on," and his genial visage vanished from the doorway.

After I had my breakfast, Zillah flitted in and out with her mother two or three times.

"Mother says I can look at thee, but I mustn't talk;" and she wouldn't.

Then Adah, with her wide-brimmed hat hanging on her arm, brought me a dainty little basket of wild strawberries.

"I promised to gather them for thee," she said, placing them on my table.

"You did? I had forgotten that," I replied. "I fear my memory is playing me sad tricks. You have just gathered them, I think?"

"What makes thee think so?"

"Because their color has got into your cheeks."

"I hope thee'll like them—the strawberries, I mean."

I laughed heartily as I answered, "I like both. I don't see how either could be improved upon."

"I think thee likes a city pallor best," she replied, shaking her head.

I imagine that a faint tinge of the strawberry came into my face, for she gave me a quick glance and turned away.

"Adah," said Mrs. Yocomb, entering, "thee can take thy sewing and sit here by the door for a while. Call me if Richard wants anything. The doctor will be here soon."

"Would thee like to have me stay?" she asked timidly.

"Indeed I would. Mrs. Yocomb, can I eat these strawberries? I've devoured them with my eyes already."

"Yes, if the doctor says so, and thee'll promise not to talk much."

I made no promise, for I was bent on talking, as convalescents usually are, I believe, and Adah forgot her sewing, and her blue eyes rested on me with an intentness that at last grew a little embarrassing. She said comparatively little, and her words had much of their old directness and simplicity; but the former flippancy and coloring of small vanity was absent. Her simple morning costume was scrupulously neat, and quite as becoming as the Sunday muslin which I had so admired, and she had fastened at her breastpin a rose that reminded me of the one I had given her on that wretched Sunday afternoon when she unconsciously and speedily dispelled the bright dream that I had woven around her.

"For some reason she has changed very much," I thought, "and I'm glad it's for the better."

Zillah came in, and leaned on her lap as she asked her a question or two. "Surely the little girl would not have done that the first day I met her," I mused, then added aloud:

"You are greatly changed, Miss Adah. What has happened to you?"

She blushed vividly at my abrupt question, and did not answer for a moment. Then she began hesitatingly:

"From what mother says, it's time I changed a little."

"I think Zillah likes you now as she does Miss Warren."

"No, she likes Emily Warren best—so does every one."

"You are mistaken. Zillah could not have looked at Miss Warren differently from the way in which she just looked at you. You have no idea what a pretty picture you two then made."

"I did not think about it."

"I imagine you don't think about yourself as much as you did. Perhaps that's the change I'm conscious of."

"I don't think about myself at all any more," and she bent low over her work.

Dr. Bates now entered with Mrs. Yocomb, and Adah slipped quietly away.

After strong professions of satisfaction at my rapid convalescence, and giving a medicine that speedily produced drowsiness, he too departed.

I roused up slightly from time to time as the day declined, and finding Reuben quietly busy at his carving, dozed again in a delicious, dreamy restfulness. In one of these half-waking moments I heard a low voice ask:

"Reuben, may I come in?"

Sleep departed instantly, and I felt that I must be stone dead before I could be unmoved by those tones, now as familiar as if heard all my life.

"Yes, please come," I exclaimed; "and you have been long in coming."

Reuben sprang up with alacrity as he said, "I'm glad thee's come, Emily. Would thee mind staying with Richard for a little while? I want to take Dapple out before night. If I don't, he gets fractious."

"I will take your place for a time, and will call Mrs. Yocomb if Mr. Morton needs anything."

"I assure you I won't need anything as long as you'll stay," I began, as soon as we were alone. "I want to thank you for the rosebuds. They were taken away this morning; but I had them brought back and placed here where I could touch them. They seemed to bring back that June evening in the old garden so vividly that I've lived the scene over and over again."

She looked perplexed, and colored slightly, but said smilingly, "Mrs. Yocomb will think I'm a poor nurse if I let you talk too much."

"Then talk to me. I promise to listen as long as you will talk."

"Well, mention an agreeable subject."

"Yourself. What have you been doing in the ages that have elapsed since I came to life. It seems as if I had been dead, and I can't recall a thing that happened in that nether world. I only hope I didn't make a fool of myself."

"I'm sorry to say you were too ill to do anything very bad. Mr. Morton, you can't realize how glad we all are that you are getting well so fast."

"I hope I can't realize how glad YOU are, and yet I would like to think that you are very glad. Do you know what has done me the most good to-day?"

"How should I know?" she asked, looking away, with something like trouble in her face.

"I heard your laugh this morning while you were at breakfast, and it filled all the old house with music. It seemed to become a part of the sunshine that was shimmering on the elm-leaves that swayed to and fro before my window, and then the robins took it up in the garden. By the way, have you seen the robin's nest that Zillah showed us?"

"Yes," she replied, "but it's empty, and the queer little things that Zillah said were all 'mouth and swallow' are now pert young robins, rollicking around the garden all day long. They remind me of Reuben and Dapple. I love such fresh young life, unshadowed by care or experience."

"I believe you; and your sympathy with such life will always keep you young at heart. I can't imagine you growing old; indeed, truth is never old and feeble."

"You are very fanciful, Mr. Morton," she said, with a trace of perplexity again on her face.

"I have heard that that was a characteristic of sick people," I laughed.

"Yes; we have to humor them like children," she added, smoothing her brow as if this were an excuse for letting me express more admiration than she relished.

"Well," I admitted, "I've never been ill and made much of before, since I was a little fellow, and my mother spoiled me, and I've no idea how to behave. Even if I did, it would seem impossible to be conventional in this house. Am I not the most singularly fortunate man that ever existed? Like a fool I had broken myself down, and was destined to be ill. I started off as aimlessly as an arrow shot into the air, and here I am, enjoying your society and Mrs. Yocomb's care."

"It is indeed strange," she replied musingly, as if half speaking to herself; "so strange that I cannot understand it. Life is a queer tangle at best. That is, it seems so to us sometimes."

"I assure you I am glad to have it tangled for me in this style," I said, laughing. "My only dread is getting out of the snarl. Indeed, I'm sorely tempted to play sick indefinitely."

"In that case we shall all leave you here to yourself."

"I think *you* have done that already."

"What would your paper do without you?" she asked, with her brow slightly knitted and the color deepening in her cheeks.

"Recalling what you said, I'm tempted to think it is doing better without me."

"You imagine I said a great deal more than I did."

"No, I remember everything that happened until I was taken ill. It's strange I was taken so suddenly. I can see you playing Chopin's nocturne as distinctly as I see you now. Do you know that I had the fancy that the cluster of roses you sent me was that nocturne embodied, and that the shades of color were the variations in the melody?"

"You are indeed very fanciful. I hope you will grow more rational as you get well."

"I remember you thought me slightly insane in the garden."

"Yes; and you promised that you would see things just as they are after leaving it."

"I can't help seeing things just as they seem to me. Perhaps I do see them just as they are."

"Oh, no! To a matter-of-fact person like myself, you are clearly very fanciful. If you don't improve in this respect, you'll have to take a course in mathematics before returning to your work or you will mislead your readers."

"No, I'm going to take a course of weeding in the garden, and you were to invite me into the arbor as soon as I had done enough to earn my salt."

"I fear you will pull up the vegetables."

"You can at least show me which are the potatoes."

In spite of a restraint that she tried to disguise, she broke out into a low laugh at this reminiscence, and said: "After that revelation of ignorance you will never trust me again."

"I will trust you in regard to everything except kitchen vegetables," I replied, more in earnest than in jest. "A most important exception," she responded, her old troubled look coming back. "But you are talking far too much. Your face is slightly flushed. I fear you are growing feverish. I will call Mrs. Yocomb now."

"Please do not. I never felt better in my life. You are doing me good every moment, and it's so desperately stupid lying helplessly here."

"Well, I suppose I must humor you a few moments longer," she laughed. "People, when ill, are so arbitrary. By the way, your editorial friends must think a great deal of you, or else you are valuable to them, for your chief writes to Mr. Yocomb every day about you; so do some others; and they've sent enough fruit and delicacies to be the death of an ostrich."

"I'm glad to hear that; it rather increases one's faith in human nature. I didn't know whether they or any one would care much if I died."

"Mr. Morton!" she said reproachfully.

"Oh, I remember my promise to you. If, like a cat, I had lost my ninth life, I would live after your words. Indeed I imagine that you were the only reason I did live. It was your will that saved me, for I hadn't enough sense or spirit left to do more than flicker out."

"Do you think so?" she asked eagerly, and a rich glow of pleasure overspread her face.

"I do indeed. You have had a subtle power over me from the first, which I cannot resist, and don't wish to."

"I must go now," she said hastily.

"Please wait," I entreated. "I've a message for Mrs. Yocomb."

She stood irresolutely near the door.

"I wish you to tell her—why is it getting dark so suddenly?"

"I fear we're going to have a shower," and she glanced apprehensively toward the window.

"When have I seen that look on your face before?" I asked quickly.

"You had a message for Mrs. Yocomb?"

"Yes. I wish you would make her realize a little of my unbounded gratitude, which every day increases. In fact, I can't understand the kindness of this family, it is so hearty, so genuine. Why, I was an entire stranger the other day. Then Adah and—pardon me—you also used expressions which puzzle me very much. I can't understand how I became ill so suddenly. I was feeling superbly that Sunday evening, and then everything became a blank. Mrs. Yocomb, from a fear of disquieting me, won't say much about it. The impression that a storm or something occurred that I can't recall, haunts me. You are one that couldn't deceive if you tried."

"You needn't think I've anything to tell when Mrs. Yocomb hasn't," she answered, with a gay laugh.

"Miss Warren," I said gravely, "that laugh isn't natural. I never heard you laugh so before. Something *did* happen."

A flash of lightning gleamed across the window, and the girl gave an involuntary and apprehensive start.

Almost as instantaneously the events I had forgotten passed through my mind. In strong and momentary excitement I rose on my elbow, and looked for their confirmation in her troubled face.

"Oh, forget—forget it all!" she exclaimed, in a low, distressed voice, and she came and stood before me with clasped hands.

"Would to God I had died!" I said, despairingly, and I sank back faint and crushed. "I had no right to speak—to think of you as I did. Good-by."

"Mr. Morton—"

"Please leave me now. I'm too weak to be a man, and I would not lose your esteem."

"But you will get well—you promised me that."

"Well!" I said, in a low, bitter tone. "When can I ever be well? Good-by."

"Mr. Morton, would you blight my life?" she asked, almost indignantly. "Am I to blame for this?"

"Nor am I to blame. It was inevitable. Curses on a world in which one can err so fatally."

"Can you not be a brave, generous man? If this should go against you— if you will not get well—you promised me to live."

"I will exist; but can one whose heart is stone, and hope dead, *live*? I'll do my best. No, yon are not to blame—not in the least. Take the whole comfort of that truth. Nor was I either. That Sunday *was* the day of my fate, since for me to see you was to love you by every instinct and law of my being. But I trust, as you said, you will find me too honorable to seek that which belongs to another."

"Mr. Morton," she said, in tones of deep distress, "you saved this home; you saved Mrs. Yocomb's life; you—you saved mine. Will you embitter it?"

"Would to God I had died!" I groaned. "All would then have been well. I had fulfilled my mission."

She wrung her hands as she stood beside me. "I can't—oh, I can't endure this!" she murmured, and there was anguish in her voice.

I rallied sufficiently to take her hand as I said: "Emily Warren, I understand your crystal truth too well not to know that there is no hope for me. I'll bear my hard fate as well as I can; but you must not expect too much. And remember this: I shall be like a planet hereafter. The little happiness I have will be but a pale reflection of yours. If you are unhappy, I shall be so inevitably. Not a shadow of blame rests on you—the first fair woman was not truer than you. I'll do my best—I'll get up again—soon, I trust, now. If you ever need a friend—but you would not so wrong me as to go to another—I won't be weak and lackadaisical. Don't make any change; let this episode in your life be between ourselves only. Good-by."

"Oh, you look so ill—so changed—what can I say—?"

Helpless tears rushed into her eyes. "You saved my life," she breathed softly; but as she turned hastily to depart she met our hostess.

"Oh, Mrs. Yocomb," she sobbed, "he knows all."

"Thee surely could not have told him—"

"Indeed I did not—it came to him like a flash."

"Mrs. Yocomb, by all that's sacred, Miss Warren is not to blame for anything—only myself. Please keep my secret; it shall not trouble any one;" and I turned my face to the wall.

"Richard Morton."

"Dear Mrs. Yocomb, give me time. I'm too sorely wounded to speak to any one."

"A man should try to do what is right under all circumstances," she said, firmly, "and it is your first and sacred duty to get well. It is time for your medicine."

I turned and said desperately, "Give me stimulants—give me anything that will make me strong, so that I may keep my word; for if ever a man was mortally weak in body and soul, I am."

"I'll do my best for thee," she said, gently, "for I feel for thee and with thee, as if thee were my own son. But I wish thee to remember now and always that the only true strength comes from Heaven."

CHAPTER VI
WEAKNESS

Soul and body are too nearly related for one to suffer without the other's sympathy. Mrs. Yocomb mercifully shielded me that evening, merely saying that I had seen enough company for one day. My sleep that night resulted from opiates instead of nature's impulses, and so was unrefreshing, and the doctor was surprised to find a change for the worse the following morning. For two or three days the scale wavered, and I scarcely held what I had gained. Mrs. Yocomb rarely left me, and I believe that I owe my life not only to her excellent nursing, but even more to her strong moral support—her gentle but unspoken sympathy. I knew she understood me, and that her mercy was infinite for my almost mortal weakness; for now that the inexplicable buoyancy which that chief of earthly hopes imparts was gone, I sank into an abyss of despondency from which I feared I could never escape. Her wisdom and intuitive delicacy led her to select Reuben as her chief assistant. I found his presence very restful; for, so far from suspecting, he could not understand a wound often more real and painful than any received on battlefields. I now could not have endured Adah's intent and curious scrutiny, and yet I deeply appreciated her kindness, for she kept my table laden with delicate fruits and flowers.

The dainty little vase was replenished daily also with clusters of roses—roses only—and I soon recognized rare and perfect buds that at this late season only a florist could supply. The pleasure they gave was almost counterbalanced by the pain. Their exquisite color and fragrance suggested a character whose perfection daily made my disappointment more intolerable. At last Mrs. Yocomb said:

"Richard Morton, is thee doing thy best to get well? Thee's incurring a grave responsibility if thee is not. Emily Warren is quite alone in the world and she came to me as to a mother when thee was taken ill, and told me of thy unfortunate attachment. As thee said, she is not to blame, and yet such is her kindly and sensitive nature that she suffers quite as much as if she were wholly to blame. Her life almost depends on thine. She is growing pale and ill. She eats next to nothing, and I fear she sleeps but little. She is just waiting in miserable suspense to see if thee will keep thy word and live. I believe thee *can* live, and grow strong and good and noble, if thee will."

"Oh, Mrs. Yocomb, how you must despise me! If you but knew how I loathe myself."

"No, I'm sorry for thee from the depths of my heart. If thee's doing thy best, I've not a word to say; but thee should know the truth. As Emily said, thee has the power either to embitter her life or to add very much to its happiness."

"Well," I said, "if I have not the strength to overcome this unmanly, contemptible weakness, I ought to die, and the sooner the better. If I'm worth life, I shall live."

If ever a weak, nerveless body yielded to an imperious will, mine did. From that hour, as far as possible, I gave my whole thought to recovery, and was as solicitous as I before had been apathetic. No captain could have been more so in regard to his ship, which he fears may not outride a storm.

I appealed to Dr. Bates to rack his brains in the preparation of the most effective tonics, I took my food with scrupulous regularity; and in the effort to oxygenize my thin pale blood, drew long respirations of the pure summer air. Mrs. Yocomb daily smiled a warmer and more hearty encouragement.

Under the impetus of a resolute purpose the wheels of life began to move steadily and at last rapidly toward the goal of health. I soon was able to sit up part of the day.

As I rallied, I could not help recognizing the richer coloring that came into the life at the farmhouse, and the fact touched me deeply.

"What is my suffering compared with the happiness of this home?" I thought. "It would have been brutally selfish to have died."

I now had my letters brought to me. My paper—my first love—was daily read, and my old interest in its welfare kindled slowly.

"Work," I said, "is the best of antidotes. It shall be my remedy. Men are respected only as they stand on their feet and work, and I shall win her respect to the utmost."

Reuben and Adah read to me. The presence of the former, like that of his father and mother, was very restful; but Adah began to puzzle me. At first I ascribed her manner to an extravagant sense of gratitude, and the romantic interest which a young girl might naturally take in one who had passed with her through peril, and who seemingly had been dangerously ill in consequence; but I was compelled at last to see that her regard was not open, frank, and friendly, but shy, absorbing, and jealous. It gave her unmingled satisfaction that I did not ask for Miss Warren, and she rarely spoke of her. When she did she watched me keenly, as if seeking to read my thoughts. Reuben, on the contrary, spoke freely of her; but, from some restraint placed upon him by his mother probably, did not ask her to relieve him in his care of me again.

After I began to sit up, Miss Warren would not infrequently come to my door, when others were present, and smilingly express her gladness that I was improving daily. Indeed there would often be quite gay repartee between us, and I think that even Adah was so blinded by our manner that her suspicions were allayed. It evidently puzzled her, and Reuben also, that I had apparently lost my interest in one who had such great attractions for me at first. But Adah was not one to seek long and deeply for subtle and hidden causes of action. She had a quick eye, however, for what was apparent, and scanned surfaces narrowly. I fear I perplexed her as sorely as she did me.

In spite of every effort to remain blind to the truth, I began to fear that she was inclined to give me a regard which I had not sought, and which would embarrass me beyond measure.

That a man can exult over a passion in a woman which he cannot requite is marvellous. That he can look curiously, critically, and complacently on this most sacred mystery of a woman's soul, that he can care no more for her delicate incense than would a grim idol, is proof that his heart is akin to the stony idol in material, and his nature like that of the gross, cruel divinity represented. The vanity that can feed on such food has a more depraved appetite than the South Sea Islander, who is content with human flesh merely. It would seem that there are those who can smile to see a woman waste the richest treasures of her spiritual life which were designed to last and sustain through the long journey of life—ay, and even boast of her immeasurable loss, of which they, wittingly or unwittingly, have been the cause.

The oddest part of it all is that women can love such men instead of regarding them as spider-like monsters that, were the doctrine of transmigration true, would become spiders again as soon as compelled to drop their human disguise.

But women usually idealize the men they love into something very different from what they are. Heaven knows that I was not a saint; but I am glad that it caused me pain, and pain only, as I saw Adah shyly and almost unconsciously bending on me glances laden with a priceless gift, which, nevertheless, I could not receive.

Her nature was too simple and direct for disguises, and when she attempted them they were often so apparent as to be comically pathetic. And yet she did attempt them. There was nothing bold and unmaidenly in her manner, and as I look back upon those days I thank God that I was never so graceless and brutal as to show or feel anything like contempt for her gentle, childlike preference. Very possibly also my own unfortunate experience made me more considerate, and it was my policy to treat her with the same frank, undisguised affection that I manifested toward Zillah, with, of course, the differences required by their different ages.

Adah was no longer repulsive to me. The events of that memorable night of storm and danger, and the experiences that followed, had apparently awakened her better nature, which, although having a narrow compass, was gentle and womanly. Her old flippancy was gone. My undisguised preference for Miss Warren after I had actually made her acquaintance, and my persistent blindness to everything verging toward sentiment, had perhaps done something toward dispelling her belief that beauty and dress were irresistible. Thus she may have been led honestly to compare herself with Emily Warren, who was not only richly endowed but highly cultivated; at any rate her small vanity had vanished also, and she was in contrast as self-distrustful and hesitating in manner as she formerly had been abrupt and self-asserting. Moreover she had either lost her interest in her neighbor's petty affairs, or else had been made to feel that a tendency to gossip was not a captivating trait, and we heard no more about what this one said or that one wore on her return from meeting. While her regard was undoubtedly sincere, I felt and hoped that it was merely a sentiment attendant on her wakening and fuller spiritual life, rather than an abiding and deep attachment; and I believed that it would soon be replaced by other interests after my departure. For my own sake as well as hers I had decided to leave the farmhouse as speedily as possible, but I soon began to entertain the theory that I could dispel her dreams better by remaining a little longer, and by proving that she held the same place in my thoughts as Zillah, and could possess no other. There would then be no vain imaginings after I had gone.

I rather wanted to stay until I had fully recovered my health, for I was beginning to take pride in my self-mastery. If I could regain my footing, and stand erect in such quiet, manly strength as to change Miss Warren's sympathy into respect only, I felt that I would achieve a victory that would be a source of satisfaction for the rest of life. That I could do this I honestly doubted, for seemingly she had enthralled my whole being, and her power over me was wellnigh irresistible.

I knew that she understood Adah even better than I did, and it seemed her wish to afford the girl every opportunity, for she never came to ask how I was when Adah was present; and the latter was honest enough to tell me that it was Miss Warren who had suggested some of the simple yet interesting stories with which my long hours of convalescence were beguiled; but in her latent jealousy she could not help adding:

"Since Emily Warren selected them, thee cannot help liking them."

"I certainly ought to like them doubly," I had quietly replied, looking directly into her eyes, "since I am indebted for them to two friends instead of one."

"There's a great difference in friends," she said significantly.

"Yes, indeed," I replied, smiling as frankly as if I had been talking to Zillah; "and your mother is the best friend I have or ever expect to have."

Adah had sighed deeply, and had gone on with her reading in a girlish, plaintive voice that was quite different from her ordinary tones.

Unconsciously she had imbibed the idea—probably from what she often heard at meeting—that anything read or spoken consecutively must be in a tone different from that used in ordinary conversation, and she always lifted up her voice into an odd, plaintive little monotone, that was peculiar, but not at all disagreeable. It would not have been natural in another, but was perfectly so to her, and harmonized with her unique character. The long words even in the simple stories were often formidable obstacles, and she would look up apprehensively, and color for fear I might be laughing at her; but I took pains to gaze quietly through the window in serene unconsciousness. She also stumbled because her thoughts evidently were often far away from her book, but at my cordial thanks when finishing the story her face would glow with pleasure. And yet she missed something in my thanks, or else saw, in the quiet manner with which I turned to my letters or paper, that which was unsatisfactory, and she would sigh as she left the room. Her gentle, patient efforts to please me, which oddly combined maidenly shyness and childlike simplicity, often touched the depths of my heart, and the thought came more than once, "If this is more than a girlish fancy, and time proves that I am essential to her happiness—which is extremely doubtful—perhaps I can give her enough affection to content a nature like hers."

But one glimpse of Emily Warren would banish this thought, for it seemed as if my very soul were already wedded to her. "The thought of another is impossible," I would mutter. "She was my fate."

Four or five of the days during which I had been sufficiently strong to sit up had passed away, and I was able to give more of my time to my mail and paper, and thus to seem preoccupied when Adah came to read. I found Zillah also a useful though unconscious ally, and I lured her into my room by innumerable stories. Reuben and Mr. Yocomb were now very busy in their harvest, and I saw them chiefly in the evening, but they were too tired to stay long. Time often hung wofully heavy on my hands, and I longed to be out of doors again; but Mrs. Yocomb was prudently inexorable. I am sure that she restrained Adah a great deal, for she grew less and less demonstrative in manner, and I was left more to myself.

Thus a week passed. It was Saturday morning, and between the harvest without and preparations for Sunday within, all the inmates of the farmhouse were very busy. The forenoon had wellnigh passed. I had exhausted every expedient to kill time, and was looking on the landscape shimmering in the fierce sunlight with an apathy that was dull and leaden in contrast, when a low knock caused me to look up; but instead of Adah, as I expected, Miss Warren stood in the doorway.

"They are all so busy to-day," she said hesitatingly, "that I thought I might help you pass an hour or two. It seems too bad that you should be left to yourself so long."

To my disgust, I—who had resolved to be so strong and self-poised in her presence—felt that every drop of blood in my body had rushed into my face. It certainly must have been very apparent, for her color became vivid also.

"I fear I was having a stupid time," I began awkwardly. "I don't want to make trouble. Perhaps Mrs. Yocomb needs your help."

"No," she said, smiling, "you can't banish me on that ground. I've been helping Mrs. Yocomb all the morning. She's teaching me how to cook. I've succeeded in proving that the family would have a fit of indigestion that might prove fatal were it wholly dependent on my performances."

"Tell me what you made?" I said eagerly. "Am I to have any of it for my dinner?"

"Indeed you are not. Dr. Bates would have me indicted."

She looked at me with solicitude, for although I had laughed with her I felt ill and faint. Despairingly, I thought, "I cannot see her and live. I must indeed go away."

"So you are coming downstairs to-morrow?" she began. "We shall give you a welcome that ought to make any man proud. Mrs. Yocomb is all aglow with her preparations."

"I wish they wouldn't do so," I said, in a pained tone. "I'd much rather slip quietly into my old place as if nothing had happened."

"I imagined you would feel so, Mr. Morton," she said gently; "but so much has happened that you must let them express their abounding gratitude in their own way. It will do them good, and they will be the happier for it."

"Indeed, Miss Warren, that very word gratitude oppresses me. There is no occasion for their feeling so. Why, Hiram, their man, could not have done less. I merely happened to be here. It's all the other way now. If ever a man was overwhelmed with kindness, I have been. How can I ever repay Mrs. Yocomb?"

"I am equally helpless in that respect; but I'm glad to think that between some of our friends the question of repaying may be forgotten. I never expect to repay Mrs. Yocomb."

"Has she done so much for you, also?"

"Yes, more than I can tell you."

"Well," I said, trying to laugh, "if I ever write another paragraph it will be due to her good nursing."

"That is my chief cause for gratitude," she said hurriedly, the color deepening again in her cheeks. "If you hadn't—if—I know of your brave effort to get well, too—she told me."

"Yes, Miss Warren," I said quietly, "I am now doing my best."

"And you are doing nobly—so nobly that I am tempted to give you a strong proof of friendship; to tell you what I have not told any one except Mrs. Yocomb. I feel as if I had rather you heard it from me than casually from others.-It will show how—how I trust you."

My very heart seemed to stand still, and I think my pallor alarmed her; but feeling that she had gone too far, she continued hurriedly, taking a letter from her pocket:

"I expect my friend to-night. He's been absent, and now writes that he will—"

I shrank involuntarily as if from a blow, and with her face full of distress she stopped abruptly.

Summoning the whole strength of my manhood, I rallied sufficiently to say, in a voice that I knew was unnatural from the stress I was under:

"I congratulate you. I trust you may be very happy."

"I had hoped—" she began. "I would be if I saw that you were happy."

"You are always hoping," I replied, trying to laugh, "that I may become sane and rational. Haven't you given that up yet? I shall be very happy tomorrow, and will drink to the health of you both."

She looked at me very dubiously, and the trouble in her face did not pass away. "Let me read to you," she said abruptly. "I brought with me Hawthorne's 'Mosses from an Old Manse.' They are not too familiar, I trust?"

"I cannot hear them too often," I said, nerving myself as if for torture.

She began to read that exquisite little character study, "The Great Stone Face." Her voice was sweet and flexible, and varied with the thought as if the words had been set to music. At first I listened with delight to hear my favorite author so perfectly interpreted; but soon, too soon, every syllable added to my sense of unutterable loss.

Possibly she intuitively felt my distress, possibly she saw it as I tried to look as stoical as an Indian chief who is tortured on every side with burning brands. At any rate she stopped, and said hesitatingly:

"You—you do not enjoy my reading."

With a rather grim smile I replied: "Nothing but the truth will answer with you. I must admit I do not."

"Would—would you like to hear something else?" she asked, in evident embarrassment.

"Nothing is better than Hawthorne," I said. "I—I fear I'm not yet strong enough." Then, after a second's hesitation, I spoke out despairingly: "Miss Warren, I may as well recognize the truth at once, I never shall be strong enough. I've overrated myself. Good-by."

She trembled; tears came into her eyes, and she silently left the room. So abrupt was her departure that it seemed like a flight.

After she had gone I tottered to my feet, with an imprecation on my weakness, and I took an amount of stimulant that Dr. Bates would never have prescribed; but it had little effect. In stony, sullen protest at my fate, I sat down again, and the hours passed like eternities.

CHAPTER VII
OLD PLOD IDEALIZED

Adah brought me up my dinner, and I at once noted that she was in a flutter of unusual excitement. Her mother had undoubtedly prepared her for the arrival of the expected guest, and made known also his relations to one of whom she had been somewhat jealous, and it would seem that the simple-hearted girl could not disguise her elation.

I was in too bitter a mood to endure a word, and yet did not wish to hurt her feelings; therefore she found me more absorbed in my paper and preoccupied than ever before.

"Thank you, Miss Adah," I said, cordially but briefly. "Editors are wretched company; their paper is everything to them, and I've something on my mind just now that's very absorbing."

"Thee isn't strong enough to work yet," she said sympathetically.

"Oh, yes," I replied, laughing bitterly; "I'm a small edition of Samson. Besides, I'm as poor as Job's impoverished turkey, and must get to work again as soon as possible."

"There is no need of thee feeling that way; we—" and then she stopped and blushed.

"I know all about 'we,'" I laughed; "your hearts are as large as this wide valley, but then I must keep my self-respect, you know. You have no idea how happy you ought to be in such a home as yours."

"I like the city better," she replied, blushing, and she hastily left the room.

My greed for work departed as abruptly. "Poor child!" I muttered. "'Life is a tangle,' as Miss Warren said, and a wretched one, too, for many of us."

Mrs. Yocomb soon after came in, and looked with solicitude at my almost untasted dinner.

"Why, Richard," she said, "thy appetite flags strangely. Isn't thy dinner to thy taste?"

"The fault is wholly in me," I replied.

"Thee doesn't look so well—nothing like so well. Has Adah said anything to trouble thee?" she asked apprehensively.

"No, indeed; Adah is just as good and kind as she can be. She's becoming as good as she is beautiful. Every day increases my respect for her;" and I spoke earnestly and honestly.

A faint color stole into the matron's cheek, and she seemed pleased and relieved, but she remarked quietly:

"Adah's young and inexperienced." Then she added, with a touch of motherly pride and solicitude, "She's good at heart, and I think is trying to do right."

"She will make a noble woman, Mrs. Yocomb—one that you may well be proud of, or I'm no judge of character," I said, with quiet emphasis. "She and Zillah have both been so kind to me that they already seem like sisters. At any rate, after my treatment in this home I shall always feel that I owe to them a brother's duty."

The color deepened in the old lady's face, that was still so fair and comely, and tears stood in her eyes.

"I understand thee, Richard," she said quietly. "I thought I loved thee for saving our lives and our home, but I love thee more now. Still thee cannot understand a mother's heart. Thee's a true gentleman."

"Dear Mrs. Yocomb, you must learn to understand me better or I shall have to run away in self-defence. When you talk in that style I feel like an arrant hypocrite. I give you my word that I've been swearing this very forenoon."

"Who was thee swearing at?" she asked, in much surprise.

"Myself, and with good reason."

"There is never good reason for such wickedness," she said gravely, but regarding me with deep solicitude. Presently she added, "Thee has had some great provocation?"

"No; I've been honored with unmerited kindness and trust, which I have ill requited." "Emily Warren has been to see thee?"

"Yes."

"Did she tell thee?"

"Yes; and I feel that I could throttle that man. Now you know what a heathen savage I am."

"Yes," she said dryly, "thee has considerable untamed human nature." Then added, smiling, "I'll trust him with thee, nevertheless. I'm inclined to think that for her sake thee'd do more for him than for any man living. Now wouldn't thee?"

"Oh, Satan take him! Yes!" I groaned. "Forgive me, Mrs. Yocomb. I'm so unmanned, so desperate from trouble, that I'm not fit for decent society, much less your company. You believe in a Providence: why was this woman permitted to enslave my very soul when it was of no use?"

"Richard Morton," she said reproachfully, "thee is indeed unmanned. Thee's wholly unjust and unreasonable. This gentleman has been Emily Warren's devoted friend for years. He has taken care of her little property, and done everything for her that her independent spirit would permit. He might have sought an alliance among the wealthiest, but he has sued long and patiently for her hand—"

"Well he might," I interrupted irritably. "Emily Warren is the peer of any man in New York."

"Thee knows New York and the world in general well enough to be aware that wealthy bankers do not often seek wives from the class to which Emily belongs, though in my estimation, as well as in thine, no other class is more respectable. But I'm not blinded by prejudice, and I think it speaks well for him that he is able to recognize and honor worth wherever he finds it. Still, he knew her family. The Warrens were quite wealthy, too, at one time."

"What is his name?" I asked sullenly.

"Gilbert Hearn." "What, Hearn the banker, who resides on Fifth Avenue?"

"The same."

"I know him—that is, I know who he is—well." Then I added bitterly, "It's just like him; he has always had the good things of this world, and always will. He'll surely marry her."

"Has thee anything against him?"

"Yes, infinitely much against him: I feel as if he were seeking to marry my wife."

"That's what thee said when out of thy mind," she exclaimed apprehensively. "I hope thee is not becoming feverish?" "Oh, no, Mrs. Yocomb, I've nothing against him at all. He is pre-eminently respectable, as the world goes. He is shrewd, wonderfully shrewd, and always makes a ten-strike in Wall Street; but his securing Miss Warren was a masterstroke.

There, I'm talking slang, and disgracing myself generally." But my bitter spirit broke out again in the words, "Never fear; Gilbert Hearn will have the best in the city; nothing less will serve him."

"Thee is prejudiced and unjust. I hope thee'll be in a better mood to-morrow," and she left my room looking hurt and grieved.

I sank back in my chair in wretched, reckless apathy, and from the depths of my heart wished I had died.

After a little time Mrs. Yocomb came hastily in, looking half ashamed of her weakness, and in her hands was a bowl of delicious broth.

"My heart relents toward thee," she said, with moist eyes. "I ought to have made more allowance for one whose mother left him much too early. Take this, every drop, and remember thy pledge to get well and be a generous man. I'll trust thee to keep thy word," and she departed before I could speak.

"Well, I should be a devil incarnate if I didn't become a man after her kindness," I muttered, and I gulped down the broth and my evil mood at the same time.

At the end of an hour I could almost have shaken hands with Gilbert Hearn, who prospered in all that he touched.

As the sun declined I heard the rustle of a silk on the stairway. A moment later Miss Warren mounted the horseblock and stood waiting for Reuben, who soon appeared in the family rockaway.

I thought the maiden looked a trifle pale in contrast with her light silk, but perhaps it was the shadow of the tree she stood under; but I muttered, "Even his critical taste can find no fault with that form and face; she'll grace his princely home, and none will recognize the truth more clearly than he."

She hesitatingly lifted her eyes toward my window, and I started back, forgetting that I was hidden by the half-closed blind; but my face suffused with pleasure as I said to myself:

"Heaven bless her! she does not forget me wholly, even on the threshold of her happiness."

At that moment Old Plod, passing through the yard in his early Saturday release from toil, gave a loud whinny of recognition. The young girl started visibly, sprang lightly down from the block and caressed her great heavy-footed pet, and then, without another glance at my window, entered the rockaway, and was driven rapidly toward the distant depot at which she would welcome the most fortunate man in the world.

I now felt sure that I had guessed her associations with the old plow-horse, and, sore-hearted as I was, I laughed long and silently over the quaint fancy.

"Truly," I muttered, "the courtly and elegant banker would not feel flattered if he knew about it. How in the world did she ever come to unite the two in her mind?"

But as I thought it all over I was led to conclude that it was natural enough. The lonely girl had no doubt found that even in the best society of a Christian city she must ever be warily on her guard. She was beautiful, and yet poor and apparently friendless; and, as she had intimated, she had found many of the young and gay ready to flatter, and with anything but sincere motives. The banker, considerably her senior, had undoubtedly proved himself a quiet, steadfast friend. He was not the fool to neglect her as did those stupid horses, for any oats the world could offer, and she always found him, like Old Plod, ready to drop everything for her, and well he might. "No matter how devoted he has been, he can never plume himself on any magnanimity," I said to myself. "She probably finds him a trifle formal and sedate, and rather lacking in ideality, just as Old Plod is very stolid till she appears; but then he is safe and strong, and very kind to a friendless girl, who might well shrink from the vicissitudes of her lot, and would naturally be attracted by the protection and position which he could offer. In spite of the disparity of years, a woman might easily love a man who could do so much for her, and the banker is still well preserved and handsome. Of course Emily Warren does love him: all the wealth of Wall Street could not buy her. Yes, in a world full of lightning flashes she has made a thrifty and excellent choice. I may as well own it, in spite of every motive to prejudice. Gilbert Hearn is not my ideal man by any means. Good things are essential to him. He would feel personally aggrieved if the weather was bad for two days in succession. He is very charitable and public-spirited, and he likes our paper to recognize the fact: I have proof of that too. Alms given in the dark are not exactly wasted—but I'm thinking scandal. He so likes to let his 'light so shine.' He's respectability personified, and the toil-worn girl will be taken into an ark of safety.

"I suppose I ought to be magnanimous enough to think that it's all for the best, since he can do infinitely more for her than I ever could. She will be the millionaire's wife, and I'll go back to my dingy little office and write paragraphs heavy enough to sink a cork ship. Thus will end my June idyll; but should I live a century I will always feel that Gilbert Hearn married my wife."

CHAPTER VIII
AN IMPULSE

For nearly an hour I sat listlessly in my chair and watched the shadows lengthen across the valley. Suddenly an impulse seized me, and I resolved to obey it.

"If I can go downstairs to-morrow, I can go just as well to-night," I said, "and go I will. She shall not have a shadow on her first evening with her lover, and she's too good-hearted to enjoy it wholly if she thinks I'm moping and sighing in my room. Moreover, I shall not let my shadows make a background for the banker's general prosperity. Stately and patronizing he cannot help being, and Miss Warren may lead him to think that he is under some obligation to me—I wish he might never hear of it—but, by Vulcan and his sledge! he shall have no cause to pity me while he unctuously rubs his hands in self-felicitation."

As far as my strength permitted, I made a careful toilet, and sat down to wait. As the sun sank below the horizon, the banker appeared. "Very appropriate," I muttered; "but his presence would make it dark at midday."

Miss Warren was talking with animation, and pointing out the surrounding objects of interest, and he was listening with a wonderfully complacent smile on his smooth, full face.

"How prosperous he looks!" I muttered. "The idea of anything going contrary to his will or wishes!"

Then I saw that a little girl sat on the front seat with Reuben, and that he was letting her drive, but with his hand hovering near the reins.

Mr. and Mrs. Yocomb came out and greeted Mr. Hearn cordially, and he in return was very benign, for it was evident that, in their place and station, he found them agreeable people, and quite to his mind.

"Why doesn't he take off his hat to Mrs. Yocomb as if she were a duchess?" I growled. "That trunk that fills half the rockaway doesn't look as if he had come to spend Sunday only. Perhaps we are destined to make a happy family. I wonder who the little girl is?".

The banker was given what was known as the parlor bedroom, on the ground floor, and I heard Adah taking the little girl to her room.

Miss Warren did not glance at my window on her return. "She would have been happy enough had I remained here and sighed like a furnace," I muttered grimly. "Well, idiot! why shouldn't she be?"

She had evidently lingered to say something to Mrs. Yocomb, but I soon heard her light step pass up to her room.

"Now's my chance," I thought. "Mrs. Yocomb is preparing for supper, and all the rest are out of the way," and I slipped down the stairs with noiseless and rather unsteady tread. Excitement, however, lent me a transient strength, and I felt as if the presence of the banker would give me sinews of steel. I entered the parlor unobserved, and taking my old seat, from which I had watched the approach of the memorable storm, I waited events.

The first one to appear was the banker, rubbing his hands in a way that suggested a habit of complacency and self-felicitation. He started slightly on seeing me, and then said graciously:

"Mr. Morton, I presume?"

"You are correct, Mr. Hearn. I congratulate you on your safe arrival."

"Thanks. I've travelled considerably, and have never met with an accident. Glad to see you able to be down, for from what I heard I feared you had not sufficiently recovered."

"I'm much better to-day, sir," I replied, briefly.

"Well, this air, these scenes ought to impart health and content. I'm greatly pleased already, and congratulate myself on finding so pleasant a place of summer sojourn. It will form a delightful contrast to great hotels and jostling crowds." I now saw Miss Warren, through the half-open door, talking to Mrs. Yocomb. They evidently thought the banker was conversing with Mr. Yocomb.

Instead of youthful ardor and bubbling happiness, the girl's face had a grave, sedate aspect that comported well with her coming dignities. Then she looked distressed. Was Mrs. Yocomb telling her of my profane and awful mood? I lent an inattentive ear to Mr. Hearn's excellent reasons for satisfaction with his present abode, and in the depths of my soul I thought, "If she's worrying about me now, how good-hearted she is!"

"I already foresee," Mr. Hearn proceeded, in his full-orbed tones, "that it will also be just the place for my little girl—safe and quiet, with very nice people to associate with."

"Yes," I said emphatically, "they are nice people—the best I ever knew."

Miss Warren started violently, took a step toward the door, then paused, and Mrs. Yocomb entered first.

"Why, Richard Morton!" she exclaimed, "what does thee mean by this imprudence?"

"I mean to eat a supper that will astonish you," I replied, laughing.

"But I didn't give thee leave to come down."

"You said I could come to-morrow, so I haven't disobeyed in spirit."

Miss Warren still stood in the hall, but seeing that I had recognized her, she came forward and gave me her hand as she said:

"No one is more glad than I that you are able to come down."

Her words were very quiet, but the pressure of her hand was so warm as to surprise me, and I also noted that what must have been a vivid color was fading from her usually pale face. I saw, too, that Mr. Hearn was watching us keenly.

"Oh, but you are shrewd!" I thought. "I wish you had cause to suspect."

I returned her greeting with great apparent frankness and cordiality as I replied, "Oh, I'm much better to-night, and as jolly as Mark Tapley."

"Well," ejaculated Mrs. Yocomb, "thee *has* stolen a march on us, but I'm afraid thee'll be the worse for it."

"Ah, Mrs. Yocomb," I laughed, "your captive has escaped. I'm going to meeting with you to-morrow."

"No, thee isn't. I feel as if I ought to take thee right back to thy room."

"Mr. Yocomb," I cried to the old gentleman, who now stood staring at me in the doorway, "I appeal to you. Can't I stay down to supper?"

"How's this! how's this!" he exclaimed. "We were going to give thee a grand ovation to-morrow, and mother had planned a dinner that might content an alderman."

"Or a banker," I thought, as I glanced at Mr. Hearn's ample waistcoat; but I leaned back in my chair and laughed heartily as I said:

"You cannot get me back to my room, Mrs. Yocomb, now that I know I've escaped an ovation. I'd rather have a toothache."

"But does thee really feel strong enough?"

"Oh, yes; I never felt better in my life."

"I don't know what to make of thee," she said, with a puzzled look.

"No," I replied; "you little knew what a case I was when you took me in hand."

"I'll stand up for thee, Friend Morton. Thee shall stay down to supper, and have what thee pleases. Thee may as well give in, mother; he's out from under thy thumb."

"My dear sir, you talk as if you were out, too. I fear our mutiny may go too far. To-morrow is Sunday, Mrs. Yocomb, and I'll be as good as I know how all day, which, after all, is not promising much."

"It must be very delightful to you to have secured such good friends," began Mr. Hearn, who perhaps felt that he had stood too long in the background. "I congratulate you. At the same time, Mr. and Mrs. Yocomb," with a courtly bend toward them, "I do not wonder at your feelings, for Emily has told me that Mr. Morton behaved very handsomely during that occasion of peril."

"Did I?" I remarked, with a wry face. "I was under the impression that I looked very ridiculous," and I turned a quick, mischievous glance toward Miss Warren, who seemed well content to remain in the background.

"Yes," she said, laughing, "your appearance did not comport with your deeds."

"I'm not so sure about that," I replied, dryly. "At any rate, I much prefer the present to reminiscences."

"I trust that you will permit me, as one of the most interested parties, to thank you also," began Mr. Hearn, impressively.

"No, indeed, sir," I exclaimed, a little brusquely. "Thanks do not agree with my constitution at all."

"Hurrah!" cried Reuben, looking in at the parlor window.

"Yes, here's the man to thank," I resumed. "Even after being struck by lightning he was equal to the emergency."

"No, thee don't, Richard," laughed Reuben. "Thee needn't think thee's going to palm that thing off on me. We've all come to our senses now."

For some reason Miss Warren laughed heartily, and then said to me, "You look so well and genial to-night that I do begin to think it was some other tramp."

"I fear I'm the same old tramp; for, as Reuben says, we have all come to our senses."

"Thee didn't lose thy senses, Richard, till after thee was sick. 'Twas mighty lucky thee wasn't struck," explained the matter-of-fact Reuben.

"You must permit me to echo the young lad's sentiment," said Mr. Hearn, feelingly. "It was really a providence that you escaped, and kept such a cool, clear head."

I fear I made another very wry face as I looked out of the window. Reuben evidently had not liked the term "young lad," but as he saw my expression he burst out laughing as he said:

"What's the matter, Richard? I guess thee thinks thee had the worst of it after all."

"So thee has," broke out Mr. Yocomb. "Thee didn't know what an awful scrape I was getting thee into when I brought thee home from meeting. Never was a stranger so taken in before. I don't believe thee'll ever go to Friends' meeting again," and the old gentleman laughed heartily, but tears stood in his eyes.

In spite of myself my color was rising, and I saw that Mrs. Yocomb and Miss Warren looked uncomfortably conscious of what must be in my mind; but I joined in his laugh as I replied:

"You are mistaken. Had I a prophet's eye, I would have come home with you. The kindness received in this home has repaid me a thousand times. With a sick bear on their hands, Mrs. Yocomb and Miss Adah were in a worse scrape than I."

"Well, thee hasn't growled as much as I expected," laughed Mrs. Yocomb; "and now thee's a very amiable bear indeed, and shall have thy supper at once," and she turned to depart, smiling to herself, but met in the doorway Adah and the little stranger—a girl of about the same age as Zillah, with large, vivid black eyes, and long dark hair. Zillah was following her timidly, with a face full of intense interest in her new companion; but the moment she saw me she ran and sprang into my arms, and, forgetful of all others, cried gladly:

"Oh, I'm so glad—I'm so glad thee's well!"

The impulse must have been strong to make so shy a child forget the presence of strangers.

I whispered in her ear, "I told you that your kiss would make me well."

"Yes; but thee said Emily Warren's roses too," protested the little girl.

"Did I?" I replied, laughing. "Well, there's no escaping the truth in this house."

I dared not look at Miss Warren, but saw that Mr. Hearn's eyes were on her.

"Confound him!" I thought. "Can he be fool enough to be jealous?"

Adah still stood hesitatingly in the doorway, as if she dared not trust herself to enter. I put Zillah down, and crossing the room in a free, frank manner, I took her hand cordially as I said:

"Miss Adah, I must thank you next to Mrs. Yocomb that I am able to be down this evening, and that I am getting well so fast. You have been the best of nurses, and just as kind and considerate as a sister. I'm going to have the honor of taking you out to supper." I placed her hand on my arm, and its thrill and tremble touched my very soul. In my thoughts I said, "It's all a wretched muddle, and, as the banker said, mysterious enough to be a providence"; but at that moment the ways of Providence seemed very bright to the young girl, and she saw Mr. Hearn escorting Miss Warren with undisguised complacency.

As the latter took her seat I ventured to look at her, and if ever a woman's eyes were eloquent with warm, approving friendliness, hers were. I seemingly had done the very thing she would have wished me to do. As we bowed our heads in grace, I was graceless enough to growl, under my breath, "My attentions to Adah are evidently very satisfactory. Can she imagine for a moment—does she take me for a weather-vane?"

When grace was over, I glanced toward her again, a trifle indignantly; but her face now was quiet and pale, and I was compelled to believe that for the rest of the evening she avoided my eyes and all references to the past.

"Why, mother!" exclaimed Mr. Yocomb from the head of the table, "thy cheeks are as red—why, thee looks like a young girl."

"Thee knows I'm very much pleased to-night," she said. "Does thee remember, Richard, when thee first sat down to supper with us?"

"Indeed I do. Never shall I forget my trepidation lest Mr. Yocomb should discover whom, in his unsuspecting hospitality, he was harboring."

"Well, I've discovered," laughed the old gentleman. "Good is always coming out of Nazareth."

"It seems to me that we've met before," remarked Mr. Hearn, graciously and reflectively.

"Yes, sir," I explained. "As a reporter I called on you once or twice for information."

"Ah, now it comes back to me. Yes, yes, I remember; and I also remember that you did not extract the information as if it had been a tooth. Your manner was not that of a professional interviewer. You must meet with disagreeable experiences in your calling."

"Yes, sir; but perhaps that is true of all callings."

"Yes, no doubt, no doubt; but it has seemed to me that a reporter's lot must frequently bring him in contact with much that is disagreeable."

"Mr. Morton is not a reporter," said Adah, a trifle indignantly; "he's the editor of a first-class paper."

"Indeed!" exclaimed Mr. Hearn, growing much more benign; "why, Emily, you did not tell me that."

"No, I only spoke of Mr. Morton as a gentleman."

"I imagine that Miss Warren thinks that I have mistaken my calling, and that I ought to be a gardener."

"That's an odd impression. Mr. Yocomb would not even trust you to weed," she retorted quickly.

"I have a fellow feeling for weeds; they grow so easily and naturally. But I must correct your impressions, Miss Adah. I'm not the dignitary you imagine-only *an* editor, and an obscure night one at that."

"Your night work on one occasion bears the light very well. I hope it may be the earnest of the future," said Mr. Hearn impressively.

I felt that he had a covert meaning, for he had glanced more than once at Miss Warren when I spoke, and I imagined him a little anxious as to our mutual impressions.

"I feel it my duty to set you right also, Mr. Hearn," I replied, with quiet emphasis, for I wished to end all further reference to that occasion. "Through Mr. and Mrs. Yocomb's kindness, I happened to be an inmate of the farmhouse that night. I merely did what any man would have done, and could have done just as well. My action involved no personal peril, and no hardship worth naming. My illness resulted from my own folly. I'd been overworking or overworked, as so many in my calling are. Conscious that I am not in the least heroic, I do not wish to be imagined a hero. Mrs. Yocomb knows what a bear I've been," I concluded, with a humorous nod toward her.

"Yes, I know, Richard," she said, quietly smiling.

"After this statement in prose, Mr. Hearn, you will not be led to expect more from me than from any ordinary mortal."

"Indeed, sir, I like your modesty, your self-depreciation."

"I beg your pardon," I interrupted a little decisively; "I hope you do not think my words had any leaning toward affectation. I wished to state the actual truth. My friends here have become too kind and partial to give a correct impression."

Mr. Hearn waved his hand very benignly, and his smile was graciousness itself as he said:

"I think I understand you, sir, and respect your sincerity. I've been led to believe that you cherish a high and scrupulous sense of honor, and that trait counts with me far more than all others."

I understood him well. "Oh, you *are* shrewd!" I thought; "but I'd like to know what obligations I'm under to you?" I merely bowed a trifle coldly to this tribute and suggestive statement, and turned the conversation. As I swept my eyes around the table a little later, I thought Miss Warren looked paler than usual.

"Does she understand his precautionary measures?" I thought. "He'd better beware—she would not endure distrust."

CHAPTER IX
A WRETCHED FAILURE

The excitement that had sustained me was passing away, and I felt myself growing miserably weak and depressed. The remainder of the meal was a desperate battle, in which I think I succeeded fairly. I talked that it might not be noticed that I was eating very little; joked with Mr. Yocomb till the old gentleman was ruddy and tremulous with laughter, and made Reuben happy by applauding one of Dapple's exploits, the history of which was easily drawn from him.

I spoke often to both Adah and Zillah, and tried to be as frank and unconscious in one case as the other. I even made the acquaintance of Mr. Hearn's little girl—indeed, her father formally presented her to me as his daughter Adela. I knew nothing of his domestic history, and gained no clew as to the length of the widowhood which he now proposed to end as speedily as possible.

I was amused by his not infrequent glances at Adah. He evidently had a keen eye for beauty as for every other good thing of this world, and he was not so desperately enamored but that he could stealthily and critically compare the diverse charms of the two girls, and I imagined I saw a slight accession to his complacency as his judgment gave its verdict for the one toward whom he manifested proprietorship by a manner that was courtly, deferential, but quite pronounced. A-stranger present could never have doubted their relationship.

A brief discussion arose as to taste, in which Mr. Hearn assumed the ground that nothing could take the place of much observation and comparison, by means of which effects in color could be accurately learned and valued. In reply I said:

"Theories and facts do not always harmonize any more than colors. Miss Adah's youth and rural life have not given her much opportunity for observation and comparison, and yet few ladies on your Avenue have truer eyes for harmony in color than she."

"Mr. Morton being the judge," said the banker, with a profound and smiling bow. "Permit me to add that Miss Adah has at this moment only to glance in a mirror to obtain an idea of perfect harmony in color," and his eyes lingered admiringly on her face.

I was worsted in this encounter, and I saw the old gleam of mirthfulness in Miss Warren's eyes. How well I remembered when I first saw that evanescent illumination—the quick flash of a bright, genial spirit. "She delights in her lover's keen thrusts," was now my thought, "and is pleased to think I'm no match for him. She should remember that it's a poor time for a man to tilt when he can scarcely sit erect." But Adah's pleasure was unalloyed. She had received two decided compliments, and she found herself associated with me in the new-comer's mind, and by my own actions.

"I frankly admit," I said, "that I'm a partial judge, and perhaps a very incompetent one." Then I was stupid enough to add: "But newspaper men are prone to have opinions. Mr. Yocomb was so sarcastic as to say that there was nothing under heaven that an editor did not know."

"Oh, if you judge by her father's authority, you are on safe ground, and I yield at once."

He had now gone too far, and I flushed angrily as we rose from the table. I saw, too, that Mr. and Mrs. Yocomb did not like it either, and that Adah was blushing painfully. It was one of those attempted witticisms that must be simply ignored.

My anxiety now was to get back to my room as speedily as possible. Again I had overrated myself. The excitement of the effort was gone, and my heart was like lead. I, too, would no longer permit my eyes to rest even a moment on one whose ever-present image was only too vivid in spite of my constant effort to think of something else; for so complete was my enthrallment that it was intolerable pain to see her the object of another's man's preferred attentions. I knew it was all right; I was not jealous in the ordinary sense of the word; I merely found myself unable longer, in my weak condition, to endure in her presence the consequences of my fatal blunder. Therefore I saw with pleasure that I might in a few moments have a chance to slip back to my refuge as quietly as I had left it. Mrs. Yocomb was summoned to the kitchen; a farm laborer was inquiring for her husband, and he and Reuben went out toward the barn. Adah would have lingered, but the two children pulled her away to the swing.

Mr. Hearn and Miss Warren stood by me a moment or two as I sat on the lounge in the hall, and then the former said: "Emily, this is just the time for a twilight walk. Come, and show me the old garden;" and he took her away, with an air of proprietorship at which I sickened, to that place consecrated by my first conscious vision of the woman that I hoped would be my fair Eve.

The moment they were off the porch I tottered to the stairway, and managed to reach the turn of the landing, and there my strength failed, and I held on to the railing for support, feeling ill and faint. A light step came quickly through the hall and up the stairway.

"Why, Mr. Morton!" exclaimed Miss Warren, "you are not going up so soon?"

"Yes, thank you," I managed to say cheerily. "Invalids must be prudent. I'm only resting on the landing a little."

"I found it rather cool and damp, and so came back for a shawl," she explained, and passed on up to her room, for she seemed a little embarrassed at meeting me on the stairs. In her absence I made a desperate effort to go on, but found that I would fall. I must wait till she returned, and then crawl up the best I could.

"You see I'm prudence personified," I laughed, as she came back. "I'm taking it so leisurely that I have even sat down about it."

"Are you not overtaxing yourself?" she asked gently. "I fear—"

"Oh, no, indeed—will sleep all the better for a change. Mr. Hearn is waiting for you, and the twilight isn't. Don't worry; I'll surpass Samson in a week."

She looked at me keenly, and hesitatingly passed down the dusky stairway. Then I turned and tried to crawl on, eager to gain my room without revealing my condition; but when I reached the topmost stair it seemed that I could not go any further if my life depended on it. With an irritable imprecation on my weakness, I sank down on the topmost step.

"Mr. Morton," said a low voice, "why did you try to deceive me? You have gone far beyond your strength."

"You here—you of all others," I broke out, in tones of exasperation. "I meant that your first evening should be without a shadow, and have failed, as I now fail in everything. Call Reuben."

"Let me help you?" she pleaded, in the same hurried voice.

"No," I replied harshly, and I leaned heavily against the wall. She held out her hand to aid me, but I would not take it.

"I've no right even to look at you—I who have been doubly enjoined to cherish such a 'scrupulous sense of honor.' I'd better have died a thousand times. Call Reuben."

"How can I leave you so ill and unhappy!" and she made a gesture of protest and distress whose strong effect was only intensified by the obscurity. "I had hoped—you led me to think to-night—"

"That I was a weather-vane. Thank you."

Steps were heard entering the hall.

"Oh! oh!" she exclaimed, in bitter protest.

"Emily," called the banker's voice, "are you not very long?"

I seized her hand to detain her, and said, in a fierce whisper: "Never so humiliate me as to let him know. Go at once; some one will find me."

"Your hand is like ice," she breathed.

I ignored her presence, leaned back, and closed my eyes.

She paused a single instant longer, and then, with a firm, decisive bearing, turned and passed quietly down the stairway.

"What in the world has kept you?" Mr. Hearn asked, a trifle impatiently.

"Can you tell me where Reuben is?" she answered, in a clear, firm voice, that she knew I must hear.

"What does thee want, Emily?" cried Reuben from the piazza.

"Mr. Morton wishes to see you," she replied, in the same tone that she would have used had my name been Mrs. Yocomb's, and then she passed out with her affianced.

Reuben almost ran over me as he came bounding up the stairs.

"Hold on, old fellow," I whispered, and I pulled him down beside me. "Can you keep a secret? I'm played out—Reuben—to speak elegantly—and I don't wish a soul to know it. I'm sitting very—comfortably on this step— you see—that's the way it looks—but I'm stuck—hard aground—you'll have to tow me off. But not a word, remember. Lift me up—let me get my arm around your neck—there. Lucky I'm not heavy—slow and easy now— that's it. Ah, thank the Lord! I'm in my refuge again. I felt like a scotched snake that couldn't wriggle back to its hole. Hand me that brandy there— like a good fellow. Now I won't kelp you—any longer. If you care—for me—never speak of this."

"Please let me tell mother?"

"No, indeed."

"But doesn't Emily Warren know?"

"She knows I wanted to see you."

"Please let me do something or get thee something."

"No; just leave me to myself a little while, and I'll be all right. Go at once, that's a good fellow."

"Oh, Richard, thee shouldn't have come down. Thee looks so pale and sick that I'm afraid thee'll die yet; if thee does, thee'll break all our hearts," and the warm-hearted boy burst out crying, and ran and locked himself in his room.

I was not left alone very long, for Mrs. Yocomb soon entered, saying:

"I'm glad thee's so prudent, and has returned to thy room. Thee acted very generously to-night, and I appreciate it. I had no idea thee could be so strong and carry it out so well. Emily was greatly surprised, but she enjoyed her first evening far more than she otherwise could have done, for she's one of the most kind-hearted, sensitive girls I ever knew. I do believe it would have killed her if thee hadn't got well. But thee looks kind of weak and faint, as far as I can see. Let me light the lamp for thee."

"No, Mrs. Yocomb, I like the dusk best. The light draws moths. They will come, you know, the stupid things, though certain to be scorched. One in the room at a time is enough. Don't worry—I'm a little tired—that's all. Sleep is all I need."

"Is thee sure?" "Yes, indeed; don't trouble about me. You won't know me in a few days."

"Thee was a brave, generous man to-night, Richard. I understood the effort thee was making, and I think Emily did. A good conscience ought to make thee sleep well."

I laughed very bitterly as I said, "My conscience is gutta-percha to-night, through and through, but please say no more, or I'll have to shock you again. I'll be in a better mood to-morrow."

"Well, good-night. Thee'll excuse a housekeeper on Seventh-day evening. If thee wants anything, ring thy bell."

She came and stroked my brow gently for a moment, and then breathed softly:

"God bless thee, Richard. May the Sabbath's peace quiet thy heart to-morrow."

CHAPTER X
IN THE DEPTHS

I awoke late Sunday morning and found Reuben watching beside me.

"Thee's better, isn't thee?" he asked eagerly.

"Well, I ought to be. You're a good fellow, Reuben. What time is it?— nearly night again, I hope."

"Oh, no, it's only about eleven; they're all gone to meeting. I made 'em leave you in my care. Adah would have stayed, but mother told her she was to go. Emily Warren's grandfather wanted to go spooning off in the woods, but she made him go to meeting too. I don't see how she ever came to like him, with his grand airs."

"She has good reasons, rest assured."

"Well, he ain't the kind of a man I'd go for if I was a girl."

"Miss Warren is not the girl to go for any man, Reuben. He had to seek her long and patiently. But that's their affair—we have nothing to do with it."

"I thought thee was taken with her at first," said Reuben innocently.

"I do admire Miss Warren very much—now as much as ever. I admire a great many ladies, especially your mother. I never knew a truer, kinder lady."

"And if it had not been for thee, Richard, she might have been burned up," and tears came into his eyes.

"Oh, no, Reuben. You could have got them all out easily enough."

"I fear I would have lost my head."

"No, you wouldn't; you are not of that kind. Please say no more about that affair. I've heard too much of it."

"Does thee think thee'll be able to come down to dinner? Mother and father and all of us will be awfully disappointed if thee isn't."

"Yes, I'll come down if you'll stand by me, and help me back when I give you the wink. I won't go down till dinner's ready; after it's over you can help me out under some tree. I'm just wild to get out of doors."

I had a consuming desire to retrieve myself, and prove that I was not weakness personified, and I passed through the ordeal of dinner much better than I expected. Mr. Hearn was benignness itself, but I saw that he was very observant. The shrewd Wall Street man had the eye of an eagle when his interests were concerned, and he very naturally surmised that no one could have seen so much of Miss Warren as I had, and still remain entirely indifferent; besides, he may have detected something in my manner or imagined that the peculiar events of the past few weeks had made us better acquainted than he cared to have us.

Miss Warren's greeting was cordial, but her manner toward me was so quiet and natural that he had no cause for complaint, and I felt that I had rather be drawn asunder by wild horses than give him a clew to my feelings. I took a seat next to Mr. Yocomb, and we chatted quietly most of the time. The old gentleman was greatly pleased about something, and it soon came out that Mr. Hearn had promised him five hundred dollars to put a new roof on the meeting-house and make other improvements. I drew all the facts readily from the zealous Friend, together with quite a history of the old meeting-house, for I proposed to make a complimentary item of the matter in my paper, well knowing how grateful such incense was to the banker's soul. Mr. Hearn, who sat nearest to us, may have heard my questions and divined my purpose, for he was peculiarly gracious.

I was not able to do very much justice to Mrs. Yocomb's grand dinner, but was unstinted in my praise. The banker made amends for my inability, and declared he had never enjoyed such a repast, even at Delmonico's. I though Miss Warren's appetite flagged a little, but to the utmost extent of my power I kept my eyes and thoughts from her.

After dinner Reuben helped me to a breezy knoll behind the dwelling, and spreading some robes from the carriage-house under a wide-branching tree, left me, at my request, to myself. The banker now had his way, and carried Miss Warren off to a distant grove. I would not look at them as they went down the lane together, but shut my eyes and tried to breathe in life and health.

Adah read to the two little girls for some time, and then came hesitatingly toward me. I feigned sleep, for I was too weak and miserable to treat the girl as she deserved. She stood irresolutely a moment or two, and then slowly and lingeringly returned to the house.

My feigning soon became reality, and when I awoke Reuben was sitting beside me, and I found had covered me well to guard against the dampness of the declining day.

"You are always on hand when I need you most," I said smilingly. "I think I will go back to my room now, while able to make a respectable retreat."

I saw Mr. Hearn and Miss Warren entering the house, and thought that they had had a long afternoon together, but that time no doubt had passed more quickly with them than with me, even though I had slept for hours. When reaching the parlor door I saw Miss Warren at the piano; she turned so quickly as almost to give me the impression that she was waiting to intercept me.

"Would you not like to hear your favorite nocturne again?" she asked, with a friendly smile.

I hesitated, and half entered the parlor. Her face seemed to light up with pleasure at my compliance. How divine she appeared in the quaint, simple room! I felt that I would gladly give the best years of my life for the right to sit there and feast my eyes on a grace and beauty that to me were indescribable and irresistible; but the heavy tread of the banker in the adjoining room reminded me that I had no right—that to see her and to listen would soon become unendurable pain. I had twice been taught my weakness.

"Thank you," I said, with a short, dry laugh; "I'm sorely tempted, but it's time I learned that for me discretion is certainly the better part of valor," and I turned away, but not too soon to see that her face grew sad and wistful.

"Heaven bless her kind heart!" I murmured as I wearily climbed the stairs.

Adah brought me up my supper long before the others were through, and I felt a faint remorse that I had feigned sleep in the afternoon, even though my motive had been consideration for her as truly as for myself.

"Miss Adah!" I exclaimed, "you are growing much too unselfish. Why didn't you get your supper first?"

"I've had all I wish. I'm not hungry to-night."

"Truly, you look as if you lived on roses; but you can't thrive long on such unsubstantial diet. It was real good of you to read to those children so long. If I had been an artist, I would have made a sketch of you three. You and that little dark-eyed girl make a lovely contrast."

"I like her," she said simply; "I feel as if I wanted some one to pet. Can't I read to you while you eat your supper?"

"I'd rather have you talk to me: what do you think of the little girl's father?"

"I haven't thought much about him."

"I wish you could see his house in New York; it's a superb one, and on your favorite Fifth Avenue."

"Yes, I know," she replied absently.

"I should think you would envy Miss Warren."

"I don't," she said emphatically; "the man is more than the house."

"I don't think you would have said that a month ago."

"I fear not. I fear thee didn't like me that Sunday afternoon when I was so self-satisfied. I've thought it over."

"Indeed, Miss Adah, I would gladly be struck by lightning myself if it would change me for the better as greatly as you are changed."

"It wasn't the lightning," she said, blushing and slowly shaking her head. "I've been thinking."

"Ah," I laughed, "you are shrewd. If women only knew it, there's nothing that gives beauty like thought, and it's a charm that increases every year. Well," I continued, with the utmost frankness, "I do like you now, and what is more, I honestly respect you. When you come to New York again, I am going to ask your mother to trust me as if I were your older brother, and I'll take you to see and hear much that I'm sure you'll enjoy."

"Oh, that will be splendid!" she cried gladly. "I know mother will let me go with thee, because—because—well, she says thee is a gentleman."

"Do you know, Miss Adah, I'd rather have your mother say that than have all Mr. Hearn's thousands. But your mother judges me leniently. To tell you the honest truth, I've come lately to have a very poor opinion of myself. I feel that I would have been a much better man if, in past years, I had seen more of such people as dwell in this house."

"Thee remembers what father said to thee," she replied, shyly, with downcast eyes; "this is thy home hereafter."

"She looks now," I thought, "as if she might fulfil the dream I wove about her on that memorable day when I first saw her in the meeting-house. How perverse my fate has been, giving me that for which I might well thank God on my knees, and yet which my heart refuses, and withholding that which will impoverish my whole life. Why must the heart be so imperious and self-willed in these matters? An elderly gentleman would say, Everything is just right as it is. It would be the absurdity of folly for Miss Warren to give up her magnificent prospects because of your sudden and sickly sentiment; and what more could you ask or wish than this beautiful girl, whose womanhood has awakened and developed under your very eyes, almost as unconsciously as if a rosebud had opened and shown you its heart? Indeed, but a brief time since I would have berated any friend of mine who would not take the sensible course which would make all happy. If I could but become 'sane and reasonable,' as Miss Warren would say, how she would beam upon me, and, the thought of my disappointment and woe-begone aspect banished, how serenely she would go toward her bright future! And yet in taking this sane and sensible course I would be false to my very soul—false to this simple, true-hearted girl, to whom I could give but a cold, hollow pretence in return for honest love. I would become an arrant hypocrite, devoid of honor and self-respect."

"Heaven bless you, Adah!" I murmured. "I love you too well for all your kindness and goodness to pretend to love you so ill."

Thoughts like these passed through my mind as I thanked her for all that she had done for me, and told her of such phases of New York life as I thought would interest her. She listened with so intent and childlike an expression on her face that I could scarcely realize that I was talking to one in whose bosom beat the heart of a woman. I felt rather as if I were telling Zillah a fairy story.

Still I had faith in her intuition, and believed that after I was gone she would recognize and accept the frank, brotherly regard that I now cherished toward her.

Reuben was not very long in joining us, and boy-like did not note that his sister evidently wished him far away. My greeting was so cordial that she noted with a sigh that I did not regard him as the unwelcome third party. Then Mr. Yocomb and the little girls came to the door and asked if there was room for a crowd. Soon after Mrs. Yocomb appeared, with her comely face ruddy from exercise.

"I've hurried all I could," she said, "but thee knows how it is with housekeepers; and yet how should thee know, living all thy life alone in dens, as thee said? Why, thee's having a reception."

"I fear your guests downstairs will feel neglected, Mrs. Yocomb."

"Don't thee worry about that, Richard," Mr. Yocomb said, laughing. "I'm not so old, mother, but I can remember when we could get through an evening together without help from anybody. I reckon we could do so again—eh? mother? Ha, ha, ha! so thee isn't too old to blush yet? How's that, Richard, for a young girl of sixty? Don't thee worry about Emily Warren. I fear that any one of us would make a large crowd in the old parlor."

This was sorry comfort, and I fear that my laugh was anything but honest, while Mrs. Yocomb stared out of the window, at which she sat fanning herself, with a fixedness that I well understood.

But they were all so kind and hearty that I could no more give way to dejection than to chill and cheerlessness before a genial wood fire. They seemed in truth to have taken me into the family. Barely was I now addressed formally as Richard Morton. It was simply "Richard," spoken with the unpremeditated friendliness characteristic of family intercourse. Heathen though I was, I thanked God that he had brought me among these true-hearted people; "and may He blast me," I muttered, "if I ever relapse into the old sneering cynicism that I once affected. Let me at least leave that vice to half-fledged young men and to bad old men."

One thing puzzled me. Miss Warren remained at her piano, and it struck me as a little odd that she did not find the music of her lover's voice preferable, but I concluded that music was one of the strongest bonds of sympathy between them, and one of the means by which he had won her affection. Sometimes, as her voice rose clear and sweet to my open windows, I answered remarks addressed to me with an inaptness that only Mrs. Yocomb understood.

Before very long, that considerate lady looked into my face a moment, and then said decisively:

"Richard, thee is getting tired. We must all bid thee good-night at once."

Adah looked almost resentfully at her mother, and lingered a little behind the others. As they passed out she stepped hastily back, and unclasping a rosebud from her breastpin laid it on the table beside me.

"It was the last one I could find in the garden," she said, breathlessly, and with its color in her cheeks. Before I could speak she was gone.

"It shall be treated with reverence, like the feeling which led to the gift," I murmured sadly. "Heaven grant that it may be only the impulse of a girlish fancy;" and I filled a little vase with water and placed the bud near the window, where the cool night air could blow upon it.

Still Miss Warren remained at the piano. "How singularly fond of music he is!" I thought.

I darkened my room, and sat at the window that I might hear every note. The old garden, half hidden by trees, looked cool and Eden-like in the light of the July moon, athwart whose silver hemisphere fleecy clouds were drifting like the traces of thought across a bright face. Motionless shadows stretched toward the east, from which the new day would come, but with a dreary sinking of heart I felt as it each coming day would bring a heavier burden.

But a little time passed before I recognized Chopin's Nocturne, to which I had listened with kindling hope on the night of the storm. Was it my own mood, or did she play it with far more pathos and feeling than on that never-to-be-forgotten evening? Be that as it may, it evoked a fiercer storm of unavailing passion and regret in my mind. In bitterness of heart I groaned aloud and insulted God.

"It was a cruel and terrible thing," I charged, "to mock a creature with such a hope. Why was such power over me given to her when it was of no use?" But I will say no more of that hour of weak human idolatry. It was a revelation to me of the depths of despair and wretchedness into which one can sink when unsustained by manly fortitude or Christian principle. It is in such desperate, irrational moods that undisciplined, ill-balanced souls thrust themselves out from the light of God's sunshine and the abundant possibilities of future good. I now look back on that hour with shame, and cannot excuse it even by the fact that I was enfeebled in mind as well as body by disease. We often never know ourselves or our need until after we have failed miserably under the stress of some strong temptation.

I was the worse the next day for my outburst of passion, and the wretched night that followed, and did not leave my room; but I was grim and rigid in my purpose to retrieve myself. I appeared to be occupied with my mail and paper much of the day, and I wrote a very complimentary paragraph concerning the banker's gift for the meeting-house. Mr. Hearn and Miss Warren were out riding much of the time. I saw them drive away with a lowering brow, and was not disarmed of my bitterness because I saw, through the half-closed blinds, that the young girl stole a swift glance at my window.

Adah was pleased as she saw how I was caring for her gift; but I puzzled and disheartened her by my preoccupation and taciturnity. She took the children off on a long ramble in the afternoon, and heaped coals of fire on my head by bringing me an exquisite collection of ferns.

The next morning I went down to breakfast resolving to take my place in the family, and make no more trouble during the brief remainder of my stay, for I proposed to go back to the city as soon as I had shown enough manhood to satisfy my pride, and had made Miss Warren believe that she could dismiss her solicitude on my account, and thus enjoy the happiness which apparently I had clouded. As I saw her pale face again I condemned my weakness unsparingly, and with the whole force of my will endeavored to act and appear as both she and Mr. Hearn would naturally wish.

"Richard," said Reuben, after breakfast, "I've borrowed a low phaeton, and I'm going to take thee out with Dapple. He'll put life in thee, never fear. He'd cure me if I were half dead."

He was right; the swift motion through the pure air braced me greatly.

When we returned, the banker sat on the piazza. Adah was near, with some light sewing, and the connoisseur was leisurely admiring her. Well he might, for in her neat morning gown she again seemed the embodiment of a June day. She rose to meet me, with a faint accession to her delicate color, and said:

"The ride has done thee good; thee looks better than thee has any day yet."

"Reuben's right," I said, laughing; "Dapple would bring a fossil to life," and the young fellow drove chuckling down toward the barn, making Dapple rear and prance in order to show off a little before Mr. Hearn.

I sat down a few moments to rest. Miss Warren must have heard our voices; but she went on with an intricate piece of music in which she was displaying no mean skill. I did not think Mr. Hearn was as much interested in it as I was. His little girl came out of the house and climbed into Adah's lap. She evidently liked being petted, and was not a little spoiled by it The banker continued to admire the picture they made with undisguised enjoyment, and I admitted that the most critical could have found no fault with the group.

After exerting myself to seem exceedingly cheerful, and laughing heartily at a well-worn jest of Mr. Hearn's, I went to my room and rested till dinner, and I slept away the afternoon as on the previous day.

My plan was now to get sufficiently strong to take my departure by the following Monday, and I was glad indeed that the tonic of out-of-door air promised an escape from a position in which I must continually seem to be what I was not—a cheerful man in the flood tide of convalescence. Were it not that my kind friends at the farmhouse would have been grievously hurt, I would have left at once.

As I returned from my ride the next day, Mr. Hearn greeted me with a newspaper in his hand.

"I'm indebted to you," he said, in his most gracious manner, "for a very kindly mention here. So small a donation was not worth the importance you give it, but you have put the matter so happily and gracefully that it may lead other men of means to do likewise at the various places of their summer sojourn. You editors are able to wield a great deal of influence."

I bowed, and said I was glad the paragraph had been worded in a way not disagreeable to him.

"Oh, it was good taste itself, I assure you, sir. It seemed the natural expression of your interest in that which interests your good friends here."

When I came down to dinner I saw that there was an unwonted fire in Miss Warren's eyes and unusual color in her cheeks. Moreover, I imagined that her replies to the few remarks that I addressed to her were brief and constrained. "She is no dissembler," I thought; "something has gone wrong."

After dinner I went to my room for a book, and as I came out I met her in the hall.

"Mr. Morton," she said, with characteristic directness, "if you had given a sum toward a good object in a quiet country place, would you have been pleased to see the fact paraded before those having no natural interest in the matter?"

"I have never had the power to be munificent, Miss Warren," I replied, with some embarrassment.

"Please answer me," she insisted, with a little impatient tap of the floor with her foot.

"No," I said bluntly.

"Did you think it would be pleasing to me?"

"Pardon me," I began, "that I did not sufficiently identify you with Mr. Hearn—"

"What!" she interrupted, blushing hotly, "have I given any reason for not being identified with him?"

"Not at all—not in one sense," I said bitterly. "Of course you are loyalty itself."

She turned away so abruptly as to surprise me a little.

"You had no more right to think it would be pleasing to him than to me," she resumed coldly.

"Miss Warren," I said, after a moment, "don't turn your back on me. I won't quarrel with you, and I promise to do nothing of the kind again;" and I spoke gravely and a little sadly.

"When you speak in that way you disarm me completely," she said, with one of the sudden illuminations of her face that I so loved to see; but I also noted that she had become very pale, and as my eyes met hers I thought

I detected the old frightened look that I had seen when I had revealed my feelings too clearly after my illness.

"She fears that I may again speak as I ought not," I thought; and therefore I bowed quietly and passed on. Mr. Hearn was reading the paper on the piazza. I took a chair and went out under the elm, not far away. In a few moments Miss Warren joined her affianced, and sat down with some light work.

"Emily," I heard the banker say, as if the topic were uppermost in his mind, "I'd like to call your attention to this paragraph. I think our friend has written it with unusual good taste and grace, and I've taken pains to tell him so."

I could not help hearing his words; but I would not look up to see her humiliation, and turned a leaf, as if intent on my author.

After a moment she said, with slight but clear emphasis:

"I can't agree with you."

A little later she went to the piano; but I never heard her play so badly. A glance at Mr. Hearn revealed that his dignity and complacency had received a wound that he was inclined to resent. I strolled away muttering:

"She has idealized him as she did Old Plod, but after all it's not a very serious foible in a man of millions."

Before the day passed she found an opportunity to ask:

"Why did you not tell me that Mr. Hearn had spoken to you approvingly of that paragraph?"

"I would not willingly say anything to annoy you," I replied quietly.

"Did you hear him call my attention to it?"

"I could not help it."

"You did not look up and triumph over me."

"That would have given me no pleasure."

"I believe you," she said, in a low tone; but she devoted herself so assiduously to the stately banker that he became benignness itself. I also observed that Mr. Yocomb looked in vain for the paper after tea. "I happened to destroy the copy," I said very innocently.

CHAPTER XI
POOR ACTING

The last week that I proposed to spend at the farmhouse was passing quietly and uneventfully away. I was gaining steadily though not rapidly in physical strength, but not in my power to endure my disappointment with equanimity, much less with resignation. In the delirium of my fever I kept constantly repeating the words—so Mrs. Yocomb told me—"It's all wrong." Each successive day found these words on my lips again with increasing frequency. It seemed contrary to both right and reason that one should so completely enslave me, and then go away leaving me a bound and helpless captive. The conviction grew stronger that no such power over me should have been given to her, if her influence was to end only in darkening my life and crippling my power to be a forceful man among men. I felt with instinctive certainty that my burden would be too heavy to leave me the elastic spring and energy required by my exacting profession. A hopeful, eager interest in life and the world at large was the first necessity to success in my calling; but already I found a leaden apathy creeping over me which even the powerful motives of pride, and my resolute purpose to seem cheerful that she might go on to her bright future unregretfully, were not sufficiently strong to banish. If I could not cope with this despondency in its inception, how could I face the future?

At first I had bitterly condemned my weakness; but now I began to recognize the strength of my love, which, so far from being a mere sudden passion, was the deep, abiding conviction that I had met the only woman I could marry—the woman whom my soul claimed as its mate, because she possessed the power to help me and inspire me to tireless effort toward better living and nobler achievement. Her absolute truth would keep me true and anchored amid the swift, dark currents of the world to which I was exposed. I feared, with almost instinctive certainty, that I would become either a brooding, solitary man or else a very ambitious and reckless one, for I was conscious of no reserve strength which would enable me to go steadfastly on my way under the calm and inexorable guidance of duty.

Such was my faith in her that I had no hope whatever. If she loved and had given her troth to another man, it would not be in her nature to change, therefore my purpose had simplified itself to the effort to get through this one week at the farmhouse in a manner that would enable me to carry away the respect of all its inmates, but especially the esteem of one to whom I feared I seemed a rash, ill-balanced man. So carefully had I avoided Miss Warren's society, and yet so freely and frankly, apparently, had I spoken to her in the presence of her affianced, that his suspicions were evidently banished, and he treated me with a gracious and patronizing benignity. He saw no reason why he should not turn on me the light of his full and smiling countenance, which might be taken as an emblem of prosperity; and, in truth, I gave him no reason. So rigid was the constraint under which I kept myself that jealousy itself could not have found fault.

With the exception of the two momentary interviews recorded in the previous chapter, we had not spoken a syllable together, except in his presence, nor had I permitted my eyes to follow her with a wistful glance that he or she could intercept. Even Mrs. Yocomb appeared to think that I was recovering in more senses than one, and by frequent romps with the children, jests and chaffing with Mr. Yocomb and Reuben, by a little frank and ostentatious gallantry to Adah, which no longer deceived even her simple mind, since I never sought her exclusive society as a lover would have done, I confirmed the impression.

And yet, in spite of all efforts and disguises, the truth will often flash out unexpectedly and irresistibly, making known all that we hoped to hide with the distinctness of the lightning, which revealed even the color of the roses on the night of the storm.

The weather had become exceedingly warm, and Miss Warren's somewhat portly suitor clung persistently to the wide, cool veranda. Adah sat there frequently also; sometimes she read to the children fairy stories, of which Adela, Mr. Hearn's little girl, had brought a great store, and she seemed to enjoy them quite as much as her eager-eyed listeners; but more often she superintended their doll dressmaking, over which there were the most animated discussions. The banker would look on with the utmost content, while he slowly waved his palm-leaf fan. Indeed the group was pretty enough to justify all the pleasure he manifested.

The rustic piazza formed just the setting for Adah's beauty, and her light summer costume well suggested her perfect and womanly form, while the companionship of the children proved that she was almost as guileless and childlike as they. The group was like a bubbling, sparkling spring, at which the rather advanced man of the world sipped with increasing pleasure.

Miss Warren also gave much of her time to the children, and beguiled them into many simple lessons at the piano. Zillah was true to her first love, but Adela gave to Adah a decided preference; and when they entered on the intense excitement of making a new wardrobe for each of the large dolls that Mr. Hearn had brought, Adah had the advantage, for she was a genius in such matters, and quite as much interested as the little girls themselves.

In my desperate struggle with myself, I tried not even to see Miss Warren, for every glance appeared to rivet my chains, and yet I gained the impression that she was a little restless and *distraite*. She seemed much at her piano, not so much for Mr. Hearn's sake as her own, and sometimes I was so impressed by the strong, passionate music that she evoked that I was compelled to hasten beyond its reach. It meant too much to me. Oh, the strange idolatry of an absorbing affection! All that she said or did had for me an indescribable charm that both tortured and delighted. Still every hour increased my conviction that my only safety was in flight.

My faithful ally, Reuben, still took me on long morning drives, and in the afternoon, with my mail and paper, I sought secluded nooks in a somewhat distant grove, which I reached by the shady lane, of which I had caught a glimpse with Miss Warren on the first evening of my arrival. But Friday afternoon was too hot for the walk thither. The banker had wilted and retired to his room. Adah and the children were out under a tree. The girl looked up wistfully and invitingly as I came out.

"I wish I were an artist, Miss Adah," I cried. "You three make a lovely picture."

Remembering an arbor at the further end of the garden, I turned my steps thither, passing rapidly by the spot where I had seen my Eve who was not mine.

I had entered the arbor before I saw it was occupied, and was surprised by the vivid blush with which Miss Warren greeted me.

"Pardon me," I said, "I did not know you were here," and I was about to depart, with the best attempt at a smile that I could muster.

She sprang up and asked, a little indignantly: "Am I infected with a pestilence that you so avoid me, Mr. Morton?"

"Oh, no," I replied, with a short, grim laugh; "if it were only a pestilence—I fear I disturbed your nap; but you know I'm a born blunderer."

"You said we should be friends," she began hesitatingly.

"Do you doubt it?" I asked gravely. "Do you doubt that I would hesitate at any sacrifice—?"

"I don't want sacrifices. I wish to see you happy, and your manner natural."

"I'm sure I've been cheerful during the past week."

"No, you have only seemed cheerful; and often I've seen you look as grim, hard, and stern as if you were on the eve of mortal combat."

"You observe closely, Miss Warren."

"Why should I not observe closely? Do you think me inhuman? Can I forget what I owe you, and that you nearly died?"

"Well," I said dejectedly, "what can I do? It seems that I have played the hypocrite all the week in vain. I will do whatever you ask."

"I was in hopes that as you grew well and strong you would throw off this folly. Have you not enough manhood to overcome it?"

"No, Miss Warren," I said bluntly, "I have not. What little manhood I had led to this very thing."

"Such—such—"

"Enthrallment, you may call it."

"No, I will not; it's a degrading word. I would not have a slave if I could."

"Since I can't help it, I don't see how you can. I may have been a poor actor, but I know I've not been obtrusive."

"You have not indeed," she replied a little bitterly; "but you have no cause for such feelings. They seem to me unnatural, and the result of a morbid mind."

"Yes, you have thought me very ill balanced from the first; but I'm constrained to use such poor wits as I possess. In the abstract it strikes me as not irrational to recognize embodied truth and loveliness, and I do not think the less of myself because I reached such recognition in hours rather than in months. I saw your very self in this old garden, and every subsequent day has confirmed that impression. But there's no use in wasting words in explanation—I don't try to explain it to myself. But the fact is clear enough. By some necessity of my nature, it is just as it is. I can no more help it than I can help breathing. It was inevitable. My only chance was never meeting you, and yet I can scarcely wish that even now. Perhaps you think I've not tried, since I learned I ought to banish your image, but I have struggled as if I were engaged in a mortal combat, as you suggested. But it's of no use. I can't deceive you any more than I can myself. Now you know the whole truth, and it seems that there is no escaping it in our experience. I do not expect anything. I ask nothing save that you accept the happiness which is your perfect right; for not a shadow of blame rests on you. If you were not happy I should be only tenfold more wretched. But I've no right to speak to you in this way. I see I've caused you much pain; I've no right even to look at you feeling as I do. I would have gone before, were it not for hurting Mrs. Yocomb's feelings. I shall return to New York next Monday; for—"

"Return to New York!" she repeated, with a sudden and deep breath; and she became very pale. After a second she added hastily, "You are not strong enough yet; we are the ones to go."

"Miss Warren," I said, almost sternly, "it's little that I ask of you or that you can give. I may not have deceived you, but I have the others. Mrs. Yocomb knows; but she is as merciful as my own mother would have been. I'm not ashamed of my love—I'm proud of it; but it's too sacred a thing, and—well, if you can't understand me I can't explain. All I ask is that you seem indifferent to my course beyond ordinary friendliness. There! God bless you for your patient kindness; I will not trespass on it longer. You have the best and kindest heart of any woman in the world. Why don't you exult a little over your conquest? It's complete enough to satisfy the most insatiable coquette. Don't look so sad. I'll be your merry-hearted friend yet before I'm eighty."

But my faint attempt at lightness was a speedy failure, for my strong passion broke out irresistibly.

"O God!" I exclaimed, "how beautiful you are to me! When shall I forget the look in your kind, true eyes? But I'm disgracing myself again. I've no right to speak to you. I wish I could never see you again till my heart had become stone and my will like steel;" and I turned and walked swiftly away until, from sheer exhaustion, I threw myself under a tree and buried my face in my hands, for I hated the warm, sunny light, when my life was so cheerless and dark.

I lay almost as if I were dead for hours, and the evening was growing dusky when I arose and wearily returned to the farmhouse. They were all on the veranda except Miss Warren, who was at her piano again. Mrs. Yocomb met me with much solicitude.

"Reuben was just starting out to look for thee," she said.

"I took a longer ramble than I intended," I replied, with a laugh. "I think I lost myself a little. I don't deserve any supper, and only want a cup of tea." Miss Warren played very softly for a moment, and I knew she was listening to my lame excuses.

"It doesn't matter what thee wants; I know what thee needs. Thee isn't out of my hands altogether yet; come right into the dining-room."

"I should think you would be slow to revolt against such a benign government," remarked Mr. Hearn most graciously, and the thought occurred to me that he was not displeased to have me out of the way so long.

"Yes, indeed," chimed in Mr. Yocomb; "we're always all the better for minding mother. Thee'll find that out, Richard, after thee's been here a few weeks longer."

"Mr. Yocomb, you're loyalty itself. If women ever get their rights, our paper will nominate Mrs. Yocomb for President."

"I've all the rights I want now, Richard, and I've the right to scold thee for not taking better care of thyself."

"I'll submit to anything from you. You are wiser than the advanced female agitators, for you know you've all the power now, and that we men are always at your mercy."

"Well, now that thee talks of mercy, I won't scold thee, but give thee thy supper at once."

"Thee always knew, Richard, how to get around mother," laughed the genial old man, whose life ever seemed as mellow and ripe as a juicy fall pippin.

Adah followed her mother in to assist her, and I saw that Miss Warren had turned toward us.

"Why, Richard Morton!" exclaimed Mrs. Yocomb, as I entered the lighted dining-room. "Thee looks as pale and haggard as a ghost. Thee must have got lost indeed and gone far beyond thy strength."

"Can—can I do anything to assist you, Mrs. Yocomb?" asked a timid voice from the doorway.

I was glad that Adah was in the kitchen at the moment, for I lost at once my ghostly pallor. "Yes," said Mrs. Yocomb heartily, "come in and make this man eat, and scold him soundly for going so far away as to get lost when he's scarcely able to walk at all. I've kind of promised I wouldn't scold him, and somebody must."

"I'd scold like Xanthippe if I thought it would do any good," she said, with a faint smile; but her eyes were full of reproach. For a moment Mrs. Yocomb disappeared behind the door of her china closet, and Miss Warren added, in a low, hurried whisper to me, "You promised me to get well; you are not keeping your word."

"That cuts worse than anything Xanthippe could have said."

"I don't want to cut, but to cure."

"Then become the opposite of what you are; that would cure me."

"With such a motive I'm tempted to try," she said, with a half-reckless laugh, for Adah was entering with some delicate toast.

"Miss Adah," I cried, "I owe you a supper at the Brunswick for this, and I'll pay my debt the first chance you'll give me."

"If thee talks of paying, I'll not go with thee," she said, a little coldly; and she seemingly did not like the presence of Miss Warren nor the tell-tale color in my cheeks.

"That's a deserved rebuke, Miss Adah. I know well enough that I can never repay all your kindness, and so I won't try. But you'll go with me because I want you to, and because I will be proud of your company. I shall be the envy of all the men present."

"They'd think me very rustic," she said, smiling.

"Quite as much so as a moss-rose. But you'll see. I will be besieged the next few days by my acquaintances for an introduction, and my account of you will make them wild. I shall be, however, a very dragon of a big brother, and won't let one of them come near you who is not a saint—that is, as far as I am a judge of the article."

"Thee may keep them all away if thee pleases," she replied, blushing and laughing. "I should be afraid of thy fine city friends."

"I'm afraid of a good many of them myself," I replied; "but some are genuine, and you shall have a good time, never fear."

"I'll leave you to arrange the details of your brilliant campaign," said Miss Warren, smiling.

"But thee hasn't scolded Richard," said Mrs. Yocomb, who was seemingly busy about the room.

"My words would have no weight. He knows he ought to be ashamed of himself," she answered from the doorway.

"I am, heartily," I said, looking into her eyes a moment.

"Since he's penitent, Mrs. Yocomb, I don't see as anything more can be done," she replied, smilingly.

"I don't think much of penitence unless it's followed by reformation," said my sensible hostess. "We'll see how he behaves the next few weeks."

"Mr. Morton, I hope you will let Mrs. Yocomb see a daily change for the better for a long time to come. She deserves it at your hands," and there was almost entreaty in the young girl's voice.

"She ought to know better than to ask it," I thought. My only answer was a heavy frown, and I turned abruptly away from her appealing glance.

"I think Emily Warren acts very queer," said Adah, after the young lady had gone; "she's at her piano half the time, and I know from her eyes that she's been crying this afternoon. If ever a girl was engaged to a good, kind man, who would give her everything, she is. I don't see—"

"Adah," interrupted her mother, "I hoped thee was overcoming that trait. It's not a pleasing one. If people give us their confidence, very well; if not, we should be blind."

The girl blushed vividly, and looked deprecatingly at me.

"You meant nothing ill-natured, Miss Adah," I said, gently; "it isn't in you. Come, now, and let me tell you and your mother what a good time I'm planning for you in New York," and we soon made the old dining-room ring with our laughter. Mr. Yocomb, Reuben, and the children soon joined us, and the lovers were left alone on the shadowy porch. From the gracious manner of Mr. Hearn the following morning, I think he rather thanked me for drawing off the embarrassing third parties.

CHAPTER XII
THE HOPE OF A HIDDEN TREASURE

The next day I lured Reuben off on a fishing excursion to a mountain lake, and so congratulated myself on escaping ordeals to which I found myself wholly unequal. We did not reach the farmhouse till quite late in the evening, and found that Mr. Hearn and Miss Warren were out enjoying a moonlight ride. As on the previous evening, all the family gathered around Reuben and me as we sat down to our late supper, the little girls arranging with delight the sylvan spoil that I had brought them. They were all so genial and kind that I grieved to think that I had but one more evening with them, and I thought of my cheerless quarters in New York with an inward shiver.

Before very long Mr. Hearn entered with Miss Warren, and the banker was in fine spirits.

"The moonlit landscapes were divine," he said. "Never have I seen them surpassed—not even in Europe."

It was evident that his complacency was not easily disturbed, for I thought that a more sympathetic lover would have noted that his companion was not so enthusiastic as himself. Indeed Miss Warren seemed to bring in with her the cold pale moonlight. Her finely-chiselled oval face looked white and thin as if she were chilled, and I noticed that she shivered as she entered.

"Come," cried Mr. Yocomb, in his hearty way; "Emily, thee and Mr. Hearn have had thy fill of moonlight, dew, and such like unsubstantial stuff. I'm going to give you both a generous slice of cold roast-beef. That's what makes good red blood; and Emily, thee looks as if thee needed a little more. Then I want to see if we cannot provoke thee to one of thy old-time laughs. Seems to me we've missed it a little of late. Thy laugh beats all thy music at the piano."

"Yes, Emily," said Mr. Hearn, a little discontentedly, "I think you are growing rather quiet and *distraite* of late. When have I heard one of your genuine, mirthful laughs?"

With a sudden wonder my mind took up his question. When had I heard her laugh, whose contagious joyousness was so infectious that I, too, had laughed without knowing why? I now remembered that it was before he came; it was that morning when my memory, more kind than my fate, still refused to reveal the disappointment that now was crushing my very soul; it was when all in the farmhouse were so glad at my assured recovery. Reuben had said that she was like a lark that day—that she equalled Dapple in her glad life. I could recall no such day since, though her lover was present, and her happiness assured. Even he was beginning to note that the light of his countenance did not illumine her face—that she was "quiet and *distraite*."

Manlike, I had to think it all out, but I thought swiftly. The echo of his words had scarcely died away before the light of a great hope flashed into my face as my whole heart put the question:

"Can it be only sympathy?"

She met my eager glance shrinkingly. I felt almost as if my life depended on the answer that she might consciously or unconsciously give. Why did she fall into painful and even piteous confusion?

But her womanly pride and strong character at once asserted themselves, for she arose quietly, saying, "I do not feel well this evening," and she left the room.

Mr. Hearn followed precipitately, and was profuse in his commiseration.

"I shall be well in the morning," she said, with such clear, confident emphasis that it occurred to me that the assurance was not meant for his ears only; then, in spite of his entreaties, she went to her room.

I wanted no more supper, and made a poor pretence of keeping Reuben company, and I thought his boy's appetite never would be satisfied. My mind was in such a tumult of hope and fear that I had to strive with my whole strength for self-mastery, so as to excite no surmises. Mrs. Yocomb gave me a few inquiring glances, thinking, perhaps, that I was showing more solicitude about Miss Warren than was wise; but in fact they were all so simple-hearted, so accustomed to express all they thought and felt, that they were not inclined to search for hidden and subtle motives. Even feigning more bungling than mine would have kept my secret from them. Adah seemed relieved at Miss Warren's departure. Mr. Hearn lighted a cigar and sat down on the piazza; as soon as possible I pleaded fatigue and retired to my room, for I was eager to be alone that I might, unwatched, look with fearful yet glistening eyes on the trace I had discovered of an infinite treasure.

I again sat down by the window and looked into the old garden. The possibility that the woman that I had there seen, undisguised in her beautiful truth, might be drawing near me, under an impulse too strong to be resisted, thrilled my very soul. "It's contrary to reason, to every law in nature," I said, "that she should attract me with such tremendous gravitation, and yet my love have no counteraction.

"And yet," I murmured, "beware—beware how you hope. Possibly she is merely indisposed. It is more probable that her feelings toward you are those of gratitude only and of deep sympathy. She is under the impression that you saved her life, and that she has unwittingly blighted yours; and, as Mrs. Yocomb said, she is so kind-hearted, so sensitive, that the thought shadows her life and robs it of zest and happiness. You cannot know that she is learning to return your love in spite of herself, simply because she is pale and somewhat sad. She would think herself, as she said, inhuman if she were happy and serene. I must seek for other tests;" and I thought long and deeply. "Oh, Will Shakespeare!" I at last murmured, "you knew the human heart, if any one ever did. I remember now that you wrote:

"'A murd'rous guilt shows not itself more soon Than love that would seem hid.'

"Oh, for the eyes of Argus. If all the mines of wealth in the world were uncovered, and I might have them all for looking, I'd turn away for one clear glimpse into her woman's heart to-night. Go to New York on Monday! No, not unless driven away with a whip of scorpions. No eagle that ever circled those skies watched as I'll stay and watch for the faintest trace of this priceless secret. No detective, stimulated by professional pride and vast reward, ever sought proof of 'murd'rous guilt' as I shall seek for evidences of this pure woman's love, for more than life depends on the result of my quest."

Words like these would once have seemed extravagant and absurd, but in the abandon of my solitude and in my strong excitement they but inadequately expressed the thoughts that surged through my mind. But as I grew calmer, Conscience asked to be heard.

"Just what do you propose?" it asked; "to win her from another, who now has every right to her allegiance and love? Change places, and how would you regard the man who sought to supplant you? You cannot win happiness at the expense of your honor."

Then Reason added, with quiet emphasis, "Even though your conscience is not equal to the emergency, hers will be. She will do what seems right without any regard for the consequences. If you sought to woo her now, she would despise you; she would regard it as an insult that she would never forgive. It would appear proof complete that you doubted her truth, her chief characteristic."

Between them they made so strong a case against me that my heart sank at the prospect. But hope is the lever that moves the world onward, and the faint hope that had dawned on my thick night was too dear and bright a one to leave me crushed again by my old despondency, and I felt that there must be some way of untangling the problem. If the wall of honor hedged me in on every side, I would *know* the fact to be true before I accepted it.

"I do not propose to woo her," I argued; and possibly my good resolution was strengthened by the knowledge that such a course would be fatal to my hope; "I only intend to discover what may possibly exist. I never have intentionally sought to influence her, even by a glance, since I knew of her relation to Mr. Hearn. I'm under no obligation to this prosperous banker; I'm only bound by honor in the abstract. They are not married. Mrs. Yocomb would say that I had been brought hither by an overruling Providence—it certainly was not a conscious choice of mine—and since I met this woman everything has conspired to bring me to my present position. I know I'm not to blame for it—no more than I was for the storm or the lightning bolt. What a clod I should be were I indifferent to the traits that she has manifested! I feel with absolute certainty that I cannot help the impression that she has made on me. If I could have foreseen it all, I might have remained away; but I was led hither, and kept here by my illness till my chains are riveted and locked, and the key is lost. I cannot escape the fact that I belong to her, body and soul.

"Now suppose, for the sake of argument, that gratitude, respect, friendliness, a sense of being unprotected and alone in the world, have led to her engagement with the wealthy, middle-aged banker, and that through it all her woman's heart was never awakened: such a thing at least is possible. If this were true, she would be no more to blame than I, and we might become the happy victims of circumstances. I'm not worthy of her, and never shall be, but I can't help that either. After all, it seems to me that that which should fulfil my hope is not a ledger balance of good qualities, but the magnetic sympathy of two natures that supplement each other, and were designed for each other in Heaven's match-making. Even now my best hope is based on the truth that she attracts me so irresistibly, and though a much smaller body morally, I should have some corresponding attraction for her. If her woman's heart has become mine, what can she give him? Her very truth may become my most powerful ally. If she still loves him, I will go away and stay away; if it be in accordance with my trembling hope, I have the higher right, and I will assert it to the utmost extent of my power.

Shall the happiness of two lives be sacrificed to his unflagging prosperity? Could it ever be right for him to lead her body to the altar and leave her heart with me? Could she, who is truth itself, go there and perjure herself before God and man? No! a thousand times no! It has become a simple question of whom she loves, and I'll find out if Shakespeare's words are true. If she has love for me, let her bury it never so deeply, my love will be the divining-rod that will inevitably discover it."

Having reached this conclusion, I at last slept, in the small hours of the night.

I thought I detected something like apprehension in her eyes when I met her in the morning. Was she conscious of a secret that might reveal itself in spite of her? But she was cheerful and decided in her manner, and seemed bent on assuring Mr. Hearn that she was well again, and all that he could desire.

Were I in mortal peril I could not have been more vigilantly on my guard. Not for the world would I permit her to know what was passing in my mind—at least not yet—and as far as possible I resumed my old manner. I even simulated more dejection than I felt, to counterbalance the flash of hope that I feared she had recognized on the previous evening.

I well knew that all her woman's strength, that all her woman's pride and exalted sense of honor would bind her to him, who was serenely secure in his trust. My one hope was that her woman's heart was my ally; that it would prove the strongest; that it would so assert itself that truth and honor would at last range themselves on its side. Little did the simple, frank old Quaker realize the passionate alternations of hope and fear that I brought to his breakfast-table that bright Sunday.

All that my guarded scrutiny could gather was that Miss Warren was a little too devoted and thoughtful of her urbane lover, and that her cheerfulness lacked somewhat in spontaneity.

It was agreed at the breakfast-table that we should all go to meeting.

"Mrs. Yocomb," I said, finding her alone for a moment, "won't you be moved this morning? I need one of your sermons more than any heathen in Africa. Whatever your faith is, I believe in it, for I've seen its fruits."

"If a message is given to me I will not be silent; if not, it would be presumptuous to speak. But my prayer is that the Spirit whom we worship may speak to thee, and that thou wilt listen. Unless He speaks, my poor words would be of no avail."

"You are a mystery to me, Mrs. Yocomb, with your genial homely farm life here, and your mystical spiritual heights at the meeting-house. You seem to go from the kitchen by easy and natural transition to regions beyond the stars, and to pass without hesitancy from the companionship of us poor mortals into a Presence that is to me supremely awful."

"Thee doesn't understand, Richard. The little faith I have I take with me to the kitchen, and I'm not afraid of my Father in heaven because he is so great and I'm so little. Is Zillah afraid of her father?"

"I suppose you are right, and I admit that I don't understand, and I don't see how I could reason it out."

"God's children," she replied, "as all children, come to believe many blessed truths without the aid of reason. It was not reason that taught me my mother's love, and yet, now that I have children, it seems very reasonable. I think I learned most from what she said to me and did for me. If ever children were assured of love by their Heavenly Father, we have been; if it is possible for a human soul to be touched by loving, unselfish devotion, let him read the story of Christ."

"But, Mrs. Yocomb, I'm not one of the children."

"Yes, thee is. The trouble with thee is that thee's ashamed, or at least that thee won't acknowledge the relation, and be true to it."

"Dear Mrs. Yocomb," I cried in dismay, "I must either renounce heathenism or go away from your influence," and I left precipitately.

But in truth I was too far gone in human idolatry to think long upon her words; they lodged in my memory, however, and I trust will never lose their influence.

CHAPTER XIII
THE OLD MEETING-HOUSE AGAIN

Reuben and I, with Dapple, skimmed along the country roads, and my hope and spirits kindled, though I scarcely knew why. We were early at the meeting-house, and, to my joy, I gained my old seat, in which I had woven my June day-dream around the fair unknown Quakeress whose face was now that of a loved sister. What ages, seemingly, had elapsed since that fateful day! What infinite advances in life's experiences I had made since I last sat there! How near I had come to the experiences of another life! The fact made me grave and thoughtful. And yet, if my fear and not my hope were realized, what a burden was imposed upon me with the life that disease had spared! Had I even Mrs. Yocomb's faith, I knew it would be a weight under which I would often stagger and faint.

Before very long the great family rockaway unloaded its precious freight at the horse-block, and Adah and Miss Warren entered, followed by the little girls. In secret wonder I saw Adah pause before the same long, straight-backed bench or pew, and Miss Warren take the place where I had first seen my "embodiment of June." Mrs. Yocomb went quietly to her place on the high seat.

"The spell continues to work, but with an important change," I thought.

In a few moments Mr. Yocomb marshalled in Mr. Hearn, and placed him in the end of the pew next to Miss Warren on the men's side, so that they might have the satisfaction of sitting together, as if at church. He then looked around for me; but I shook my head, and would not go up higher.

Soon all the simple, plainly apparelled folk who would attend that day were in their places, and the old deep hush that I so well remembered settled down upon us. The sweet low monotone of the summer wind was playing still among the maples. I do believe that it was the same old bumblebee that darted in, still unable to overcome its irate wonder at a people who could be so quiet and serene. The sunlight flickered in here and there, and shadowy leaves moved noiselessly up and down the whitewashed wall. Only the occasional song of a bird was wanting to reproduce the former hour, but at this later season the birds seem content with calls and chirpings, and in the July heat they were almost as silent as we were.

But how weak and fanciful my June day-dream now seemed. Then woman's influence on my life was but a romantic sentiment. I had then conjured up a pretty vista full of serene, quiet domestic joys, which were to be a solace merely of my real life of toil and ambition. I had thought myself launched on a shining tide that would bear me smoothly to a quiet home anchorage; but almost the first word that Emily Warren spoke broke the spell of my complacent, indolent dream, and I awoke to the presence of an earnest, large-souled woman, who was my peer, and in many respects my superior; whom, so far from being a mere household pet, could be counsellor and friend, and a daily inspiration. Instead of shrinking from the world with which I must grapple, she already looked out upon its tangled and cruel problems with clear, intelligent, courageous eyes; single-handed she had coped with it and won from it a place and respect. And yet, with all her strength and fearlessness, she had kept her woman's heart gentle and tender. Oh, who could have better proof of this than I, who had seen her face bending over the little unconscious Zillah, and who had heard her low sob when she feared I might be dying.

The two maidens sat side by side, and I was not good enough to think of anything better or purer than they. Adah, with her face composed to its meeting-house quiet, but softened and made more beautiful by passing shades of thought; still it seemed almost as young and childlike as that of Zillah. Miss Warren's profile was less round and full, but it was more finely chiselled, and was luminous with mind. The slightly higher forehead, the more delicately arched eyebrow, the deeper setting of her dark, changing eyes, that were placed wide apart beneath the overhanging brow, the short, thin, tremulous upper lip, were all indications of the quick, informing spirit which made her face like a transparency through which her thoughts could often be guessed before spoken; and since they were good, noble, genial thoughts, they enhanced her beauty. And yet it had occurred to me more than once that if Miss Warren were a depraved woman she could give to evil a deadly fascination.

"Are her thoughts wandering like mine?" I mused. With kindling hope I saw her face grow sad, and I even imagined that her pallor increased. For a long time she looked quietly and fixedly before her, as did Adah, and then she stole a shy, hesitating glance at Mr. Hearn by her side; but the banker seemingly had found the silent meeting a trifle dull, for his eyes were heavy, and all life and animation had faded out of his full white face. Was it my imagination, or did she slightly shrink from him? In an almost instantaneous flash she turned a little more and glanced at me, and I was caught in the act of almost breathless scrutiny. A sudden red flamed in her cheeks, but not a Friend of them all was more motionless than she at once became.

My conscience smote me. Though I watched for her happiness as truly as my own, the old meeting-house should have been a sanctuary even from the eyes of love. I knew from the expression of her face that she had not liked it; nor did I blame her.

I was glad to have the silence of the meeting broken; for a venerable man rose slowly from the high seat and reverently enunciated the words:

"'The Lord of Hosts is with us; the God of Jacob is our refuge.

"'He maketh wars to cease unto the end of the earth; He breaketh the bow and cutteth the spear in sunder; He burneth the chariot in the fire.

"'Be still, and know that I am God.'

"The quiet, reverent bowing of the heart to His will is often the most acceptable worship that we can offer," he began, and if he had stopped there the effect would have been perfect; but he began to talk and to ramble. With a sense of deep disappointment I dreaded lest the hour should pass and that Mrs. Yocomb would not speak; but as the old gentleman sat down, that rapt look was on her face that I remembered seeing on the night of the storm. She rose, took off her deep Quaker bonnet, and laid it quietly on the seat beside her; but one saw that she was not thinking of it or of anything except the truth which filled her mind.

Clasping her hands before her she looked steadfastly toward heaven for a few moments, and then, in a low, sweet, penetrating monotone, repeated the words:

"'Peace I leave with you, my peace I give unto you: not as the world giveth, give I unto you. Let not your heart be troubled, neither let it be afraid.'"

She paused a moment, and I gazed in wonder at her serene, uplifted face. She had spoken with such an utter absence of self-consciousness or regard for externals as to give the strong impression that the words had come again from heaven through her lips, and were endowed with a new life and richer meaning; and now she seemed waiting for whatever else might be given to her.

Could that inspired woman, who now looked as if she might have stood unabashed on the Mount of Transfiguration, be my genial, untiring nurse, and the cheery matron of the farmhouse, whose deft hands had made the sweet, light bread we had eaten this morning? I had long loved her; but now, as I realized as never before the grand compass of her womanly nature, I began to reverence her. A swift glance at Miss Warren revealed that the text had awakened an interest so deep as to suggest a great and present need, for the maiden was leaning slightly toward the speaker and waiting with parted lips.

"As I sat here," Mrs. Yocomb began, looking down upon us with a grave, gentle aspect, "these words came to me as if spoken in my soul, and I am constrained to repeat them unto you. I'm impressed with the truth that peace is the chief need of the world—the chief need of every human heart. Beyond success, beyond prosperity, beyond happiness, is the need of peace—the deep, assured rest of the soul that is akin to the eternal calmness of Him who spake these words.

"The world at large is full of turmoil and trouble. The sounds of its wretched disquietude reach me even in this quiet place and at this quiet hour. I seem to hear the fierce uproar of battle; for while we are turning our thoughts up to the God of peace, misguided men are dealing death-blows to their fellow men. I hear cries of rage, I hear the groans of the dying. But sadder than these bloody fields of open strife are the dark places of cruelty. I hear the clank of the prisoner's chain, and the crack of the slave-driver's whip. I see desperate and despairing faces revealing tortured souls to whom the light of each day brings more bitter wrongs, viler indignities, until they are ready to curse God for the burden of life. Sadder still, I hear the dark whisperings of those who would destroy the innocent and cast down the simple. I hear the satanic laugh of such as are false to sacred trusts and holy obligations, who ruthlessly as swine are rending hearts that have given all the pearls they had. From that sacred place, home, come to me hot words of strife, drunken, brutal blows, and the wailing of helpless women and children. Saddest of all earthly sounds, I hear the wild revelry of those who are not the victims of evil in others, but who, while madly seeking happiness, are blotting out all hope of happiness, and who are committing that crime of crimes, the destruction of their own immortal souls. Did I say the last was the saddest of earthly sounds? There comes to me another, at which my heart sinks; it is the sound of proud arrogant voices, who are explaining that faith is a delusion, that prayer is wasted breath, that the God of the Bible is a dream of old-time mystics, and that Christ died in vain. I hear the moan of Mary at the sepulchre repeated from thousands of hearts, 'They have taken away my Lord.' O God, forgive those who would blot out the dearest hope which has ever sustained humanity. Can there be peace in a world wherein we can never escape these sad, terrible, discordant sounds? The words that I have repeated were spoken in just such a world when the din of evil was at its worst, and to those who must soon suffer all the wrong that the world could inflict."

After a brief pause of silent waiting she continued:

"But is the turmoil of the world a far-away sound, like the sullen roar of angry waves beating on a shore that rises high and enduring, securing us safety and rest? Beyond the deep disquietude of the world at large is the deeper unrest of the human heart. No life can be so secluded and sheltered but that anxieties, doubts, fears, and foreboding will come with all their disturbing power. Often sorrows more bitter than death are hidden by smiling faces, and in our quiet country homes there are men and women carrying burdens that are crushing out hope and life: mothers breaking their hearts over wayward sons and daughters; wives desperate because the men who wooed them as blushing maidens have forgotten their vows, and have become swinish sots; men disheartened because the sweet-faced girls that they thought would give them a home have become vile slatterns, busybodies, shrill-tongued shrews, who banish the very thought of peace and rest, who waste their substance and eat out their hearts with care. Oh, the clouds of earth are not those which sweep across the sun, but those which rise out of unhappy hearts and evil lives. These are the clouds that gather over too many in a leaden pall, and it seems as if no light could ever break through them. There are hearts to whom life seems to promise one long, hopeless struggle to endure an incurable pain. Can there be peace for such unhappy ones? To just such human hearts were the words spoken, 'Peace I leave with you, my peace I give unto you.'"

Then came one of those little pauses that were quite as impressive as the preceding words. Although my interest was almost breathless, I involuntarily looked toward one whom I now associated with every thought.

"O God!" I exclaimed mentally, "can that be the aspect of a maiden happy in her love and hope?" Her face had become almost white, and across the pallor of her cheeks tear followed tear, as from a full and bitter fountain.

"Never, in all this evil world," the speaker resumed, "was there such cruel, bitter mockery as these words would be if they were not true—if He who spake them had no right to speak them. And what right would He have to speak them if He were merely a man among men—a part of the world which never has and never can give peace to the troubled soul? How do we know these words are true? How do we know He had a right to speak them? Thank God! I know, because He has kept His word to me. Thank God! Millions know, because He has proved His power to them. The scourged, persecuted, crucified disciples found that He was with them always, even unto the end. Oh, my friends, it is this living, loving, spiritual Presence that uplifts and sustains the sinking heart when the whole great world could only stand helplessly by. 'Not as the world giveth, give I unto you.' Yes, thank thee, Lord, 'not as the world.' In spite of the world and the worst it can do, in spite of our evil and the worst it can do, in spite of our sorrows, our fears, our pains and losses, our bitter disappointments, thou canst give peace; thou hast given peace. No storm can harm the soul that rests on the Rock of Ages, and by and by He will say to the storm, 'Peace, be still,' and the light of heaven will come. Then there shall be no more night. 'God shall wipe away all tears from their eyes; and there shall be no more death, neither sorrow nor crying, neither shall there be any more pain; for the former things are passed away.'"

The light and gladness of that blessed future seemed to have come into her sweet, womanly face. I looked out of the window to hide tears of which I was fool enough to be ashamed.

When she spoke again her voice was low and pitiful, and her face full of the divinest sympathy. "Dear friends," she said, "it was not merely peace that he promised, but his peace. 'My peace I give unto you.' Remember, it was the man of sorrows who spoke; remember that he was acquainted with grief; remember that years of toil and hardship were behind him, and that Gethsemane and Calvary were before him; remember that one would betray him, and that all would desert him. When he spoke, the storm of the world's evil was breaking upon him more cruelly and remorselessly than it ever has on any tempted soul. He suffered more because more able to suffer. But beneath all was the sacred calm of one who is right, and who means to do right to the end, cost what it may. The peace that he promises is not immunity from pain or loss, or the gratification of the heart's earthly desires. His natural and earthly desires were not gratified; often ours cannot be. His peace came from self-denial for the good of others, from the consciousness that he was doing his Father's will, and from the assurance that good would come out of the seeming evil. Suffer he must, because he was human, and in a world of suffering; but he chose to suffer that we might know that he understands us, and sympathizes with us when we suffer. To each and to all he can say, I was tempted in all points like unto thee. When we wander he goes out after us; when we fall he lifts us up; when we faint he takes us in his arms and carries us on his bosom. O great heart of love! thy patience never tires, never wearies. Thou canst make good to us every earthly loss; thy touch can heal every wound of the soul. Even though life be one long martyrdom, yet through thy Presence it may be a blessed life, full of peace.

"Because our Lord was a man of sorrows, was he in love with sorrows? or does he love to see storms gathering around his people? No. It was not with *his* sorrows, but with *our* sorrows, that he was afflicted. He so loved the world that he could not be glad when we were sad. It is said that there is no record that Jesus ever smiled; but those little children whom he took in his arms and blessed know that he smiled. I doubt whether he ever saw a flower but that, no matter how weary from the hot day's long journey, he smiled back upon it. The flowers are but his smiles, and the world is full of them. Still he is naturally and very justly associated with sorrow; for when on earth he sought out those in trouble, and the distressed and the suffering soon learned to fly to him. What was the result? Were the shadows deepened? Was the suffering prolonged? Let the sisters of Bethany answer you; let the widow of Nain answer you. Let the great host of the lame, blind, diseased, and leprous answer. Look into the gentle, serene eyes of Mary Magdalene, once so desperate and clouded by evil, and then know whether he brings sorrow or joy to the world. Just as the sun follows the night that it may bring the day, so the Sun of Righteousness seeks out all that is dark in our lives that he may shine it away. Gladness, then, should be the rule of our lives. Nothing to him is so pleasing as gladness, if it comes from the heart of pilgrims truly homeward bound; but if sorrow comes, oh, turn not to the world, for the best thing in it can give no peace, no rest. Simply do right, and leave the results with him who said, even under the shadow of his cross, 'My peace I give unto you.' Accept this message, dear friends, and 'Let not your hearts be troubled, and neither let them be afraid.'" And she sat down quietly and closed her eyes.

There was here and there a low sob from the women, and the eyes of some of the most rugged-featured men were moist. The hush that followed was broken by deep and frequent sighs. Mr. Yocomb sat with his face lifted heavenward, and I knew it was serene and thankful. The eyes of Reuben, who was beside me, rested on his mother in simple, loving devotion. As yet she was his religion. Adah was looking a little wonderingly but sympathetically at Miss Warren, whose bowed head and fallen veil could not hide her deep emotion. The banker, too, looked at her even more wonderingly. At last the most venerable man on the high seat gave his hand to another white-haired Friend beside him, and the congregation began slowly and quietly to disperse.

"Come, Reuben," I said, in a whisper, "let us get away, quick."

He looked at me in surprise, but in a few moments the old meeting-house was hidden behind us among the trees. Dapple's feet scarcely touched the ground; but I sat silent, absorbed, and almost overwhelmed.

"Didn't—didn't thee like what mother said?" Reuben asked, after a while, a little hurt.

I felt at once that he misunderstood my silence, and I put my arm around his neck as I said, "Reuben, love and honor your mother the longest day you live. She is one among a million. 'Liked!' It mattered little whether I liked it or not; she made it seem God's own truth."

"And to think, Richard, that if it hadn't been for thee—"

"Hush, Reuben. To think rather that she waited on me for days and nights together. Well, I could turn Catholic and worship one saint."

"I'm glad she's only mother," said the boy, with a low laugh; "and, Richard, she likes me to have a good time as much as I do myself. She always made me mind, but she's been jolly good to me. Oh, I love her; don't thee worry about that."

"Well, whatever happens," I said, with a deep breath, "I thank God for the day that brought me to her home."

"So do I," said the boy; "so do we all; but confound Emily Warren's grandfather! I don't take to him. He thinks we're wonderfully simple folks, just about good enough to board him and that black-eyed witch of his. I do kind of like her a little bit, she's so saucy-like sometimes. One day she commenced ordering me around, and I stood and stared at the little miss in a way that she won't forget."

"She'll learn to coax by and by, and then you'll do anything for her, Reuben."

"P'raps," he said, with a half smile on his ruddy face.

CHAPTER XIV
LOVE TEACHING ETHICS

On reaching the farmhouse I went directly to my room, and I wished that I might stay there the rest of the day; but I was soon summoned to dinner. In Miss Warren's eyes still lingered the evidences of her deep feeling, but her expression was quiet, firm, and resolute. The effect of the sermon upon her was just what I anticipated in case my hope had any foundation—it had bound her by what seemed the strongest of motives to be faithful to the man who she believed had the right to her fealty.

"Well," I thought bitterly, "life might have brought her a heavier cross than marrying a handsome millionaire, even though considerably her senior. I'm probably a conceited fool for thinking it any very great burden at all. But how, then, can I account—? Well, well, time alone can unravel this snarl. One thing is certain: she will do nothing that she does not believe right; and after what Mrs. Yocomb said I would not dare to wish her to do wrong."

Mrs. Yocomb did not come down to dinner, and the meal was a quiet one. Mr. Yocomb's eyes glistened with a serene, happy light, but he ate sparingly, and spoke in subdued tones. He reminded me of the quaint old scripture—"A man's wisdom maketh his face to shine." Whatever might be said against his philosophy, it produced good cheer and peace. Adah, too, was very quiet; but occasionally she glanced toward Miss Warren as if perplexed and somewhat troubled. Mr. Hearn seemed wrought up into quite a religious fervor. He was demonstratively tender and sympathetic toward the girl at his side, and waited on her with the effusive manner of one whose feelings must have some outlet. His appetite, however, did not flag, and I thought he seemed to enjoy his emotions and his dinner equally.

"Mr. Morton," he said impressively, "you must have liked that sermon exceedingly."

"Indeed, sir," I replied briefly, "I have scarcely thought whether I liked it or not."

Both he and Miss Warren looked at me in surprise; indeed all did except Reuben.

"I beg your pardon, but I thought Mrs. Yocomb expressed herself admirably," he said, with somewhat of the air of championship.

"She certainly expressed herself clearly. The trouble with me is that the sermon is just what Mrs. Yocomb would call it—a message—and one scarcely knows how to dodge it. I never had such a spiritual blow between the eyes before, and think I'm a little stunned yet."

A smile lighted up Miss Warren's face. "Mrs. Yocomb would like your tribute to her sermon, I think," she said.

"What most bewilders me," I resumed, "is to think how Mrs. Yocomb has been waiting on me and taking care of me. I now feel like the peasant who was taken in and cared for by the royal family."

"I think our friend Mr. Morton is in what may be termed 'a frame of mind,'" said Mr. Hearn a little satirically.

"Yes, sir, I am," I replied emphatically. "I believe that adequate causes should have some effects. It does not follow, however, that my frame of mind is satisfactory to any one, least of all to Mrs. Yocomb."

"Your contact with the truth," said Mr. Hearn, laughing, "is somewhat like many people's first experience of the ocean—you are much stirred up, but have not yet reached the point of yielding to the mysterious malady."

I was disgusted, and was about to reply with a sarcastic compliment upon the elegance of his illustration, when a look of pain upon Miss Warren's face checked me, and I said nothing. Lack of delicacy was one of Mr. Hearn's gravest faults. While courtly, polished, and refined in externals, he lacked in tact and nicety of discrimination. He often said things which a finer-fibred but much worse man would never have said. He had an abundance of intellect, great shrewdness, vast will force, and organizing power, but not much ideality or imagination. This lack rendered him incapable of putting himself in the place of another, and of appreciating their feelings, moods, and motives. The most revolting thought to me of his union with Miss Warren was that he would never appreciate her. He greatly admired and respected her, but his spiritual eyes were too dim to note the exquisite bloom on her character, or to detect the evanescent lights and shades of thought and feeling of which to me her mobile face gave so many hints. He would expect her to be like the July days now passing—warm, bright, cloudless, and in keeping with his general prosperity.

"They will disappoint each other inevitably," I thought, "and it's strange that her clear eyes cannot see it when mine can. It is perhaps the strongest evidence of her love for him, since love is blind. Still she may love and yet be able to see his foibles and failings clearly; thousands of women do this.

But whether the silken cord of love or the chain of supposed duty binds her to him now, I fear that Mrs. Yocomb's sermon has made her his for all time."

Her manner confirmed my surmise, for she apparently gave me little thought, and was unobtrusively attentive and devoted to him. He had the good taste to see that further personal remarks were not agreeable; and since his last attempted witticism fell flat, did not attempt any more. Our table-talk flagged, and we hastened through the meal. After it was over he asked:

"Emily, what shall we do this afternoon?"

"Anything you wish," she replied quietly.

"That's the way it will always be," I muttered as I went dejectedly to my room. "Through all his life it has been 'anything you wish,' and now it would seem as if religion itself had become his ally. There is nothing to me so wonderful as some men's fortune. Earth and heaven seem in league to forward their interests. But why was she so moved at the meeting-house? Was it merely religious sensibility? It might have been we were all moved deeply. Was it my imagination, or did she really shrink from him, and then glance guiltily at me? Even if she had, it might have been a momentary repulsion caused by his drowsy, heavy aspect at the time, just as his remark at dinner gave her an unpleasant twinge. These little back eddies are no proof that there is not a strong central current.

"Can it be that she was sorrowful in the meeting-house for my sake only? I've had strong proof of her wonderful kindness of heart. Well, God bless her anyway. I'll wait and watch till I know the truth. I suppose I'm the worst heathen Mrs. Yocomb ever preached to, but I'm going to secure Emily Warren's happiness at any cost. If she truly loves this man, I'll go away and fight it out so sturdily that she need not worry. That's what her sermon means for me. I'm not going to pump up any religious sentiment. I don't feel any. It's like walking into a bare room to have a turn with a thumb-screw; but Mrs. Yocomb has hedged me up to just this course. Oh, the gentle, inexorable woman! Satan himself might well tremble before her. There is but one that I fear more, and that's the woman I love most. Gentle, tender-hearted as she is, she is more inexorable than Mrs. Yocomb. It's a little strange, but I doubt whether there is anything in the universe that so inspires a man with awe as a thoroughly good, large-minded woman."

I could not sleep that afternoon, and at last I became so weary of the conflict between my hope and fear that I was glad to hear Miss Warren at the piano, playing softly some old English hymns. The day was growing cool and shadowy, but I hoped that before it passed I might get a chance to say something to her which would give a different aspect to the concluding words of Mrs. Yocomb's sermon. I had determined no longer to avoid her society, but rather to seek it, whenever I could in the presence of others, and especially of her affianced. They had returned from a long afternoon in the arbor, which I knew must occasion Miss Warren some unpleasant thoughts, and the banker was sitting on the piazza chatting with Adah.

I strolled into the parlor with as easy and natural a manner as I could assume, and taking my old seat by the window, said quietly: "Please go on playing, Miss Warren."

She turned on me one of her swift looks, which always gave me the impression that she saw all that was in my mind. Her color rose a little, but she continued playing for a time. Then with her right hand evoking low, sweet chords, she asked, with a conciliatory smile:

"Have you been thinking over Mrs. Yocomb's words this afternoon?"

"Not all the time—no. Have you?"

"How could I all the time?"

"Oh, I think you can do anything under heaven you make up your mind to do," I said, with a slight laugh. The look she gave now was a little apprehensive, and I added hastily: "I've had one thought that I don't mind telling you, for I think it may be a pleasant one, though it must recall that which is painful. The thought occurred to me when Mrs. Yocomb was speaking, and since, that your brother had perfect peace as he stood in that line of battle."

She turned eagerly toward me, and tears rushed into her eyes.

"You may be right," she said, in a low, tremulous tone.

"Well, I feel sure I'm right. I know it, if he was anything like you."

"Oh, then I doubt it. I'm not at all brave as he was. You ought to know that."

"You have the courage that a veteran general most values in a soldier. You might be half dead from terror, but you wouldn't run away. Besides," I added, smiling, "you would not be afraid of shot and shell, only the noise of a battle. In this respect your brother, no doubt, differed from you. In the grand consciousness of right, and in his faithful performance of duty, I believe his face was as serene as the aspect of Mr. Yocomb when he looked at the coming storm. As far as peace is concerned, his heaven began on earth. I envy him."

"Mr. Morton, I thank you for these words about my brother," she said very gently, and with a little pathetic quaver in her voice. "They have given me a comforting association with that awful day. Oh, I thank God for the thought. Remembering what Mrs. Yocomb said, it reconciles me to it all, as I never thought I could be reconciled. If Herbert believed that it was his duty to be there, it was best he should be there. How strange it is that you should think of this first, and not I!"

"Will you pardon me if I take exception to one thing you say? I do not think it follows that he ought to have been there simply because he felt it right to be there."

"Why, Mr. Morton! ought one not to do right at any and every cost? That seemed to me the very pith of Mrs. Yocomb's teaching, and I think she made it clear that it's always best to do right."

"I think so too, most emphatically; but what is right, Miss Warren?"

"That's too large a question for me to answer in the abstract; but is not the verdict of conscience right for each one of us?"

"I can't think so," I replied, with a shrug. "About every grotesque, horrible act ever committed in this world has been sanctioned by conscience. Delicate women have worn hair-cloth and walked barefooted on cold pavements in midnight penance. The devil is scarcely more cruel than the Church, for ages, taught that God was. It's true that Christ's life was one of self-sacrifice; but was there any useless, mistaken self-sacrifice in it? If God is anything like Mrs. Yocomb, nothing could be more repugnant to him than blunders of this kind."

She looked at me with a startled face, and I saw that my words had unsettled her mind.

"If conscience cannot guide, what can?" she faltered. "Is not conscience God's voice within us?"

"No. Conscience may become God's worst enemy—that is, any God that I could worship or even respect."

"Mr. Morton, you frighten me. How can I do right unless I follow my conscience?"

"Yes," I said sadly, "you would, in the good old times, have followed it over stony pavements, in midnight penance, or now into any thorny path which it pointed out; and I believe that many such paths lead away from the God of whom Mrs. Yocomb spoke to-day. Miss Warren, I'm a man of the world, and probably you think my views on these subjects are not worth much. It's strange that your own nature does not suggest to you the only sure guide. It seems to me that conscience should always go to truth for instructions. The men who killed your brother thought they were right as truly as he did; but history will prove that they were wrong, as so many sincere people have been in every age. He did not suffer and die uselessly, for the truth was beneath his feet and in his heart."

"Dear, brave, noble Herbert!" she sighed. "Oh, that God had spared him to me!"

"I wish he had," I said, with quiet emphasis. "I wish he was with you here and now."

Again she gave me a questioning, troubled look through her tears.

"Then you believe truth to be absolutely binding?" she asked, in a low voice.

"Yes. In science, religion, ethics, or human action, nothing can last—nothing can end well that is not built squarely on truth."

She became very pale; but she turned quietly to her piano as she said:

"You are right, Mr. Morton; there can be no peace—not even self-respect—without truth. My nature would be pitiful indeed did it not teach me that."

She had interpreted my words in a way that intensified the influence of Mrs. Yocomb's sermon. To be false to the trust that she had led her affianced to repose in her still seemed the depth of degradation. I feared that she would take this view at first, but believed, if my hope had any foundation, she would think my words over so often that she would discover a different meaning.

And my hope was strengthened. If she loved Mr. Hearn, why did she turn, pale and quiet, to her piano, which had always appeared a refuge to her, when I had seemingly spoken words that not only sanctioned but made the course which harmonized with her love imperative? Even the possibility that in the long days and nights of my delirium I had unconsciously wooed and won her heart, so thrilled and overcame me that I dared not trust myself longer in her presence, and I went out on the piazza—a course eminently satisfactory to Mr. Hearn, no doubt. I think he regarded our interview as becoming somewhat extended. He had glanced at me from time to time, but my manner had been too quiet to disturb him, and he could not see Miss Warren's face. The words he overheard suggested a theological discussion rather than anything of a personal nature. It had been very reassuring to see Miss Warren turn from me as if my words had ceased to interest her, and my coming out to talk with Adah confirmed the impression made by my manner all along, that we were not very congenial spirits. It also occurred to me that he did not find chatting with Adah a very heavy cross, for never had she looked prettier than on that summer evening. But now that Miss Warren was alone he went in and sat down by her, saying so loudly that I could not help hearing him, as I stood by the window:

"I think you must have worsted Mr. Morton in your theological discussion, for he came out looking as if he had a great deal to think about that was not exactly to his taste; but Miss Adah will—" and then his companion began playing something that drowned his voice.

CHAPTER XV
"DON'T THINK OF ME"

Mrs. Yocomb appeared at supper, serene and cheerful; but she was paler than usual, and she still looked like one who had but just descended from a lofty spiritual height. No reference whatever was made to the morning. Mrs. Yocomb no longer spoke on religious themes directly, but she seemed to me the Gospel embodied, as with natural kindly grace she presided at her home table. Her husband beamed on her, and looked as if his cup was overflowing. Reuben's frank, boyish eyes often turned toward her in their simple devotion, while Zillah, who sat next to her, had many a whispered confidence to give. Adah's accent was gentle and her manner thoughtful. Miss Warren looked at her from time to time with a strange wistfulness— looked as if the matron possessed a serenity and peace that she coveted.

"Emily," said Mr. Yocomb, "thee doesn't think music's wicked, does thee?"

"No, sir, nor do you either."

"What does thee think of that, mother?"

"I think Emily converted thee over to her side before she had been here two days."

"Thee's winked very hard at my apostasy, mother. I'm inclined to think thee was converted too, on the third or fourth day, if thee'd own up."

"No," said Mrs. Yocomb, with a smile at her favorite, "Emily won my heart on the first day, and I accepted piano and all."

"Why, Mrs. Yocomb!" I exclaimed—for I could not forego the chance to vindicate myself—"I never considered you a precipitate, ill-balanced person."

Miss Warren's cheeks were scarlet, and I saw that she understood me well. I think Mrs. Yocomb guessed my meaning, too, for her smile was a little peculiar as she remarked demurely, "Women are different from men: they know almost immediately whether they like a person or not. I liked thee in half a day."

"You like sinners on principle, Mrs. Yocomb. I think it was my general depravity and heathenism that won your regard."

"No, as a woman I liked thee. Thee isn't as bad as thee seems."

"Mr. Yocomb, I hope you don't object to this, for I must assure you most emphatically that I don't."

"Mother's welcome to love thee all she pleases," said the old gentleman, laughing. "Indeed, I think I egg her on to it."

"Good friends," said Miss Warren, with her old mirthful look, "you'll turn Mr. Morton's head; you should be more considerate."

"I am indeed bewildered. Miss Warren's keen eyes have detected my weak point."

"A man with so stout a heart," Mr. Hearn began, "could well afford —" and then he hesitated.

"To be weak-headed," I said, finishing his sentence. "I fear you are mistaken, sir. I can't afford it at all."

"Thee was clear-headed enough to get around mother in half an hour," said the old gentleman again, laughing heartily. "It took me several months."

"Thee was a little blind, father. I wasn't going to let thee see how much I thought of thee till I had kept thee waiting a proper time."

"That's rich!" I cried, and I laughed as I had not since my illness. "How long is a proper time, Mrs. Yocomb? I remember being once told that a woman was a mystery that a man could never solve. I fear it's true."

"Who told you that?" asked Mr. Hearn; for I think he noticed my swift glance at Miss Warren, who looked a little conscious.

"As I think of it, I may have read it in a newspaper," I said demurely.

"I'm not flattered by your poor memory, Mr. Morton," remarked Miss Warren quietly. "I told you that myself when you were so mystified by my fearlessness of Dapple and my fear of the cow."

"I've learned that my memory is sadly treacherous, Miss Warren."

"A man who is treacherous only in memory may well be taken as a model," remarked Mr. Hearn benignly.

"Would you say that of one who forgot to pay you his debts?"

"What do you owe me, Mr. Morton?"

"I'm sure I don't know. Good-will, I suppose Mrs. Yocomb would suggest."

"Well, sir, I feel that I owe you a great deal; perhaps more than I realize, as I recall your promptness on that memorable night of the storm."

"I was prompt—I'll admit that," I said grimly, looking at the ceiling.

"Mr. Yocomb, how long would it have taken the house to burn up if the fire had not been extinguished?" Mr. Hearn asked.

"The interior," replied Mr. Yocomb very gravely, "would all have been in flames in a very few moments, for it's old and dry."

"Ugh!" exclaimed Adah, shudderingly. "Richard—"

I put my finger on my lips. "Miss Adah," I interrupted, "I'd rather be struck by lightning than hear any more about that night."

"Yes," said Miss Warren desperately, "I wish I could forget that night forever."

"I never wish to forget the expression on your face. Miss Warren, when we knew Zillah was alive. If that didn't please God, nothing in this world ever did."

"Oh, hush!" she cried.

"Emily, I think you cannot have told me all that happened."

"I can't think of it any more," she said; and her face was full of trouble. "I certainly don't know, and have never thought how I looked."

"Mr. Morton seems to have been cool enough to have been very observant," said the banker keenly.

"I was wet enough to be cool, sir. Miss Warren said I was not fit to be seen, and the doctor bundled me out of the room, fearing I would frighten Zillah into hysterics. Hey, Zillah! what do you think of that?"

"I think the doctor was silly. I wouldn't be afraid of thee any more than of Emily."

"Please let us talk and think of something else," Miss Warren pleaded.

"I don't want to forget what I owe to Richard," said Reuben a little indignantly. I trod on his foot under the table. "Thee needn't try to stop me, Richard Morton," continued the boy passionately. "I couldn't have got mother out alone, and I'd never left her. Where would we be, Emily Warren, if it hadn't been for Richard?"

"In heaven," I said, laughing, for I was determined to prevent a scene.

"Well, I hope so," Reuben muttered; "but I don't mind being in mother's dining-room."

Even Mrs. Yocomb's gravity gave way at this speech.

As we rose from the table, Zillah asked innocently:

"Emily, is thee crying or laughing?"

"I hardly know myself," she faltered, and went hastily to her room; but she soon came down again, looking very resolute.

"Emily," said Mr. Yocomb, "since thee and mother doesn't think music's wicked, I have a wonderful desire to hear thee sing again, 'Tell me the Old, Old Story,' as thee did on the night of the storm."

In spite of her brave eyes and braver will, her lip trembled.

I was cruel enough to add, "And I would be glad to listen to the Twelfth Nocturne once more."

For some reason she gave me a swift glance full of reproach.

"I will listen to anything," I said quickly.

Mr. Hearn looked a little like a man who feared that there might be subterranean fires beneath his feet.

"I will not promise more than to be chorister to-night," she said, sitting down to the piano with her back toward us. "Let us have familiar hymns that all can sing. Miss Adah has a sweet voice, and Mr. Morton, no doubt, is hiding his talent in a napkin. There's a book for you, sir. I'm sorry it doesn't contain the music."

"It doesn't matter," I said; "I'm equally familiar with Choctaw."

"Adela and Zillah, you come and stand by me. Your little voices are like the birds'."

We all gathered in the old parlor, and spent an hour that I shall never forget. I had a tolerable tenor, and an ear made fairly correct by hearing much music. Mr. Hearn did not sing, but he seemingly entered into the spirit of the occasion. Before very long Miss Warren and I were singing some things together. Mr. Hearn no doubt compared our efforts unfavorably with what he had heard in the city, but the simple people of the farmhouse were much pleased, and repeatedly asked us to continue. As I was leaning over Miss Warren's shoulder, finding a place in the hymn-book on the stand, she breathed softly:

"Have you told them you are going to-morrow?"

"No," I replied.

"Can you leave such friends?"

"Yes."

"You ought not. It would hurt them cruelly;" and she made some runs on the piano to hide her words.

"If *you* say I ought not to go, I'll stay—Ah, this is the one I was looking for," I said, in a matter-of-fact tone; but she played the music with some strange slips and errors; her hands were nervous and trembling, and never was the frightened look that I had seen before more distinctly visible.

After we had sung a stanza or two she rose and said, "I think I'm getting a little tired, and the room seems warm. Wouldn't you like to take a walk?" she asked Mr. Hearn, coming over to his side.

He arose with alacrity, and they passed out together. I did not see her again that night.

The next morning, finding me alone for a moment, she approached, hesitatingly, and said:

"I don't think I ought to judge for you."

"Do you wish me to go?" I asked, sadly, interpreting her thought.

She became very pale, and turned away as she replied, "Perhaps you had better. I think you would rather go."

"No, I'd rather stay; but I'll do as you wish."

She did not reply, and went quickly to her piano.

I turned and entered the dining-room where Mrs. Yocomb and Adah were clearing away the breakfast. Mr. Yocomb was writing in his little office adjoining.

"I think it is time I said good-by and went back to New York."

In the outcry that followed, Miss Warren's piano became silent.

"Richard Morton!" Mrs. Yocomb began almost indignantly, "if thee hasn't any regard for thyself, thee should have some for thy friends. Thee isn't fit to leave home, and this is thy home now. Thee doesn't call thy hot rooms in New York home, so I don't see as thee has got any other. Just so sure as thee goes back to New York now, thee'll be sick again. I won't hear to it. Thee's just beginning to improve a little."

Adah looked at me through reproachful tears, but she did not say anything. Mr. Yocomb dropped his pen and came out, looking quite excited:

"I'll send for Doctor Bates and have him lay his commands on thee," he said. "I won't take thee to the depot, and thee isn't able to walk half way there. Here, Emily, come and talk reason to this crazy man. He says he's going back to New York. He ought to be put in a strait-jacket. Doesn't thee think so?"

Her laugh was anything but simple and natural.

As she said "I do indeed," Mr. Hearn had joined her.

"What would thee do in such an extreme case of mental disorder?"

"Treat him as they did in the good old times: get a chain and lock him up on bread and water."

"Would thee then enjoy thy dinner?"

"That wouldn't matter if he were cured."

"I think Mr. Morton would prefer hot New York to the remedies that Emily prescribes," said Mr. Hearn, with his smiling face full of vigilance.

"Richard," said Mrs. Yocomb, putting both her hands on my arm, "I should feel more hurt than I can tell thee if thee leaves us now."

"Why, Mrs. Yocomb! I didn't think you would care so much."

"Then thee's very blind, Richard. I didn't think thee'd say that."

"You cut deep now; suppose I must go?"

"Why must thee go, just as thee is beginning to gain? Thee is as pale as a ghost this minute, and thee doesn't weigh much more than half as much as I do. Still, we don't want to put an unwelcome constraint on thee."

I took her hand in both of mine as I said earnestly, "God forbid that I should ever escape from any constraint that you put upon me. Well, I won't go to-day, and I'll see what word my mail brings me." And I went up to my room, not trusting myself to glance at the real controller of my action, but hoping that something would occur which would make my course clear. As I came out of my room to go down to dinner, Miss Warren intercepted me, saying eagerly:

"Mr. Morton, don't go. If you should be ill again in New York, as Mrs. Yocomb says—"

"I won't be ill again."

"Please don't go," she entreated. "I—I shouldn't have said what I did. You *would* be ill; Mrs. Yocomb would never forgive me."

"Miss Warren, I will do what you wish."

"I wish what is best for you—only that."

"I fear I cloud your happiness. You are too kind-hearted."

She smiled a little bitterly. "Please stay—don't think of me."

"Again, I repeat, you are too kind-hearted. Never imagine that I can be happy if you are not;" and I looked at her keenly, but she turned away instantly, saying:

"Well, then, I'll be very happy, and will test you," and she returned to her room.

"Mrs. Yocomb," I said quietly at the dinner-table, "I've written to the office saying that my friends do not think I'm well enough to return yet, and asking to have my leave extended."

She beamed upon me as she replied:

"Now thee's sensible."

"For once," I added.

"I expect to see thee clothed and in thy right mind yet," she said, with a little reassuring nod.

"Your hopeful disposition is contagious," I replied, laughing.

"I'd like to see thee get to the depot till we're ready to let thee go," said Reuben, emphatically.

"Yes," added Mr. Yocomb, with his genuine laugh, "Reuben and I are in league against thee."

"You look like two dark, muttering conspirators," I responded.

"And to think thee was going away without asking me!" Zillah put in, shaking her bright curls at me.

"Well, you all have made this home to me, true enough. The best part of me will be left here when I do go."

At these words Adah gave me a shy, blushing smile.

"Mr. Morton, will you please pass me the vinegar?" said Miss Warren, in the most matter-of-fact tone.

"Wouldn't you prefer the sugar?" I asked.

"No; I much prefer the vinegar."

Mr. Hearn also smiled approvingly.

"Don't be too sure of your prey," I said, mentally. "If she's not yours at heart—which I doubt more than ever—you shall never have her." But she puzzled me for a day or two. If she were not happy she simulated happiness, and made my poor acting a flimsy pretence in contrast. She and the banker took long rides together, and she was always exceedingly cheerful on her return—a little too much so, I tried to think. She ignored the past as completely as possible, and while her manner was kind to me she had regained her old-time delicate brusqueness, and rarely lost a chance to give me a friendly fillip. Indeed I had never known her to be so brilliant, and her spirits seemed unflagging. Mr. Yocomb was delighted and in his large appetite for fun applauded and joined in every phase of our home gayety. There was too much hilarity for me, and my hope failed steadily.

"Now that her conscience is clear in regard to me—now that I have remained in the country, and am getting well—her spirits have come up with a bound," I reasoned moodily. I began to resume my old tactics of keeping out of the way and of taking long rambles; but I tried to be cheerfulness itself in her presence.

On Wednesday Miss Warren came down to breakfast in a breezy, airy way, and, scarcely speaking to me as I stood in the doorway, she flitted out, and was soon romping with Zillah and Adela. As she returned, flushed and panting, I said, with a smile:

"You are indeed happy. I congratulate you. I believe I've never had the honor of doing that yet."

"But you said that you would be happy also?"

"Am I not?"

"No."

"Well, it doesn't matter since you are."

"Oh, then, I'm no longer kind-hearted. You take Reuben's view, that I'm a heartless monster. He scarcely speaks to me any more. You think I propose to be happy now under all circumstances."

"I wish you would be; I hope you may be. What's the use of my acting my poor little farce any longer? I don't deceive you a mite. But I'm not going to mope and pine, Miss Warren. Don't think of me so poorly as that. I'm not the first man who has had to face this thing. I'm going back to work, and I am going next Monday, surely."

"I've no doubt of it," she said, with sudden bitterness, "and you'll get over it bravely, very bravely;" and she started off toward the barn, where Reuben was exercising Dapple, holding him with a long rope. The horse seemed wild with life and spirit, and did I not know that the beautiful creature had not a vicious trait I should have feared for the boy. Just at this moment, Dapple in his play slipped off his headstall and was soon careering around the dooryard in the mad glee of freedom. In vain Reuben tried to catch him; for the capricious beast would allow him to come almost within grasp, and then would bound away. Miss Warren stood under a tree laughing till the boy was hot and angry. Then she cried:

"I'll catch him for you, Reuben."

I uttered a loud shout of alarm as she darted out before the galloping horse and threw up her arms.

Dapple stopped instantly; in another second she had her arm around his arched neck and was stroking his quivering nostrils. Her poise was full of grace and power; her eyes were shining with excitement and triumph, and, to make her mastery seem more complete, she leaned her face against his nose.

Dapple looked down at her in a sort of mild wonder, and was as meek as a lamb.

"There, Reuben, come and take him," she said to the boy, who stared at her with his mouth open.

"Emily Warren, I don't know what to make of thee," he exclaimed.

Never before had I so felt my unutterable loss, and I said to her almost savagely, in a low tone, as she approached:

"Is that the means you take to cure me—doing the bravest thing I ever saw a woman do, and looking like a goddess? I was an unspeakable fool for staying."

Her head drooped, and she walked dejectedly toward the house, not seeming to think of or care for the exclamations and expostulations which greeted her.

"Why, Emily, were you mad?" cried Mr. Hearn above the rest; and now that the careering horse was being led away he hastened down to meet her.

"No, I'm tired, and want a cup of coffee," I heard her say, and then I followed Reuben to the barn.

"She's cut me out with Dapple," said the boy, with a crestfallen air.

Already I repented of my harshness, into which I had been led by the sharpest stress of feeling, and was eager to make amends. Since the night of the storm honest Reuben had given me his unwavering loyalty. Still less than Adah was he inclined or able to look beneath the surface of things, and he had gained the impression from Miss Warren's words that she was inclined to make light of their danger on that occasion, and to laugh at me generally. In his sturdy championship in my behalf he had been growing cold and brusque toward one whom he now associated with the wealthy middle-aged banker, and city style generally. Reuben was a genuine country lad, and was instinctively hostile to Fifth Avenue. While Mr. Hearn was polite to his father and mother, he quite naturally laid more stress on their business relations than on those of friendship, and was not slow in asking for what he wanted, and his luxurious tastes led him to require a good deal. Reuben had seen his mother worried and his father inconvenienced not a little. They made no complaint, and had no cause for any, for the banker paid his way liberally. But the boy had not reached the age when the financial phase of the question was appreciated, and his prejudice was not unnatural, for unconsciously, especially at first, Mr. Hearn had treated them all as inferiors. He now was learning to know them better, however. There was nothing plebeian in Adah's beauty, and he would have been untrue to himself had he not admired her very greatly.

It was my wish to lead the boy to overcome his prejudice against Miss Warren, so I said:

"You are mistaken, Reuben; Dapple is just as fond of you as ever. It was only playfulness that made him cut up so; but, Reuben, Dapple is a very sensible horse, and when he saw a girl that was brave enough to stand right out before him when it seemed that he must run over her, he respected and liked such a girl at once. It was the bravest thing I ever saw. Any other horse would have trampled on her, but Dapple has the nature of a gentleman. So have you, Reuben, and I know you will go and speak handsomely to her. I know you will speak to her as Dapple would could he speak. By Jove! it was splendid, and you are man enough to know it was."

"Yes, Richard, it was. I know that as well as thee. There isn't a girl in the county that would have dared to do it, and very few men. And to think she's a city girl! To tell the truth, Emily Warren is all the time making game of thee, and that's why I'm mad at her."

"I don't think you understand her. I don't mind it, because she never means anything ill-natured; and then she loves your mother almost as much as you do. I give you my word, Reuben, Miss Warren and I are the best of friends, and you need not feel as you do, because I don't."

"Oh, well, if thee puts it that way, I'll treat her different. I tell thee what it is, Richard, I'm one that sticks to my friends through thick and thin."

"Well, you can't do anything so friendly to me as to make everything pleasant for Miss Warren. How is her favorite, Old Plod?" I asked, following him into the barn.

"Old Plod be hanged! She hasn't been near him in two weeks."

"What!" I exclaimed exultantly.

"What's the matter with thee, Richard? Thee and Emily are both queer. I can't make you out."

"Well, Reuben, we mean well; you mustn't expect too much of people."

CHAPTER XVI
RICHARD

I came in to breakfast with Reuben, feeling that Dapple had been more of a gentleman than I had, for he had treated the maiden with gentleness and courtesy, while I had thought first of myself. She looked up at me as I entered so humbly and deprecatingly that I wished that I had bitten my tongue out rather than have spoken so harshly.

Straightforward Reuben went to the girl, and, holding out his hand, said:

"Emily, I want to ask thy forgiveness. I've been like a bear toward thee. Thee's the bravest girl I ever saw. No country girl would have dared to do what thee did. I didn't need to have Richard lecture me and tell me that; but I thought thee was kind of down on Richard, and I've a way of standing by my friends."

With a face like a peony she turned and took both of the boy's hands as she said warmly:

"Thank you, Reuben. I'd take a much greater risk to win your friendship, and if you'll give it to me I'll be very proud of it. You are going to make a genuine man."

"Yes, Reuben, thee'll make a man," said his mother, with a low laugh. "Thee is as blind as a man already."

I looked at her instantly, but she dropped her eyes demurely to her plate. I saw that Mr. Hearn was watching me, and so did not look at Miss Warren.

"Well," said he irritably, "I don't like such escapades; and Emily, if anything of the kind happens again, I'll have to take you to a safer place."

His face was flushed, but hers was very pale.

"It won't happen again," she said quietly, without looking up.

"Richard," said Mr. Yocomb, as if glad to change the subject, "I've got to drive across the country on some business. I will have to be gone all day. Would thee like to go with me?"

"Certainly. I'll go with you to the ends of the earth."

"That would be too far away from mother. Thee always pulls me back very soon, doesn't thee?"

"Well, I know thee comes," replied his wife. "Don't tire Richard out; he isn't strong yet."

"Richard," said Mr. Yocomb, as we were driving up a long hill, "I want to congratulate thee on thy course toward Emily Warren. Thee's a strong-minded, sensible man. I saw that thee was greatly taken with her at first, and no wonder. Besides, I couldn't help hearing what thee said when out of thy mind. Mother and I kept the children away then, and Doctor Bates had the wink from me to be discreet; but thee's been a sensible man since thee got up, and put the whole thing away from thee very bravely."

"Mr. Yocomb, I won't play the hypocrite with you. I love her better than my own soul."

"Thee does?" he said, in strong surprise.

"Yes, and I ought to have gone away long ago, I fear. How could I see her as she appeared this morning, and not almost worship her?"

The old gentleman gave a long, low whistle. "I guess mother meant me when she said men were blind."

I was silent, not daring, of course, to say that I hoped she meant me, but what I had heard and seen that morning had done much to confirm my hope.

"Well," said the old gentleman, "I can scarcely blame thee, since she is what she is, and I can't help saying, too, that I think thee would make her happier than that man can, with all his money. I don't think he appreciates her. She will be only a part of his great possessions."

"Well, Mr. Yocomb, I've but these requests to make. Keep this to yourself, and don't interpose any obstacles to my going next Monday. Don't worry about me. I'll keep up; and a man who will have to work as I must won't have time to mope. I won't play the weak fool, for I'd rather have your respect and Mrs. Yocomb's than all Mr. Hearn's millions; and Miss Warren's respect is absolutely essential to me."

"Then thee thinks that mother and—and Emily know?"

"Who can hide anything from such women! They look through us as if we were glass."

"Mother's sermon meant more for thee than I thought."

"Yes, I felt as if it were preached for me. I hope I may be the better for it some day; but I've too big a fight on my hands now to do much else. You will now understand why I wish to get away so soon, and why I can't come back till I've gained a strength that is not bodily. I wouldn't like you to misunderstand me, after your marvellous kindness, and so I'm frank. Besides, you're the kind of man that would thaw an icicle. Your nature is large and gentle, and I don't mind letting you know."

"Richard, we're getting very frank, and I'm going to be more so. I don't like the way Mr. Hearn sits and looks at Adah."

"Oh, you needn't worry about him. Mr. Hearn is respectability itself; but he's wonderfully fond of good things and pretty things. His great house on Fifth Avenue is full of them, and he looks at Miss Adah as he would at a fine oil painting."

"Thee speaks charitably of him under the circumstances."

"I ought to try to do him justice, since I hate him so cordially."

"Well," said the old gentleman, laughing, "that's a new way of putting it. Thee's honest, Richard."

"If I wasn't I'd have no business in your society."

"I'm worried about Emily," broke out my companion. "She was a little thin and worn from her long season of work when she came to us lately; but the first week she picked up daily. While thee was so sick she seemed more worried than any one, and I had much ado to get her to eat enough to keep a bird alive; but it's been worse for the last two weeks. She has seemed much brighter lately for some reason, but the flesh just seems to drop off of her. She takes a wonderful hold of my feelings, and I can't help troubling about her."

"Mr. Yocomb, your words torture me," I cried. "It is not my imagination then. Can she love that man?"

"Well, she has a queer way of showing it; but it is one of those things that an outsider can't meddle with."

I was moody and silent the rest of the day, and Mr. Yocomb had the tact to leave me much to myself; but I was not under the necessity of acting my poor farce before him.

The evening was quite well advanced when we reached the farmhouse; but Mrs. Yocomb had a royal supper for us, and she said every one had insisted on waiting till we returned. Mr. Hearn had quite recovered his complacency, and I gathered from this fact that Miss Warren had been very devoted. Such was his usual aspect when everything was pleasing to him.

But she who had added so much to his life had seemingly drained her own, for she looked so pale and thin that my heart ached. There were dark lines under her eyes, and she appeared exceedingly wearied, as if the day had been one long effort.

"She can't love him," I thought. "It's impossible. Confound him! he's the blindest man of us all. Oh that I had her insight, that I might unravel this snarl at once, for it would kill me to see her looking like that much longer. What's the use of my going away? I've been away all day; she has had the light of his smiling countenance uninterruptedly, and see how worn she is. Can it be that my hateful words hurt her, and that she is grieving about me only? It's impossible. Unselfish regard for another could not go so far if her own heart was at rest. She is doing her best to laugh and talk and to seem cheerful, but her acting now is poorer than mine ever was. She is tired out; she seems like a soldier who is fighting mechanically after spirit, courage, and strength are gone."

Mr. Hearn informed Mr. Yocomb that important business would require his presence in New York for a few days. "It's an enterprise that involves immense interests on both sides of the ocean, and there's to be quite a gathering of capitalists. Your paper will be full of it before very long, Mr. Morton."

"I'm always glad to hear of any grist for our mill," I said. "Mrs. Yocomb, please excuse me. I'm selfish enough to prefer the cool piazza."

"But thee hasn't eaten anything."

"Oh, yes, I have, and I made a huge dinner," I replied carelessly, and sauntered out and lighted a cigar. Instead of coming out on the piazza, as I hoped, Miss Warren bade Mr. Hearn good-night in the hall, and, pleading fatigue, went to her room.

She was down to see him off in the morning, and at his request accompanied him to the depot. I was reading on the piazza when she returned, and I hastened to assist her from the rockaway.

"Miss Warren," I exclaimed, in deep solicitude, "this long, hot ride has been too much for you."

"Perhaps it has," she replied briefly, without meeting my eyes. "I'll go and rest."

She pleaded a headache, and did not come down to dinner. Mrs. Yocomb returned from her room with a troubled face.

I had resolved that I would not seek to see her alone while Mr. Hearn was away, and so resumed my long rambles. When I returned, about supper time, she was sitting on the piazza watching Adela and Zillah playing with their dolls. She did not look up as I took a seat on the steps not far away.

At last I began, "Can I tell you that I am very sorry you have been ill to-day?"

"I wasn't dangerous, as country people say," she replied, a little brusquely.

"You look as if Dapple might run over you now."

"A kitten might run over me," she replied briefly, still keeping her eyes on the children.

By and by she asked, "Why do you look at me so intently, Mr. Morton?"

"I beg your pardon."

"That's not answering my question."

"Suppose I deny that I was looking at you. You have not condescended to glance at me yet."

"You had better not deny it."

"Well, then, to tell you the truth, as I find I always must, I was looking for some trace of mercy. I was thinking whether I could venture to ask forgiveness for being more of a brute than Dapple yesterday."

"Have your words troubled you very much?"

"They have indeed."

"Well, they've troubled me too. You think I'm heartless, Mr. Morton;" and she arose and went to her piano.

I followed her instantly. "Won't you forgive me?" I asked; "I've repented."

"Oh, nonsense, Mr. Morton. You know as well as I do that I'm the one to ask forgiveness."

"No, I don't," I said, in a low, passionate tone. "I fear you are grieving about what you can't help."

"Can't help?" she repeated, flushing.

"Yes, my being here makes you unhappy. If I knew it, I'd go to-night."

"And you think that out of sight would be out of mind," she said, with a strange smile.

"Great God! I don't know what to think. I know that I would do anything under heaven to make you look as you did the first night I saw you."

"Do I look so badly?"

"You look as if you might take wings and leave us at any moment."

"Then I wouldn't trouble you any more."

"Then my trouble would be without remedy. Marry Mr. Hearn; marry him to-morrow, if you wish. I assure you that if you will be honestly and truly happy, I won't mope a day—I'll become the jolliest old bachelor in New York. I'll do anything within the power of man to make you your old joyous self."

Now at last she turned her large, glorious eyes upon me, and their expression was sadness itself; but she only said quietly:

"I believe you, Mr. Morton."

"Then tell me, what can I do?"

"Come to supper;" and she rose and left me.

I went to my old seat by the window, and the tumult in my heart was in wide contrast with the quiet summer evening.

"You are mistaken, Emily Warren," I thought. "You have as much as said that I can do nothing for you. I'll break your chain. You shall not marry Gilbert Hearn, if I have to protest in the very church and before the altar. You are mine, by the best and divinest right, and with your truth as my ally I'll win you yet. From this hour I dedicate myself to your happiness. Heavens, how blind I've been!"

"Come, Richard," said Mrs. Yocomb, putting her head within the door.

Miss Warren sat in her place, silent and apathetic. She had the aspect of one who had submitted to the inevitable, but would no longer pretend she liked it. Mr. Yocomb was regarding her furtively, with a clouded brow, and Adah's glances were frequent and perplexed. I felt as if walking on air, and my heart was aglow with gladness; but I knew her far too well to show what was in my mind. My purpose now was to beguile the hours till I could show her what truth really required of her. With the utmost tact that I possessed, and with all the zest that hope confirmed inspired, I sought to diffuse a general cheerfulness, and I gradually drew her into the current of our talk. After supper I told them anecdotes of public characters and eminent people, for my calling gave me a great store of this kind of information. Ere she was aware, the despondent girl was asking questions, and my answers piqued her interest still more; at last, quite late in the evening, Mr. Yocomb exclaimed:

"Look here, Richard, what right has thee to keep me out of my bed long after regular hours? I'm not a night editor. Good people, you must all go to bed. I'm master of this house. Now, don't say anything, mother, to take me down."

Finding myself alone with Miss Warren a moment in the hall, I asked:

"Have I not done more than merely come to supper?"

She turned from me instantly, and went swiftly up the stairway.

But the apathetic, listless look was on her face when she came down in the morning, and she appeared as if passively yielding to a dreaded necessity. I resumed my old tactics, and almost in spite of herself drew her into the genial family life. Mr. Yocomb seconded me with unflagging zeal and commendable tact, while Mrs. Yocomb surpassed us both. Adah seemed a little bewildered, as if there were something in the air which she could not understand. But we made the social sunshine of the house so natural and warm that she could not resist it.

"Reuben," I said, after breakfast, "Miss Warren is not well. A ride after Dapple is the best medicine I ever took. Take Miss Warren out for a swift, short drive; don't let her say no. You have the tact to do the thing in the right way."

She did decline repeatedly, but he so persisted that she at last said:

"There, Reuben, I will go with you."

"I think thee might do that much for a friend, as thee calls me."

When she returned there was a faint color in her cheeks. The rapid drive had done her good, and I told her so as I helped her from the light wagon.

"Yes, Mr. Morton, it has, and I thank *you* for the drive very much. Let me suggest that Reuben is much too honest for a conspirator."

"Well, he was a very willing one; and I see by his face, as he drives down to the barn, that you have made him a happy one."

"It doesn't take much to make him happy."

"And would it take such an enormous amount to make you happy?"

"You are much too inclined to be personal to be an editor. The world at large should hold your interest;" and she went to her room.

At the dinner-table the genial spell worked on; she recognized it with a quiet smile, but yielded to its kindly power. At last she apparently formed the resolution to make the most of this one bright day, and she became the life of the party.

"Emily," said Mrs. Yocomb, as we rose from the table, "father proposes that we all go on a family picnic to Silver Pond, and take our supper there. It's only three miles away. Would thee feel strong enough to go?"

Mrs. Yocomb spoke with the utmost simplicity and innocence; but the young girl laughed outright, then fixed a penetrating glance on Mr. Yocomb, whose florid face became much more ruddy.

"Evidences of guilt clearly apparent," she said, "and Mr. Morton, too, looks very conscious. 'The best laid schemes of mice and men'—you know the rest. Oh, yes, I'd go if I had to be carried. When webs are spun so kindly, flies ought to be caught."

"What is the matter with you all?" cried Adah.

"Miss Adah, if you'll find me a match for my cigar you'll make me happy," I said hastily, availing myself of the first line of retreat open.

"Is that all thee needs to make thee happy?"

"Well, one thing at a time, Miss Adah, if you please."

As the day grew cool, Reuben came around with the family rockaway. Mrs. Yocomb and Adah had prepared a basket as large as their own generous natures. I placed Miss Warren beside Mrs. Yocomb on the back seat, while I took my place by Adah, with Zillah between us. Little Adela and Reuben had become good friends, and she insisted on sitting between him and his father.

As we rolled along the quiet country roads, chatting, laughing, and occasionally singing a snatch of a song, no one would have dreamed that any shadows rested on the party except those which slanted eastward from the trees, which often hung far over our heads.

I took pains not to feign any forced gayety, nor had I occasion to, for I was genuinely happy—happier than I had ever been before. Nothing was assured save the absolute truth of the woman that I loved, but with this ally I was confident. I was impartial in my attentions to Adah and Zillah, and so friendly to both that Adah was as pleased and happy as the child. We chaffed the country neighbors whom we met, and even chattered back at the barking squirrels that whisked before us along the fences. Mr. Yocomb seemed almost as much of a boy as Reuben, and for some reason Miss Warren always laughed most at his pleasantries. Mrs. Yocomb looked as placid and bright as Silver Pond, as it at last glistened beneath us in the breathless, sunny afternoon; but like the clear surface fringed with shadows that sank far beneath the water, there were traces of many thoughts in her large blue eyes.

There was a cow lying under the trees where we meant to spread our table. I pointed her out to Miss Warren with humorous dismay. "Shall we turn back?" I asked.

"No," she replied, looking into my eyes gratefully. "You have become so brave that I'm not afraid to go on."

I ignored her reference to that which I intended she should forget for one day, believing that if we could make her happy she would recognize how far her golden-haloed lover came short of this power. So I said banteringly, "I'll wager you my hat that you dare not get out and drive that terrific beast away."

"The idea of Emily's being afraid of a cow, after facing Dapple!" cried Reuben.

"Well, we'll see," I said. "Stop the rockaway here."

"What should I do with your hat, Mr. Morton?"

"Wear it, and suffer the penalty," laughed Adah.

"You would surely win it," retorted the girl, a little nettled.

"I'll wager you a box of candy then, or anything you please."

"Let it be anything I please," she agreed, laughing. "Mr. Morton, you are not going to let me get out alone?"

"Oh, no," and I sprang out to assist her down.

"She wants you to be on hand in case the ferocious beast switches its tail," cried Adah.

The hand she gave me trembled as I helped her out, and I saw that she regarded the placid creature with a dread that she could not disguise. Picking up a little stick, she stepped cautiously and hesitatingly toward the animal. While still ridiculously far away, she stopped, brandished her stick, and said, with a quaver in her threatening tone, "Get up, I tell you!"

But the cow ruminated quietly as if understanding well that there was no occasion for alarm.

The girl took one or two more faltering steps, and exclaimed, in a voice of desperate entreaty, "Oh, please get up!"

We could scarcely contain ourselves for laughter.

"Oh, ye gods! how beautiful she is!" I murmured. "With her arm over Dapple's neck she was a goddess. Now she's a shrinking woman. Heaven grant that it may be my lot to protect her from the real perils of life!"

The cow suddenly switched her tail at a teasing gadfly, and the girl precipitately sought my side.

Reuben sprang out of the rockaway and lay down and rolled in his uncontrollable mirth.

"Was there anything ever so ridiculous?" cried Adah; for to the country girl Miss Warren's fear was affectation.

At Adah's words Miss Warren's face suddenly became white and resolute.

"You, at least, shall not despise me," she said to me in a low tone; and shutting her eyes she made a blind rush toward the cow. I had barely time to catch her, or she would have thrown herself on the horns of the startled animal that, with tail in air, careered away among the trees. The girl was so weak and faint that I had to support her; but I could not forbear saying, in a tone that she alone heard:

"Do we ever despise that which we love supremely?"

"Hush!" she answered sternly.

Mrs. Yocomb was soon at our side with a flask of currant wine, and Adah laughed a little bitterly as she said, "It was 'as good as a play'!" Miss Warren recovered herself speedily by the aid of the generous wine, and this was the only cloud on our simple festivity. In her response to my ardent words she seemingly had satisfied her conscience, and she acted like one bent on making the most of this one occasion of fleeting pleasure.

Adah was the only one who mentioned the banker. "How Mr. Hearn would have enjoyed being here with us!" she exclaimed.

Miss Warren's response was a sudden pallor and a remorseful expression; but Mr. Yocomb and I speedily created a diversion of thought; I saw, however, that Adah was watching her with a perplexed brow. The hours quickly passed, and in the deepening shadows we returned homeward, Miss Warren singing some sweet old ballads, to which my heart kept time.

She seemed both to bring the evening to a close, and sat down at the piano. Adah and I listened, well content. Having put the children to bed Mrs. Yocomb joined us, and we chatted over the pleasant trip while waiting for Mr. Yocomb and Reuben, who had not returned from the barn. At last Mrs. Yocomb said heartily, as if summing it all up:

"Well, Richard, thee's given us a bright, merry afternoon."

"Yes, Richard," Miss Warren began, as if her heart had spoken unawares—"I beg your pardon—Mr. Morton—" and then she stopped in piteous confusion, for I had turned toward her with all my unspeakable love in my face.

Adah's laugh rang out a little harshly.

I hastened to the rescue of the embarrassed girl, saying, "I don't see why you should beg my pardon. We're all Friends here. At least I'm trying to be one as fast as a leopard can change his spots and the Ethiopian his skin. As for you, a tailor would say you were cut from the same cloth as Mrs. Yocomb."

But for some reason she could not recover herself. She probably realized, in the tumult of her feeling, that she had revealed her heart too clearly, and she could not help seeing that Adah understood her. She was too confused for further pretence, and too unnerved to attempt it. After a moment of pitiful hesitation she fled with a scarlet face to her room.

"Well," said Adah, with a slight hysterical laugh, "I understand Emily Warren now."

"Pardon me, Miss Adah, I don't think you do," I began.

"If thee doesn't, thee's blind indeed."

"I am blind."

"Be assured I'm not any longer," and with a deep angry flush she, too, left us.

I turned to Mrs. Yocomb, and taking both of her hands I entreated, "As you have the heart of a woman, never let Emily Warren marry that man. Help me—help us both!"

"My poor boy," she began, "this is a serious matter—"

"It is indeed," I said, passionately; "it's a question of life and death to us both."

"Well," she said, thoughtfully, "I think time and truth will be on thy side in the end; but I would advise thee not to do or say anything rash or hasty. She is very resolute. Give her time."

Would to God I had taken her advice!

CHAPTER XVII
MY WORST BLUNDER

I scarcely could foresee how we should get through the following day. I both longed for and dreaded it, feeling that though it might pass quietly enough, it would probably be decisive in its bearing on the problem of my life. Miss Warren would at last be compelled to face the truth squarely, that she had promised a man what she could not give, and that to permit him to go on blindly trusting would be impossible. The moment she realized fully that she had never truly loved him, and now never could, she would give up the pretence. Then why should she not see that love, duty, and truth could go together? That she had struggled desperately to be loyal to Mr. Hearn was sadly proved by her thin face and wasted form; but with a nature like hers, when once her genuine love was evoked, the effort to repress it was as vain as seeking to curb a rising tide. I now saw, as I looked back over the past weeks, that her love had grown steadily and irresistibly till it had overwhelmed all save her will and conscience; that these stood, the two solitary landmarks of her former world. And I knew they would stand, and that my only hope was to stand with them. Her love had gone out to me as mine had to her, from a constraint that she could not resist, and this fact I hoped would reveal to her its sacred right to live. With every motive that would naturally bind her to a man who could give her so much, her heart claimed its mate in one who must daily toil long hours for subsistence. It would be like her to recognize that a love so unthrifty and unselfish must spring from the deepest truths and needs of her being rather than from any passing causes. She would come to believe as I did, that God had created us for each other.

But it seemed as if the whole world had changed and gone awry when we sat down to breakfast the next morning. Adah was polite to me, but she was cool and distant. She no longer addressed me in the Friendly tongue. It was "you" now. I had ceased to be one of them, in her estimation. Her father and mother looked grave and worried, but they were as kind and cordial to me as ever. Reuben and the little girls were evidently mystified by the great change in the social atmosphere, but were too inexperienced to understand it. I was pained by Adah's manner, but did not let it trouble me, feeling assured that as she thought the past over she would do me justice, and that our relations would become substantially those of a brother and sister.

But I was puzzled and alarmed beyond measure by Miss Warren's manner and appearance, and my feelings alternated between the deepest sympathy and the strongest fear. She looked as if she had grown old in the night, and was haggard from sleeplessness. Her deep eyes had sunken deeper than ever, and the lines under them were dark indeed, but her white face was full of a cold scorn, and she held herself aloof from us all.

She looked again as if capable of any blind, desperate self-sacrifice.

Simple, honest Mr. Yocomb was sorely perplexed, but his wife's face was grave and inscrutable. If I had only gone quietly away and left the whole problem to her, how much better it would have been!

I tried to speak to Miss Warren in a pleasant, natural way; her answers were brief and polite, but nothing more. Before the meal was over she excused herself and returned to her room. I felt almost indignant. What had I—most of all, what had her kind, true friends, Mr. and Mrs. Yocomb— done to warrant that cold, half—scornful face? Her coming to breakfast was but a form, and she clearly wished to leave us at the earliest possible moment. Adah smiled satirically as she passed out, and the expression did not become her fair face.

I strode out to the arbor in the garden and stared moodily at the floor, I know not how long, for I was greatly mystified and baffled, and my very soul was consumed with anxiety.

"She shall listen to reason," I muttered again and again. "This question must be settled in accordance with truth—the simple, natural truth—and nothing else. She's mine, and nothing shall separate us—not even her perverse will and conscience;" and so the heavy hours passed in deep perturbation.

At last I heard a step, and looking through the leaves I saw the object of my thoughts coming through the garden, reading a letter. My eyes glistened with triumph. "The chance I coveted has come," I muttered, and I watched her intently. She soon crushed the letter in her hand and came swiftly toward the arbor, with a face so full of deep and almost wild distress that my heart relented, and I resolved to be as gentle as I before had intended to be decisive and argumentative. I hastily changed my seat to the angle by the entrance, so that I could intercept her should she try to escape the interview.

She entered, and throwing herself down on the seat, buried her face in her arm.

"Miss Warren," I began.

She started up with a passionate gesture. "You have no right to intrude on me now," she said, almost sternly.

"Pardon me, were I not here when you entered, I would still have a right to come. You are in deep distress. Why must I be inhuman any more than yourself? You have at least promised me friendship, but you treat me like an enemy."

"You have been my worst enemy."

"I take issue with you there at once. I've never had a thought toward you that was not most kind and loyal.

"Loyal!" she replied, bitterly; "that word in itself is a stab."

"Miss Warren," I said, very gently, "you make discord in the old garden to-day."

She dropped her letter on the ground and sank on the seat again. Such a passion of sobs shook her slight frame that I trembled with apprehension. But I kept quiet, believing that Nature could care for her child better than I could, and that her outburst of feeling would bring relief. At last, as she became a little more self-controlled, I said, gravely and kindly:

"There must be some deep cause for this deep grief."

"Oh, what shall I do?" she sobbed. "What shall I do? I wish the earth would open and swallow me up."

"That wish is as vain as it is cruel. I wish you would tell me all, and let me help you. I think I deserve it at your hands."

"Well, since you know so much, you may as well know all. It doesn't matter now, since every one will soon know. He has written that his business will take him to Europe within a month—that we must be married—that he will bring his sister here to-night to help me make arrangements. Oh! oh! I'd rather die than ever see him again. I've wronged him so cruelly, so causelessly."

In wild exultation I snatched a pocketbook from my coat and cried:

"Miss Warren—Emily—do you remember this little York and Lancaster bud that you gave me the day we first met? Do you remember my half-jesting, random words, 'To the victor belong the spoils'? See, the victor is at your feet."

She sprang up and turned her back upon me. "Rise!" she said, in a voice so cold and stern that, bewildered, I obeyed.

She soon became as calm as before she had been passionate and unrestrained in her grief; but it was a stony quietness that chilled and disheartened me before she spoke.

"It does indeed seem as if the truth between us could never be hidden," she said, bitterly. "You have now very clearly shown your estimate of me. You regard me as one of those weak women of the past whom the strongest carry off. You have been the stronger in this case—oh, you know it well! Not even in the house of God could I escape your vigilant scrutiny. You hoped and watched and waited for me to be false. Should I yield to you, you would never forget that I had been false, and, in accordance with your creed, you would ever fear—that is, if your passion lasted long enough—the coming of one still stronger, to whom in the weak necessity of my nature, I again would yield. Low as I have fallen, I will never accept from a man a mere passion devoid of respect and honor. I'm no longer entitled to these, therefore I'll accept nothing."

She poured out these words like a torrent, in spite of my gestures of passionate dissent, and my efforts to be heard; but it was a cold, pitiless torrent. Excited as I was, I saw how intense was her self-loathing. I also saw despairingly that she embraced me in her scorn.

"Miss Warren," I said, dejectedly, "since you are so unjust to yourself, what hope have I?"

"There is little enough for either of us," she continued, more bitterly; "at least there is none for me. You will, no doubt, get bravely over it, as you said. Men generally do, especially when in their hearts they have no respect for the woman with whom they are infatuated. Mr. Morton, the day of your coming was indeed the day of *my* fate. I wish you could have saved the lives of the others, but not mine. I could then have died in peace, with honor unstained. But now, what is my life but an intolerable burden of shame and self-reproach? Without cause and beyond the thought of forgiveness, I've wronged a good, honorable man, who has been a kind and faithful friend for years. He is bringing his proud, aristocratic sister here to-night to learn how false and contemptible I am. The people among whom I earned my humble livelihood will soon know how unfit I am to be trusted with their daughters—that I am one who falls a spoil to the strongest. I have lost everything—chief of all my pearl of great price—my truth. What have I left? Is there a more impoverished creature in the world? There is nothing left to me but bare existence and hateful memories. Oh, the lightning was dim compared with the vividness with which I've seen it all since that hateful moment last night, when the truth became evident even to Adah Yocomb. But up to that moment, even up to this hour, I hoped you pitied me—that you were watching and waiting to help me to be true and not to be false. I did not blame you greatly for your love—my own weakness made me lenient—and at first you did not know. But since you now openly seek that which belongs to another; since you now exult that you are the stronger, and that I have become your spoil, I feel, though I cannot yet see and realize the depths into which I have fallen. Even to-day you might have helped me as a friend, and shown me how some poor shred of my truth might have been saved; but you snatch at me as if I were but the spoil of the strongest. Mr. Morton, either you or I must leave the farmhouse at once."

"This is the very fanaticism of truth," I cried, desperately. "Your mind is so utterly warped and morbid from dwelling on one side of this question that you are cruelly unjust."

"Would that I had been less kind and more just. I felt sorry for you, from the depths of my heart. Why have you had no pity for me? You are a man of the world, and know it. Why did you not show me to what this wretched weakness would lead? I thought you meant this kindness when you said you wished my brother was here. Oh that I were sleeping beside him! I thought you meant this when you said that nothing would last, nothing could end well unless built on the truth. I hoped you were watching me with the vigilance of a man who, though loving me, was so strong and generous and honorable that he would try to save me from a weakness that I cannot understand, and which was the result of strange and unforeseen circumstances. When you were so ill I felt as if I had dealt you your death-blow, and then, woman-like, I loved you. I loved you before I recognized my folly. Up to that point we could scarcely help ourselves. For weeks I tried to hide the truth from myself. I fought against it. I prayed against it through sleepless nights. I tried to hide the truth from you most of all. But I remember the flash of hope in your face when you first surmised my miserable secret. It hurt me cruelly. Your look should have been one of dismay and sorrow. But I know something of the weakness of the heart, and its first impulse might naturally be that of gladness, although honor must have changed it almost instantly into deep regret. Then I believed that you were sorry, and that it was your wish to help me. I thought it was your purpose yesterday to show me that I could be happy, even in the path of right and duty, that had become so hard, though you spoke once as you ought not. But when I, unawares, and from the impulse of a grateful heart, spoke your name last night as that of my truest and best friend, as I thought, you turned toward me the face of a lover, and to-day—but it's all over. Will you go?"

"Are Mr. and Mrs. Yocomb false?" I cried.

"No, they are too simple and true to realize the truth. Mr. Morton, I think we fully understand each other now. Since you will not go, I shall. You had better remain here and grow strong. Please let me pass."

"I wish you had dealt me my death-blow. It were a merciful one compared with this. No, you don't understand me at all. You have portrayed me as a vile monster. Because you cannot keep your engagement with a man you never truly loved, you inflict the torments of hell on the man you do love, and whom Heaven meant you to love. Great God! you are not married to Gilbert Hearn. Have not engagements often been broken for good and sufficient reasons? Is not the truth that our hearts almost instantly claimed eternal kindred a sufficient cause? I watched and waited that I might know whether you were his or mine. I did not seek to win you from him after I knew—after I remembered. But when I knew the truth, you *were* mine. Before God I assert my right, and before His altar I would protest against your marriage to any other."

She sank down on the arbor seat, white and faint, but made a slight repellent gesture.

"Yes, I'll go," I said, bitterly; "and such a scene as this might well cause a better man than I to go to the devil;" and I strode away.

But before I had taken a dozen steps my heart relented, and I returned. Her face was again buried in her right arm and her left hand hung by her side.

I took it in both of my own as I said, gently and sadly:

"Emily Warren, you may scorn me—you may refuse ever to see my face again; but I have dedicated my life to your happiness, and I shall keep my vow. It may be of no use, but God looketh at the intent of the heart. Heathen though I am, I cannot believe he will let the June day when we first met prove so fatal to us both: the God of whom Mrs. Yocomb told us wants no harsh, useless self-sacrifice. You are not false, and never have been. Mrs. Yocomb is not more true. I respect and honor you, as I do my mother's memory, though my respect now counts so little to you. I never meant to wrong you or pain you; I meant your happiness first and always. If you care to know, my future life shall show whether I am a gentleman or a villain. May God show you how cruelly unjust you are to yourself. I shall attempt no further self-defence. Good-by."

She trembled; but she only whispered:

"Good-by. Go, and forget."

"When I forget you—when I fail in loving loyalty to you, may God forget me!" I replied, and I hastened from the garden with as much sorrow and bitterness in my heart as the first man could have felt when the angel drove him from Eden. Alas! I was going out alone into a world that had become thorny indeed.

As I approached the house Mrs. Yocomb happened to come out on the piazza.

I took her hand and drew her toward the garden gate. She saw that I was almost speechless from trouble, and with her native wisdom divined it all.

"I did not take your advice," I groaned, "accursed fool that I was! But no matter about me. Save Emily from herself. As you believe in God's mercy, watch over her as you watched over me. Show her the wrong of wrecking both of our lives. She's in the arbor there. Go and stay with her till I am gone. You are my only hope. God bless you for all your kindness to me. Please write: I shall be in torment till I hear from you. Good-by."

I watched her till I saw her enter the arbor, then hastened to the barn, where Reuben was giving the horses their noonday feeding.

"Reuben," I said, quietly, "I'm compelled to go to New York at once. We can catch the afternoon train, if you are prompt. Not a word, old fellow. I've no time now to explain. I must go, and I'll walk if you won't take me;" and I hastened to the house and packed for departure with reckless haste.

At the foot of the moody stairway I met Adah.

"Are you going away?" she tried to say distantly, with face averted.

"Yes, Miss Adah, and I fear you are glad."

"No," she said, brokenly, and turning she gave me her hand. "I can't keep this up any longer, Richard. Since we first met I've been very foolish, very weak, and thee—thee has been a true gentleman toward me."

"I wish I might be a true brother. God knows I feel like one."

"Thee—thee saved my life, Richard. I was wicked to forget that for a moment. Will thee forgive me?"

"I'll forgive you only as you will let me become the most devoted brother a girl ever had, for I love and respect you, Adah, very, very much."

Tears rushed into the warm-hearted girl's eyes. She put her arms around my neck and kissed me. "Let this seal that agreement," she said, "and I'll be thy sister in heart as well as in name."

"How kind and good you are, Adah!" I faltered. "You are growing like your mother now. When you come to New York you will see how I keep my word," and I hastened away.

Mr. Yocomb intercepted me in the path.

"How's this? how's this?" he cried.

"I must go to New York at once," I said. "Mrs. Yocomb will explain all. I have a message for Mr. Hearn. Please say that I will meet him at any time, and will give any explanations to which he has a right. Good-by; I won't try to thank you for your kindness, which I shall value more and more every coming day."

For a long time we rode in silence, Reuben looking as grim and lowering as his round, ruddy face permitted.

At last he broke out, "Now, I say, blast Emily Warren's grandfather!"

"No, Reuben, my boy," I replied, putting my arm around him, "with all his millions, I'm heartily sorry for Mr. Hearn."

CHAPTER XVIII
MRS. YOCOMB'S LETTERS

I will not weary the reader with my experiences after arriving at New York. I could not have felt worse had I been driven into the Dismal Swamp. My apartments were dusty and stifling, and as cheerless as my feelings.

My editorial chief welcomed me cordially, and talked business. "After you had gone," he was kind enough to say, "we learned your value. Night work is too wearing for you, so please take that office next to mine. I feel a little like breaking down myself, and don't intend to wait until I do, as you did. I shall be off a great deal the rest of the summer, and you'll have to manage things."

"Pile on work," I said; "I'm greedy for it."

"Yes," he replied, laughing, "I appreciate that rare trait of yours; but I shall regard you as insubordinate if you don't take proper rest. Give us your brains, Morton, and leave hack work to others. That's where you blundered before."

Within an hour I was caught in the whirl of the great complicated world, and, as I said to Mr. Yocomb, I had indeed no time to mope. Thank God for work! It's the best antidote this world has for trouble.

But when night came my brain was weary and my heart heavy as lead. It seemed as if the farmhouse was in another world, so diverse was everything there from my present life.

I had given my uptown address to Mrs. Yocomb and went home—if I may apply that term to my dismal boarding-place—Tuesday night, feeling assured that there must be a letter. Good Mrs. Yocomb had not failed me, for on my table lay a bulky envelope, addressed in a quaint but clear hand. I was glad no one saw how my hand trembled as I opened her missive and read:

"My Dear Richard—I know how anxious thee is for tidings from us all, and especially from one toward whom thy heart is very tender. I will take up the sad story where thee left it. Having all the facts, thee can draw thy own conclusions.

"I found Emily in an almost fainting condition, and I just took her in my arms and let her cry like a child until tears brought relief. It was no time for words. Then I brought her into the house and gave her something that made her sleep in spite of herself. She awoke about an hour before Gilbert Hearn's arrival, and her nervous trepidation at the thought of meeting him was so great that I resolved she should not see him—at least not that night—and I told her so. This gave her great relief, though she said it was cowardly in her to feel so. But in truth she was too ill to see him. Her struggle had been too long and severe, and her nervous system was utterly prostrated. I had Doctor Bates here when Gilbert Hearn came, and the doctor is very discreet. I told him that he must manage so that Emily need not see the one she so feared to meet again, and hinted plainly why, though making no reference to thee, of course. The doctor acted as I wished, not because I wished it, but on professional grounds. 'Miss Warren's future health depends on absolute rest and quiet,' he said to her affianced. 'I not only advise that you do not see her, but I forbid it,' for he was terribly excited—so was his sister, Charlotte Bradford—and it was as much as we could do to keep them from going to her room. If they had, I believe the excitement would have destroyed either her life or reason. Gilbert Hearn plainly intimated that something was wrong. 'Very well, then,' I said, 'bring thy own family physician, and let him consult with Doctor Bates,' and this he angrily said he would do on the morrow. The very fact they were in the house made the poor girl almost wild; but I stayed with her all night, and she just lay in my arms like a frightened child, and my heart yearned over her as if she were my own daughter. She did not speak of thee, but I heard her murmur once, 'I was cruel—I was unjust to him.'

"In the morning she was more composed, and I made her take strong nourishment, I can tell thee. Thee remembers how I used to dose thee in spite of thyself. _

"Well, in the morning Emily seemed to be thinking deeply; and by and by she said: 'Mrs. Yocomb, I want this affair settled at once. I want you to sit by me while I write to him, and advise me.' I felt she was right. Her words were about as follows: (I asked her if I could tell thee what she wrote. She hesitated a little, and a faint color came into her pale face. 'Yes,' she said at last, 'let him know the whole truth. Since so much has occurred between us, I want him to know everything. He then may judge me as he thinks best. I have a horror of any more misunderstanding.')

"'You can never know, Mr. Hearn,' she wrote, 'the pain and sorrow with which I address to you these words. Still less can you know my shame and remorse; but you are an honorable man, and have a right to the truth. My best hope is that when you know how unworthy I am of your regard your regret will be slight. I recall all your kindness to me, and my heart is tortured as I now think of the requital I am making. Still, justice to myself requires that I tell you that I mistook my gratitude and esteem, my respect and genuine regard, for a deeper emotion. You will remember, however, that I long hesitated, feeling instinctively that I could not give you what you had a right to expect. Last spring you pressed me for a definite answer. I said I would come to this quiet place and think it all over, and if I did not write you to the contrary within a few days you might believe that I had yielded to your wishes. I found myself more worn and weary from my toilsome life than I imagined. I was lonely; I dreaded my single-handed struggle with the world, and my heart overflowed with gratitude toward you—it does still—for your kindness, and for all that you promised to do for me. I had not the will nor the disposition to say no, or to put you off any longer. Still I had misgiving; I feared that I did not feel as I ought. When I received your kind letter accepting my silence as consent, I felt bound by it—I was bound by it. I have no defence to make. I can only state the miserable truth. I cannot love you as a wife ought, and I know now that I never can. I've tried—God knows I've tried. I'm worn out with the struggle. I fear I am very ill. I wish I were dead and at rest. I cannot ask you to think mercifully of me. I cannot think mercifully of myself. To meet again would be only useless suffering. I am not equal to it. My one effort now is to gain sufficient strength to go to some distant relatives in the West. Please forget me. "In sorrow and bitter regret, "'Emily Warren.'"

I started up and paced the room distractedly. "The generous girl!" I exclaimed, "she lays not a particle of blame on me. But, by Jove! I'd like to take all the blame, and have it out with him here and now. Blame! What blame is there? The poor child! Why can't she see that she is white as snow?"

Again I eagerly turned to Mrs. Yocomb's words:

"Emily seemed almost overwhelmed at the thought of his reading this letter. She is so generous, so sensitive, that she saw only his side of the case, and made scarcely any allowance for herself. I was a little decided and plain-spoken with her, and it did her good. At last I said to her, 'I am not weak-minded, if I am simple and plain. Because I live in the country is no reason why I do not know what is right and just. Thee has no cause to blame thyself so bitterly.' 'Does Mr. Yocomb feel and think as you do?' she asked. 'Of course he does,' I replied. She put her hands to her head and said pitifully, 'Perhaps I am too distracted to see things clearly. I sometimes fear I may lose my reason.' 'Well, Emily,' I said, 'thee has done right. Thee cannot help feeling as thee does, and to go on now would be as great a wrong to Gilbert Hearn as to thyself. Thee has done just as I would advise my own daughter to do. Leave all with me. Thee need not see him again. I am going to stand by thee;' and I left her quite heartened up."

"Oh, but you are a gem of a woman!" I cried. "A few more like you would bring the millennium."

"Gilbert Hearn was dreadfully taken aback by the letter; but I must do him the justice to say that he was much touched by it too, for he called me again into the parlor, and I saw that he was much moved. He had given his sister the letter to read, and she muttered, 'Poor thing!' as she finished it. He fixed his eyes sternly on me and said, 'Mr. Morton is at the bottom of this thing.' I returned his gaze very quietly, and asked, 'What am I to infer by this expression of thy opinion to me?' His sister was as quick as a flash, and she said plainly, 'Gilbert, these people were not two little children in Mrs. Yocomb's care.' 'Thee is right,' I said; 'I have not controlled their actions any more than I have those of thy brother. Richard Morton is absent, however, and were we not under peculiar obligations to him I would still be bound to speak for him, since he is not here to speak for himself. I have never seen Richard Morton do anything unbecoming a gentleman. Has thee, Gilbert Hearn? If so, I think thee had better see him, for he is not one to deny thee any explanation to which thee has a right.' 'Why did he go to the city so suddenly?' he asked angrily. 'I will give thee his address,' I said coldly. 'Gilbert,' expostulated his sister, — we have no right to cross—question Mrs. Yocomb.' 'Since thee is so considerate,' I said to her, 'I will add that Richard Morton intended to return on Second Day at the latest, and he chose to go to-day. His action enables me to give thee a room to thyself.' 'Gilbert,' said the lady, 'I do not see that we have any reason to regret his absence. As Mrs. Yocomb says, you can see him in New York; but unless you have well founded and specific charges to make, I think it would compromise your dignity to see him. Editors are ugly customers to stir up unless there is good cause.'"

"I know one," I growled, "that would be a particularly ugly customer just now."

"'In Emily Warren's case,' I said, 'it is different,'" Mrs. Yocomb continued. "'She is a motherless girl and has appealed to me for advice and sympathy. In her honest struggle to be loyal to thee she has worn herself almost to a shadow, and I have grave fears for her reason and her life, so great is her prostration. She has for thee, Gilbert Hearn, the sincerest respect and esteem, and the feeling that she has wronged thee, even though she cannot help it, seems almost to crush her.' 'Gilbert,' said his sister warmly, 'you cannot blame her, and you certainly ought to respect her. If she were not an honest-hearted girl she would never have renounced you with your great wealth.' He sank into a chair and looked very white. 'It's a terrible blow,' he said; 'it's the first severe reverse I've ever had.' 'Well,' she replied, 'I know from your character that you will meet it like a man and a gentleman.' 'Certainly,' he said, with a deep breath, 'I cannot do otherwise.' I then rose and bowed, saying: 'You will both excuse me if I am with my charge much of the time. Adah will attend to your wants, and I hope you will feel at home so long as it shall please you to stay.'"

"By Jove! but her tact was wonderful. Not a diplomat in Europe could have done better. The innocent-looking Quakeress was a match for them both."

"Then I went back to Emily," Mrs. Yocomb wrote, "and I found her in a pitiable state of excitement. When I opened the door she started up apprehensively, as if she feared that the man with whom she had broken would burst in upon her with bitter reproaches. I told her everything; for even I cannot deceive her, she is so quick. Her mind was wonderfully lightened, and I soon made her sleep again. She awoke in the evening much quieter, but she cried a good deal in the night, and I surmise she was thinking of thee more than of herself or of him. I wish thee had waited until all this was over, but I think all will come out right."

"Oh, the unutterable fool that I was!" I groaned; "I'm the champion blunderer of the world."

"Well, Richard, this is the longest letter I ever wrote, and I must bring it to a close, for my patient needs me. I will write soon again, and tell thee everything. Goodnight.

"Second Day. P.S.—I left my letter open to add a postscript. Gilbert Hearn and his sister left this morning. The former at last seemed quite calm and resigned, and was very polite. His sister was too. She amused me not a little. I do not think that her heart was greatly set on the match, and she was not so troubled but that she could take an interest in our quiet, homely ways. I think we seemed to her like what you city people call *bric-a-brac*, but she was too much of a lady to let her curiosity become offensive. She took a great fancy to Adah, especially as she saw that Adela was very fond of her, and she persuaded her brother to leave the child here in our care, saying that she was improving wonderfully. He did not seem at all averse to the plan. Adah is behaving very nicely, if I do say it, and showed a great deal of quiet, gentle dignity. She and Charlotte Bradford had a long chat in the evening about Adela. Adah says, 'Send Richard my love'; and if I put in all the messages from father, Reuben, and Zillah, they would fill another sheet.

"I asked Emily if she had any message for thee. She buried her face in the pillow and murmured, 'Not now, not yet'; but after a moment she turned toward me, looking white and resolute. 'Tell him,' she said, 'to forgive me and forget.' Be patient, Richard. Wait. "Thine affectionately,

"Ruth Yocomb."

"Forget!" I shouted. "Yes, when I am annihilated," and I paced my room for hours. At last, exhausted, I sought such rest as I could obtain, but my last thought was, "God bless Ruth Yocomb. I could kiss the ground she had trodden."

The next morning I settled down to my task of waiting and working, resolving that there must be no more nights like the last, in which I had wasted a vast amount of vital force. I wrote to Mrs. Yocomb, and thanked her from a full heart. I sent messages to all the family, and said, "Tell Adah I shall keep her love warm in my heart, and that I send her twice as much of mine in return. Like all brothers, I shall take liberties, and will subscribe in her behalf for the two best magazines in the city. Give Miss Warren this simple message: The words I last spoke to her shall ever be true."

I also told Mrs. Yocomb of my promotion, and that I was no longer a night-owl.

Toward the end of the week came another bulky letter, which I devoured, letting my dinner grow cold.

"Our life at the farmhouse has become very quiet," she wrote. "Emily improves slowly, for her nervous system has received a severe strain. I told her that thee had sent messages to all the family, and asked if she did not expect one. 'I've no right to any—there's no occasion for any,' she faltered; but her eyes were very wistful and entreating. 'Well,' I said, 'I must clear my conscience, and since he sent thee one, I must give it. He writes, 'Say to Miss Warren in reply that the last words I spoke to her shall ever be true.' I suppose thee knows what he means,' I said, smiling; 'I don't.' She buried her face in the pillow again; but I think thy message did her good, for she soon fell asleep, and looked more peaceful than at any time yet."

At last there came a letter saying, "Emily has left us and gone to a cousin—a Mrs. Vining—who resides at Columbus, Ohio. She is much better, but very quiet—very different from her old self. Father put her on the train, and she will have to change cars only once. 'Emily,' I said to her, 'thee can not go away without one word for Richard.' She was deeply moved, but her resolute will gained the mastery. 'I am trying to act for the best,' she said. 'He has appealed to the future: the future must prove us both, for there must be no more mistakes.' 'Does thee doubt thyself, Emily?' 'I have reason to doubt myself, Mrs. Yocomb,' she replied. 'But what does thy heart tell thee?' A deep solemn look came into her eyes, and after a few moments she said, 'Pardon me, my dear friend, if I do not answer you fully. Indeed, I would scarcely know how to answer you. I have entered on an experience that is new and strange to me. I am troubled and frightened at myself. I want to go away among strangers, where I can think and grow calm. I want to be alone with my God. I should always be weak and vacillating here. Moreover, Mr. Morton has formed an impression of me, of which, perhaps, I cannot complain. This impression may grow stronger in his mind. It has all been too sudden. His experiences have been too intermingled with storm, delirium, and passion. He has not had time to think any more than I have. In the larger sphere of work to which you say he has been promoted he may find new interests that will be absorbing. After a quiet and distant retrospect he may thank me for the course I am taking.' 'Emily!' I exclaimed, 'for so tender-hearted a girl thee is very strong.' 'No,' she replied, 'but because I have learned my weakness I am going away from temptation.' I then asked, 'Is thee willing I should tell Richard what thee has said?' After thinking for some time she answered, 'Yes, let everything be based on the simple truth. But tell him he must respect my action—he must leave me to myself.' The afternoon before she left us, Adah and Reuben went over to the village and got some beautiful rosebuds, and Adah brought them up after tea. Emily was much touched, and kissed her again and again. Then she threw herself into my arms and cried for nearly an hour, but she went away bravely. I never can think of it with dry eyes. Zillah was heart-broken, and Reuben clung to her in a way that surprised me. He has been very remorseful that he treated her badly at one time. Adah and I were mopping our eyes, and father kept blowing his nose like a trumpet. She gave way a little at the last moment, for Reuben ran down to the barn and brought out Dapple that she might say good-by to him, and she put her arms around the pretty creature's neck and sobbed for a moment or two. I never saw a horse act so. He followed her right up to the rockaway steps. At last she said, 'Come, let us go, quick!' I shall never forget the scene, and I think that she repressed so much feeling that we had to express it for her. She kissed little Adela tenderly, and the child was crying too. It seemed as if we couldn't go on and take up our every-day life again. I wouldn't have believed that one who was a stranger but a short time ago could have gotten such a hold upon our hearts, but as I think it all over I do not wonder. Dear little Zillah reminds me of what I owe to her. She is very womanly, but she is singularly strong. As she was driven away she looked up at thy window, so thee may guess that thee was the last one in her thoughts. Wait, and be patient. Do just as she says."

I am glad that my editorial chief did not see me as I read this letter, for I fear I should have been deposed at once. Its influence on me, however, was very satisfactory to him, for if ever a man was put on his mettle I felt that I had been.

"Very well, Emily Warren," I said, "we have both appealed to the future: let it judge us." I worked and tried to live as if the girl's clear dark eyes were always on me, and her last lingering glance at the window from which I had watched her go to meet the lover that, for my sake, she could not marry, was a ray of steady sunshine. She did not realize how unconsciously she had given me hope.

A few days later I looked carefully over our subscription list. Her paper had been stopped, and I felt this keenly; but as I was staring blankly at the obliterated name a happy thought occurred to me, and I turned to the letter V. With a gleam of deep satisfaction in my eyes I found the address, Mrs. Adelaide Vining, Columbus, Ohio.

"Now through the editorial page I can write to her daily," I thought.

Late in September my chief said to me:

"Look here, Morton, you are pitching into every dragon in the country. I don't mind fighting three or four evils or abuses at a time, but this general onslaught is raising a breeze."

"With your permission, I don't care if it becomes a gale, as long as we are well ballasted with facts."

"Well, to go back to my first figure, be sure you are well armed before you attack. Some of the beasts are old and tough, and have awful stings in their tails. The people seem to like it, though, from the way subscriptions are coming in."

But I wrote chiefly for one reader. He would have opened his eyes if I had told him that a young music-teacher in Columbus, Ohio, had a large share in conducting the journal. Over my desk in my rooms I had had framed, in illuminated text, the words she had spoken to me on the most memorable day of my life:

"The editor has exceptional opportunities, and might be the knight-errant of our age. If in earnest, and on the right side, he can forge a weapon out of public opinion that few evils could resist. He is in just the position to discover these dragons and drive them from their hiding-places."

The spirit that breathed in these words I tried to make mine, for I wished to feel and think as she did. While I maintained my individuality of thought I never touched a question but that I first looked at it from her standpoint. I labored for weeks over an editorial entitled "Truth versus Conscience," and sent it like an arrow into the West.

CHAPTER XIX
ADAH

I heard often from the farmhouse, and learned that Mr. Hearn had gone to Europe almost immediately, but that he had returred in the latter part of September, and had spent a week with his little girl, Mrs. Bradford, his sister, accompanying him. "They seem to think Adela is doing so well," Mrs. Yocomb wrote, "that they have decided to leave her here through October. Adah spends part of every forenoon teaching the little girls." In the latter part of November I received a letter that made my heart beat thick and fast.

"We expect thee to eat thy Thanksgiving dinner with us, and we expect also a friend from the West. I think she will treat thee civilly. At any rate we have a right to invite whom we please. We drew up a petition to Emily, and all signed it. Father added a direful postscript. He said, 'If thee won't come quietly, I will go after thee. Thee thinks I am a man of peace, but there will be commotion and violence in Ohio if thee doesn't come; so, strong-willed as thee is, thee has got to yield for once.' She wrote father the funniest letter in reply, in which she agreed, for the credit of the Society of Friends, not to provoke him to extremities. She doesn't know thee is coming, but I think she knows me well enough to be sure that thee would be invited. Emily writes that she will not return to New York to live, since she can obtain more scholars than she needs at Columbus."

Mrs. Yocomb also added that Adah had left home that day for an extended visit in the city, and she gave me her address.

I had written to Adah more than once, and had made out a programme of what we should do when she came to town.

Quite early in the evening I started out to call upon her, but as I drew near the house I saw that a handsome coupe stood before the door, drawn by two horses, and that the coachman was in livery. My steps were speedily arrested, for the door of the dwelling was opened, and Mr. Hearn came out, accompanied by Adah. They entered the coupe and were driven rapidly toward Fifth Avenue. I gave a long, low whistle, and took two or three turns around the block, muttering, "Gilbert Hearn, but you are shrewd. If you can't have the best thing in the world, you'll have the next best. Come to think of it, she is the best for you. If this comes about for Adah, I could throw my hat over yonder steeple."

I went back to the house, proposing to leave my card, and thus show Adah that I was not inattentive. The interior of the dwelling, like its exterior, was plain, but very substantial and elegant. The servant handed my card to a lady passing through the hall.

"Oh, thee is Richard Morton?" she said. "Cousin Ruth and Adah have told us all about thee. Please come in, for I want to make thy acquaintance. Adah will be so sorry to miss thee. She has gone out for the evening."

"If she will permit me," I said, "I will call to-morrow, on my way downtown, for I wish to see her very much."

"Do so, by all means. Come whenever thee can, and informally. Thee'll always find a welcome here."

Before I was aware I had spent an hour in pleasant chat, for with the Yocombs as mutual friends we had common interests.

Mrs. Winfield, my hostess, had all the elegance of Mrs. Bradford; but there was also a simple, friendly heartiness in her manner that stamped every word she spoke with sincerity. I was greatly pleased, and felt that the wealthy banker and his sister could find no fault with Adah's connections.

She greeted me the next morning like the sister she had become in very truth.

"Oh, Richard!" she exclaimed, "I'm so glad to see thee. Why! thee's so improved I'd hardly know thee. Seems to me thee's grown taller and larger every way."

"I fear I looked rather small sometimes in the country."

"No, Richard, thee never looked small to me; but when I think what I was when thee found me, I don't wonder thee went up to thy room in disgust. I've thought a great deal since that day, and I've read some too."

"If you knew how proud of you I am now, it would turn your head."

"Perhaps it isn't very strong. So thee's going to eat thy Thanksgiving dinner at home. I shall be well out of the way."

"You will never be in my way; but perhaps I might have been in somebody's way had I come earlier last night."

"I thought thee was blind," she said, an exquisite color coming into her beautiful face.

"Never to your interests, Adah. Count on me to the last drop."

"Oh, Richard, thee has been so kind and helpful to me. Thee'll never know all that's in my heart. When I think what I was when I first knew thee, I wonder at it all."

"Adah," I said, taking her hand, "you have become a genuine woman. The expression of your face has changed, and it has become a fine example of the truth, that even beauty follows the law of living growth—from within outward. Higher thoughts, noble principle, and unselfishness are making their impress. After our long separation I see the change distinctly, and I feel it still more. You have won my honest respect, Adah; I predict for you a happy life, and, what is more, you will make others happy. People will be the better for being with you."

"Well, Richard, now that we are brother and sister. I don't mind telling thee that it was thee who woke me up. I was a fool before thee came."

"But the true, sweet woman was in your nature ready to be awakened. Other causes would soon have produced the same effect."

"Possibly; but I don't know anything about other causes. I do know thee, and I trust thee with my whole heart, and I'm going to talk frankly with thee because I want to ask thy advice. Thee knows how near to death I came. I've thought a great deal about it. Having come so near losing life, I began to think what life meant—what it was—and I was soon made to see how petty and silly my former life had been. My heart just overflowed with gratitude toward thee. When thee was so ill I would often lie awake whole nights thinking and trembling lest thee should die. I felt so strangely, so weak and helpless, that I stretched out my hands to thee, and thy strong hands caught and sustained me through that time when I was neither woman nor child. Thee never humiliated me by even a glance. Thee treated me with a respect that I did not deserve, but which I want to deserve. I am not strong, like Emily Warren, but I am trying to do right. Thee changed a blind impulse into an abiding trust and sisterly affection. Thee may think I'm giving thee a strange proof of my trust. I am going to tell thee something that I've not told any one yet. Last evening Gilbert Hearn took me to see his sister, Mrs. Bradford, and I spent the evening with them and little Adela. Coming home he asked me to be his wife. I was not so very greatly surprised, for he spent every First Day in October at our house while Adela was with us, and he was very attentive to me. Father and mother don't like it very much, but I think they are a little prejudiced against him on thy account. I believe thee will tell me the truth about him."

"Adah dear, you *have* honored me greatly. I will advise you just as I would my own sister. What did you answer him last evening?"

"I told him that I was a simple country girl, and not suited to be his wife. Then he said that he had a right to his own views about that. He said he wanted a genuine wife—one that would love him and his little girl, and not a society woman, who would marry him for his money."

"That is exceedingly sensible."

"Yes, he said he wanted a home, and that he was fond of quiet home life; that I came of a quiet, sincere people, and that he had seen enough of me to know that he could trust me. He said also that I could be both a mother and a companion to Adela, and that the child needed just such a disposition as I had."

I laughed as I said, "Mr. Hearn is sagacity itself. Even Solomon could not act more wisely than he is seeking to act. But what does your heart say to all this, Adah?"

Her color deepened, and she averted her face. "Thee will think I'm dreadfully matter-of-fact, Richard, but I think that perhaps we are suited to each other. I've thought about it a great deal. As I said before, my head isn't very strong. I couldn't understand half the things thee thinks and writes about. I've seen that clearly. He wouldn't expect a wife to understand his business, and he says he wants to forget all about it when he comes home. He says he likes a place full of beauty, repose, and genial light. He likes quiet dinner parties made up of his business friends, and not literary people like thee. We haven't got great, inquiring minds like thee and Emily Warren."

"You are making fun of me now, Adah. I fear Miss Warren has thrown me over in disgust."

"Nonsense, Richard. She loves thy little finger more than I am capable of loving any man. She is strong and intense, and she could go with thee in thought wherever thee pleases. I'm only Adah."

"Yes, you are Adah, and the man who has the reputation of having the best of everything in the city wants you badly, and with good reason. But I want to know what *you* want."

"I want to know what thee thinks of it. I want thee to tell me about him. Does thee know anything against him?"

"No, Adah. Even when I feared he would disappoint my dearest hope, I told your mother that he was an honorable man. He is exceedingly shrewd in business, but I never heard of his doing anything that was not square. I think he would make you a very kind, considerate husband, and, as he says, you could do so much for his little girl. But, rich as he is, Adah, he is not rich enough for you unless you can truly love him."

"I think I can love him in my quiet way. I think I would be happy in the life I would lead with him. I'm fond of housekeeping, and very fond of pretty things and of the city, as thee knows. Then I could do so much for them all at home. Father and mother are growing old. Father lent money some years ago, and lost it, and he and mother have to work too hard. I could do so much for them and for Zillah, and that would make me happy. But I am so simple, and I know so little, that I fear I can't satisfy him."

"I have no fear on that score. What I am anxious about is, will he satisfy you? You can't realize how bent upon your happiness I am."

"I thank thee, Richard. I was not wrong in coming to thee. Well, I told him that I wanted to think it all over, and I asked him to do the same. He said he had fully made up his mind and that his sister heartily approved of his course, and had advised it. He said that he would wait for me as long as I pleased. Now if thee thinks it's best, thy words would have much influence with father and mother."

I raised her hand to my lips, and said, feelingly: "Adah, I am very grateful for this confidence. I feel more honored that you should have come to me than if I had been made Governor. In view of what you have said, I do think it's best. Mr. Hearn will always be kind and considerate. He will be very proud of you, and you will grow rapidly in those qualities that will adorn your high social position. Do not undervalue yourself. Gilbert Hearn may well thank God for you every day of his life."

I went down to the office in a mood to write an interminable Thanksgiving editorial, for it seemed as if the clouds were all breaking away.

CHAPTER XX
THANKSGIVING DAY

On the day before Thanksgiving one of my associates clapped me on the shoulder, and said, laughing: "Morton, what's the matter? You are as nervous as a girl on her wedding-day. I've spoken to you twice, and you've not answered. Has one of the dragons got the best of you?"

I woke up, and said quietly, "It isn't a dragon this time."

Oh, how vividly that evening comes back to me, as I walked swiftly uptown! It would have been torture to have ridden in a lumbering stage or crawling street-car. I scarcely knew what I thrust into my travelling bag. I had no idea what I ate for dinner, and only remember that I scalded myself slightly with hot coffee. Calling a coupe, I dashed off to a late train that passed through the village nearest to the farmhouse.

It had been arranged that I should come the following morning, and that Reuben should meet me, but I proposed to give them a surprise. I could not wait one moment longer than I must. I had horrible dreams in the stuffy little room at the village inn, but consoled myself with the thought that "dreams go by contraries."

After a breakfast on which mine host cleared two hundred per cent, I secured a light wagon and driver, and started for the world's one Mecca for me. My mind was in a tumult of mingled hope and fear, and I experienced all a young soldier's trepidation when going into his first battle. If she had not come: if she would not listen to me. The cold perspiration would start out on my brow at the very thought. What a mockery Thanksgiving Day would ever become if my hopes were disappointed. Even now I cannot recall that interminable ride without a faint awakening of the old unrest.

When within half a mile of the house I dismissed my driver, and started on at a tremendous pace; but my steps grew slower and slower, and when the turn of the road revealed the dear old place just before me, I leaned against a wall faint and trembling. I marked the spot on which I had stood when the fiery bolt descended, and some white shingles indicated the place on the mossy roof where it had burned its way into the home that even then enshrined my dearest treasures. I saw the window at which Emily Warren had directed the glance that had sustained my hope for months. I looked wistfully at the leafless, flowerless garden, where I had first recognized my Eve. "Will her manner be like the present aspect of that garden?" I groaned. I saw the arbor in which I had made my wretched blunder. I had about broken myself of profanity, but an ugly expression slipped out (I hope the good angel makes allowances for human nature). Recalling the vow I had made in that arbor, I snatched up my valise and did not stop till I had mounted the piazza. Further suspense was unendurable. My approach had been unnoted, nor had I seen any of the family. Noiselessly as possible I opened the door and stood within the hallway. I heard Mrs. Yocomb's voice in the kitchen. Reuben was whistling upstairs, and Zillah singing her doll to sleep in the dining-room. I took these sounds to be good omens. If she had not come there would not have been such cheerfulness.

With silent tread I stole to the parlor door. At my old seat by the window was Emily Warren, writing on a portfolio in her lap. For a second a blur came over my vision, and then I devoured her with my eyes as the famishing would look at food.

Had she changed? Yes, but only to become tenfold more beautiful, for her face now had that indescribable charm which suffering, nobly endured, imparts. I could have knelt to her like a Catholic to his patron saint.

She felt my presence, for she looked up quickly. The portfolio dropped from her lap; she was greatly startled, and instinctively put her hand to her side; still I thought I saw welcome dawning in her eyes; but at this moment Zillah sprang into my arms and half smothered me with kisses. Her cries of delight brought Reuben tearing down the stairs, and Mrs. Yocomb, hastening from the kitchen, left the mark of her floury arm on the collar of my coat as she gave me a motherly salute. Their welcome was so warm, spontaneous, and real that tears came into my eyes, for I felt that I was no longer a lonely man without kindred.

But after a moment or two I broke away from them and turned to Miss Warren, for after all my Thanksgiving Day depended upon her.

She had become very pale, but her eyes were glistening at the honest feeling she had witnessed.

I held out my hand, and asked, in a low voice, "May I stay?"

"I could not send you away from such friends, Mr. Morton," she said gently, "even had I the right," and she held out her hand.

I think I hurt it, for I grasped it as if I were drowning.

Reuben had raced down to the barn to call his father, who now followed him back at a pace that scarcely became his age and Quaker tenets.

"Richard," he called, as soon as he saw me, "welcome home! Thee's been a long time coming, and yet thee's stolen a march on us after all. Reuben was just going for thee. How did thee get here? There's no train so early."

"Oh, I came last night. A ship's cable couldn't hold me the moment I could get away."

"Mother, I think that's quite a compliment to us old people," he began, with the humorous twinkle that I so well remembered in his honest eyes. "Has thee seen Adah?"

"Yes, indeed, and she sent more love than I could carry to you all. She looked just lovely, and I nearly forgot to go down town that morning."

Miss Warren was about to leave the room, but the old gentleman caught her hand and asked:

"Where is thee going, Emily?"

"Pardon me; I thought you would all have much to say to Mr. Morton."

"So we have, to be sure. We won't get half through to-day, but that's no reason for thy leaving us. We are all one family under this roof, thank God, and I'm going to thank Him to-day in good old style and no make-believe;" and he kept her hand as she sat down by him.

"If you knew how homesick I've often been you would realize how much good your words do me," she replied gratefully.

"So thee's been homesick, has thee? Well, thee didn't let us know."

"What good would it have done? I couldn't come before."

"Well, I am kind of glad thee was homesick. The missing wasn't all on our side. Why, Richard, thee never saw such a disconsolate household as we were after Emily left. I even lost my appetite—didn't I, mother?—and that's more than I've done for any lady since Ebenezer Holcomb cut me out of thy company at a picnic—let me see, how many years ago is it, mother?"

"Thee doesn't think I remember such foolishness, I hope," said the old lady; but with a rising color almost pretty as the blush I had seen so recently on Adah's face.

Mr. Yocomb leaned back and laughed. "See mother blush," he cried. "Poor Ebenezer!"

"Thee'll want more than light nonsense for thy dinner by and by, so I must go back to the kitchen."

As she turned away she gave a sweet suggestion of the blushing girl for whom Ebenezer had sighed in vain, and I said emphatically, "Yes, indeed,

Mr. Yocomb, you may well say 'Poor Ebenezer!' How in the world did he ever survive it?"

"Thee's very sympathetic, Richard."

Miss Warren looked at him threateningly.

I tried to laugh it off, and said, "Even if he had a millstone for a heart, it must have broken at such a loss."

"Oh, don't thee worry. He's a hale and hearty grandfather to-day."

Miss Warren broke into a laugh that set all my nerves tingling. "Yes," she cried, "I thought it would end in that way."

"Why, Emily, bless thee!" said Mrs. Yocomb, running in, "I haven't heard thee laugh so since thee came."

"She's at her old tricks," said her husband; "laughing at Richard and me."

I found her merriment anything but reassuring, and I muttered under my breath: "Perdition on Ebenezer and his speedy comfort! I hope she don't class me with him."

Very soon Mrs. Yocomb appeared again, and said: "Father, thee must take them all out to drive. I can't do anything straight while I hear you all talking and laughing, for my thoughts are with you. I've put salt into one pie already. A Thanksgiving dinner requires one's whole mind."

"Bustle, bustle, all get ready. Mother's mistress of this house on Thanksgiving Day, if at no other time. We're commanded to obey the 'powers that be,' and if the woman who can get up such a dinner as mother can isn't a 'power,' I'd like to know where we'll find one. I'm very meek and respectful on Thanksgiving morning. Get on thy wraps, Emily. No mutiny before dinner."

She seemed very ready to go, for I think she dreaded being left alone with me. I, too, was glad to gain time, for I was strangely unnerved and apprehensive. She avoided meeting my eyes, and was inscrutable.

In a few moments we were in the family rockaway, bowling over the country at a grand pace.

"Mother's shrewd," said Mr. Yocomb; "she knew that a ride like this in the frosty air would give us an appetite for any kind of a dinner, but it will make hers taste like the Feast of Tabernacles. Let 'em go, Reuben, let 'em go!"

"Do you call this a Quaker pace?" asked Miss Warren, who sat with Zillah on the back seat.

"Yes, I'm acting just as I feel moved. Thee's much too slow for a Friend, Emily. Now I'll wager thee a plum that Richard likes it. Doesn't thee, Richard?"

"Suppose a wheel should come off," I suggested. "I'm awfully nervous to-day. I was sure the train would break down or run off the track last night; then I had horrible dreams at the hotel."

"Why, Mr. Morton!" Miss Warren exclaimed, "what did you eat for supper?"

"Bless me! I don't know. Come to think of it, I didn't have any."

"Did thee have any breakfast?" asked Mr. Yocomb, who seemed greatly amused.

"I believe so. I went through the motions."

"Drive slow, Reuben; Richard's afraid he'll have his neck broken before dinner;" and they all had a great laugh at my expense.

"I've won the plum this time," cried Miss Warren.

"Thee has indeed, and thee deserves it sure enough."

I looked around at her, but could not catch her eyes. My efforts to emulate Mr. Yocomb's spirit were superhuman, but my success was indifferent. I was too anxious, too doubtful concerning the girl who was so gentle and yet so strong. She had far more quietude and self-mastery than I, and with good reason, for she was mistress of the situation. Still, I gathered hope every hour, for I felt that her face would not be so happy, so full of brightness, if she proposed to send me away disappointed, or even put me off on further probation. Nevertheless, my Thanksgiving Day would not truly begin until my hope was confirmed.

Dinner was smoking on the table when we returned, and it was so exceedingly tempting that I enjoyed its aroma with much of Mr. Yocomb's satisfaction, and I sat down at his right, feeling that if one question were settled I would be the most thankful man in the land.

We bowed our heads in grace; but after a moment Mr. Yocomb arose, and with uplifted face repeated words that might have been written for the occasion, so wonderfully adapted to human life is the Book of God.

"'Bless the Lord, O my soul: and all that is within me, bless His holy name.

"'Bless the Lord, O my soul, and forget not all His benefits: "'Who forgiveth all thine iniquities; who healeth all thy diseases;

"'Who redeemeth thy life from destruction; who crowneth thee with loving kindness and tender mercies.

"'Who satisfieth thy mouth with good things; so that thy youth is renewed like the eagle's.'"

Never was there a grace so full of grace before. If a kind earthly father looks with joy on his happy children, so surely the divine Father must have smiled upon us. In the depths of my heart I respected a faith that was so simple, genuine, and full of sunshine. Truly, it had come from heaven, and not from the dyspeptic creeds of cloistered theologians.

"Father," cried Zillah, "thee looked like my picture of King David."

"Well, I'm in a royal mood," replied her father, "and I don't believe King David ever had half so good a dinner as mother has provided. Such a dinner, Richard, is the result of genius. All the cookbooks in the world couldn't account for it, and I don't believe mother has read one of them."

"Thee must give Cynthia part of the credit," protested his wife.

"She's the woman who says 'Lord a massy,' and insists that I was struck with lightning, isn't she?" and I glanced toward Miss Warren, but she wouldn't meet my eye. Her deepening color told of a busy memory, however. Mr. Yocomb began to laugh so heartily that he dropped his knife and fork on the table and leaned back in his chair quite overcome.

"Father, behave thyself," his wife remonstrated. At last the old gentleman set to work in good earnest. "Emily," he said, "this is that innocent young gobbler that thee so commiserated. Thee hasn't the heart to eat him, surely."

"I'll take a piece of the breast, if you please."

"Wouldn't thee like his heart?"

"No, I thank you."

"What part would thee like, Richard?"

"Anything but his wings and legs. They would remind me how soon I must go back to awful New York."

"Not before Second Day."

"Yes, sir, to-morrow morning. An editor's play-spells are few and far between."

"Well, Richard, thee thrives on work," said Mrs. Yocomb.

"Yes. I've found it good for me."

"And you have done good work, Mr. Morton," added Miss Warren. "I like your paper far better now."

"But you stopped it."

"Did you find that out?"

"Indeed I did, and very quickly."

"My cousin, Mrs. Vining, took the paper."

"Yes, I know that, too."

"Why, Mr. Morton! do you keep track of all your readers? The circulation of your paper cannot be large."

"I looked after Mrs. Vining carefully, but no further."

"I shall certainly tell her of your interest," she said, with her old mirthful gleam.

"Please do. The people at the office would be agape with wonder if they knew of the influence resulting from Mrs. Vining's name being on the subscription list."

"Not a disastrous influence, I trust?"

"It has occasioned us some hot work. My chief says that nearly all the dragons in the country are stirred up."

"And some of them have been sorely wounded-I've noted that too," said the girl, flushing with pleasure in spite of herself.

"Yes, please tell Mrs. Vining that also. Credit should be given where it's due."

Her laugh now rang out with its old-time genuineness. "Cousin Adelaide would be more agape than the people of your office. I think the dragons owe their tribulations to your disposition to fight them."

"If you could see some words in illuminated text over my desk you would know better."

"Mr. Yocomb, don't you think we are going to have an early winter?" she asked abruptly, with a fine color in her face.

"I don't think it's going to be cold—not very cold, Emily. There are prospects of a thaw to-day;" and the old gentleman leaned back in his chair and shook with suppressed merriment.

"Father, behave thyself. Was there ever such a man!" Mrs. Yocomb exclaimed reproachfully.

"I know you think there never was and never will be, Mrs. Yocomb," I cried, controlling myself with difficulty, for the old gentleman's manner was irresistibly droll and instead of the pallor that used to make my heart ache, Miss Warren's face was like a carnation rose. My hope grew apace, for her threatening looks at Mr. Yocomb contained no trace of pain or deep annoyance, while the embarrassment she could not hide so enhanced her loveliness that it was a heavy cross to withhold my eager eyes. Reuben kindly came to our relief, for he said:

"I tell thee what it is, mother: I feel as if we ought to have Dapple in here with us."

"Emily, wouldn't thee rather have Old Plod?" Mr. Yocomb asked.

"No!" she replied brusquely; and this set her kind tormentor off once more.

But an earnest look soon came into his face, and he said, with eyes moist with feeling:

"Well, this is a time of thanksgiving, and never before in all my life has my heart seemed so full of gladness and gratitude. Richard, I crept in this old home when I was a baby, and I whistled through the house just as Reuben does. In this very room my dear old father trimmed my jacket for me, God bless him! Oh, I deserved it richly; but mother's sorrowful looks cut deeper, I can tell thee. It was to this home I brought the prettiest lass in the county—what am I saying?—the prettiest lass in the world. No offence to thee, Emily; thee wasn't alive then. If every man had such a home as thee has made for me and the children, mother, the millennium would begin before next Thanksgiving. In this house my children were born, and here they have played. I've seen their happy faces in every nook and corner, and with everything I have a dear association. In this home we bade good-by to our dear little Ruth; she's ours still, mother, and she is at home, too, as we are; but everything in this house that our little angel child touched has become sacred to me. Ah, Richard, there are some things in life that thee hasn't learned yet, and all the books couldn't teach thee; but what I have said to thee reveals a little of my love for this old home. How I love those whom God has given me, only He knows. Well, He directed thy random steps to us one day last June, and we welcomed thee as a stranger. But thee has a different welcome to-day, Richard—a very different welcome. Thee doesn't like to hear about it; but we never forget."

"No, Richard, we never forget," Mrs. Yocomb breathed softly.

"Do you think, sir, that I forget the unquestioning hospitality that brought me here? Can you think, Mrs. Yocomb, I ever forget the words you spoke to me in yonder parlor on the evening of my arrival? or that I should have died but for your devoted and merciful care? This day, with its hopes, teaches me how immeasurable would have been my loss, for my prospects then were not bright for either world. Rest assured, dear friends, I have my memories too. The service I rendered you any man would have given, and it was my unspeakable good-fortune to be here. But the favors which I have received have been royal; they are such as I could not receive from others, because others would be incapable of bestowing them."

"You are right, Mr. Morton," Miss Warren began impetuously, her lovely eyes full of tears. "I, too, have received kindnesses that could not come from others, because others would not know how to confer them with your gentleness and mercy, Mrs. Yocomb. Oh! oh! I wish I could make you and your husband know how I thank you. I, too, never forget. But if we talk this way any more, I shall have to make a hasty retreat." "Well, I should say this *was* a thanksgiving dinner," remarked Reuben sententiously.

Since we couldn't cry, we all laughed, and I thanked the boy for letting us down so cleverly. The deep feeling that memories would evoke in spite of ourselves sank back into the depths of our hearts. The shadow on our faces passed like an April cloud, and the sunshine became all the sweeter and brighter.

"If Adah were only here!" I cried. "I miss her more and more every moment, and the occasion seems wholly incomplete without her."

"Yes, dear child, I miss her too, more than I can tell you," said Mrs. Yocomb, her eyes growing very tender and wistful. "She's thinking of us. Doesn't thee think she has improved? She used to read those magazines thee sent her till I had to take them away and send her to bed."

"I can't tell you how proud I am of Adah. It was like a June day to see her fair sweet face in the city, and it would have had done your hearts good if you could have heard how she spoke of you all."

"Adah is very proud of her big brother, too, I can tell thee. She quotes thy opinions on all occasions."

"The one regret of my visit is that I shall not see her," Miss Warren said earnestly. "Mrs. Yocomb, I have those roses she gave me the day before I left you last summer, and I shall always keep them. I told Cousin Adelaide that they were given to me by the best and most beautiful girl in the world."

"God bless the girl!" ejaculated Mr. Yocomb; "she has become a great comfort and joy to me;" and his wife smiled softly and tenderly.

"Adah is so good to me," cried Zillah, "that if Emily hadn't come I wouldn't have half enjoyed the day."

"What does thee think of that view of the occasion, Richard?" asked Mr. Yocomb.

"Zillah and I always agreed well together," I said; "but I wish Adah knew how much we miss her."

"She shall know," said her mother. "I truly wish we had all of our children with us to-day; for, Richard, we have adopted thee and Emily without asking your consent. I think the lightning fused us all together."

I looked with a quick flash toward Miss Warren, but her eyes were on the mother, and they were full of a daughter's love.

"Dear Mrs. Yocomb," I replied, in a voice not over-steady, "you know that as far as fusing was concerned I was the worst struck of you all, and this day proves that I am no longer without kindred."

But how vain the effort to reproduce the light and shade that filled the quaint, simple room! How vain the attempt to make the myriad ripples of that hour flow and sparkle again, each one of us meanwhile conscious of the depths beneath them!

CHAPTER XXI
RIPPLES ON DEEP WATER

After dinner was over, Reuben cried, "Come, Zillah, I'm going out with Dapple, and I'll give thee a ride that'll settle thy dinner. Emily, thee hasn't petted Dapple to-day. Thee's very forgetful of one of thy best friends."

"Do you know," said Miss Warren to me as we followed the boy, "Reuben sent Dapple's love to me every time he wrote?"

"It's just what Dapple would have done himself if he could. Did you refuse to receive it?"

"No, indeed. Why should I?"

"Oh, I'm not jealous; only I can't help thinking that the horse had greater privileges than I."

She bit her lip, and her color deepened, but instead of answering she tripped away from me toward the barn. Dapple came prancing out, and whinnied as soon as he saw her.

"Oh, he knows thee as well as I do," said Reuben. "He thinks thee's a jolly good girl. Thee's kind of cut me out; but I owe thee no grudge. See how he'll come to thee now," and sure enough, the horse came and put his nose in her hand, where he found a lump of sugar.

"I won't give you fine words only, Dapple," she said, and the beautiful animal's spirited eyes grew mild and gentle as if he understood her perfectly.

"Heaven grant that she gives me more than words!" I muttered.

While Reuben was harnessing Dapple, Miss Warren entered the barn, saying:

"I feel a little remorseful over my treatment of Old Plod, and think I will go and speak to him."

"May I be present at the interview?"

"Certainly."

Either the old horse had grown duller and heavier than ever, or else was offended by her long neglect, for he paid her but little attention, and kept his head down in his manger.

"Dapple would not treat you like that, even if you hadn't a lump of sugar in your hand."

"Dapple is peculiar," she remarked.

"Do you mean a little ill-balanced? He was certainly very precipitate on one occasion."

"Yes, but he had the grace to stop before he did any harm."

"But suppose he couldn't stop? Did Old Plod give you any more advice?"

"Mr. Morton, you must cub your editorial habit of inquiring into everything. Am I a dragon?"

"I fear you more than all the dragons put together."

"Then you are a brave man to stay."

"Not at all. To run away would be worse than death."

"What an awful dilemma you are in! It seems to me, however, the coolest veteran in the land could not have made a better dinner while in such peril."

"I had scarcely eaten anything since yesterday morning. Moreover, I was loyally bound to compliment Mrs. Yocomb's efforts in the only way that would have satisfied her."

"That reminds me that I ought to go and help Mrs. Yocomb clear away the vast debris of such a dinner."

"Miss Warren, I have only this afternoon and evening."

"Truly, Mr. Morton, the pathos in your tones would move a post"

"But will it move you? That's the question that concerns me. Will you take a walk with me?"

"Indeed, I think I must go now, if I would not be thought more insensible than a post. Wait till I put on more wraps, and do you get your overcoat, sir, or you will take cold."

"Yes, I'm awfully afraid I shall be chilled, and the overcoat wouldn't help me. Nevertheless, I'll do your bidding in this, as in all respects."

"What a lamblike frame of mind!" she cried; but her step up the piazza was light and quick.

"She could not so play with me if she meant to be cruel, for she has not a feline trait," I murmured, as I pulled on my ulster. "This genial day has been my ally, and she has not the heart to embitter it. So far from finding 'other interests,' she must have seen that time has intensified the one chief interest of my life. Oh, it would be like death to be sent away again. How beautiful she has become in her renewed health! Her great spiritual eyes make me more conscious of the woman-angel within her than of a flesh-and-blood girl. Human she is indeed, but never of the earth, earthy. Even when I take her hand, now again so plump and pretty, I feel the exquisite thrill of her life within. It's like touching a spirit, were such a thing possible. I crushed her hand this morning, brute that I was! It's been red all day. Well, Heaven speed me now!"

"What! talking to yourself again, Mr. Morton?" asked Miss Warren, suddenly appearing, and looking anything but spirit-like, with her rich color and substantial wraps.

"It's a habit of lonely people," I said.

"The idea of a man being lonely among such crowds as you must meet!"

"I have yet to learn that a crowd makes company."

"Wouldn't you like to ask Mr. Yocomb to go with us?"

"No," I replied, very brusquely.

"I fear your lamblike mood is passing away."

"Not at all. Moreover, I'm a victim of remorse—I hurt your hand this morning."

"Yes, you did."

"I've hurt you a great many times."

"I'm alive, thank you, and have had a good dinner."

"Yes, you are very much alive. Are you very amiable after dinner?"

"No; that's a trait belonging to men alone. I now understand your lamblike mood. But where are you going, Mr. Morton? You are walking at random, and have brought up against the barn."

"Oh, I see. Wouldn't you like to visit Old Plod again?"

"No, I thank you; he has forgotten me."

"By the way, we are friends, are we not, and can be very confidential?"

"If you have any doubt, you had better be prudent and reticent."

"I wish I could find some sweetbrier; I'd give you the whole bush."

"Do you think I deserve a thorny experience?"

"You know what I think. When was there an hour when you did not look through me as if I were glass. But we are confidential friends, are we not?"

"Well, for the sake of argument we may imagine ourselves such."

"To be logical, then, I must tell you something of which I have not yet spoken to any one. I called on Adah the evening I learned she was in town, and I saw her enter an elegant coupe driven by a coachman in stunning livery. A millionaire of your acquaintance accompanied her."

"What!" she exclaimed, her face becoming fairly radiant.

I nodded very significantly.

"For shame, Mr. Morton! What a gossip you are!" but her laugh rang out like a chime of silver bells.

At that moment Mr. Yocomb appeared on the piazza, and he applauded loudly, "Good for thee, Emily," he cried, "that sounds like old times."

"Come away, quick," I said, and I strode rapidly around the barn.

"Do you expect me to keep up with you?" she asked, stopping short and looking so piquant and tempting that I rejoined her instantly.

"I'll go as slow as you please. I'll do anything under heaven you bid me."

"You treat Mr. Yocomb very shabbily."

"You won't make me go after him, will you?"

"Why, Mr. Morton? What base ingratitude and after such a dinner, too."

"You know how ill-balanced I am."

"I fear you are growing worse and worse."

"I am, indeed. Left to myself, I should be the most unbalanced man in the world."

"Mr. Morton, your mind is clearly unsettled. I detected the truth the first day I saw you."

"No, my mind, such as it is, is made up irrevocably and forever. I must tell you that I can't afford to keep a coupe."

"There is a beautiful sequence in your remarks. Then you ought not to keep one. But why complain. There are always omnibuses within call."

"Are you fond of riding in an omnibus?"

"What an irrelevant question! Suppose I followed your example, and ask what you think of the Copernican system?" "You can't be ill-balanced if you try, and your question is not in the least irrelevant. The Copernican system is true, and illustrates my position exactly. There is a heavenly body, radiant with light and beauty, that attracts me irresistibly. The moment I came within her influence my orbit was fixed."

"Isn't your orbit a little eccentric?" she asked, with averted face. "Still your figure may be very apt. Another body of greater attraction would carry you off into space."

"There is no such body in existence."

"Mr. Morton, we were talking about omnibuses."

"And you have not answered my question."

"Since we are such confidential friends, I will tell you a profound secret. I prefer street cars to omnibuses, and would much rather ride in one than in a carriage that I could not pay for."

"Well, now, that's sensible."

"Yes, quite matter-of-fact. Where are you going, Mr. Morton?"

"Wherever you wish—even to Columbus."

"What! run away from your work and duty? Where is your conscience?"

"Where my heart is."

"Oh, both are in Columbus. I should think it inconvenient to have them so far off."

I tried to look in her eyes, but she turned them away.

"I can prove that my conscience was in Columbus; I consulted you on every question I discussed in the paper."

"Nonsense! you never wrote me a line."

"I was enjoined not to in a way that made my blood run cold. But I thought Mrs. Vining's opinions might be influenced by a member of her family, and I never wrote a line unmindful of that influence."

Again her laugh rang out. "I should call the place where you wrote the Circumlocution Office. Well, to keep up your way of doing things, that member of the family read most critically all you wrote."

"How could you tell my work from that of others?"

"Oh, I could tell every line from your hand as if spoken to me."

"Well, fair critic?"

"Never compliment a critic. It makes them more severe."

"I could do so much better if you were in New York."

"What! Do you expect me to go into the newspaper business?"

"You are in it now—you are guiding me. You are the inspiration of my best work, and you know it."

We had now reached a point where the lane wound through a hemlock grove. My hope was glad and strong, but I resolved at once to remove all shadow of fear, and I shrank from further probation. Therefore I stopped decisively, and said in a voice that faltered not a little:

"Emily, our light words are but ripples that cover depths which in my case reach down through life and beyond it. You are my fate. I knew it the day I first met you. I know it now with absolute conviction."

She turned a little away from me and trembled.

"Do you remember this?" I asked, and I took from my pocketbook the withered York and Lancaster rosebud.

She gave it a dark glance, and her crimson face grew pale.

"Too well," she replied, in a low tone.

I threw it down and ground it under my heel; then, removing my hat, I said:

"I am at your mercy. You are the stronger, and your foot is on my neck."

She turned on me instantly, and her face was aflame with her eager imperious demand to know the truth. Taking both my hands in a tense, strong grasp, she looked into my eyes as if she would read my very soul. "Richard," she said, in a voice that was half entreaty, half command, "in God's name, tell me the truth—the whole truth. Do you respect me at heart? Do you trust me? Can you trust me as Mr. Yocomb trusts his wife?"

"I will make no comparisons," I replied, gently. "Like the widow in the Bible, I give you all I have."

Her tense grasp relaxed, her searching eyes melted into love itself, and I snatched her to my heart.

"What were the millions I lost compared with this dowry!" she murmured. "I knew it—I've known it all day, ever since you crushed my hand. Oh, Richard, your rude touch healed a sore heart."

"Emily," I said, with a low laugh, "that June day was the day of fate after all."

"It was, indeed. I wish I could make you know how gladly I accept mine. Oh, Richard, I nearly killed myself trying not to love you. It was fate, or something better."

"Then suppose we change the figure, and say our match was made in heaven."

I will not attempt to describe that evening at the farmhouse. We were made to feel that it was our own dear home—a safe, quiet haven ever open to us when we wished to escape from the turmoil of the world. I thank God for our friends there, and their unchanging truth.

I accompanied Emily to Columbus, but I went after her again in the spring and for a time she made her home with Mrs. Yocomb.

Adah was married at Mrs. Winfield's large city mansion, for Mr. Hearn had a host of relatives and friends whom he wished present. The farmhouse would not have held a tithe of them, and the banker was so proud of his fair country flower that he seemed to want the whole world to see her.

We were married on the anniversary of the day of our fate, and in the old garden where I first saw my Eve, my truth. She has never tempted me to aught save good deeds and brave work.